# WEASELS RIPPED MY FLESH!

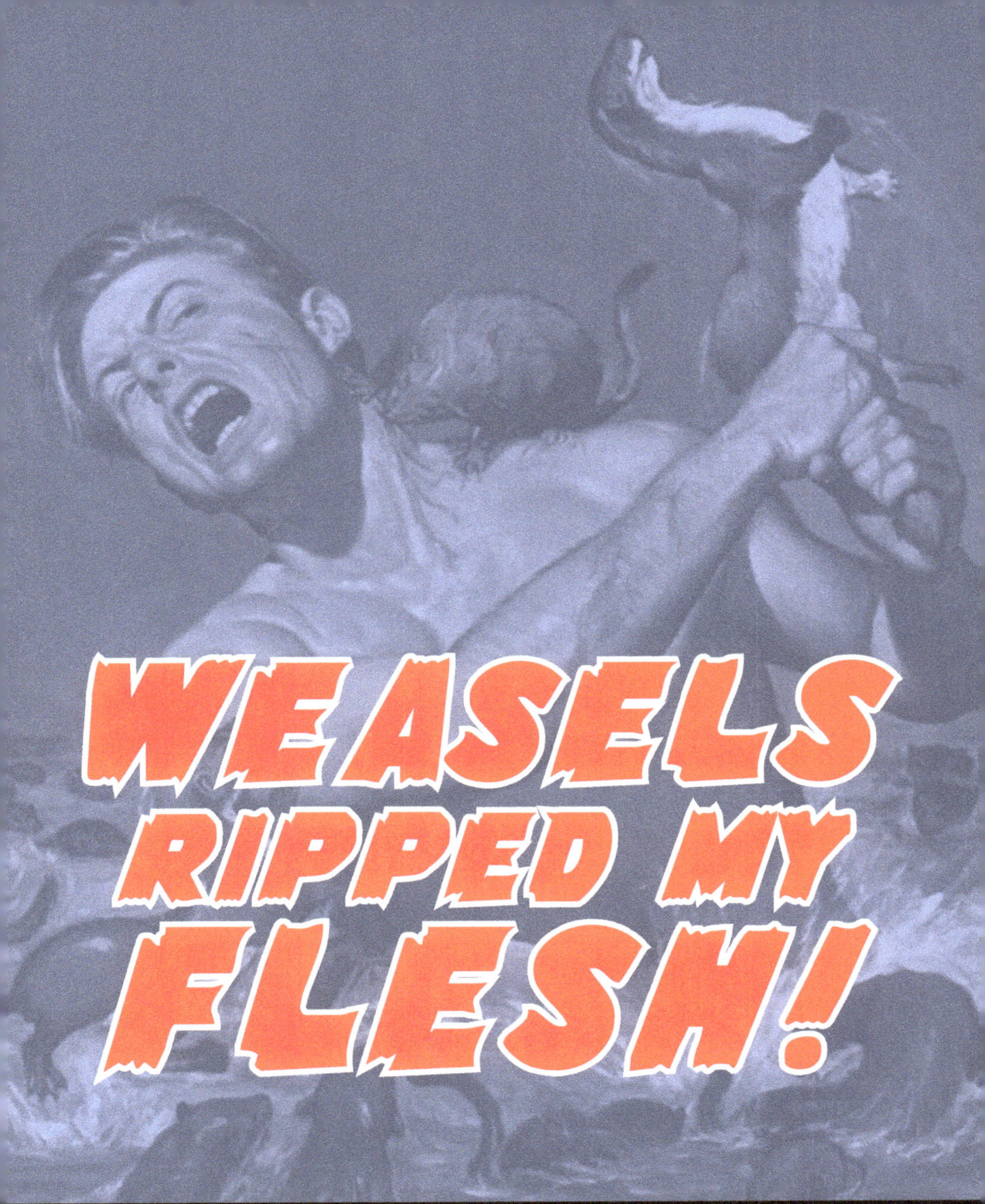

# WEASELS RIPPED MY FLESH!

EDITED BY **ROBERT DEIS** & **WYATT DOYLE**

WITH **JOSH ALAN FRIEDMAN**

MensPulpMags.com

# new texture

A New Texture book

Copyright © 2024 Subtropic Productions LLC

Archival materials supplied by The Robert Deis Archive

All Rights Reserved.

Cover: "Weasels Ripped My Flesh" by Wil Hulsey

Proofreaders: Rob Morris, Bernice A. .Jones (editor.bernice@gmail.com)
            Sandee Curry (2012 edition)

Designed by Wyatt Doyle for The Men's Adventure Library

NewTexture.com

  @ThisIsNewTexture

MensAdventureLibrary.com          MensPulpMags.com

**Booksellers: *Weasels Ripped My Flesh!*** and other New Texture books
are available through Ingram Book Company

ISBN 978-1-943444-66-3

First color softcover edition: August 2024

Printed in the United States of America

10 9 8 7 6 5 4 3 2 1

# Men's Adventure Magazines [MAMs]

A bona fide publishing phenomenon that emerged in the 1950s and thrived through the 1970s, the tropes and aesthetic established by **men's adventure magazines** (**MAMs**) have proven so durable and have been absorbed so totally into the American consciousness that even decades after their demise, MAMs remain an incontestable—if invisible—hand behind key events and directions in entertainment and popular culture.

Incorporating the colorful, eye-catching cover paintings and pulse-pounding action/adventure fiction of pre-World War II pulp fiction magazines, MAMs added non-fiction adventures to the mix, and blurred the line between the two by frequently claiming the outrageous, high-octane fiction was *also* true, even when such claims were implausible, preposterous, or demonstrably false. This blend quickly became standard for the genre, and pulp "fact" ran side by side with pulp fiction.

The **MAM** formula cannily incorporated aspects of other popular magazines that appealed to the working-class readership they targeted, including racy "bachelor" and pin-up mags, outdoor and travel periodicals, true crime and detective magazines, and celebrity scandal rags.

The format was adopted by multiple publishers, who produced magazines of varying quality. All told, more than 160 different periodicals fit the classification. Some lasted decades, others, only a few issues—or just one. While the more lurid varieties (sometimes called "sweats" or "sweat mags") often draw the most attention (and criticism), the range and quality of MAM content is more varied than is generally understood.

Though dismissed in their time as downmarket, lowbrow entertainment, the magazines were an enduring success, enjoyed by millions of readers over three decades. MAMs published popular writers of the day, and artwork by many of the era's top illustration artists. The terse, hard-boiled intensity of the writing and the dynamic, explosive, and racy illustration art—on their covers and in their pages—are essential to their appeal, then and now. The potency of these words and images remains undiminished; their excesses still spark gobsmacked wonder, and their artistry inspires fascination on its own terms.

*I gratefully dedicate this book to my wife,*
Barbara Jo Butler Deis,
*who benignly tolerates my fascination with musty old men's adventure*
*magazines and the piles of them I leave around the house,*
*and to my friend and mentor*
Rich Oberg,
*the world's foremost collector of men's pulp magazine art, who has graciously*
*provided me access to his collection and invaluable knowledge.*

—Bob Deis

# CONTENTS

"The Street of a Hundred Sins" by Joe Chamberlain
*Man's Conquest*, March 1958

"Yankee Lynch Mob" by Bruce J. (Jay) Friedman
*Climax*, November 1959

*This illustration by Brendan Lynch would inspire the penultimate panel of the comix story "The Andy Griffith Show" by BJF's sons, Drew and Josh Alan Friedman, published in* Kar-tunz' *(April 1979),* Raw *(Fall 1980),* High Times *(March 1981), and the Friedman Bros. collection* Any Similarity to Persons Living or Dead Is Purely Coincidental *(Fantagraphics).*

# PREFACE

## —— JOSH ALAN FRIEDMAN ——

**WHO** are today's equivalent of yesteryear's men's adventure magazine writers? Are they frat boys who sit before plasma TVs, downing Dos Equis as they grind out computer code for guerilla warfare video games? Are they Hollywood hustlers who write by committee for network TV? Skateboarding editors of "lads' mags," who wax rhapsodic over consumer gadgets, cars and mud wrestling?

Their world is hard to romanticize when compared to the Mad Men of Madison Avenue. I still cherish childhood memories of the Magazine Management offices, where I visited my father, Bruce Jay Friedman, in the early '60s (though I was unaware of the angst and misery some of these men suffered). Men were men, women were secretaries. Typewriters winged, banged and whizzed through the cigar smoke. Artists painted magnificent action covers at their easels. They all loved the office.

Where do kids with journalism degrees apply for work today—directly to their own blogs? Newspapers that barely exist have closed most of their bureaus and cut reporting staff down to a ghost shift. (Is it true the New York *Daily News* only has three city reporters—where once there were hundreds?)

But not all is lost. Real-world jobs can be good for writers. Even ditch digging. Novelists who labor by day as English professors tend to write books about…English professors. Expertise in any field other than literature or journalism provides a wellspring of material. Michael Crichton was an MD, Scott Turow a practicing attorney. The problem is, where to train for the immensely complicated art of writing itself? There are no trenches or spawning grounds like the late, great men's adventure mags (or "armpit slicks," if you prefer). Rookies (one-in-a-thousand?) who break into TV seem to go straight from *Scriptwriting*

**Male, December 1955**
**Cover by George Gross**

*for Dummies* to the industry. And you can detect the clumsy architecture of Screenplay 101 creaking loudly through their scripts; they really know how to set margins and slug lines. (Episodic cable TV produces far superior writing than the current movie landscape.)

As such, some of us have more appreciation for stories that first transpired by means of typewriter to hot press to low-grade paper stock. And what you are about to read here is transcribed from the surviving paper pulp. We now know that hardcore geeks who began as Nintendo boys have remained gamers into their 30s; they will probably remain gamers throughout life. For the rest of us, sit back in your recliner by the fireplace with your silk robe and snifter of cognac, stuff the pipe and read on. ///

# FOREWORD

— WYATT DOYLE —

**IF YOU** want to know where a society's head was at, dig through their stuff. Nothing opens up the nooks and crannies of the American consciousness like pop culture detritus.

Yet somehow, despite decades of eager archaeology by collectors, tastemakers, and obsessives, the men's adventure magazines (MAMs) of the 1950s, '60s and '70s—largely forgotten, but hardly esoteric—have remained, for the most part, un(re)discovered country.

The covers have endured on the cultural periphery, and the phrase *"weasels ripped my flesh"* delivered in a stern, movie-trailer baritone is bound to elicit some half-remembered pop *frisson* among the culturally astute, even if they can't quite place its context. (Something from an old movie? Something from a *parody* of an old movie?)

This cultural amnesia would be more understandable if MAMs were some short-lived fluke of the publishing industry, if they'd come and gone before the public at large was able to take note of their existence. But these magazines were a fixture of newsstands, barber shops, and garage restrooms for the better part of *three decades*, with circulations in the hundred thousands. And though collectors disagree on the exact number of men's adventure titles unleashed on the American marketplace over those decades, estimates place the figure at over 150.

Certainly they were never intended to last. As Josh Alan Friedman puts it in his interview with *Godfather* (and men's adventure) scribe Mario Puzo (pg. 231), they were "comic books for grown-ups"—and, like comics of the time, they were regarded as cheap, plentiful and disposable. The magazines were entertainment, first and foremost, diversion without pretension. They were impulse buys, with temptations aimed well south of the brain for the softer targets of gut and groin.

Cheap, lurid and sensational. Lowbrow, in the years before the term had cachet.

Who read MAMs? Celebrated writer Bruce Jay Friedman, who worked on several of the most popular mags in his years as Managing Editor for Magazine Management Company, explains in his essay "Even the Rhinos Were Nymphos" that closes this volume, even the fellows producing the mags weren't entirely sure:

> *We never did find out with any precision exactly who "our guys" were. They seemed to be multiple men's magazine readers who would buy* Argosy *and* True *and then return, with a certain petulance, and buy one or two of ours. Much in the style of someone who has eaten dinner, but requires a cup of chili to be put properly over the top. We were reasonably sure our readers drank beer and had some affiliation with Iwo. There may have been some migrant workers mixed in among them. My brother-in-law was the only reader I was able to pinpoint with any certainty.*

Working stiffs and average Joes with a taste for earthy (and often kinky) escapism; these were the men higher-end, higher-profile publications like *Playboy* and *Esquire* left behind. It's reasonable to presume that the typical *Action For Men* reader's life lacked the glamour, the expense accounts, the nightclub memberships and the hi-fi systems seemingly expected of *Playboy* readers. (Much of *Playboy*'s readership lacked these as well, but MAM readers had fewer illusions about it.)

*Playboy*'s intellectual pretensions and white collar consumerism drew a line in the newsstand, and the mag wasted no time distancing itself from those periodicals on the *other* side of the men's magazine shelf. "*Playboy*," editor and publisher Hugh Hefner opined in 1953, "is an entertainment magazine for the indoor man…a pleasure-primer for the sophisticated, city-bred male…that select group of urbane fellows who were less concerned with hunting, fishing, and climbing mountains than good food, drink, proper dress, and the pleasure of female company." And Hef's million-dollar idea of showcasing "the girl next door" in cozy cheesecake layouts was a reaction against the beehive-and-black-eyeliner models and stark motel room monochrome that had been standard features of men's mags 'til then.

Even their standards of masculinity differed. Where *Playboy*'s male ideal hovered somewhere between James Bond and a white-collar corporate ladder-climber, MAMs emphasized earthier protagonists; lustier, devil-may-care kinds of men: bounders, brawlers, bastards.

*Peril*, October 1957
Cover by John Duillo

Broad-shouldered Burt Lancaster types.

A whole generation of former GIs may have found themselves white picket fenced-in by the suburbs, but their fantasy lives were lived far outside its borders. There was a whole world of excitement, danger and adventure outside those fences. For those home from their war and trying to reconcile themselves to a 9-to-5 lifestyle, MAMs temporarily sated their thirst for exotic action and high adventure, while reinforcing attitudes they were already comfortable with. This was what escapist entertainment was all about.

World War II—later Korea, then Vietnam—were still fresh and vivid experiences for American men, and war stories were a significant and enduring component of MAMs—though both the writers of these stories and their readers agree that the mags' battlefield sagas can be broken down into three loose categories: *total fiction, highly embellished* and *reasonably accurate, if not entirely true.* Though far from authoritative,

**Man's Magazine, February 1961
Cover by Rafael DeSoto**

any legitimate accounts of American fighting men tended to receive
sincere and respectful treatment. This was particularly true when
stories were entrusted to author-historians like the prolific Robert F.
Dorr. As the writer put it in conversation with Robert Deis:

> *Many readers of those stories were veterans, who'd been
> there. So, when I wrote about warfare for them, I had to have
> the personalities and the details right and avoid puffery.
> What these men wouldn't tolerate was to have themselves or
> the military brass glorified or to have war made glamorous,
> so I didn't do those things.*

Dorr's own "Bayonet Killer of Heartbreak Ridge" (pg. 107) makes
fine use of this approach to biography, men's adventure style. Going out
of their way to establish and maintain an everyman tone, writers often

played down their erudition to better suit the format. Even "educational" articles by purported experts might resist adopting *too* much authority in their authorial voices. See the opening paragraphs of Ken Krippene's "I Married a Jungle Savage" (pg. 289), as the sophisticated writer, world traveler and amateur anthropologist reads like a randy hound dog straining his leash. Or Lawrence Block's pseudonymous prostitution exposé, "She Doesn't Want You" (pg. 79), with its *"Let me tell you, brother"* delivery and highly corruptible narrator. Or even Joanne Beardon's wide-eyed report on same-sex attraction, "I Went to a Lesbian Party" (pg. 389).

IT'S EASY to see the stories in MAMs as tall tales for the postwar era. Like tall tales (and ancient myth before them), in a changing world of new questions, the magazines did provide a curious reassurance: monthly confirmation that their views and experiences were still meaningful and valid. Only a few years before, these men had circled the globe to trounce Tojo and the Gerrys in foreign cities, oceans, deserts, and jungles. Now they faced futures defined by significantly more.

*(cont'd on pg. 22)*

"I Escaped Louisiana's Killer Barracuda"
By Walter Kaylin (as Roland Empey)
*Male,* January 1973
Illustration by Bob Larkin

*Adventure*, October 1955
Cover by Frank McCarthy

This anthology's focus is MAM writing, not MAM artwork. But MAM covers are easily the best known aspects of the magazines, and deserve comment here. Designed for maximum visual impact, MAM covers were a defining aspect of the magazines, from depictions of the calm before (or amid) the storm (as in the tense Frank McCarthy *Adventure* cover above) to those that thrust the viewer squarely into the heat of the action. It's the latter category that regularly tips into the

*Rage*, January 1961
Cover by John Duillo

outrageous, assaulting the viewer with the barely contained chaos of clanging headlines and inset images elbowing for space, vying for attention, and unleashing bizarre juxtapositions of word and image. (John Duillo's 1961 *Rage* cover above is a particularly frantic visual cacophony.)

The goal was to make MAMs irresistible on newsstands. So in their publishers' efforts to attract the largest possible readership, MAMs were lots of things. Sometimes all at once.

*(cont'd from pg. 19)*

workaday experiences and weighty new responsibilities: wives, kids, domesticity; gainful employment, and the daily grind. It's not difficult to see where a Joe might want to relive old glories in his choice of reading material, and catch up on the life he might have led, if not for… (fill in the blank). This wasn't literary junk food; this was literary *comfort* food.

The magazines offered both temporary escape from the modern world and tips on how to understand and cope with it. Readers ate up the kind of alleged inside knowledge the mags professed to share, man to man, with their readers. This was the mid-20th Century, when societal changes came quicker than most could keep up with, and sex education could be a legal offense punishable by jail time. When it came to certain subjects, the average guy didn't have a wide variety of resources available to him, and MAMs offered answers.

*Real,* October 1962
Cover by Shannon Stirnweis

BUT FOR stories made to go down easy, the harsh turns some of these narratives take can be surprising. Though storybook morality only occasionally factors into events, the stories aren't always grim or ironic enough to meet the criteria for *noir*. (Walter Kaylin's "Bar Room Girl Who Touched Off a Tribal War" (pg. 59) and Harlan Ellison's twisty "Death Climb" (pg. 91) are two notable exceptions.)

Bruce Jay Friedman again:

> *We failed, finally, to come up with a concise formula, one that could be as crisply stated as that of, say, the confession magazines: "Sin, confess, repent." With a bit of tap dancing and some Nielsen-type research, we discovered what "our guys," whoever they were, liked and didn't... What we did find was a ferocious craving for what was actual and real... Our staple product became the verifiably true story of some fellow who had survived a Japanese "rat cage," made a record-breaking Death Trek though Borneo, raided Schweinfurt, or helped to storm the Remagen Bridge. Dutifully, we served these up to "our guys," who were appreciative.*

While adventures often stretched plausibility, they were not strictly wish-fulfillment dreams. Unless the heroes were American fighting men, readers weren't treated to many unqualified victories in MAMs. Stories were as likely to conclude with a stoic acceptance of grim fate as end on a note of triumph.

He-man castaways might have appeared to live every hetero man's fantasy as "love slaves" to gorgeous vixens (EC Schurmacher's "I Was a Slave of the Savage Blonde," pg. 343), or compelled to play stud bull to an entire tribe of alluring jungle maidens ("Mattern's 50 Days as an Amazon Love Slave," by Robert Silverberg, pg. 209), but the protagonists invariably wanted out, effecting bold and daring escapes. And though the hardy outdoorsmen who provided "first-person" accounts of animal savagery may have lived to tell the tale, they never failed to remind the reader of the *severe and ongoing psychological trauma* that continued to plague them, even years later. And rare was the animal brawler who didn't lose at least a few body parts to his attackers. (Tallies were graphically delineated in epilogues.)

FOR THREE decades, these magazines and the stories in them at once reflected the fantasies and fueled the daydreams of more than one

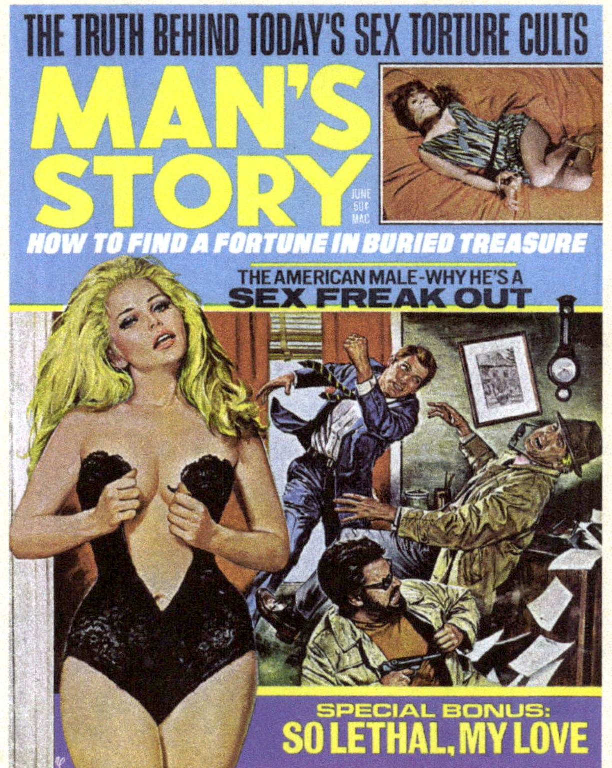


**Man's Story,** June 1970
Cover by Norm Eastman

generation of American males (and surely some females). If those dreams are sometimes crude or obvious, silly, salacious, or naïve, they're no less accurate a reflection of who we were.

And if some of the stories are easy to poke fun at today, their power as metaphor has only grown more potent. A man alone, sane and rational, growing increasingly desperate as he beats back an army of crazed, bloodthirsty weasels/monkeys/lizards/lemmings, all champing to bite off pieces of him… Readers of MAMs identified readily with even these impossible, outrageous yarns. They too wondered if machismo alone could be enough to survive a life of a thousand cuts. ///

# INTRODUCTION

## — ROBERT DEIS —

**BETWEEN** the late 1940s and the mid-1970s, a unique genre of magazines for men developed, flourished, then faded away.

They are most commonly known as *men's adventure magazines*. Sometimes they're referred to as *men's pulp adventure magazines* or *men's pulp mags*—reflecting their link to earlier digest-size pulp fiction periodicals. To prevent repetitive typing injuries, we call them *MAMs*.

They have also been called *men's postwar pulp magazines*, to distinguish them from their pre-World War II pulp forbears. *Sweat magazines* is yet another popular nickname for the genre, used derogatorily by critics and adopted affectionately by fans.

Like most modern collectors of vintage MAMs, I was initially attracted by their cover and interior paintings: amazing pulp illustration art showing gritty war scenes, gonzo animal attacks by everything from anteaters to weasels, exotic action and adventure, Western gunfights, pulp sleaze-style "Good Girl Art," and jaw-dropping depictions of evil Nazis, Commies, natives, bikers, Satanists and psychos tormenting gorgeous, well-endowed, scantily clad damsels in distress.

When I started reading the magazines I bought, I found many of the stories to be as wildly imaginative and artfully crafted as the illustrations. Some are top notch stories by writers who went on to wider renown. Some are ripping yarns penned by unknown or forgotten pulp hacks.

Others, while hardly great literature, are interesting and often unintentionally hilarious windows on history and American culture that are probably even more fun to read now than when they were originally published.

You'll understand what I mean when you read the stories in this anthology.

Of course, this collection provides just a partial look at the wild, weird world of vintage MAMs. From the early '50s to the mid-'70s, more than 150 different MAMs were published in the United States. Some were long-lasting titles published in all three decades, such as

**Adventure, December 1957**
**Cover by Harry Schaare**

*Adventure, Argosy, Battle Cry, Bluebook, For Men Only, Male, Man's Life, Man's Magazine, Man's World, Real Men, Saga, Stag, True* and *True Adventures.* Dozens of others ran for just a few years; some for just a few issues. Several failed to make it beyond a single issue. Only a few MAMs had circulations in the hundreds of thousands (the average print run was about 100,000). But collectively, at their peak in the '50s and '60s, MAMs were read by millions of American men. They were sold at newsstands, drug stores and supermarkets throughout the country. Some also had sizeable subscriber bases.

By the 1970s, the "girlie slick" magazines like *Playboy, Hustler* and *Penthouse*—and even harder-core porn mags—began to dominate the men's magazine market. The pulpy MAMs seemed increasingly out-of-date and unhip. Some survived a while longer by running more and more nude photos, less artwork and fewer action and adventure stories. But by 1980, there were no more magazines that fit the term *men's adventure magazine*. The genre was essentially extinct. By the 1990s, it was largely forgotten.

Then, starting about a decade ago, several things sparked renewed interest in these old magazines. Two highly praised, heavily illustrated books helped revive awareness and appreciation of the genre.

One was Adam Parfrey's *It's a Man's World: Men's Adventure Magazines, The Postwar Pulps* (Feral House, 2003). That book includes contributions from writer-musician Josh Alan Friedman, co-editor of this anthology, and from Josh's father, Bruce Jay Friedman, who worked as a writer and editor for MAMs before he became a famous novelist and playwright.

**Man's Look, December 1961**
**Cover by Jay Scott Pike**

The other seminal book was *Men's Adventure Magazines in Postwar America* (Taschen, 2004). It features the legendary art and magazine collection of my friend Rich Oberg, the world's foremost collector of MAMs and the original artwork used for their covers and stories.

Another reason for the renewed interest in MAMs is the internet.

The pioneering collector Bill Devine, author of *Devine's Guide to Men's Adventure Magazines,* has estimated that only about one percent of the MAMs published have survived the trash heap. Bill also estimates that only about one percent of that one percent is up for sale somewhere at any given time.

Collectors used to have to seek out copies at used book stores, flea markets and yard sales. Now they're accessible to anyone with an Internet connection. Websites like eBay have made it easy to find and buy old MAMs and turned them into increasingly popular collectors' items.

There are also a growing number of websites, blogs and Facebook groups where fans post scans of the cover and interior paintings and discuss MAMs (including my own **MensPulpMags.com** site and FB group). Nonetheless, most people today are only dimly aware of this "lost" genre of magazines, if at all. And, the recognition that exists still tends to focus on their covers, especially those that have the most over-the-top scenes and wildest headlines.

It's definitely noteworthy that MAMs feature cover and interior paintings by some of the best illustration artists of the 20th Century—artists like James Bama, Stan Borack, Gil Cohen, Charles Copeland, Charles, Mel Crair, Rafael DeSoto, John Duillo, Norm Eastman, Basil Gogos, George Gross, Wil Hulsey, Mort Künstler, John Leone, Frank McCarthy, James Meese, Bruce Minney, Rudy Nappi, Earl Norem, Samson Pollen, Walter Popp, Vic Prezio, Norman Saunders, Bob Schulz, and Syd Shores. But behind the cool illustrations that these and other artists created for MAMs are many equally cool stories.

Yet, while many anthologies of stories from pre-WWII pulp fiction magazines have been published, this is the first anthology made up of stories from postwar men's pulp adventure magazines. If my co-editors and I get our way, there will be more; we're already plotting to unleash future volumes on an unsuspecting world. This is just the beginning.[1]

*RELEASE THE WEASELS!* ///

---

[1]      *It certainly was! See the back pages of this book for information on the many subsequent releases in The Men's Adventure Library series.*

# ABOUT "WEASELS RIPPED MY FLESH"

Tens of thousands of stories were written for MAMs from the early 1950s to the mid-1970s, when the genre faded away. The most famous story should be "Weasels Ripped My Flesh." And it is famous, in a way. However, few people have ever read it and, until now, it has never been reprinted in any collection.

It certainly has the most famous title of any story written specifically for publication in a men's pulp mag. That's because in 1970, Frank Zappa immortalized it as the title of an album by his band, The Mothers of Invention. (It was also the title of a song on that LP.) Zappa had a copy of the magazine the story was first published in: the September 1956 issue of Man's Life.

"Weasels Ripped My Flesh" was the featured cover story for that issue, illustrated with a wild painting by Wilbur "Wil" Hulsey, one of the great MAM artists. Hulsey's painting shows a horde of vicious weasels attacking a bleeding, bare-chested man who's waist-deep in water.

Zappa didn't use Hulsey's painting as the cover art for his album. Instead, he showed it to an up-and-coming album artist he knew named Neon Park. According to legend, Zappa asked Park, "What can you do that's worse than this?"

Park came up with his own bizarre image for the album cover. He based it on a 1953 Schick print ad that shows a smiling man in a suit and tie shaving with the company's new "Schick 20" electric shaver.

The man in Park's painting looks just like the guy in the Schick ad. But in Park's version he's "shaving" with what appears to be an electric weasel and the weasel's teeth are ripping a bloody gouge in his cheek.

Zappa fans later uncovered the fact that the title "Weasels Ripped My Flesh" came from the September 1956 issue of Man's Life. When the age of the internet arrived in the 1990s, scans of that issue's cover were posted on various sites and it became famous in its own right. Indeed, it's probably the best known of all MAM covers.

Yet, aside from a small number of avid Zappa and pulp fiction fans, few people have seen or read the story "Weasels Ripped My Flesh."

It's a story that's as entertainingly gonzo as Wil Hulsey's cover

THERE'S NOTHING like being on a cheap drunk under 300 feet of ice-cold water. They got a pretty name for it: rapture of the deep.

But it isn't pretty at all. It's got nothing to do with liquor; it just feels almost the name. Mostly you don't give a damn. No matter what kind of fix you're in. Thats the horror of it: if the fix is bad enough, and if you're drunk enough on all that high-pressure oxygen sizzling through your system—well, kid, that's it. No more hang-overs.

Your eyes turn until they only show the white. You spit out the life-giving mouthpiece of your air tube. Water gurgles into your throat and lungs. You choke. Your vomit mixes with the water and you drink it back. There's a last stab of consciousness, a sudden panic: Oh God! And a searing pain as your heart bursts.

Then death takes you by the hand, almost gently, and you smile a drunken welcome, and you and grinning death drift down together slowly and softly in a stiff embrace that nobody will ever break. Down until your pale body drapes itself over some rock. Down and out. For good and always.

Mel Finchley and I, we were in a fix all right. 300 feet down in a water cave, and no help on top. We were weak from loss of blood, sucked from us by the cave salamanders. In the light of our lanterns I could see the water turning pink from the ooze of our shredded, tortured flesh.

We had long ago lost our guide rope. We had lost contact with Jack Wozniak who carried spare oxygen tanks. He was off somewhere in the impenetrable blackness of our water labyrinth. Maybe he was already dead, killed by the worm-like olms.

Our own air supplies were running out; there was hardly enough left to see us to the top—if we could ever find it.

And here we were on the biggest rapture jag of our skin diving career. The terrible reality of our situation hovered way off somewhere in the deeper crevices of our sluggish minds.

It was now or never. But we didn't know it.

Mel drifted, hunched over, his arms dangling at his sides. He looked very funny, like a science-fiction puppet dangling on an invisible string. Very funny. I wanted to laugh. But it hardly seemed worth the trouble. My mask pressed painfully against my nose. I could fix it by snorting, but that wasn't worth the trouble either. I felt a million miles away from my own body.

"Hank," an inner voice whispered to me. "this is it. You've had it."

I didn't listen. Death winked at me, and I winked back.

We hung in the wet nowhere, waiting for rigor mortis.

IT HAD ALL started a few weeks before. Jack Wozniak and I, we had bummed around Europe for several years now, making a few bucks here and a few bucks there, easy money and an easy life. Mostly we hired out for salvage work on ships that had been sunk along the coast during World War II, and then we blew our dough in Paris, Rome and on the Riviera. Plenty of women and plenty of cognac: the way life can be once you make up your mind to kiss off surburbia and installment plan hucksters.

And then, a few weeks ago in Vienna, we'd run into Mel Finchley. Skin divers (Continued on page 58)

***Man's Action*, September 1957**
**Illustration by Bruce Minney**

**Another little known threat to humanity: killer salamanders! (Newts, actually.) Naturally, they have shadowy ties to Hitler.**

*painting suggests. It's also a good example of the "killer creature" subgenre of stories that were popular in MAMs in the 1950s and 1960s. Some of those stories featured attacks by animals that are typically considered to pose a possible threat to humans, such as bears, lions, crocodiles and sharks. But in the surreal world of men's pulp adventure yarns, critters from every branch of the animal kingdom could be bloodthirsty man-killers, including everything from lemmings and crabs to anteaters and flying squirrels.*

*Like many stories in MAMs, "Weasels Ripped My Flesh" is portrayed as a true account. In fact, it's pulp fiction and the name used for the author, Mike Kamens, is undoubtedly equally fictitious. Unlike some stories in this anthology, the real author behind the pseudonym is unknown.*

*Like many of the stories here, it's a bloody good read in more ways than one.*

*—Robert Deis*

**Opposite: The Schick "20," weasel not included. (From *The Saturday Evening Post*, October 3, 1953)**

When "Weasels" met the Mothers. *Weasels Ripped My Flesh*, Art by Neon Park copyright © 1970, 2024 Universal Music Group (UMG)

A (by no means complete) accounting of the fearsome and not so fearsome creatures that have made trouble for MAM protagonists:

| | | | |
|---|---|---|---|
| alligators | coyotes | lemmings | scorpions |
| anacondas | crabs | leopards | sea snakes |
| anteaters | crocodiles | lions | sharks |
| antelopes | eagles | mandrills | snakes |
| ants | electric eels | manta rays | snow leopards |
| baboons | elephants | marlins | spiders |
| badgers | elk | monkeys | spider monkeys |
| barracuda | flying squirrels | moray eels | squid |
| bats | giant otters | moose | stingrays |
| bighorn sheep | gila monsters | octopi | Tasmanian tigers |
| boars | gorillas | orangutans | tigers |
| bobcats | grizzly bears | ostriches | turtles |
| bears | hippos | pangolins | vultures |
| bees | horses | panthers | water buffalo |
| bison | hyenas | piranhas | weasels |
| bulls | iguanas | polar bears | whale sharks |
| caimans | jaguars | rats | whales |
| chimpanzees | killer whales | rattlesnakes | wild dogs |
| condors | komodo dragons | razorbacks | wolverines |
| cougars | leeches | rhinos | wolves |

Killer anteater (?) from "The Thing in the Pit," by Jon Hartt
***Escape to Adventure***, October 1960
**Artist uncredited**

## "WEASELS RIPPED MY FLESH"

— MIKE KAMENS —

*Man's Life*, September 1956
COVER ARTIST: WIL HULSEY

RIPPED MY FLESH

(Continued from page 23)

# WEASELS RIPPED MY FLESH

**Many claws tore at my skin putting razor sharp teeth in easy reach of my flesh.—The furry animals came from all directions—chewing—gnawing—turning the water red with my blood**

## by MIKE KAMENS

I WAS sprawled on a mound of hay—shotgun cradled in my arms and my head drooping fiercely from want of sleep—when that first ripple of alarm surged through the duck house.

Instinctively my finger curled on the trigger as I slowly sat upright, blinking at the soft amber glow of the kerosene lamp suspended from the rafter. I heard nothing. Only the breeders shifting timorously in their pens and their quacking.

I had two loads of 4's in the shotgun and a spare double-dose in my pocket in case of trouble. Fox—skunk—bobcat trouble. I felt good then. I brought the gun up and lined it along the rafter, waiting and praying for a shot.

Then I saw movement silhouetted against the rafters, rapid and distorted, and I stared incredulously as two pinpoints of sheer fire suddenly loomed down at me. I squinted at the animal for a long moment and when, an instant later, another appeared directly behind it and I saw the undulating tail and streak of white running down the center of its breast, I knew the cause of my headaches—weasels. In two nights, ninety ducks lost to these murderers!

I was so mad, I didn't think to look at the dropboards and see more weasels scampering over a pitchfork toward me. At least a dozen of them, big ones, a foot long, and they hit me at the precise moment I squeezed the trigger.

Something tore into my right leg, clawing and biting me so that the shot deflected downward striking the kerosene lamp. Rivulets of flame coursed along the hay as I fell to the floor, screaming and smashing my fists against the hideous furred body. I saw flesh and blood rip loose as I pulled it off me and then the duckhouse became a pyre.

For as long as was humanly possible, I tried to smother the flames. I tried despite the fact that weasels were clinging to my clothes and crawling up my back. I could smell the sickening odor of burning fur and hear the piteous lament of the trapped ducks. But I couldn't get them out because I was rolling on the floor ripping weasels off my face. . . .

It was 1954, a day after Hurricane Carol, and we were still without electricity. That's the equivalent of a

(Continued from page 39)

man in a gun battle with no gun. Incubators die, freshly killed ducks go bad, and all the vermin in the world have a field day in the dark night. Without electricity, the small company which I owned was speeding unalterably toward bankruptcy. I knew it, yet there wasn't a damned thing could be done but pray they'd restore power in sufficient time.

My farm was on the east shore of Connecticut, convenient to the hurricane but somehow, miraculously, it had been spared. Naturally, a few shingles got blown off and a hunk of roofing went flying, but on the main we were lucky. We—my wife, Mary, and I.

Actually, we were lucky in several respects. Because of the holiday weekend, Labor Day, I'd sold most of my freshly killed ducks. There was damned little left except some reserve stock and the ducklings-to-be still in incubation. Plus the live stock. We were lucky —until the weasels, I mean.

THE first night of the weasel trouble, we were so beat up from trying to keep the roof on the house, I slept right through the frantic quacking that meant sixty dead breeders. Mary broke the news gently the following dawn, "Mike, here's a cup of coffee. You'd better get up."

"Time is it?" I mumbled groggily.

"Six-thirty. Joe's back from the feed. He's downstairs in the kitchen, waiting—"

"For what?" I said, leaning up on one elbow and sipping the coffee. "More bad news?"

"You're psychic, Mike—"

"What? Tell me gently—"

"A lot of dead ducks. Something got into the breeder house last night. (Continued on page 50)



Illustration by **Wil Hulsey**

*I WAS* sprawled on a mound of hay—shotgun cradled in my arms and my head drooping fiercely from want of sleep—when that first ripple of alarm surged through the duck house.

Instinctively my finger curled on the trigger as I slowly sat upright, blinking at the soft amber glow of the kerosene lamp suspended from the rafter. I heard nothing. Only the breeders shifting timorously in their pens and their quacking.

I had two loads of 4's in the shotgun and a spare double-dose in my pocket in case of trouble. Fox-skunk-bobcat trouble. I felt good then. I brought the gun up and lined it along the rafter, waiting and praying for a shot.

Then I saw movement silhouetted against the rafters, rapid and distorted, and I stared incredulously as two pinpoints of sheer fire suddenly loomed down at me. I squinted at the animal for a long moment and when, an instant later, another appeared directly behind it and I saw the undulating tail and streak of white running down the center of its breast, I knew the cause of my headaches—weasels. In two nights, ninety ducks lost to these murderers!

I was so mad, I didn't think to look at the dropboards and see more weasels scampering over a pitchfork toward me. At least a dozen of them, big ones, a foot long, and they hit me at the precise moment I squeezed the trigger.

Something tore into my right leg, clawing and biting me so that the shot deflected downward striking the kerosene lamp. Rivulets of flame coursed along the hay as I fell to the floor, screaming and smashing my fists against the hideous furred body. I saw flesh and blood rip loose as I pulled it off me and then the duck house became a pyre.

For as long as was humanly possible, I tried to smother the flames. I tried despite the fact that weasels were clinging to my clothes and crawling up my back. I could smell the sickening odor of burning fur and hear the piteous lament of the trapped ducks. But I couldn't get them out because I was rolling on the floor ripping weasels off my face....

It was 1954, a day after Hurricane Carol, and we were still without electricity. That's the equivalent of a man in a gun battle with no gun. Incubators die, freshly killed ducks go bad, and all the vermin in the world have a field day in the dark night. Without electricity, the small company which I owned was speeding unalterably toward bankruptcy. I knew it, yet there wasn't a damned thing could be done but pray they'd restore power in sufficient time.

My farm was on the east shore of Connecticut, convenient to the hurricane but somehow, miraculously, it had been spared. Naturally, a few shingles got blown off and a hunk of roofing went flying, but on the main we were lucky. We—my wife, Mary, and I.

Actually, we were lucky in several respects. Because of the holiday weekend, Labor Day, I'd sold most of my freshly killed ducks. There was damned little left except some reserve stock and the ducklings-to-be still in incubation. Plus the live stock. We were lucky—until the weasels, I mean.

The first night of the weasel trouble, we were so beat up from trying to keep the roof on the house, I slept right through the frantic quacking that meant sixty dead breeders. Mary broke the news gently the following dawn, "Mike, here's a cup of coffee. You'd better get up."

"Time is it?" I mumbled groggily.

"Six-thirty. Joe's back from the feed. He's downstairs in the kitchen, waiting—"

"For what?" I said, leaning up on one elbow and sipping the coffee. "More bad news?"

"You're psychic, Mike—"

"What? Tell me gently—"

"A lot of dead ducks. Something got into the breeder house last night. Joe found a fair sized hole he said."

I nodded, gulped the coffee, dressed and went. down to the kitchen to talk with my foreman.

Joe Haines and I'd been friends for a long while. Since the Army, to be exact. I knew Joe and Joe's thoughts before he did, I think. He and I and two pluckers made it a four man operation with Mary doing the cash registering and bookkeeping. It was a small outfit, only a year and a half old, at the time.

"Fox?" I said, nodding.

"Don't think so, Mike. Looks like maybe a big cat of some sort. Maybe a mink or a family of skunks. Maybe a weasel? Can't tell for sure. Whatever it was he went through that house like—"

"Let's go!" I snapped. "Might as well see the worst now."

Thirty yards from the house Joe nodded at the fencing. He speculated some of the wind might've ripped holes along the bottom of the meshing. I suppose I said you're right or something; I don't remember. I was sick at heart and in my wallet where it hurt more.

ALL THAT season we'd had predator trouble, the usual thing—rats— skunk—even a bobcat or two. I expected to find the usual collection of half eaten ducks, but I was wrong. Of the sixty dead fowl we'd counted, only three had been chewed apart. The balance had been killed for the sheer love of spilling blood.

"No lights, Mike!" Haines sighed. "Bastard got in here and had a ball—"

"Kerosene lamp didn't faze him a damn," I nodded dourly. "Let's see where he got in."

So we looked, for more than an hour we checked the whole length of the duckhouse. On our hands and knees we covered every bit of running floorspace. Nothing. Then Haines took the ladder to the roof and checked there. Nothing.

"C'mon, Joe!" I called finally. "I'll figure something out. We've got other work to do."

Rest of the day I and Joe and the boys got the farm squared away as best we could without electricity.

Mary drove into town to plead with the electric company, and they told her there'd be service maybe that evening. Maybe we'd be in business after all!

BUT EVENING came and the power was still off. I swore upside down I'd hock my soul for an independent motor generator system.

After dinner that night I walked down to the ducks and checked six lanterns I'd hung over the pens. Then I went back to my gunrack. I was still putting on my jacket, figuring it'd be a long night's vigil sitting in the hay, when one of the hands came charging up.

"Mike! Something got in the house a few minutes ago!"

Right when my back was turned it had come again and ripped the throats of another 30 ducks…and so it was that I was well on my way down the drain. I'm not saying that 90 ducks would break us—but 90 in two days and how many more after that! Feel? How did I feel? I wanted to crawl into the ground and pull the lid over me.

So I'd gone down that third night—still no electricity—and stationed myself in a corner of the duck house, the big 12 gauge double cradled in my arms, waiting and praying for a shot. And the murdering devils returned for more and now I had them lined in my barrels.

But it didn't quite work out as I'd planned. Not now, it didn't. Now the barn was a roaring inferno with hundreds of ducks cooking alive and I was being ripped to pieces by foot-long weasels, their bodies wet with my blood.

In the stark reflections of the pyre I could see them running out of the duckhouse. I clawed great fistfuls of wet hair from my legs as they piled on the others already tearing me to pieces. I shrieked as the pain burned my flesh, but I stumbled back to the duckhouse and found the pitchfork.

Then, like some poor demented animal, I began spearing everything that moved before me. I saw the long double-pronged steel gouge through squirming bodies…one…two…four! I was out of my mind with pain and grief, yet I didn't stop skewering them even as I drove the pitchfork into my own leg to stop them.

I was soaked with blood, gushing down my face, blinding me, staggering around like a madman and shrieking at the top of my lungs—jabbing—jabbing with that pitchfork until I thought my arms would come off.

Behind me the heat of the holocaust singed my hair. I could smell burning feathers; I could hear the weird din of roasting live duck and it sickened me. I turned for a moment and stared at the barn, then turned again and drove the pitchfork into the shining white breast that was smeared with my blood.

My hands were torn to pieces every time I stopped to claw at some part of me being attacked. I had to drop the pitchfork 1n those moments, clubbing and tearing with my bare hands. I'd get one and another two would hit me from behind and start raking my face.

Time after time I'd drop to the river bank and roll over trying to smother them, but they'd squirm out from under, their fetid breath full in my lungs, feinting like

boxers for a new attack. I caught a weasel under his throat and dropped
the pitchfork and held onto his neck with both hands, squeezing until
the narrow mouth popped open and the tongue slid between the bloody
mouth. I squeezed until his body went limp, then turned and heaved it
fully into the fire.

The sound of my voice screaming Mary was like an insane person's,
and no doubt I was insane at that point. My body from the skull down
felt as though hundreds of hot pokers had been driven into the skin—
driven there and held by some devilish horror which I'd never believed
existed in real life.

And then it happened: I began to feel queasy from loss of blood
and the terrible panic in my heart. I couldn't hold the pitchfork and I
couldn't stand. The ground moved up and knocked the wind out of me
and I began rolling. I felt hairy bodies racing over my face. I clawed one
from my cheeks and tried shielding my face.

My blood—the taste of warm human blood excited them still
further—and the weasels drew back in a cluster to drink it from my
clothing. I felt a hairy tail cross my face and I opened my mouth and bit
solidly on a leg. I heard a squeaking sound in my vagueness and opened
my eyes to see drawn fangs gnashing before me. I lurched and missed
and crawled to my knees and began moving away.

VAGUELY I heard my wife's voice above the roar of the nightmare. I
screamed as I fell again, my chin banging against the handle of the
pitchfork. But it didn't knock me unconscious. It reminded me I was still
in the world of the living and if I wanted to go on living I'd have to get
up. I did, and the nightmare continued, but there were less of them now
and I could protect myself better now.

I WAS a long time in recovering. Four months. Plastic surgery and the
best of care gave me a face that seemed strange to me. I didn't recognize
it even after they finished restoring my sight. It was the face of a new
man because the old one had been eaten away. They gave me metal
fingers for my left hand in exchange for the hand I'd lost, too.

But they didn't give me a new memory. The old one still sends me
into paroxysms of fear every time someone mentions the duck business.
The night I died, slowly, by degrees, comes back in all its fantastic
horror, and I see the weasels again. And I remember the smell of blood
and feathers. It makes me wish they'd have eaten my memory along with
the rest of me. **///**

# ABOUT " 'BEAT' GIRLS"

UNTAMED *is one of my favorite vintage MAMs.*

*It featured painted covers by two great pulp artists who are more widely known for their science fiction magazine covers: Ed "Emsh" Emshwiller and Leo Morey. It also featured some wild stories that I find highly entertaining, though probably for different reasons than originally intended.*

*Consider, for example, this supposedly true story about beatniks from the February 1959 issue. In this exposé-style piece, author Gilbert Nash sets out to answer that question with his buddy Bob. Gil is a New Yorker who knows some Beats in the city. Bob is said to be a writer of detective novels from Bloomington, Indiana. Bob tells Gil he wants "to get a close look at this Beat Generation he'd been hearing so much about, and see if he could get some idea what makes it tick."*

*Bob isn't a fan of Jack Kerouac or Allen Ginsberg, or any of the other legendary Beat writers. But he is especially intrigued by a recent article he'd read "about the kids who held plush Madison Avenue jobs on weekdays and indulged their Beatness on weekends, at 'cool' parties." That article "described how all the girls take off their blouses and bras and walk around with nothing on top." With this tantalizing image in mind, Gil and Bob set off on their "quest for Beatness."*

*During the course of the evening they go to a beatnik party and actually do encounter one topless "Beat Girl," plus some others who are like, real crazy, Daddy-O.*

*For example, there's Joannie. She's a 21-year-old who has already bedded hundreds of guys. Joannie "keeps track of the number of men she sleeps with and announces the running total out loud at the appropriate moment." The "moment" is during sex. Joannie likes to shout out the guy's number ("297 or 369 or whatever the number is") while they're going at it. "It can be pretty disconcerting," Gil notes.*

*Then there's the blonde girl "who was not nude from the waist up, but might as well have been":*

"She was talking in a low, steady drone. 'Baby,' she said. 'Don't tell me about the past, baby. There is no past. The past is dead. The past is dead, baby. The future isn't here yet. Maybe there'll be a future, maybe there won't. We're in between. And in between is nowhere, baby. Nowhere."

*Man oh man, I dig that groovy beatnik lingo!*

*I also dig the story's unintentionally funny anecdote about how Beats liked to smoke peyote:*

"'Pot' is a word that is used loosely, like most words these Beat kids use," Gil explains in the story. "But generally it means the dried leaves of the peyote cactus, which are made into cigarettes and smoked. Though the stuff has obvious narcotic effects, for some odd reason it has not been made illegal in New York yet, and lots of the kids use it to get 'high,' or 'far out.' Aldous Huxley wrote a whole book about the sensations he had when he tried it, and now uncounted young people in New York grow the plants, dry the leaves, and smoke the stuff for kicks."

*The part about Aldous Huxley has a basis in fact. It refers to his groundbreaking 1954 book* The Doors of Perception.

*It's also true that peyote and the psychedelic alkaloid it contains—mescaline—were not yet illegal in most states or under federal drug laws when Gil wrote his story in 1959.*

*Of course, the part about smoking peyote leaves is hilariously absurd. Peyote is a cactus plant that has no leaves. And, it's not smoked. Indeed, it's not even smokable.*

*I also seriously doubt if many people in New York were growing peyote in 1959. And, I don't recall ever hearing anyone refer to anything but marijuana as "pot."*

*If you think Gil's knowledge gap about peyote and his search for topless Beat Girls sounds amusing, I suspect you'll enjoy reading his story, "'Beat' Girls: Worshippers of Zen and Sin?"*

—*Robert Deis*

## " 'BEAT' GIRLS: WORSHIPPERS OF ZEN AND SIN?"

— GILBERT NASH —

*Untamed*, February 1959
COVER ARTIST: LEO MOREY

her narrow chest, and now was
g her whole body closer to mine.
ped my hands and pulled away
, noticing Bob's look of amuse-
The girl tried to play it cool as I
off.
zily, she dropped onto the bed—
y just a thin mattress on a set of
—and roll
ed sheets
ly. "That
erybody
I'm contac
message
h . . ."
ling Bob
y. We mo
was even
w. The
e mixtur
unwash
d clothes,
spectable
red the g
were no
irls all
tter how
appened t
d it.
girl, a p
utstandin
completely
arent blou
ter anoth
to a con
his, and
nds, up
d and wa
him awa
m. "Hate
."
e the oth
e. I knew
oth read
were con
t. I pause
was.
swayed,
wine, an
inside
ly. "Pass
as about
soft, si
rtains. "
ge stuck
he said.
, Gil Na
Send him
ge stood
aved us in
rtains.
re were n
but plen
ough the dirty, uncurtained and
ed window. Sarah was sitting up
a crumpled sheet drawn up just
past her thighs. Otherwise, she
otally nude—and Sarah has one

bed beside her, inviting us to sit and talk
with her. She was utterly, cheerfully
drunk, and completely unconscious of
her nudity. Her lovely body gleamed in
the moonlight, rich, firm, cherry-tipped
breasts rising and falling rapidly as she
tried to take our hands and pull both of
us down beside her.

I couldn't help but be excited as I

ence between them
I've known is that
on the average,
special about the

I grinned. "It's
"If you asked any
if they were Beat
No, or claim they
But each of them

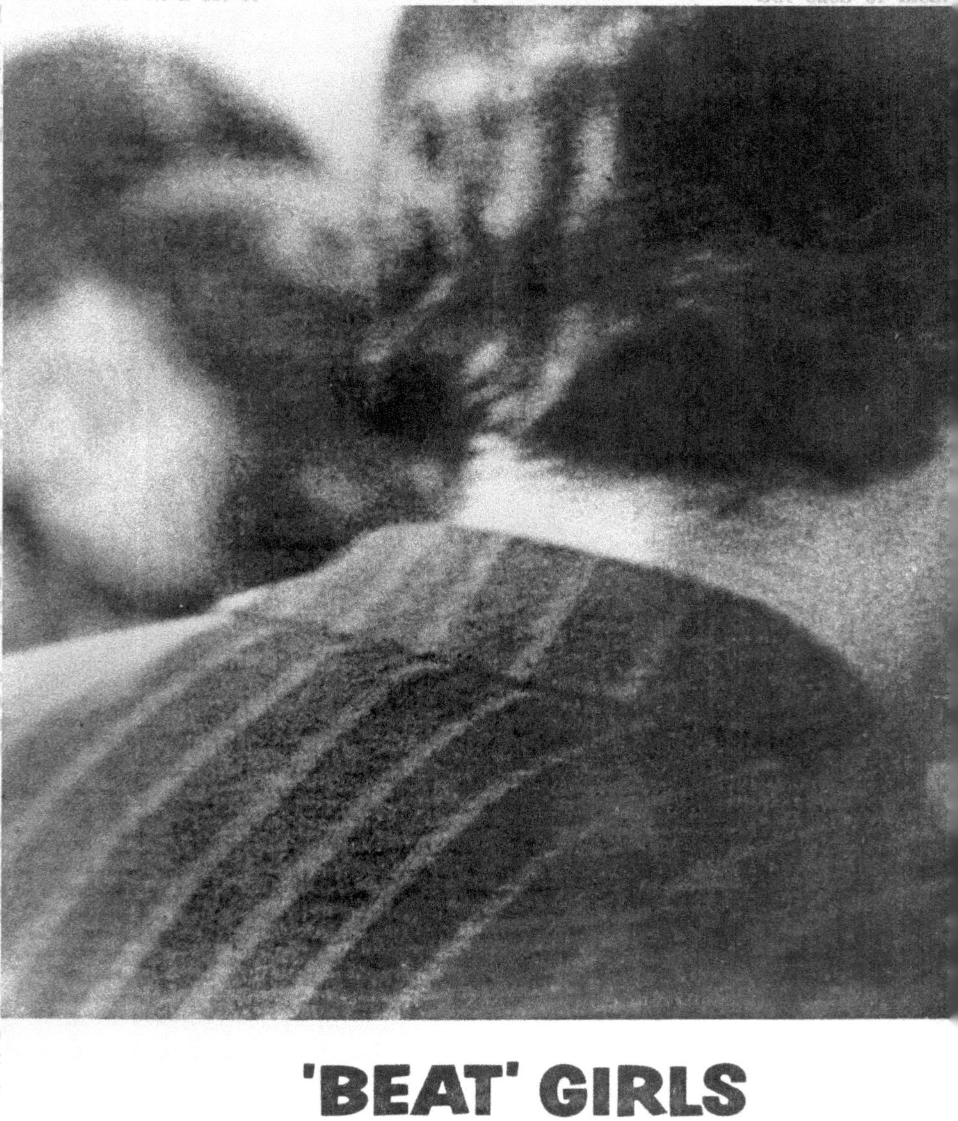

# 'BEAT' GIRLS

## Worshippers of Zen and Sin?

**By Gilbert Nash**

30

They're confused, neurotic, bored and often just pla
phony . . . but their one common obsession is with s

# 'Beat' Girls

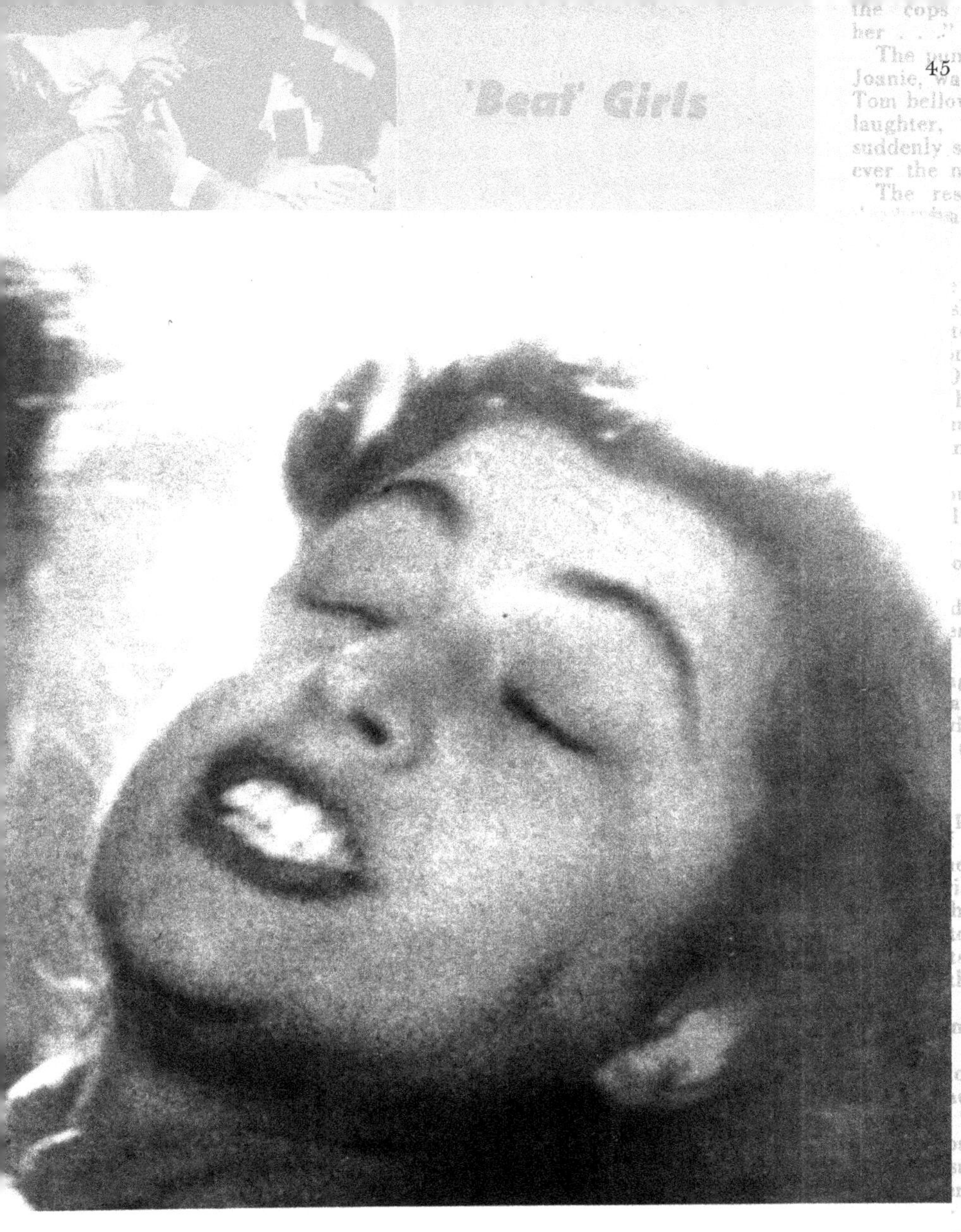

THE GIRL was short, dark, and sullen-looking. She stood slouched against the big built-in bookcases, [id]ly flipping the pages of a book, although she could [ha]rdly have been able to make out the type in the dim [lig]ht. Her black hair hung straight to her shoulders, and [m]atched the color of her over-sized sweater and baggy [sl]acks. The costume made her look shapeless and lumpy [at] first glance, but at second glance you could sort out [wh]ich lumps were which. It became obvious that the [fir]m young body under the thick cloth must be quite [sp]ectacular.

My friend Bob Wilson decided to try to get acquainted. He wandered over and made some remark I didn't catch. It must have concerned the book, though, for with a sudden, almost angry movement she slammed it back into the shelves. "Books!" she said contemptuously. "Who needs books? I read for twenty years, and now I don't read any more, except by accident. They all say the same thing in different ways . . . I could tell you what's in any one of them without reading it, if I want to think about it."

She turned abruptly and wandered away. Bob looked

31

**THE GIRL** was short, dark, and sullen-looking. She stood slouched against the big built-in bookcases, idly flipping the pages of a book, although she could hardly have been able to make out the type in the dim light. Her black hair hung straight to her shoulders, and matched the color of her over-sized sweater and baggy slacks. The costume made her look shapeless and lumpy at first glance, but at second glance you could sort out which lumps were which. It became obvious that the firm young body under the thick cloth must be quite spectacular.

My friend Bob Wilson decided to try to get acquainted. He wandered over and made some remark I didn't catch. It must have concerned the book, though, for with a sudden, almost angry movement she slammed it back into the shelves. "Books!" she said contemptuously. "Who needs books? I read for twenty years, and now I don't read any more, except by accident. They all say the same thing in different ways… I could tell you what's in anyone of them without reading it, if I want to think about it."

She turned abruptly and wandered away. Bob looked at me in bewilderment. I just smiled and shrugged. He had asked for this guided tour, and he had a lot to see yet. This was merely the beginning.

Bob is an old friend, who makes a comfortable living writing detective novels. In his home town of Bloomington, Indiana, this makes him something of an intellectual, but when he comes to New York, he looks more like a bumpkin. Since he's tall, rangy and muscular, very few operators ever try to put anything over on him. On the other hand, not many people discover what a bright and inquiring mind he has, either. I'm one of the few, and we've been friends for a long time.

This was one of his infrequent trips to town to see his literary agent—but this time he had another purpose as well. He confessed it to me within a few minutes of our first meeting in our regular bar. He wanted to get a close look at this Beat Generation he'd been hearing so much about, and see if he could get some idea what makes it tick.

"I've read Kerouac and Ginsberg and all the so-called spokesmen for the Beats," he confessed, his brow furrowed. "I've read all the books and articles I can find claiming to explain the whole thing. And frankly, all I get is more confused. The explanations don't explain anything, in the first place—and in the second, they all disagree with each other."

I nodded sagely. It was already clear that Bob figured I must be an expert on the subject, that I could not only fill him in on the picture but actually show it to him in person. Well, maybe I could.

I asked Bob if he'd read the article about the kids who held plush Madison Avenue jobs on weekdays and indulged their Beatness on weekends, at "cool" parties. The question got the expected result.

"The one where the writer described how all the girls take off their blouses and bras and walk around with nothing on top?" he asked. "And the fellows don't dare so much as try to touch the merchandise, because that would make them un-cool? Yeah, I read it. And brother, I hate to think how long *I'd* stay cool at a party like that! Any girl that flashes her uppers at me is asking for a pass!"

I grinned. Not that I don't know plenty of normal people in New York, mixed in with the weird ones, but Bob is so normal it hurts. It's refreshing to have him around.

"Don't believe all you read," I told him. "I've been to some of those Madison Avenue parties. Once in a while a girl strips to the waist, but it's usually pretty obvious that she's read that article too, and does it because she thinks she's supposed to. Mostly, when some of the males in the vicinity start to warm up, she finds some excuse to cover up again."

Bob looked disappointed. "You mean it's all phony?" he asked. "Everybody trying to live up to the legends some writer invented, or something like that?"

"I don't want to prejudice you," I said. "Suppose we see what we can dig up, so you can decide for yourself. I ought to be able to find some reasonably Beat parties tonight."

"Madison Avenue?" He lifted an eyebrow.

"Nope," I said. "That kind of party is usually just dull. Those cats aren't Beat; they're just bored—and boring. Besides, this is a week night, and you don't find many week night parties uptown. We go downtown."

GREENWICH Village is not what it used to be. That's putting it mildly, in fact. There has been a gradual change during the twenty-odd years I've been in New York, a change that has accelerated tremendously during the past couple of years. The area became a desirable place to live, and that ruined it. Rents became too high for the genuine artists, intellectuals and bohemians, and they moved out. But the myth remains. Nowadays you can scarcely force your way through the crowds on the sidewalks on weekend nights. Hundreds of well-dressed and well-heeled people from uptown, the Bronx and Queens come down to stare at the antics of the bohemians, and hundreds of high school kids from the same areas dress up in odd costumes and come down to make like bohemians and be stared at. The strip joints and sidewalk artists do a thriving business, but none of it is for real. The Village is now almost 100 percent tourist trap and 100 percent phony.

But the bohemians haven't died out. For the most part, they've just moved east of Third Avenue, into the tenement apartments, stores and lofts there. A few of them have gone north of 14th Street, but most of them have managed to stay south of it. The area doesn't have anything like the quaint, old world charm the Village used to have and now tries to imitate, but it has low rents—and interesting people.

I started Bob's tour at the Chapel, which is a facetious name for a loft inhabited by a couple of young fellows who write and paint sporadically and spend most of their time, dreaming up ways to live without working. The Chapel is on the northern end of the Bowery, in a building supposedly devoted to manufacturing lofts. Theoretically, it is illegal to live in such places, but the housing shortage is still so bad in New York that many such violations are winked at by the authorities, in return for small bribes in some cases and in others out of pure pity or realism. Charlie and Tom claim the Chapel is merely an art studio if anyone asks, and they never have trouble except when their parties get too noisy.

We stepped over the drunk sleeping in the doorway and went up three flights of dimly lit, sagging stairs. The party was already in full swing when we got there. I warned Bob to keep his pint of bourbon carefully concealed—the usual freeloaders would make short work of it if he didn't—and we went in.

As usual, the place was in semi-darkness and filled with slowly swirling clouds of smoke. At least, the few lights the boys have were on, though; somebody must have paid the light bill for a change. There was already an impressive array of empty bottles lined up just inside the door: mostly very cheap wine, beer and ale bottles, but a few whiskey and gin bottles as well. We skirted these carefully and were immediately absorbed in the crowd.

I managed to introduce Bob to one of the hosts, but after that I gave up. Nobody bothers with introductions at these parties, and if you wait to be introduced you're sunk. For a short while, I just wandered about with Bob in tow, letting him get the feel of the place. The loft is roughly divided up into rooms by flimsy partitions, erected seemingly at random. The furniture is scant, and what there is is pretty rickety, so most people were standing. There were so many there that night it was hardly possible to do much else, anyway.

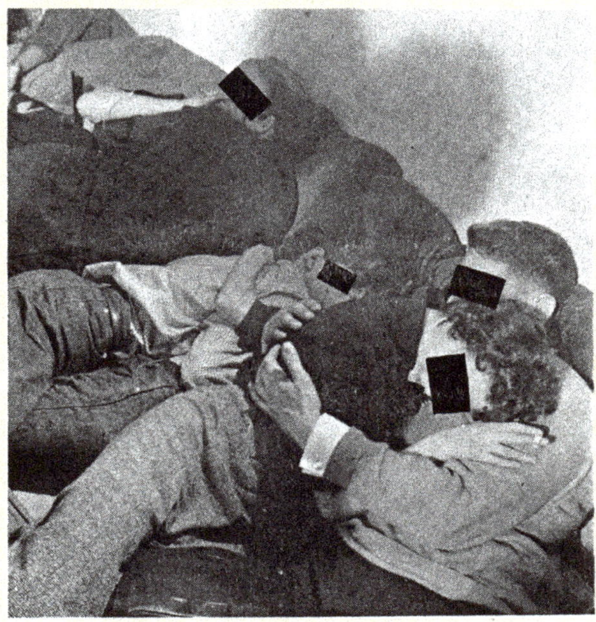

Bob's attempt to get acquainted with the girl with the book discouraged him for a while, and he rejoined me. We ducked into a corner for a quick pull at our bottles, then resumed the quest for Beatness. There was a likely-looking group in the corner which Tom has walled off with huge rubber plants, so we made for that.

The bet paid off. Standing with her back almost touching the clammy brick wall was a plump blonde girl who was not nude from the waist up, but might as well have been. She wore a thin, faded man's shirt, wide open at the throat and tied in a knot beneath her large breasts. There was a huge expanse of skin visible between it and her ragged shorts, which were obviously the barely surviving remains of a pair of dungarees. There was no line of her body that could not be detected either around the cloth or through it. Her posture and movements help a lot, too.

She had her hands clasped behind her head, her elbows jutting out, and she was moving her body constantly in what amounted to a fantastically slow burlesque grind. The effect was stimulating, to say the least. But the blonde herself was anything but stimulated.

She was talking in a low, steady drone. "Baby," she said. "Don't tell me about the past, baby. There is no past. The past is dead. The past is dead, baby. The future isn't here yet. Maybe there'll be a future, maybe there won't. We're in between. And in between is nowhere, baby. Nowhere."

Though there were many people in the circle around her, she seemed to be addressing herself solely to a fantastically tall, pale, scrawny boy in a turtle-necked sweater. His head bobbed up and down, keeping time with the undulations of her body. "I get the message, kid," he whispered throatily. "I get the message. We're like dead. Nowhere."

The conversation, if you can call it a conversation, went on like that. They kept going over and over the same theme, only varying the phrases slightly. Once in a while, others in the group repeated a few words in a sort of litany. And all the ,while the blonde kept swaying, writhing, her breasts jiggling against the taut cloth of the shirt as her hips twitched erratically.

Suddenly, as if at a signal, the group turned and melted away. All but the blonde girl and the tall boy, that is. As Bob and I left with the others, we saw that the pair had sunk to a mattress on the bare floor, wrapped in each other's arms. As the rest of us moved away, somebody nudged me. "Poor Zack," the fellow said, shaking his head. "He thinks he's going to make out with Polly—but he won't. Nobody ever does..."

IN ANOTHER corner we found Tom, one of the hosts, a mountainous fellow with a deceptively placid face who is the greatest expert I've ever seen at heaving out the Bowery winos who occasionally try to crash these parties. He was standing guard over his precious hi-fi set, to make sure nobody scratched or "borrowed" the records or damaged the equipment. But his usual grin was broader than ever and his voice boomed jovially as he welcomed us to the circle around him. "Hi," he said briefly, then returned to the story he had been telling. "Man, that was a brawl," he rumbled. "Party, last night at Joanie's pad, I mean. Probably would have been all right if Otto hadn't gotten jealous of Joanie—can you imagine being jealous of Joanie?—started throwing bottles out the window, and then run off screaming into the street. That's what *really* brought the cops!

"It looked rough for a while there. They didn't just tell us to keep things quiet, the way the cops usually do. They threatened to run us all in. But then Joanie took over. She slid up to the cops and started to unbutton her dress, and asked them if they wouldn't like to go in the bedroom to talk it over. Well, the cop went in the bedroom with her..."

The punchline, to anybody who knows Joanie, was obvious. "Can you imagine," Tom bellowed, almost doubling over with laughter, "how they felt when Joanie suddenly squealed '297' or '369' or whatever the number is by now?"

The rest of the crowd laughed enthusiastically. I glanced at Bob, and saw him looking completely puzzled. "Joanie," I explained, "has a peculiar habit. She keeps track of the number of men she sleeps with, and announces the running total out loud at the appropriate moment. It can be pretty disconcerting. Oh yes, it's also her ambition to go to bed with more men than any other woman in history. She isn't doing badly, considering she isn't twenty-one yet…"

The story about Joanie over with the crowd fell to discussing other girls who were not present. In particular, they talked about wives and girl-friends who happened to be in Hillside, Rockland State, and other mental institutions at the moment. It was important to know who was in, who was out, who might be coming out soon. Somebody suggested that we should all rent bicycles the following Sunday, and visit the girls at one of the institutions, to cheer them up…

AT THIS point, Bob was beginning to look as if he needed air, so I took him up to the roof. This is one of the more enviable features of the Chapel, one of the things that make it look superior to people who live in ordinary apartments, and who do not stop to consider the lack of heat and hot water. Tom has built several plant boxes out of old lumber and extended his jungle up there, and it is unarguably a fine place to loaf, drink and smoke.

Like the interior of the loft, it was crowded. There were couples necking, and groups discussing politics. The latter groups usually centered around intense young men telling how they planned to take over some vital faction in some splinter group of some totally unknown political party or club, but there were plenty of intense young girls present, too. Bob and I looked at the stars a while, and then went back inside.

As we virtually groped our way inside, Bob suddenly grabbed my elbow. "Hey!" he said. "I know what's been bothering me! There are a lot of things about this set-up that don't correspond with my ideas about the Beat Generation, but there's one in particular. Where are all the Zen Buddhists?"

I'd been waiting for that. I knew the gang owned at least one copy of a book explaining Zen Buddhism, just as it owned one copy of *On the Road.* That is, somebody had pilfered it from a bookstore, gotten it from a book club under an alias, or in some manner acquired it without paying. After reading it himself, the first owner passed it on, and it kept making the rounds. To be absolutely honest, though, when *On the Road* was first published one of the girls was so anxious to read it that she visited all the pads collecting deposit bottles and returning them until she had enough cash to buy the book.

I steered Bob toward one of the bedrooms—small areas separated from the rest of the loft by crude Masonite panels and cloth and bamboo curtains hung up any which way. A thin girl with glasses and short hair fell in beside us as we entered. "Give me a couple of cigarettes, Gil," she demanded.

I handed her my pack, and she took two cigarettes. From the pocket of her skirt came a roll of Scotch tape. Placing the cigarettes end to end, she taped them together. She was nervous, and her movements got more and more excited. When she had her double-length cigarette put together, she looked at me beseechingly, and I quietly handed her a pack of matches. Bob, meanwhile, was watching the whole performance in fascination.

The girl got the thing lit, and took deep, gasping puffs. Her whole body shuddered from the effort. Between drags she stood, very straight and erect, with her hands held away from her sides. Then she would take another puff, pulling in huge quantities of smoke, and you could almost feel it coursing through her entire body.

When the double cigarette was almost half smoked, she dropped it carelessly on the floor and ground it under her foot. She leaned back against a battered bureau, and ecstatic look on her face, and smiled at us. Slowly, her eyes closed and her arms came together, hugging herself warmly. I waited, knowing she'd soon come back to Earth somewhat.

Finally she opened one eye and looked at us. "Man," she breathed huskily. "That's great! That's my kick. The best way of getting far out I know of!"

"Better than pot?" I asked.

"Pot" is a word that is used loosely, like most words these Beat kids use. But generally it means the dried leaves of the peyote cactus, which are made into cigarettes and smoked. Though the stuff has obvious narcotic effects, for some odd reason it has not been made illegal in New York yet, and lots of the kids use it to get "high," or "far out." Aldous Huxley wrote a whole book about the sensations he had when he tried it, and now uncounted young people in New York grow the plants, dry the leaves, and smoke the stuff for kicks.

The thin girl looked at me. "For me it's better," she said happily. "For me pot is nothing. Plain tobacco is better. The idea is to get the smoke directly into your lungs, without even taking it into your mouth first. It puts me so far out, like, I could die. Want to try it?"

I shook my head. I've seen a lot of kids get really drugged on pot, but others, when they speak of getting high or far out, seem to mean merely drunk. Personally, I prefer to get drunk on liquor, if at all. I took the thin girl's hand to hold her attention, and asked her if she'd finished reading the Zen philosophy.

She looked at me dreamily. "Doll," she murmured, and I wondered if she meant me or Zen. "Doll. I read the first chapter, and I got the message. I didn't have to read any more. I'm with him, like. It cleared up everything. Now I don't have any worries or troubles at all. Like, great, man."

Taking her hand had been a mistake. She had pulled it and was holding it against her narrow chest, and now was drawing her whole body closer to mine. I dropped my hands and pulled away hastily, noticing Bob's look of amusement. The girl tried to play it cool as I backed off.

Woozily, she dropped onto the bed—actually just a thin mattress on a set of springs—and rolled back among the dirty, crumpled sheets. "Telepathy!" she said suddenly. "That's my kick now. I can dig everybody and anybody that way. Like, I'm contacting you, man. I'm getting a message from you. You're getting through…"

Hauling Bob after me, I departed in a hurry. We moved on through the loft, which was even darker and more crowded now. The people were the usual strange mixture, some looking completely unwashed and wearing old, patched clothes, other quite well-dressed and respectable looking. The men outnumbered the girls, and in most cases people were not paired off in couples. The girls all got plenty of attention, no matter how attractive or unattractive they happened to be, and they obviously enjoyed it.

One girl, a particularly beautiful one with outstanding high, firm breasts almost completely revealed by a low-cut, transparent blouse, was approaching one boy after another. She backed each victim into a corner, pressed her body against his, and made rapid motions with her hands, up and down his body. Bob stopped and watched, fascinated, but I pulled him away. "She's a lesbian," I told him. "Hates men, and likes to hurt them…"

OUTSIDE the other bedroom, we ran into George. I knew that he and his wife had both read Zen pretty thoroughly, and were considered experts on the subject. I paused and asked him where Sarah was.

He swayed, clutching his bottle of cheap wine, and peered at us owlishly. "She's inside on the bed," he smiled foolishly. "Passed out."

I was about to turn away, when Sarah's soft, silky voice came through the curtains. "Who's that?" she said. George stuck his head in. "It's Gil Nash," he said.

"Ooh, Gil Nash!" she squealed. "How *nice!* Send him in! *Nice* old Gil Nash!"

George stood aside, grinning foolishly, and waved us in. We pushed on through the curtains.

There were no. lights at all on in the room, but plenty of moonlight filtered in through the dirty, uncurtained and unshaded window. Sarah was sitting up in bed, a crumpled sheet drawn up just barely past her thighs. Otherwise, she was totally nude—and Sarah has one of the most beautiful bodies I've even seen.

"Gil!" she exclaimed. "How *nice!* And a friend! Who's your *nice* friend, Gil!"

I introduced Bob, adding needlessly that he was from Bloomington, Indiana. Sarah said that Bloomington, Indiana, was nice, and patted the edges of the bed beside her, inviting us to sit and talk with her. She was utterly, cheerfully drunk, and completely unconscious of her nudity. Her lovely body gleamed in the moonlight, rich, firm, cherry-tipped breasts rising and falling rapidly as she tried to take our hands and pull both of us down beside her.

I couldn't help but be excited as I looked at her, though I tried not to be. I knew she wasn't trying to seduce us. Sarah sincerely believes that everything is nice, and she wants to be friends with everybody. Being friendly can include going to bed together, or just going naked in front of other people without feeling embarrassed. She's really a sweet girl, but a little frustrating to be around sometimes.

Bob and I sat down next to her, and I could see he was having a hard time keeping his hands off her. She lay back, put her head on the pillow, smiled happily at us—and passed out.

We left quietly. George was nowhere in sight.

LATER, over black coffee in an all-night cafeteria, we talked it over. I couldn't resist needling Bob a bit.

"Well, you saw one girl without her blouse," I said. "And some of the others would have been glad to take theirs off if you'd asked them to."

He rubbed a hand across his forehead, looking tired and confused. "Yeah, I know," he said. "But it certainly wasn't like the descriptions I've read. Those kids may be all mixed up in lots of ways, but I wouldn't call them *cool*. They get all excited about all kinds of things. They may be loose and wild, and some of them may be too neurotic for their own good. But the only difference between them and other bohemians I've known is that they're a little younger, on the average. I don't see anything special about the Beats!"

I grinned. "It's a funny thing," I said. "If you asked any of those boys or girls if they were Beat, they'd probably say No, or claim they were only partly Beat. But each of them would say the *others* were Beat. It's a nice, convenient label, and they stick it on each other because it's easy and popular—but I don't know anyone that feels *completely* Beat."

Bob looked at me seriously, and I could see the wheels turning in his head. "Yes," he said. "But they do have some things in common. They're all afraid of the future, and don't want to face it. They don't seem to like work. They talk about art, but not many of them work very hard at being artists or writers or anything, either..."

"You'd be surprised at how many of them are being supported by the folks back home," I put in. "And back home may be no farther away than Brooklyn!"

There was a real light in Bob's eyes. "I guess they're not so different from any bohemian kids anywhere," he said. "Just a little more worried about the world, and a little more self-conscious about the role they're playing. Still, I want to find out more. There may be more to it, somewhere!"

I had my doubts, personally, but the night wasn't over yet. It never is, for Beats. We paid for our coffee, and I led him off to another party. **///**

Among easily demonized groups MAMs sought to cast as menaces to society, beatniks were never real contenders—though MAMs certainly tried.

Often serving as explainers and clarifiers for readers feeling lost amid sweeping cultural changes, MAMs tracked subcultures that challenged accepted norms. As a cultural phenomenon, beatniks inspired both curiosity and disdain, titillation and judgment—that sweet spot between catnip and kryptonite underpinning so much MAM content. Beatniks were a ripe subject for overheated analysis and exposés.

But while MAM non-fiction focused on satisfying readers' curiosities (and catered to readers' prejudices), MAM *fiction* sparked thrills by targeting readers' fears, anxieties, and concerns. Where MAM non-fiction might be exploratory, approaching subjects with some level of nuance, MAM fiction relied on readers' unequivocal agreement that the bad guys were bad guys—real, and legitimate threats. And ultimately, beatniks just weren't that threatening. Their public image lacked the unified vision and violent tendencies that made such effective MAM antagonists of foreign adversaries and, closer to home, leather-jacketed gangs of juvenile delinquents brandishing switchblades and chains.

So while a 1959 article like "'Beat' Girls" addressed readers' uncertainty about an emerging counter-cultural scene (while tantalizing readers about what went on within that scene), mainstream perception of Beats and beatniks would soon skew comedic, represented by *Dobie Gillis'* work-averse Maynard G. Krebs, *Beany and Cecil's* Wild Man of Wildsville, and any number of beret-wearing, finger-popping bongo enthusiasts employed as comic relief.

There's a desperation in *For Men Only*'s struggle to villainize beatniks in its November 1966 issue, with the

*For Men Only,* November 1966
Cover by Mort Künstler

CK Winston story, "Beatnik Raiders Who Pulled the Riviera's Great Gambling Ship Highjack." Mort Künstler's cover illustration *(above)* is packed with guns, bikinis, and engaging bits of business, but absolutely nothing about the scene or characters says "beatnik," any more than a shipboard heist does. As MAM villains, they were miscast and underqualified.

Fortunately for MAMs, beatniks begat hippies, with their threatening ties to protest movements and more radical strains of activism. Charles Manson and the notion of homicidal hippies would push the trope into high gear, and editors found hippies blended easily with popular and emerging villains in MAM fiction such as violent biker gangs, murderous occultists, and Satan worshippers.

—*Wyatt Doyle*

# ABOUT WALTER KAYLIN

THE LATE *writer Walter Kaylin [1921–2017] was one of the grand masters of MAM stories and overdue for rediscovery. He is name-checked by famous authors in two pieces reprinted in this anthology. In Josh Alan Friedman's interview with the late Mario Puzo, the* Godfather *author said of Kaylin: "He was great!" In the memoir that concludes this volume, "Even the Rhinos Were Nymphos," Josh's father, Bruce Jay Friedman, used the same adjective, calling him "the great Walter Kaylin."*

*From the late 1950s to the mid-1970s, he wrote hundreds of stories for the genre under his own name, his common pseudonym Roland Empey, or his less frequent* nom de plume *David Mars.*

*Many of Kaylin's men's adventure stories are gritty action/adventure yarns, ranging from war stories to Westerns. Some are fact-based historical pieces. Most are superior examples of the faux "true" stories that were a hallmark of MAMs.*

*A couple of years ago, I asked Josh if he knew whether Kaylin was still alive. He told me he wasn't sure. But he gave me contact info for Walter's daughter Lucy Kaylin, who is herself a luminary in the realm of modern magazines. Lucy was a top editor at* GQ *and* Marie Claire *and Deputy Editor of* O, The Oprah Magazine.

*I was happy to find out from her that Walter is still kicking and living in Old Lyme, Connecticut. I was ecstatic when I got the chance to interview him for the MensPulpMags.com blog and later got his permission to reprint some of his MAM stories.*

*The following tale, "Bar Room Girl Who Touched Off a Tribal War," was published, straight-faced, as a true story in the June 1960 issue of* Male *magazine. It's illustrated with a terrific duotone painting by the masterful pulp illustration artist Charles Copeland. But to add an air of reality, the layout also includes a newsclip and news photos related to the place and events mentioned in the story.*

*Of course, it was all a product of the combined talents of Walter Kaylin and the staff of* Male, *led at the time by Editorial Director Bruce Jay Friedman.*

*—Robert Deis*

**"BAR ROOM GIRL WHO TOUCHED OFF A TRIBAL WAR"**

— WALTER KAYLIN —

*Male,* June 1960
COVER ARTIST: MORT KÜNSTLER

POISON MURDERS brought Belgian troops to Luluabourg but carnage had already turned town into a morgue

By WALTER KAYLIN
Art by CHARLES COPELAND

# BAR ROOM GIRL WHO TOUCHED OFF A TRIBAL WAR

**From her throne in Baluba land, she offered a Yank a season's pass to her affections provided he brought along the head of her worst enemy to use as a door stop . . .**

▶ The kidnaping of Ruzi Dugg took place one night during the first week of December, 1959. The Baluba sub-chief was returning to his village by jeep from a meeting with Belgian officials in Luluabourg. He rode in the back with a body guard beside him and another in front next to the driver. The discussions had dealt with the growing unrest in the Congo, particularly as it concerned the threat of conflict between the Baluba and Lulua tribes. The Baluba was a huge man of great calm and composure and he had no difficulty falling asleep as the jeep picked its way along the jungle trail that led to his village. He woke only when it stopped, so suddenly he wound up on the driver's neck. His first thought was to hit everyone within

## DEATH TOLL GROWS IN CONGO

### Female "Poison Mixer" Incites War

LULUABOURG, Belgian Congo, Dec. 11—A naked screaming Lulua "diviner" named Tono Muj last night led a howling mob of her Lulua tribesmen in a raid against the Baluba tribe.

Estimates of the dead and injured ran as high as 500.

It is assumed in government circles that the attack was the result of the abduction of a Baluba chief by the Luluas.

The diviner, or *misheke* (r
of poisons) is dedicated to
ing out witches through
trials," in which the vi
a lethal potion pre

**Illustrations by Charles Copeland**

**THE KIDNAPPING** of Ruzi Dugg took place one night
during the first week of December, 1959. The Baluba subchief was
returning to his village by jeep from a meeting with Belgian officials
in Luluabourg. He rode in the back with a body guard beside him and
another in front—next to the driver. The discussions had dealt with the
growing unrest in the Congo, particularly as it concerned the threat
of conflict between the Baluba and Lulua tribes. The Baluba was a
huge man of great calm and composure and he had no difficulty falling
asleep as the jeep picked its way along the jungle trail that led to his
village. He woke only when it stopped, so suddenly he wound up on
the driver's neck. His first thought was to hit everyone within reach,
but he was discouraged from attempting it by the sight of a tall, white
man standing beside the jeep covering its occupants with a rifle. He
recognized the man as a lion hunter named Buddy Grace.

"I was hoping you'd be alone," Grace said. "This part of it don't
give me any pleasure."

His first shot hit the back seat guard somewhere in the face. Just
where couldn't be decided. There wasn't enough face left for the
investigators to work with.

"The way of violence is the way of the ignorant and ungodly," Ruzi
Dugg said in disapproval while the two in front scrambled to get out
the other side of the jeep. "What did he ever do to you to deserve such
unkind treatment?"

"Nothing," Grace said. "I never saw him before."

He shot the nearer of the front seat men as he tried to squeeze past
the wheel and the other when he was ten yards beyond the jeep. The
second man fell, but got up almost immediately and Grace had to shoot
him again to bring him down for keeps.

"You have similar plans for me?" Ruzi Dugg inquired.

"I did all right with this one, but 1 sure won't get any medals for
knocking off that second bird," Grace said poking the man in the front
seat with his rifle. "That first shot must have hit him right in the can.
No, you don't have anything to worry about. I'm just bringing you to
this sweet and gentle lady that thinks you're—"

He'd had to poke hard to dislodge the body stuck under the wheel.

He had lost his balance
when it tumbled out of the
jeep and in that moment a
hand like a bag of bricks
came down on his neck. He
went flat on the seats and
turned over to see Ruzi
Dugg coming down on him.
He put a hand over his face
and jabbed it straight up,
the heel of it catching the
African under the chin. It
jarred a grunt out of him,
drove his great bull's head
sideways, and permitted
Grace to get out from
under and roll the other

down to the floor with his head coming to rest against the gear shift.
As he landed there Grace stood up with a foot on each seat and as the
Baluba started to get up Grace kicked viciously at his head to drop him
where he'd been.

"What do you say?" the hunter said, sitting on the back of the
driver's seat. "I ain't getting any more fun out of this than you are.
You'll have to do the driving so 1 can keep an eye on you. I'll point you
out the way to go."

Ruzi Dugg pushed himself up till his head was at seat level. Blood
poured down his face from where Grace's foot had caved in his forehead,
but the eye he raised to the waiting hunter was alert and calculating.

"Don't try it," Grace said. "You're all tied up in the machinery there
and you wouldn't have a chance. Come on, it might not be as bad as you
think. I'll put the boots to you again if you push me into it, but I'd just
as soon I didn't have to."

"It's Tono Muj, isn't it?" the Baluba said.

"Yes."

She was a startling woman to look at, Tono Muj; a curious
combination of raw, surging Africa and the mocking cynicism of the
Orient. Her body was straight and strong as any Lulua woman's, the
breasts outthrust and high in hard-sell advertisement of her physical
needs and capacities. Yet, her features were neat and precise, her skin the
soft amber tone of wine syrup, and her wide-slanted eyes cool as a pool
hall hustler's. She ran an *azifo* (native bar) in the great, sprawling camp
housing the men who built the paved road from Luluabourg to Solwezi

in Rhodesia, but she considered this just a sideline. By training and natural interest (mother killed as a witch, father a Japanese missionary who went mad with religious fervor), she was a diviner, a person dedicated to the rooting out of witches and sorcerers from an otherwise healthy populace.

"A hundred and eleven dollars." she had said one fateful night to Buddy Grace, the hunter brought down from Kenya to stop the lions from mangling the men building the road. "A hundred and eleven dollars for Ruzi Dugg. He poisons the minds of his people against the Lulua. I would try him as a sorcerer."

"That ain't an awful lot of dough," Grace said, a long, loose-bodied man with a distaste for speed or extra effort. "Why not get a couple of your own guys to do it? Maybe they come cheaper than me."

"They have become too soft and lazy for such a job," the woman said. "It means nothing to them that Ruzi Dugg tells the Baluba to scorn us. My people have lost their pride and self-respect. There is none I could trust to do what I ask."

"Well, I can't do that kind of work for that kind of money," Grace said. "Hell I get that much every week just for shooting a couple of cats."

"It is all I have," Tono Muj said sullenly.

"It ain't enough," Grace said.

"In that case—"

He had been sitting on a cot in his tent wearing just a pair of shorts the woman standing and facing him. He grinned now and sank back on his elbows as she kissed his chest and touched her tongue to the palms of his hands.

"I got a feeling I'd be safer bedding down with a cobra," he said drawing her to him and turning sideways so they were lying against each other and her asking-taking-tasting-wanting kisses were on his throat and eyes and mouth. "Only you're too good to pass up. You're too good to pass up no matter what."

He was an aggressive man where women were concerned, but with Tono Muj that night he gave up his customary role and permitted things to be done to him rather than calling the plays himself. Yet, so subtle was her approach that at no point did he feel himself unmanned. An amazing use of finger tips, tongue, sweet-pressing thighs and soft moans of pleasure-pain featured her approach, the whole of it merged into a package so tender and worshipping that Grace wound up feeling more of a bull than ever before.

It was a performance combining the skills of modern bohemia's

CLEAN-UP SQUADS toured ruins day after riots, picking up hacked Baluba bodies

GUILTY ARROWS, tipped with *ihumi* poison, were used for "witch trials", always proved victim was a "devil"

most creative experimenters and Sultan Saladin's medieval courtesans, those legendary women trained in the art and science of love from infancy for the sole purpose of pleasing the lords of Arabia. It left Grace feeling relaxed and exalted, cleansed and comforted.

"Did I please you?" she inquired lying with her head in his lap and smiling up at him. "If so, perhaps even for only a hundred and eleven dollars you will not object to—"

"Now let's not get started on politics again," he said. "Killing these cats is a government job and since it pays okay and I like the work I'm in no rush to lose it. It might happen if I started running around popping people into sacks. So what do you say we forget it and concentrate on scheduling ourselves a next time? Or better still why don't you bring your toothbrush over and move right in with—?"

"I have already scheduled our next time," the woman said spilling snake-like out of his lap and standing up. "It will be the night you bring me Ruzi Dugg."

He didn't want any part of her deal—but he was, as has been noted, an aggressive man where women were concerned. This is clearly indicated in the letter of recommendation sent to Congolese officials on his behalf by a former associate in Kenya:

*Mr. Grace is a most remarkable shot, a sure and experienced tracker, and a man who takes his responsibilities seriously,* it read in part. *Liquor presents no problem to him, nor do women if they are sufficiently available. We are under the impression here that the women of our Aberdare forest tribes are among the most repulsive in all Africa, but Mr. Grace seemed not to find that true. The attention he paid them was truly astonishing. A rather crudely stated joke among the other hunters has it that should all women disappear from the face of the earth, Mr. Grace would not find it objectionable paying court to a lady rhinoceros. Nevertheless, I recommend him highly—*

Grace's preoccupation with women had been evidenced in the Lulua villages before his night with Tono Muj and was demonstrated again immediately after it. The tempo even increased. He became a familiar sight jumping out of his jeep before some jungle mud hut and darting inside for 10-15 minutes with one or another of the savage, grunting women who serviced him, then running out again to drive off and get back on the job. He began to sleep less and drink more. His work suffered and a tracker was mauled to death by a lion Grace should have killed, but only managed to wound.

He became known in those vile, steaming, stifling pits that were the Luluabourg brothels and here his playmates were the walking corpses of women ravaged by drugs and illness and a lifetime of neglect and excess. He was a staggering, bellowing, vomiting wild man in these places and there were women who feared the violence of his needs and

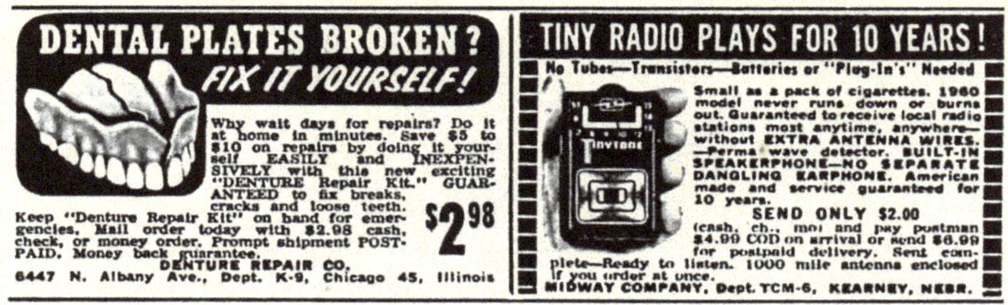


fled at his approach. And finally he began to drop into Tono Muj's dim-lighted, low-ceilinged *azifo* to drink native beer with the Lulua road builders and jeer good naturedly at the calm-eyed diviner moving back and forth behind her plank bar.

"Make way for the Queen of Sheba," he might call out in comment on her proud stride. "How do you get all that equipment to swing that way, honey? Come on honey, give the boys a treat."

The Africans standing along the bar or sitting at the tables behind him would laugh dutifully, but nudge each other too, and form the word *buzolo* with their silent mouths, a white man who has lost his grip because of a native woman. Days went by and his comments became louder and more vicious, the earlier good nature no longer there, the pretense of indifference all gone. He called her "whore" and bragged to the quiet grinning room that he had had her. "The biggest whore in the Congo and I ought to know"—and the men laughed outright and slapped their knees and laughed still harder when he slipped in a puddle of beer and sprawled on the floor.

*"Buzolo! Buzolo!"* they chanted at him as though it were a football cheer and pounded their heavy metal drinking mugs on the tables in unison. *"Buzolo! Buzolo!"*—and Grace staggered along the bar howling insults at them and challenging them to come fight. *"Buzolo! Buzolo! Buzolo! Bu—"*

HE BURST into her hut later that night and dragged her off her cot by the hair. She fell to the floor, but bounced up as though she were equipped with springs and began to run around the tiny room. He caught up to her, bulled her into a corner and punched her to the floor. She covered up as best she could while he kicked at her and when at last he was through she took his muddy, booted foot upon her trembling body and called him her king, her god, her emperor.

"But I have sworn an oath," she whispered. "I must deny myself the glories of your passion until you bring me Ruzi Dugg."

He cursed her obscenely and threatened to beat her till the blood

ran out of her ears. She sadly acknowledged this as his right, but
continued to murmur there was nothing she could do about it because
of her oath. He flung himself out the hut like one demented and was
back at the *azifo* the next night, entering a few minutes after she had
begun the slow, sensuous Lulua *uzluma* dance with a road worker
named Zezi Lo, a powerfully built man, emphatic and confident in the
dance's elaborate movements. For some moments Grace watched them
in brooding silence and men' at the bar and tables touched each other
lightly to call attention to him. Then he walked toward the dancers,
turned Zezi Lo toward him by pulling on his arm, and drove his fist into
the big man's face.

"I think I kill you for that," the Lulua said calmly and brushed blood
from his mouth with the back of his hand while Tono Muj stepped away
from them, her black eyes slitting down to the thickness of dimes. "I
think I will break your back."

Behind that thoughtful threat he moved in, a massive, gliding figure
with arms thick as hawsers and hands dangling loosely as though poorly
fitted at the wrists. Then the hands moved to take Grace at the waist
and lift him off the floor. The hunter's fists raised instant welts on the
African's broad face but failed to disturb his immediate plans. Up Grace
went and over the bar, his flying body a good yard above it. A brick wall
would have killed him, but he went up against thick-stacked cardboard
instead and was reaching around for discarded beer bottles even as he
hit the floor.

As the oncoming Lulua loomed over him, Grace swung smashing
a bottle full into that broad, calm face, then rolled over the bar flailing
with both hands at the bewildered giant backing up before him. The
bottle had hit with stunning force and shattered and blood spilled
through Zezi Lo's fingers as he pressed his hands to his face. Grace bent
low to punish the big man's body, switched to overhand punches when
the other's thick arms came down, and finally put him on the floor with
a straight right that almost took his jaw off. Zezi Lo was not out, but
through despite it, and Grace didn't wait to see if he would get up.

"You win, whore," he said, addressing Tono Muj. "Get your Mickey
Finn ready. I'll get your sorcerer for you…"

> Be it said that any person thought a witch
> or sorcerer shall be given poison from the
> powdered bark of the *ihumi* tree.
>
> Be it said that the poison shall be given
> only in the correct amount as decided by
> one trained in the art of the diviner.

> Be it said that if the person given the
> poison eject it and live, he or she shall
> be judged innocent of the offense of
> practicing witchcraft; but if the person
> given the poison cry out in pain and roll
> upon the floor and die, he or she shall be
> judged guilty.
>
> Be it said that burial shall not be
> permitted to anyone judged a witch or
> sorcerer, but that person's body shall
> he placed in the forest for the jackals to
> feed upon.
>
> —*from the* Duzardu *(Tribal Laws) of the
> Lulua tribe of the Belgian Congo.*

"DRINK it," Tono Muj said when the Baluba, Ruzi Dugg, had been taken from the jeep and forced to his knees before her. "Don't be a fool. You know we can make you."

She held a wooden cup to his lips and all about them, forming a great, silent, crowding circle on the floor of the *azifo*, men and women of the Lulua stood watching. Grace was the only outsider. Buddy Grace with three killings under his belt and one more on the drawing board. Buddy Grace, a man aware that he'd gone too far.

"Drink it," the woman said with a strong hand on the Baluba's throat and the wooden cup held to his lips. "Drink."

Ruzi Dugg opened his mouth and the crowd murmured and shifted its feet uneasily as the yellow, pulpy liquid was seen to enter. When the cup had been drained, the woman threw it aside and put her hand firmly over the Baluba's mouth. His throat moved convulsively and his

"TAKE A LONG DRINK," Grace said, leaping at the taunting natives. "Before my foot clogs your throats"

eyes were wide and staring over the edge of her hand. The people crowded closer and sighed collectively as Ruzi Dugg suddenly collapsed and rolled on the floor emitting the high-pitched, yapping sounds of a pain-frightened dog. His writhings sent him up against one segment of the crowd, but several of its members promptly kicked him back into the center of the circle. The people were no longer quiet now, or reserved. They shouted and shoved each other in an effort to get close to the dying man and Tono Muj spoke commandingly to them, ordering them back, then stood over him to confine him within the arch formed by her slim, strong legs. Two yards in front of her Grace stood watching and as their eyes met she smiled, nodded and in one easy motion drew off the print dress that was her only garment.

At sight of her gleaming nakedness, lusty howls rose from the Lulua; others began to rip their clothes off. Still smiling, Tono Muj walked toward Grace leaving the Baluba to meet his death beneath the pounding feet of the roaring tribesmen. Now men and women met in violent embrace, some on the tables, others under them, the entire *azifo* a seething, mauling mass of humanity covering the floor with Grace and Tono Muj picking their way across it to leave the building and enter her hut ten yards behind it.

"This never hurts for a starter," she said and reached under her cot to bring out a whiskey bottle of American make. Grace drank deep of it, then snatched it away from his mouth. But by then the woman was on him. A physical freak, strong as a man when she wanted to be, she got a hand on his mouth before he could spit anything out. At the same time her other hand grabbed for the bottle and sent it smashing against his head even while his own hand was still on it. He fell, trying to drag her down with him, but she slipped out of his hands as easily as though soaped allover and stepped back to watch as he went to hands and knees, his bloodied head hanging down.

"Bitch to end all bitches," he panted. "You poisoned me."

"I could not wait to do what you wanted," she explained. "My people are ready to fall on the Baluba now. If I stayed here with you the moment might pass."

She ran from the hut without bothering to close the door and Grace saw her re-enter the *azifo*. The tumult inside died down and he heard her voice, high-pitched and intense with most of the words inaudible, but *"Kill! Kill! Kill!"* sounded with perfect clarity.

He crawled through the door of the hut but before he could stand up, he felt something heavy roll over his leg and pin it to the ground. It was the front wheel of his jeep. A native with a leopard-fur headpiece shut the motor off and jumped down. "Big white boss stuck now," the

native said with a grin and ran off to the *azifo*. Grace tried to pull out but didn't have the strength. He could only claw the soft ground weakly.

Then the Lulua were streaming from the building behind Tono Muj, the naked women running beside their bellowing men and urging them on with kicks and screaming voices.

It was only when they had passed from his sight and their voices were growing rapidly fainter that he was able to think clearly about his own situation. His stomach felt as though it were trying to digest a hack saw. His chest felt as though it might explode. A great knotting and turning-over had started inside him.

He was rolling on his back now, his free knee lifted high, his lingers still clawing inside his mouth. Then all the world's pain met in one lump somewhere behind his navel and he screamed and tried to swallow his hand as a stream of yellow liquid jelled up past it and out his mouth.

He collapsed with his face in it and for minutes was too weak to move. He was dead. He knew that. Dead, but with a few hours of grace before they tucked him away out of sight. A little later he woke up again, and with a desperate surge of strength pushed against the jeep bumper until it rolled off his leg. Then he got up, climbed slowly into the jeep' and set out the jeep and set out for Luluabourg.

THE MONGOLS under Genghis Khan's go-go-go leadership were perfect little gentlemen compared to the Lulua that night behind Tono Muj. They were violence in flood form, a tidal wave of destruction pouring into the native quarter to engulf its inhabitants. The Baluba ran screaming before them and were slashed about the body and ran on with blood spilling to the ground and ran on to be cut again and again and fell to be cut still again. Blood made streams in the narrow alleys and

the Lulua invaded the tiny, dark dwellings hacking away at everything that moved.

Grace arrived a little after the Government's Congolese troops had gone into the native quarter. Tall, stalwart Africans under the command of Belgian officers hardly out of their teens, they moved in clubbing their rifles at frenzied faces in a methodical suppression of Lulua energy. In some cases tribesmen were shot or bayoneted and as the wave of Lulua terror began to roll back, Grace slipped into it, his eyes jumping from one struggling, cursing group to the next until at last halfway down a semi-dark alley he saw a naked figure backing out of a doorway and realized it was Tono Muj. He ran toward her and was within feet of her when she turned.

"Back in there," he said grabbing her wrist and twisting so that the bloodied knife she had been holding dropped to the ground. "The boys will be picking you up any minute now, but this is a matter I'd rather handle myself."

He pushed her back inside and went in after her. A dead man lay on the floor with his head in a puddle of blood.

"Do not kill me," the woman said in a low voice. "I swear you will not regret it."

"Make your case," Grace said sitting down on a cot.

"You will never forget me after tonight," she promised, kneeling to remove his boots. "You will live to be 100 and know 1000 women, but you will never forget Tono Muj."

It was a confident claim, but a reliable one. If there is such a thing as genius in the art of giving pleasure, the slant-eyed woman possessed it. She was passion-controlled and a moment later passion-unchecked. She gave of herself as only one man in a million ever knows a woman to do.

"How masterfully you possess me," she smiled up at the hunter when it was over. "How gloriously—sweetheart!"

He had put both hands on her throat and begun to press down.

"But there will be other times," she said quickly, her voice going shrill. "I will be everything—"

"How can there he other times?" Grace asked bunching himself over her and pouring all the strength left in his body into his hands. "You killed me."

He was still choking her minutes later when two Congolese soldiers burst in. She was dead, but he didn't know it. The two men had to drag him off her…

*LULUABOURG, BELGIAN CONGO, DEC. 8—Congolese troops still patrol the native quarter of this city, but things are slowly returning to normal. An uneasy trust exists between the Lulua and Baluba tribesmen who were battling each other so violently just two days ago.*

*The hunter, Aaron "Buddy" Grace, died early this morning despite strenuous efforts by Government doctors to keep him alive. It was Mr. Grace's testimony, taken at his hospital bed, that provides the Government with most of its information on the Lulua uprising. Mr. Grace was particularly graphic in speaking of Tono Muj, the Lulua medicine woman who led the tribesmen in their incredible assault. When one realizes that Mr. Grace killed three men and kidnapped a fourth at her request, it must be wondered if perhaps her powers of persuasion were not even more striking than he suggested. But this is merely conjecture, of course. Both are now dead.* ▌▌▌

# MAKE MONEY
## WHILE MEETING BEAUTIFUL GIRLS!

YOU CAN MAKE AN EXTRA $100.00 FOR SAYING HELLO TO PRETTY GIRLS. MAKE NEW FRIENDS, THE KIND YOU ALWAYS WANTED.

IF YOU HAVE AN EYE FOR BEAUTY AND ARE WILLING TO LEARN OUR PROVEN METHOD OF THE PROPER APPROACH, WE CAN START YOU IMMEDIATELY.

NO AGE OR EDUCATION BARRIERS. FULL OR PART TIME. CHOOSE YOUR OWN AREA AND HOURS.

We need scouts for one of America's newest Airline Recruiting Programs. We need hundreds of girls NOW! You can recruit for us anywhere there are beautiful girls, on the beach, at dances, at work, anywhere.

Not only will you make money but girls will actually thank you for recommending them for this wonderful opportunity

We will teach you how to pick the RIGHT GIRLS and obtain their names and addresses anytime or place you see a beauty. Absolutely no closing of sales.

We have been offering trainees to over 29 scheduled airlines for years and need additional scouts NOW to meet the ever increasing demands for the most beautiful girls in the world, AIRLINE GIRLS.

To get started you will need personal Airline Scout authorization and identification cards, etc., instructions on the proper approach method, referral cards for girls you select and of course, details on earnings. WRITE IMMEDIATELY. Send $2.00 to cover cost of authorization and identification cards, etc., and approach method.

WE GUARANTEE THAT YOU MUST BE 100% SATISFIED WITH THE MONEY AND NEW FRIENDS YOU MAKE, OR RETURN IN SEVEN DAYS AND RECEIVE FULL REFUND.

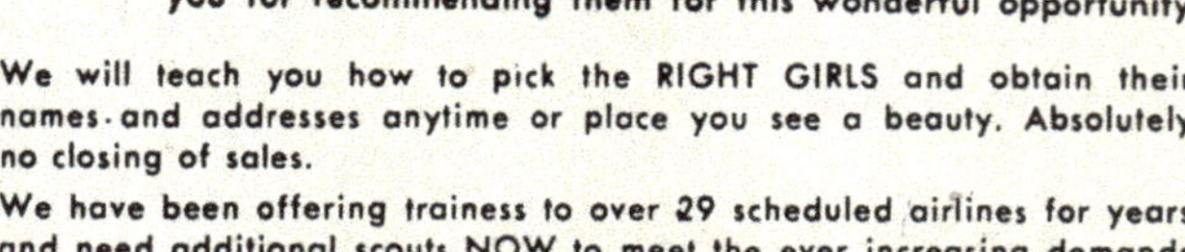

SEND TO:

**AIRLINES Dept. 29**
**285 Market Street**
**Newark, New Jersey**
Please rush authorization and identification cards, etc., Enclosed is $2.00.

MAIL NO-RISK TRIAL COUPON NOW!

Name ..............................................

Address ..........................................

City ....................... State .......................

Check

I promise to use authorization and identification cards, etc., proprely ☐

# ABOUT LAWRENCE BLOCK

*Like science fiction and mystery magazines, MAMs provided a welcome and important market for many up-and-coming writers in the 1950s and 1960s. Lawrence Block is one of those writers. In his younger days he helped pay his bills by selling spicy stories to several men's pulp mag publishers. Now he's one the most prolific and acclaimed crime writers in the world.*

*Block has penned more than a hundred books since the 1960s. They've been read by millions of readers and brought him a long list of awards, including a Grand Master Award from the Mystery Writers of America, four Edgar and Shamus Awards, the Nero and Philip Marlowe Awards, a Lifetime Achievement Award from the Private Eye Writers of America, and the Cartier Diamond Dagger from the Crime Writers Association of the United Kingdom.*

*Of course, Lawrence Block didn't start out famous. He didn't even start out writing under his own name. His first writing jobs, for publishers of mystery digests, MAMs, and erotic "sleaze" paperbacks, were written under the pen name Sheldon Lord.*

*The sexposé "She Doesn't Want You" is an early "Sheldon Lord" story from the June 1958 issue of* Real Men, *one of more than a dozen MAMs published by Stanley Publications.*

*I asked Block if he remembered the context for this story.*

In the summer of 1957, after I'd completed a second year at Antioch College, I answered a blind ad and landed a job as an editor at Scott Meredith Literary Agency, where I read over-the-transom submissions and wrote their authors lengthy encouraging rejections. It was ideal training for a writer-to-be and after a couple of weeks I dropped out of college in order to stay with it. I was there until May or June of 1958, when I decided I'd learned most of what the job had to teach me and elected to drop back into college again.

One of the perks of the job was the opportunity to grab quickie magazine assignments. An editor would get in touch, saying he needed something overnight for an issue with a hole in it. Or an editor would have an idea and want someone to write it up.

Ted Hecht at Stanley Publications was one such editor, and I wrote a batch of articles for him. Some of the ideas were his, while others were ones I proposed. 'She Doesn't Want You' was, I think, my idea. I'd recently learned that some prostitutes were actually lesbians by inclination, and I rushed to share this knowledge with the world.

A friend of mine, Laurence Janifer, claimed that there was a fortune waiting for the man who found a new animal to be eaten by. I don't think I wrote any lemmings-gnawed-my-genitalia pieces, but I could be wrong.

'Just Window Shopping' *[the second Sheldon Lord piece in this collection]* was fiction. (Well, so were most of the articles, but they pretended otherwise.)

*In Block's recent autobiographical book* Afterthoughts *(which I highly recommend), he recalled the origin of his Sheldon Lord pen name:*

I'd first used the name when I had two stories slated for the same issue of one of the digest-sized detective story magazines. The editor wanted to use a pen name on one of the stories, and I came up with Sheldon Lord….

I'd known a girl at Antioch College named Marcia Lord, and I really liked her last name. And I liked the name Sheldon, too, though I can't offhand think of anyone who bore it. Sheldon Lord. I used it on that second short story, and I used it on a batch of articles I wrote for a couple of male adventure magazines. (I mean, would you want your own name on 'Reinhard Heydrich, Blond Beast of the SS'? Well, neither would I.)

*Note to self: Find Lawrence Block's pseudonymous story "Reinhard Heydrich, Blond Beast of the SS" and ask him if we can reprint it in our next collection. It sounds like a classic.*

—*Robert Deis*
[2011]

*DEIS did indeed find "Reinhard Heydrich, Blond Beast of the SS." He located it in the May 1961 issue of* All Man *as "They Called Him 'King of Pain'." The story is credited to Sheldon Lord.*

*But it wasn't until years later, while working on* Exotic Adventures of Robert Silverberg *that we received this casual suggestion at the end of an email from Block's old friend and colleague Silverberg:*

> Lawrence Block, by the way, did a lot of stuff for the Stanley magazines in the Sixties, and after I told him about my *Exotic Adventures* (project), he wondered whether you might want to reprint some of his.

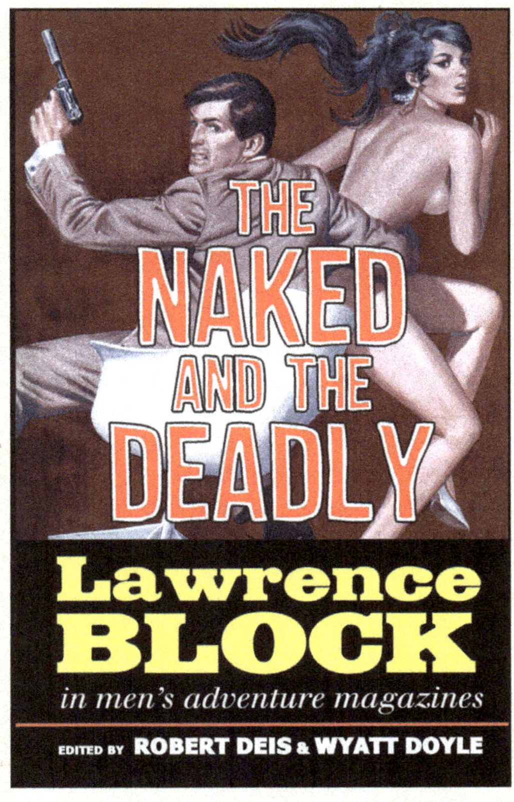


**Cover of the mass market paperback and ebook editions.**

*Deis and I were floored. We'd previously connected with Block to secure the rights to the stories included here, but hadn't considered he'd be willing to collaborate on an entire volume of his MAM pieces.*

*Thanks to Robert Silverberg, thus was hatched* The Naked and the Deadly, *the 17th (!) volume in* The Men's Adventure Library. *We made the most of the opportunity, determined to give Block the kind of handsome presentations he deserved. We've issued a signed and numbered hardcover, a standard hardcover, a deluxe softcover, an ebook, and a mass-market paperback edition, created as an homage to Block's many successes in paperback.*

*We remain deeply grateful for the trust, confidence, and generosity of a pair of former MAM writers we're proud to know as Bob and Larry.*

*—Wyatt Doyle*
⌈2024⌉

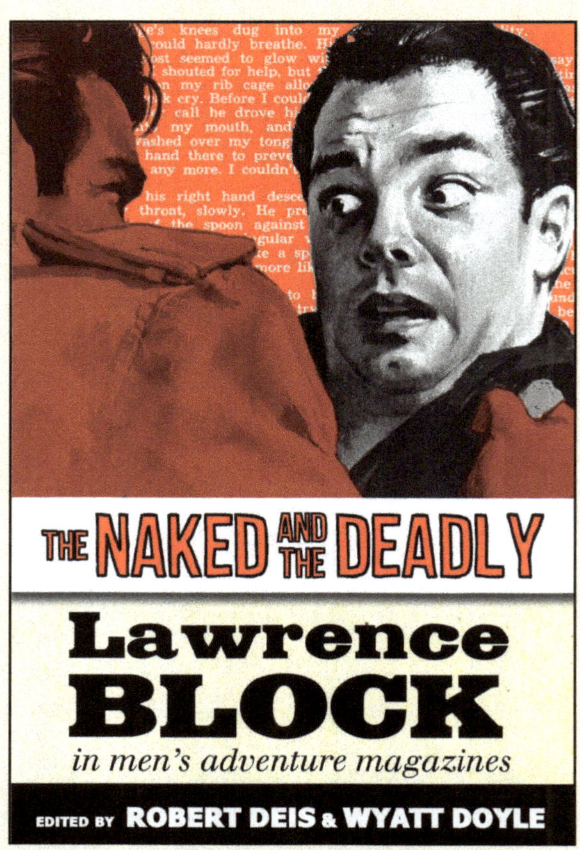



**Cover of the hardcover and deluxe softcover editions.**

## "SHE DOESN'T WANT YOU"

— LAWRENCE BLOCK (AS SHELDON LORD) —

*Real Men*, June 1958

COVER ARTIST: Vic Prezio

She loves the color of your money, but . . .
she doesn't want you!
by SHELDON LORD
Illustration specially posed by professional models

**ing the truth about the girls who earn their living at love.**

**as she's concerned, you're just another sucker on her little list!**

**Y**OU'RE IN A ROOM at the other end of town, and you're tired. And why not? You've got a right to be tired.

You've paid your ten dollars or five dollars or whatever the price was, and if you were lucky you got your money's worth. Now it's time to go home —the show is over. But like most men, you look once again at the girl you've just been visiting. And, like most men, you can't help wondering . . .

What was it like for her? All work and no play? *Or did she enjoy it too?*

Go home quick, brother. Don't even think about it—it's better that way. Because unless you're something pretty special, the little gal didn't get any kind of a thrill outside of the keep provided by the money you gave her. And there's a helluva good chance no man in the world can give her anything *but* money. It's almost even money that you just got a smile from a gal *who likes gals!*

Surprised? You shouldn't be. If you've read your Kinsey, you'd know that an amazingly high percentage of this country's prostitutes are lesbians. They get their wages from men—*and their love from each other.*

At first it doesn't make sense. People should like their work. Veterinarians like animals, bakers like bread. So why shouldn't prostitutes like men?

When you come right down to it, there are a good many reasons. And you can't fight the facts, for this sort of thing has been going on for a good long while. Prostitution doesn't have the reputation of being the oldest profession in the world for nothing. It dates all the way back to the Greeks.

In case you didn't realize it, the Greeks gave the world more than just Socrates. The bordellos of the ancient isles were the ultimate in pleasure palaces, the likes of which the world has never seen since.

If you were an ancient Greek with enough drachmas in your jeans, you were in for a treat. The gal you sported with was no tramp from the wrong side of the tracks. When she woke up mornings she had more perfumes rubbed into her skin than she could count. She was never too thin and never too fat. Her skin was a mixture of ivory and silk.

And she knew her trade, too. She started learning around the age of ten, and by the time she got her union card she knew every trick in the business. When an ancient Greek male tiptoed up the back stairs to his wife after an evening of "pinochle," he was a contented Greek indeed!

What do you suppose happened when all the paying customers tiptoed out of the place of "ill-repute?" You guessed it, friend. That was the signal for Little Miss Ivory-and-Silk to flash a smile of her own. She didn't waste any time in finding another "companion"—with long hair and curves —and having some fun for herself.

**N**OR WAS THIS sort of thing confined to Greece. Around the turn of the century, when Chicago was the way it used to be, there was a brothel on North Clark Street with an unusual set of house rules. The last man left at three AM, and the gals retired for a beauty sleep. And if any beauty had the unmitigated gall to insist on sleeping alone, she could jolly well hustle up another job in the morning.

Just because Chicago stopped being the way it used to be, there was no reason for the lassies to change their lives. And they didn't. Rome conquered Greece, Attilla conquered Rome, and Capone conquered Chicago, but you still can put down plenty of cold cash for a sweetie-pie who is a lesbian—and you'll never know it!

What's the reason for all this? That depends on the gal, of course, but there are several basic personality types.

First of all is the babe who has developed a hate for men over the years. A man seduced her in the first place, another man started her hustling, and other men—customers—give her a bad time every day. The upshot of all this is that she winds up loathing the male gender like the plague. After working hours, a man becomes about as welcome as the seven year itch.

Louise was this type of gal—I first met her on a street a little way off the Bowery, New York's Skid Row. She must have been pretty once upon a time, but that was long ago. Like so many other prostitutes in that neighborhood, *Louise was a lesbian.* She blamed men for all her difficulties.

"Men!" she snorted. "When I was twelve years old, a man raped me in an alleyway two blocks from my house. Then I made the mistake of tellin' my old man. He called me a tramp, belted me till I couldn't sit down, and didn't speak to me for the next three weeks. After that, I couldn't wait to get out of the house."

When Louise was sixteen, she ran away from home and never came back. But men kept making life miserable for her.

"I even fell in love with one of them," she said, bitterly. "The rotten heel! He got me into this racket—wouldn't work for a living, so he let me support the both of us. First I was "entertaining" some of his friends. The guy had more "friends" than Hitler had enemies. Then I was entertaining half the town, and lover-boy was pocketing every cent. One night I found out that there were three other girls doing the same thing for him. That was when I walked out. *Men!"*

Why, I asked, didn't she quit the racket then? Why keep going with men if they were all so miserable? She had a quick answer for that one.

"Let 'em pay," she said. "They got enough from me—now let 'em pay *my way.* They think they're getting a big deal, but they don't show me a thing. *Not a damn thing!"*

That last statement holds a clue to the whole problem. A good many girls drift into prostitution and lesbianism for the (Continued on page 56)

**YOU'RE** in a room at the other end of town, and you're tired. And why not? You've got a right to be tired.

You've paid your ten dollars or five dollars or whatever the price was, and if you were lucky you got your money's worth. Now it's time to go home—the show is over. But like most men, you look once again at the girl you've just been visiting. And, like most men, you can't help wondering… What was it like for her? All work and no play? *Or did she enjoy it too?*

Go home quick, brother. Don't even think about it—it's better that way. Because unless you're something pretty special, the little gal didn't get any kind of a thrill outside of the keep provided by the money you gave her. And there's a helluva good chance no man in the world can give her anything but money. It's almost even money that you just got a smile from a gal *who likes gals!*

Surprised? You shouldn't be. If you've read your Kinsey, you'd know that an amazingly high percentage of this country's prostitutes are lesbians. They get their wages from men—*and their love from each other.*

At first it doesn't make sense. People should like their work. Veterinarians like animals, bakers like bread. So why shouldn't prostitutes like men?

When you come right down to it, there are a good many reasons. And you can't fight the facts, for this sort of thing has been going on for a good long while. Prostitution doesn't have the reputation of being the oldest profession in the world for nothing. It dates all the way back to the Greeks.

In case you didn't realize it, the Greeks gave the world more than just Socrates. The bordellos of the ancient isles were the ultimate in pleasure palaces, the likes of which the world has never seen since.

If you were an ancient Greek with enough drachmas in your jeans, you were in for a treat. The gal you sported with was no tramp from the wrong side of the tracks; When she woke up mornings she had more perfumes rubbed into her skin than she could count. She was never too thin and never too fat. Her skin was a mixture of ivory and silk.

And she knew her trade, too. She started learning around the age of ten, and by the time she got her union card she knew every trick in the business. When an ancient Greek male tiptoed up the back stairs to his wife after an evening of "pinochle," he was a contented Greek indeed!

What do you suppose happened when all the paying customers tiptoed out of the place of "ill repute?" You guessed it, friend. That was the signal for Little Miss Ivory-and-Silk to flash a smile of her own. She didn't waste any time in finding another "companion"—with long hair and curves and having some fun for herself.

Nor was this sort of thing confined to Greece. Around the turn of the century, when Chicago was the way it used to be, there was a brothel on North Clark Street with an unusual set of house rules. The last man left at 3 AM, and the gals retired for a beauty sleep. And if any beauty had the unmitigated gall to insist on sleeping alone, she could jolly well hustle up another job in the morning.

Just because Chicago stopped being the way it used to be, there was no reason for the lassies to change their lives. And they didn't. Rome conquered Greece, Attila conquered Rome, and Capone conquered Chicago, but you still can put down plenty of cold cash for a sweetie-pie who is a lesbian—and you'll never know it!

What's the reason for all this? That depends on the gal, of course, but there are several basic personality types.

First of all is the babe who has developed a hate for men over the years. A man seduced her in the first place, another man started her hustling, and other men—customers—give her a bad time every day. The upshot of all this is that she winds up loathing the male gender like the plague. After working hours, a man becomes about as welcome as the seven-year itch.

Louise was this type of gal—I first met her on a street a little way off the Bowery, New York's Skid Row. She must have been pretty once upon a time, but that was long ago. Like so many other prostitutes in that neighborhood, *Louise was a lesbian*. She blamed men for all her difficulties.

"Men!" she snorted. "When I was twelve years old, a man raped me in an alleyway two blocks from my house. Then I made the mistake of tellin' my old man. He called me a tramp, belted me till I couldn't sit down, and didn't speak to me for the next three weeks. After that, I couldn't wait to get out of the house."

When Louise was sixteen, she ran away from home and never

came back. But men kept making life miserable for her.

"I even fell in love with one of them," she said, bitterly. "The rotten heel! He got me into this racket—wouldn't work for a living, so he let me support the both of us. First I was "entertaining" some of his friends. The guy had more "friends" than Hitler had enemies: Then I was entertaining half the town, and lover-boy was pocketing every cent. One night I found out that there were three other girls doing the same thing for him. That was when I walked out. *Men!*"

Why, I asked, didn't she quit the racket then? Why keep going with men if they were all so miserable? She had a quick answer for that one.

"Let 'em pay," she said. "They got enough from me—now let 'em pay *my way*. They think they're getting a big deal, but they don't show me a thing. *Not a damn thing!*"

That last statement holds a clue to the whole problem. A good many girls drift into prostitution and lesbianism for the same reason—to avenge a deep and abiding hatred for all men. This hatred usually goes a long way back—even to childhood. They may have started by hating their fathers, and wound up hating and despising *everything* in pants.

To these women, lesbianism becomes a means of "getting even" with men. When one gal finds physical satisfaction with another, she proves to herself that she can *exist independently* of men. She can do anything a man can do, and through her lesbianism she flaunts her self-sufficiency before the world. She requires another woman to fulfill herself, and this makes the male inadequate and superfluous.

IN THE same way, her hatred of men manifests itself in prostitution. She goes through the motions of enjoyment, usually fooling her partner. She feels that, in actuality, she is giving him nothing at all. She's *faking* pleasure, and thus, in her own mind, making a fool out of the man.

Shirley was like this. She was young—eighteen when I met her, and she'd already been working the streets for a year-and-a-half. She had a pretty babyface, and the type of body which one would hardly associate with a lesbian. Her curves were all there, in the right places.

Shirley's mother managed to run through four husbands in six years. Instead of swearing off men, she floated from one to another. One-third of the time she was with a man—any man. Another third of her time was spent in an alcoholic stupor. The rest of the time was spent in pouring out her troubles to Shirley.

"Men ruined my mother," she explained to me. "They got her so she didn't know which end was up. I felt sorry for her, and I loved her. But I made up my mind *I wouldn't let any man make a sap out of me.*"

Shirley makes saps out of men instead, and makes what she calls "a respectable living" at her trade. She's young now, and gets a minimum of ten dollars for her favors. And when *she* wants to be loved, she goes to another girl.

"No men for me!" she asserts. "That's what ruined my mother. A girl's every bit as good as a man and she won't make a tramp out of you. A man'll make a tramp out of you every time!"

There are those unkind souls who might class Shirley as a tramp, but she would argue the point. It's just business with her, *and business is business.*

Business is business, and that's where the acting comes into play. The good businesswoman not only acts as though she's enjoying every minute of it, but she makes her lover feel as though he's the best man in the world.. If she's a good enough actress, he goes away feeling that he's done her a favor. There's no ego like the male ego. He'll come back again and again, anxious to pay for the privilege of making her happy.

And a lesbian can give a fantastic performance. A friend of mine kept a girl in an apartment and dressed her in mink. He loved his wife, but complained that she was cold. *He* wanted a woman who could give him sincere affection and satisfaction.

He had the money, and he was willing to pay the price. He didn't really feel as though he was paying, insisting that he and his mistress were the most perfectly matched couple since Adam and Eve.

He got a rude awakening. One afternoon, he dropped in unexpectedly. But someone had beat him to it. Where there should have been one head, there were two, *and they both had long hair.* After my friend picked himself up off the floor, he reclaimed the mink and gave it to his "frigid" wife. He's sadder but wiser today.

So DON'T think about it, buddy. You'll just drive yourself nuts, because no man likes to feel that his playmate is bored stiff with the whole show. It just isn't recommended for the ego. It makes a man feel about as valuable as a second appendix.

Take the gals in Germany. GIs thought they had a paradise over there during the first few years of the occupation. The Berlin Babes were built like brick bomb-shelters and were about as available as flies in a fertilizer plant. And the price was ridiculously low.

But the performance left a good deal to be desired. One married serviceman had his first fling overseas, and hasn't strayed from the straight-and-narrow since he donned civvies.

"I met this gal," he recounted, "and she was a doll. A living doll! All she wanted was a bar of chocolate and a comic book. At first I couldn't believe it.

"So I went to the PX and picked up the candy and the comic, and we

went to her room.

"I still can't believe what came next. She picked up the candy bar and started munching away on it, then grabbed the comic book and buried her face in it. I just stood there watching.

"After a minute or so she asked me what I was waiting for—*she was ready!* Then she went back to the comic book. I got the hell out of there fast!"

Admittedly, that's a rather extreme example. But one thing is certain—a good many men are paying a good many dollars for a misrepresented commodity. You just can't buy passion.

There's a third class of prostitute who take their pleasure with their own sex. These are the kind who have had so many men so many ways, that they need something different in order to enjoy *themselves.* Variety, they argue, is the spice and "seasoning" of life.

These gals have nothing against the male of the species; in fact, they'll even *enjoy* him once in a while. But they need a change from time to time, and lesbianism provides this change for them.

"I *like* men," Marcia insisted. "I've liked men from the time I was fifteen, and I'm not going to quit now. But," she said with a wink, "you can get tired of ice cream, too."

I started to protest at that point, but Marcia squelched me. "Look," she said, "a guy pays for sex and he gets sex. That's all you can buy. A man hands over his money and expects to be loved, but you can't turn love on and off like a faucet. *It just doesn't work that way.*

"A good hustler can make a grandfather feel like he's twenty again, and she can make a high school kid feel more experienced than Casanova. The scrawniest, mealiest jerko in creation thinks he's Superman when he's with her. He wants love too?"

She stretched playfully. She watched me stare, her eyes twinkling with amusement. "Like what you see?"

I nodded.

"You got the price?"

I nodded again.

"You know," she said when I hesitated, "some days I just *love* ice cream."

And you know, when I finally left, I couldn't help wondering.... ▟▟▟

*Real*, December 1962
Cover by George Gross

# ABOUT HARLAN ELLISON

WRITERS *can inspire curiously conflicted responses in a way few other professionals do. Too much of the time, it's either a pedestal or the back of the bus—and it hardly seems a coincidence that the first attitude is generally assumed after a writer's death, while the latter comes into play when writers seek compensation commensurate with their talent.*

*Harlan Ellison has never had much patience for either position, and has dedicated countless lines and hours to educating readers in a few simple realities of his profession: A writer must be a dedicated craftsman, first and foremost. It is the work that deserves attention, not the hand behind it. And if you want a writer's work, pay him—same as one would pay* any *skilled laborer.*

*Ironically, the eloquence and verve he's employed in expressing his philosophy has resulted in increased attention on Ellison himself—both as an outsized literary personality and as something of an ethical guidepost for writers still calibrating their own moral and professional compasses. And, as you might expect of someone living on his own terms and unquietly, he's ticked off about as many as he's inspired—though that appears to bother him little.*

*For Ellison, a name on the spine of a book does not a writer make. There's a significant difference between a "writer" and an "author" as he sees it, and it comes down to commitment. Anyone can be an* author, *he's argued, from White House pets to fad dieticians to Snooki from* Jersey Shore. *But a* writer *is "someone who gets hemorrhoids from sitting on his ass all his life…writing."*

*His dedication to these principles, together with his acknowledged mastery of the short story form, make Harlan Ellison a welcome, even essential, presence in this collection. The definition of a working writer (and editor) during the MAM era, Ellison covered a lot of ground in the early stages of his illustrious career: In addition to his better known work for science fiction and fantasy mags, he contributed to EC comics, mystery, crime and detective magazines like* The Saint *and* Crime and Justice, *bachelor magazines like* Playboy *and* Rogue *(where he also served as Associate Editor), even* True Confessions-*style magazines for women.*

*The Ellison tale we include here, "Death Climb," is a tight, terse piece of crime fiction that shows off the young writer's storytelling chops to good effect. And while Alpine* noir *might seem an unlikely milieu for those only familiar with his work in the field of the fantastic, the writer's voice is unmistakable.*

*Rife with amoral, nasty characters, marital infidelity, blackmail, double-crosses and murder, the shifty protagonist's constant wheedling and manipulation a contrast to the icy, impassive face of the lethal and ever-present Mt. Keppler. It's one of a handful of stories Ellison sold to MAMs, and though it's perhaps the most traditional narrative in our collection, it's also one of the most satisfying stories in the book.*

*Five decades on from "Death Climb," Ellison's still going strong—and we might need him more than ever. In a time when titles are all but stripped of meaning and legitimacy by flatterers and those with something to sell, Ellison fights on for the integrity of words and wordsmiths. Is Diddy distilling that vodka he calls his? Did Kim Kardashian actually blend the perfume sold under her name? Is Jennifer Lopez designing the outfits for Kohl's that bear her label? Well, Harlan Ellison is sure as hell writing those stories.*

*As the actor Peter O'Toole succinctly put it when asked about his own craft, "It's my job, it's what I do, it's what I'm on earth to do, and it's who I am."*

*—Wyatt Doyle*
⌈2011⌉

## UPDATE FOR THE NEW EDITION

*We lost Harlan in 2018, though his legacy in print lives on with recent releases of his* Greatest Hits, *as well as reissues of his historic* Dangerous Visions *anthologies and, at long last, the premiere publication of the final volume in that series,* The Last Dangerous Visions. *And he allowed us to purchase reprint rights for* another *lost Ellison yarn that will appear in this book's sequel.*

*As part of this book's initial release in 2013, Marc Campbell hosted a contest to win signed copies via the* Dangerous Minds *site. "Win a* Weasels!*" entrants competed to see who could cook up the most outrageously entertaining "Weasels Ripped My Flesh"-style MAM headline.*

*Though he was ineligble to win the competition, Ellison—who knew from fighting weasels, four-legged or two—entered anyway, the only* Weasels *contributor to do so.*

*His entry?*

"Ants Assailed My Anus!"

*Age did not mellow him.*

*—Wyatt Doyle*
⌈2024⌉

## "DEATH CLIMB"

—— Harlan Ellison ——

*True Men Stories*, February 1957

COVER ARTIST: Wil Hulsey

"I've watched you for more than a week, Charlie," she said. He felt his stomach leap up at him, his legs felt rubbery at the knees.

# DEATH CLIMB

Big money was his if he'd leave the small time to be a killer—the dame had the dough and a proposition—but once you're small time you are always small time

## by HARLAN ELLISON

IT was either climb Mt. Keppler—or die!

Charlie Kennoy had a big choice: he could kill Vera Steig's husband Arnold, or get his face shot off by Zegondy's trigger men.

Zegondy had sent his boys all the way from the Riviera. He had taken badly to Kennoy walking out on a ten thousand dollar gambling debt, and now the gunmen waited at the chalet, at the base of Mt. Keppler. They waited for Kennoy to come back from guiding the Steigs to the top. They waited for Kennoy to come back from his climb—so they could introduce him to death.

All around him the whistle of the sleeting snow was a frozen melody, as he guided beautiful Vera and fat, little Arnold to the summit. But he didn't hear the wind, or feel the snow. Kennoy was scared . . . real scared. He'd been a sport-bum all his life, traveling between ski resorts and mountain retreats, living off the money he could pick up by instructing. Or living off the money he'd gotten from the women he had encountered. He'd been able to do all right that way; but times had started to get rougher.

The crowds at the resorts weren't the same any more. The women were more cautious . . . there weren't as many jobs to be had . . . and then this loss to Zegondy on the Riviera, and now the gambler's men waiting.

Kennoy was frightened. His stomach—which was strong to the dangers of mountain-climbing—knotted up terribly when he thought of the three gunmen. Sitting in the chalet, sipping brandy cordials, just waiting for him.

This wasn't like the other times when he could laugh his way out of a tight situation, or run away. This was different! Zegondy wasn't playing games. He couldn't afford to let someone skip a bet. It wasn't good business. That was why Kennoy had to get the money.

That was why he was climbing the mountain with Vera Steig and her husband. That was why he had listened to Vera when she'd come to him asking him to kill Arnold.

KENNOY wrapped his muffler closer about his mouth. The wind seemed to want to rip it from the buttoned-up neck of his anorak. It was getting mad on the mountain. There had been an unfavorable weather report before they'd left— sliding passes, heavy winds, slipping moraines of debris all down the *massif*. Disturbances all the way to the summit—but Vera had insisted they go. Kennoy knew why, but dumpy little Arnold didn't. And never would.

Kennoy looked below him. Attached to the line, ten feet under his spiked crampons, he could see the anxious face of beautiful Vera. Even the heavy *cagoule* jacket, coming down below her knees, could not conceal her lush figure. Her snow-glasses blocked off the expression in her eyes, but Kennoy knew what it was: desire for death!

*Well, you finally made it, Kennoy,* he thought to himself, chinking out a foothold with his pike. *You finally took the last step. You aren't a small-time chiseler any more. Today you become a murderer. Just think: Charlie Kennoy from Spokane, Washington . . . a hatchet-man!*

Somehow, he managed to grimace, inside the protection of the muffler. It didn't bother him as much as it had when Vera had suggested it. Killing Arnold was a job now. The only things that bothered him were thoughts of Zegondy's gunsels—and Vera Steig.

The whipping, grainy snow of the Alps and the cold pearl-grey of the

(Continued on page 54)

25

***IT WAS*** either climb Mt. Keppler—or die!

Charlie Kennoy had a big choice: he could kill Vera Steig's husband Arnold, or get his face shot off by Zegondy's trigger men.

Zegondy had sent his boys all the way from the Riviera. He had taken badly to Kennoy walking out on a ten thousand dollar gambling debt, and now the gunmen waited at the chalet, at the base of Mt. Keppler. They waited for Kennoy to come back from guiding the Steigs to the top. They waited for Kennoy to come back from his climb—so they could introduce him to death.

All around him the whistle of the sleeting snow was a frozen melody, as he guided beautiful Vera and fat, little Arnold to the summit. But he didn't hear the wind, or feel the snow. Kennoy was scared… real scared. He'd been a sport-bum all his life, traveling between ski resorts and mountain retreats, living off the money he could pick up by instructing. Or living off the money he'd gotten from the women he had encountered. He'd been able to do all right that way; but times had started to get rougher.

The crowds at the resorts weren't the same any more. The women were more cautious…there weren't as many jobs to be had…and then this loss to Zegondy on the Riviera, and now the gambler's men waiting.

Kennoy was frightened. His stomach—which was strong to the dangers of mountain climbing—knotted up terribly when he thought of the three gunmen. Sitting in the chalet, sipping brandy cordials, just waiting for him.

This wasn't like the other times when he could laugh his way out of a tight situation, or run away. This was different. Zegondy wasn't playing games. He couldn't afford to let someone skip a bet. It wasn't good business. That was why Kennoy had to get the money.

That was why he was climbing the mountain with Vera Steig and her husband. That was why he had listened to Vera when she'd come to him asking him to kill Arnold.

KENNOY wrapped his muffler closer about his mouth. The wind seemed to want to rip it from the buttoned-up neck of his anorak. It was getting mad on the mountain. There had been an unfavorable weather report before they'd left—sliding passes, heavy winds, slipping moraines of debris all down the *massif*. Disturbances all the way to the summit—but Vera had insisted they go. Kennoy knew why, but dumpy little Arnold didn't. And never would.

Kennoy looked below him. Attached to the line, ten feet under his spiked crampons, he could see the anxious face of beautiful Vera. Even the heavy *cagoule* jacket, coming down below her knees, could not conceal her lush figure. Her snow-glasses blocked off the expression in her eyes, but Kennoy knew what it was: desire for death!

*Well, you finally made it, Kennoy,* he thought to himself, chinking out a foothold with his pike. *You finally took the last step. You aren't a small-time chiseler any more. Today you become a murderer. Just think: Charlie Kennoy from Spokane, Washington…a hatchet man!*

Somehow, he managed to grimace, inside the protection of the muffler. It didn't bother him as much as it had when Vera had suggested it. Killing Arnold was a job now. The only things that bothered him were thoughts of Zegondy's gunsels—and Vera Steig.

The whipping, grainy snow of the Alps and the cold pearl-grey of the sky faded around him. His thoughts went back to the night he had met Vera in the chalet.

He had seen her several times: on the slope, near the shuffleboards, at the bar. And each time, she had turned to stare at him. Her eyes had told him a great deal; they had told him she was rich—and hungry.

That night he had met her formally, in the cocktail lounge. She had been throwing subtle looks in his direction, and he had watched her carefully, making no move. He had watched her in the bar mirror, as she sat alone in a booth.

Then she became almost flagrant about her come-on. She wetted her full lips with her tongue, and slid about in the booth as though she were burning up. Kennoy knew he was handsome—he had counted on that many times to keep him eating, and living as high as he enjoyed.

"Karl," Kennoy had asked the bartender, "who's the woman with the blonde hair, in the booth near the window?"

"That's Mrs. Steig, sir. She and her husband are Americans. They are here for climbing, sir."

Kennoy had bolted his drink and slid off the stool. She watched him as a tiger watches its prey, as he walked toward her.

"Mrs. Steig?" he inquired, smiling down at her.

She smiled up in return, and slid over. "I was wondering how long it would take you."

"I understand you're here for the climbing?" he decided to play it guardedly.

"Among other things," she said, arching her back slightly, as though the tight-fitting ski sweater and slacks were constricting her.

"Care to go skiing?" he asked "I've discovered several excellent slopes."

She slid around toward him, her thigh touching his. "I was hoping you'd ask me. They tell me around here you're one of the best."

He smiled slowly. "I try to be."

And so they went skiing.

And several times after that. One day they had even gone to explore the crannies of the little Swiss town below the chalet.

As the week ebbed away, Vera became nervous, as though she wanted to ask an important question. She introduced Kennoy to her husband Arnold. Kennoy shook the fat, little man's hand, wondering how a fiery item like Vera had gotten saddled-up with this…this wart!

Finally, one night, she came to him in his rooms. Alone.

Kennoy felt no cold, felt no sleeting, as he climbed Mt. Keppler, remembering Vera Steig that night, remembering the question she had finally asked.

THE DOOR closed, and she leaned against it. Kennoy stared at her for a brief moment, catching the full length of her in the tight ski-sweater and the even tighter ski-slacks.

Her hair was a rich, auburn mass, drawn back at the base of her neck in a tight knot. Her eyes were green as the snow of the Alps, high up. They were green, and very deep…they seemed to be saying something, though the full mouth was unmoving.

Her body was rich and full—high-breasted. He had wanted her since he had met her, but there was always the faint chance she didn't want to play that hard. Now, it seemed, she was bringing the game to him.

He watched her push away from the door, and come toward him.

"Where's Arnold?" he asked, not giving a damn.

"I left him discussing the merits of the devalued franc note with a Frenchman," she said, and her words said more than they should.

She grinned at him, as a little girl doing something she shouldn't would have grinned, and came closer. "I've been watching you over a week. You haven't made a pass at me."

"You're married."

"Not *that* married." Her arms even through the sweater, slipped around his neck. He felt his stomach leap up at him, and his legs felt watery at the back of the knees.

Her face was very close then, and as he ran his hands up her back, he felt the soft wool of the sweater slide up. She stepped back for a moment, and the sweater came off. She had known she wasn't going out into the biting cold of the Swiss Alps that day—and so she had worn no underthings.

He stared silently. Why was this beautiful woman tossing herself at him? There must have been other men, equally as attractive, in the chalet-lodge.

She moved toward him again, slowly, and he backed up till the edge of the bed caught him in the back of the knees.

Then she gave him part of the answer. "I want to talk to you about a business deal," she murmured, slipping into his waiting arms, "later…"

KENNOY squinted through his goggles. The summit was another forty feet, across the snow-bridge, over the ledged rise—the tiny *Arete*—and then the cave. The snow whipped past him in small flurries, and he dug the crampons in tightly, felt the weight of Vera and Arnold behind him on the line.

He weighed the offer she had made him, as he felt the icepick bite into the crusted snow.

"I want you to push Arnold off the top, and I'll give you five thousand dollars," she had said. "I came to you first because you're the guide who was recommended to me, but now…it's more than that."

She had offered him more than five thousand. She had offered herself. And that was an offer Kennoy didn't find hard to consider. And yet…

His face had become shocked. "You *what?*"

"I want you to kill my husband," she had said emphatically.

"But…but…why? Why can't you just leave him?"

"He won't give me a divorce. And if I leave him, I'll be cut off without a cent. I like his money too much for that, Charlie."

Kennoy had shaken his head as though to clear it of clinging cobwebs, not quite believing what he had heard. It was obvious that Vera Steig hated her husband, but *this* much?

She had sensed his reluctance, and edged closer, her breath coming raggedly.

"Look, Charlie, I've been married to that fat slug for eight years. I'm beautiful. I *am* beautiful, aren't I, Charlie?" She had grabbed at him frantically, and he'd seen the wild look in her eyes.

"Yeah, sure, there's no doubt about that, Vera, but my God!"

"My beauty's slipping away from me, Charlie. I want to be young again. I want to be young—with you!"

And it had set Kennoy thinking. He had worried it through his mind for over a week, before he had proposed the trip to the top of Mt. Keppler.

It would be so simple.

The summit was cut off from sight below by the violent weather. One healthy shove when they reached the cave and ledge…and Arnold Steig would plummet ten thousand feet, with no questions asked by the authorities…and a staggering fortune left to Vera.

All that money, and Vera, too.

They kept climbing. Kennoy had harbored at least a small doubt, but the day they had left yesterday—he had seen Zegondy's men arriving. And that had decided him. He was really frightened. If he didn't have the ten thousand, he would surely be dead by tomorrow! He was stuck, and he would have to do it.

*Maybe it isn't such a bad deal after all,* he thought, the mountain around him. *I can give Zegondy's boys the five thousand, and beg Vera for the other five. Then I'll marry her, and spend the rest of my life on soft cushions— with her money!*

They kept climbing.

At the next plateau, Vera sank down against the ice wall, panting and Arnold disengaged the towrope, scuttled over to where Kennoy was sitting, hunched into his anorak, trying to shut out the fury of the mountain, trying to shut in the conscience that warned him against murder.

"I want to talk to you," Steig said, over the keening of the wind.

"What is it?" Kennoy asked.

Steig slipped down next to the guide. He put his mouth close to Kennoy's ear. "I want you to do something for me. I'll pay you… handsomely."

Kennoy sat up straighter. He looked around sharply. Steig's face, even overhung with ice particles, was anxious. The fat little man swept nervous glances at Vera from time to time. She slumped against the ice wall, drawing in breath heavily.

"I want you to kill Vera," Arnold Steig said, haltingly. "I'll give you twenty thousand if you push her." Steig's fatty, puffy face was beaded with flakes of snow, and the rosy glow of his cherub-cheeks was bright against the ice of his eyebrows and moustache.

Kennoy felt a strange quiver cross his chest. This was unbelievable. Steig wanted to murder his wife, and his wife wanted Steig dead! They *both* wanted to hire him.

"You can't be kidding, Steig. Nobody would kid about a thing like that, but…" Kennoy's face was incredulous.

*"Don't look at me like that!"* Steig snapped. "You don't understand! You couldn't possibly! You aren't married to her."

Kennoy fumbled for some logic to this situation.

"Why? Why do you want me to kill her?"

"She's nothing but a money-mad bitch! She won't let me alone… I can't get away from her. If I try to divorce her, she'll get everything I have. I've got to get rid of her—she's making my life miserable. You've got to help me!"

Kennoy considered for a moment. He could have either twenty thousand dollars flat cash, or Vera and five thousand. It was a toss-up.

"I'll have to think about it," he said. Then he rose to his feet. The crampons bit into the ice. "Come on!" he screamed into the whipping snow, "it's only twenty-five feet to the summit!"

They began the long climb once more.

He was having more difficulty digging out handholds with the pike. Finally he resorted to the piton—a metal spike with a ring in the head—driving it into the ice deeply. He rested on the piton a moment, then used his pick. It wouldn't take big enough chunks, and he buckled it back on his belt, and removed the ice-axe.

The snow had gotten worse; more dense, and they climbed almost blindly. Soon he was able to start again, and the ice-axe did its work with relative ease.

Kennoy found his thoughts slipping away from the tedious work of climbing Keppler, and thought more of this other matter. Which offer should he take? He was certain now that he would take one of them. At first the idea of murder had appalled him—but now he was accustomed to it.

Should he settle for Vera and the five thousand—with a chance for the entire fortune later? But what if she decided she had no further use for him, after he'd done the job and refused to marry him? What if she gave him only the five and dared him to talk? He couldn't, of course. What if…?

Or should he accept Arnold Steig's twenty thousand, which was in the bag if he pushed Vera? It would leave him with ten thousand after Zegondy's men had been paid off. It was very little, actually. And the way he was living, it wouldn't last more than six months. What if Arnold refused to give him the money? What if… ?

Then it came to him. He could, indeed, have his cake and eat it too.

When they stopped for breath, he carefully inched his way down to Vera.

"Arnold wants me to kill you," he said.

Her face went deadly white, and behind the dark glasses her eyes grew large and frightened.

"H-he w-what?"

"He wants me to shove you. If you don't give me the five thousand, I'll do it."

"How? How can I get it? I don't have any money with me? You can't! You can't do it, Charlie… I love you!"

He laughed roughly. "Love is fine, Vera, and maybe I'll have time for it later. But right now I want to insure your…ah, shall we say… good faith."

She stared at him bleakly for a moment, the beautiful mouth twisting in disbelief. "How much did he offer you?"

"Twenty thousand."

"I haven't got that much of my own—even at the chalet. I won't have it till he's dead."

Kennoy laughed lightly. He could not trust her after Arnold was dead. She might cut him off with nothing. "Then we'll have to make other arrangements." Savagely he pulled off her mitten. She closed her fist instinctively against the raw cold of the Alps, but he grasped her hand tightly, stared at it.

"Your rings will do nicely as a down-payment," he said. He yanked without care at the diamond wedding and engagement bands, and in a few moments they were in his hand.

"You can't!" she wailed. "They're my wedding rings! They're worth over twenty thousand alone! Arnold will see they're missing!"

"Not if you keep your mitten on," he answered, throwing the glove back at her. She put it on hurriedly. "And if you say they're worth twenty, maybe I can hock them for twelve. Maybe. But anyhow, it's a start.

"We'll just say another five thousand a month from now on—how about it, Vera baby?"

She stared at him, and her face tightened with fury. "You stinking rat!" she breathed. It was lost instantly in the keening roar of the wind.

"Not a rat, baby. Just smart. Just smart." He began to slip down past her to Arnold's position. "See you back at the chalet, honey. And we can talk some more about love."

He laughed shortly, and she stared after him as he slipped down past her.

Then he went to work on Arnold.

"Vera wants me to kill you," he said. "But if you can come up with the twenty thousand now, I won't tell her you want me to do the same. If I do, she'll be able to sue you for every dollar you've got!"

Steig's face crumbled. He stared wordlessly at the mountaineer. "You surely aren't serious?" he finally coughed out.

"You bet your sweet life I am, Mister, and I might even do the job for her if you don't come across."

"But how? I don't have any money with me!"

Kennoy's face' assumed a sharp look. "Have you got any valuables on you? Any rings? A watch?"

Steig ground his jaws for a second, then slipped the sleeve of the *cagoule* back, revealing a ruby-encrusted watch. It was an expensive chronometer, and Kennoy took but a moment to slip it off the man's wrist. Steig replaced his mitten, and muttered, "That watch is expensive, Kennoy. Will it do for a down-payment. On the twenty thousand?"

Kennoy grinned wolfishly. "It'll do dandy for a down-payment. But not just on twenty thousand. I want more, Steig. Much more. Say, ten thousand a month from now on?"

Steig began to scream something at him, but Kennoy didn't wait for an answer. He knew he had the man in the corner. Right where he wanted him. He'd collect the balance of the pay-off when they got back to the chalet, and then he'd have a steady income of

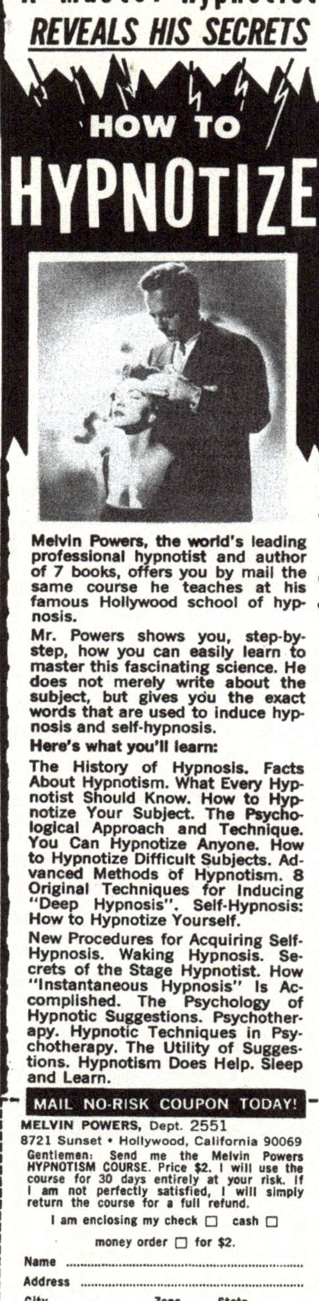

fifteen thousand a month, for the rest of his life. Neither one of them wanted the other to know about the death-plans they'd prepared. It was a foolproof set-up.

With the burden of decision off his mind, they began climbing again.

WHEN they reached the summit, Kennoy wasn't surprised that they dropped their tow-lines and stayed away from him. He had double-crossed them both, and they still weren't sure that he might not accept the other's offer to kill.

He stared at them, sitting huddled together, talking. Kennoy was certain they'd pay up. They knew he had too much on them.

After all these years of being a sport-bum, of having to make do with the sharpness of his mind and his good looks, he was finally coming into the big money! It felt good, real good!

He watched them as they got up and stretched. The poor saps! Particularly Vera, who had fallen for him. Like all the other damned dumb females in the world, a smart man had outfoxed her. And there was probably still some more rolling in the hay there—but he wouldn't settle for anything less than the money.

They came toward him, walking with care across the slippery ice of the cave mouth.

"We've been thinking, Kennoy," said Steig.

"Yes, we've been deciding something, Charlie," Vera chimed in.

"We still want to get rid of each other, but you're too expensive. We've decided to try our luck elsewhere. Your services come too high."

Kennoy stepped toward them, the wind of the ledge whistling past. "What do you two think you're pulling? I've, got you cold! I'll tell the cops everything! You rather I'd do *that?* Or would you like me to carry out the job for one of you?" His face was flushed, and the anger rolled in his voice, as he saw the money fading before him, They were trying to double-cross him!

They kept coming forward, steadily.

"Just wait till I get down!" he exploded angrily.

Suddenly they rushed, and he felt hands jarring against his chest. As the ice slipped from under. his feet, and his arms flailed into emptiness, he slid out into space, he heard Vera scream over the wind:

"You'll get down all right. And they'll find you with our valuables. You shouldn't have tried to rob us poor innocent tourists. So long, Charlie baby!"

He didn't hear the last of her speech. The night, the cold, the space of Mt. Keppler swallowed him. **///**

# ABOUT ROBERT F. DORR

ROBERT F. Dorr [1939–2016] was one of America's top military aviation historians. Author of over 70 books, his final releases included two critically-acclaimed World War II history books about American pilots and their crews: Hell Hawks (co-authored with former US astronaut Thomas D. Jones) and Mission to Berlin.

From the late 1950s to the mid-1970s, before Bob specialized as a history writer, he penned hundreds of stories for MAMs.

He wrote war stories, exotic adventure yarns, spy stories, sex exposés (sometimes called sexposés), and just about every type of story typically found in MAMs.

"Bayonet Killer of Heartbreak Ridge" is an interesting early example of his military history writing. It's about US Army Sergeant Donn F. Porter, a real-life hero and Medal of Honor recipient who was killed during the Korean War. When I asked Bob about it in 2009, here's what he told me:

> In 1957, I graduated high school and joined the Air Force. I'd had a couple of short, paid items published in magazines and wanted to become an author. The Air Force wanted me to go to Korea. While in Korea, I tried writing literary fiction but I noticed that some authors were appearing frequently in the men's adventure magazines. The Korean War was fresh in memory then, and Americans had a lot of interest in heroes like Donn Porter, a recipient of the Medal of Honor. In the late 1950s and early 1960s, I began reading whatever I could find about soldiers like Porter and tried writing about their experiences. It hadn't yet occurred to me to try to interview anyone but I did know a little about digging stuff out of historical archives. If I could write about someone like Porter accurately, I did. If I was missing anything, I made it up. That was the standard for the men's adventure magazines. I'd like to believe that the Porter story, while it includes soldiers with pseudonyms and made-up dialogue, gets right some of what it was like to fight in Korea just a few short years before I

got there.

Beginning around 1960 when I got out of the Air Force, I became a regular contributor to the men's adventure magazines. I typed out manuscripts on a manual typewriter, using typewriter paper, an eraser, carbon paper, cigarettes and booze. I submitted stories to several editors in the men's field. Phil Hirsch of *Man's Magazine*, which ran the Porter story, was an early supporter and later became the only men's adventure editor I met in person. Noah Sarlat of *Stag* magazine initially used my stamped, self-addressed envelopes to return each manuscript with a handwritten note that said, "Sorry, no"—until, one day, he said yes. One of my early stories for Noah was about American B-17 Flying Fortress bomber crews in World War II, the very same subject as my recent book *Mission to Berlin*. Carl Sifakis, editor of *Male* magazine, later became a supporter and encouraged me to write on far-out topics on which I had little expertise, like the intimate lives of airline stewardesses.

I began working for the government in 1965 and got to see a lot of the exotic places that became locales for men's adventure stories. I can't remember whether I ever set a men's adventure story in Madagascar, the site of my first overseas assignment, 1965-67. I did a lot of writing about Vietnam but the government kept ignoring my requests to be sent there. I retired from the Foreign Service in 1989, more than a decade after the men's adventure magazines vanished from our culture. By then, and until now, I've been a writer mostly on military subjects. From 2000 to 2009, I wrote a series of 1,700 history columns for the *Military Times* newspapers and was able to revisit heroes like Donn Porter and write about them with better focus and greater accuracy. More recently, I've written about military heroes for the online publication *Defense Media Network*. The story about Porter in *Man's* was among early examples of many to follow.

*Bob's history book,* Mission to Tokyo: The American Airmen Who Took the War to the Heart of Japan, *was released as the initial edition of this anthology originally went to press in 2012.*

*We so enjoyed working with Bob on the initial edition of this book, and we so admired his writing that we approached him about assembling one collecting the cream of his work for MAMs. That project would become the Men's Adventure Library collection* A Handful of Hell, *released as an illustrated softcover, ebook, and in an expanded hardcover edition.*

*On November 17, 2015, Bob posted to his blog that he had been diagnosed with glioblastoma cancer. In the months after that shocking announcement, the effects of the brain tumor increasingly robbed him of his ability to hit the right keys on a computer keyboard.*

*Nonetheless, in the first few months after his diagnosis, he managed to complete and self-publish his second novel,* Crime Scene: Fairfax County, *a follow-up to his 2014 alternate history novel,* Hitler's Time Machine.

*Bob would go on to wrote a series of blog posts about his life, his recent books, and people who influenced and inspired him. The titles of many of*

**Cover of the expanded hardcover edition.**

*those posts include the number of days since Bob's brain tumor had been discovered. It seemed an acknowledgment of the fact that many people diagnosed with a glioblastoma tumor die within a few months, and of his determination to exceed that timeline and continue to work as a writer as long as he could. (Those posts remain online at RobertFDorr.blogspot.com.)*

*He posted his telephone number, encouraging friends and readers to get in touch. "I'm in good spirits and having a great time," he wrote on his blog. "People are fussing over me. People who never picked up the tab in their lives are taking me to lunch. Thanks to my family, friends, and readers for a great time."*

*The courage and optimism Bob Dorr showed in those final days was nothing short of remarkable. There was no self-pity, no cursing his fate; only determination to keep doing what he did so well for as long as he was able.*

—*Robert Deis & Wyatt Doyle*

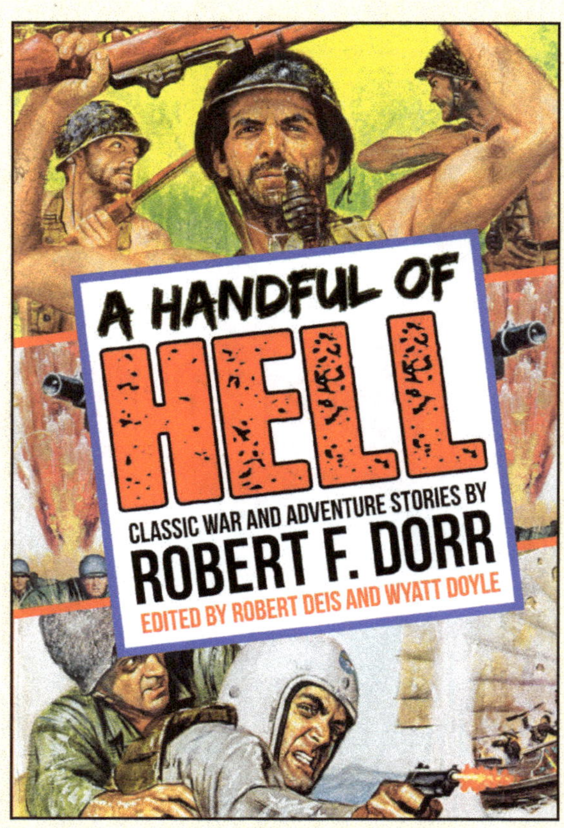


**Cover of the softcover edition.**

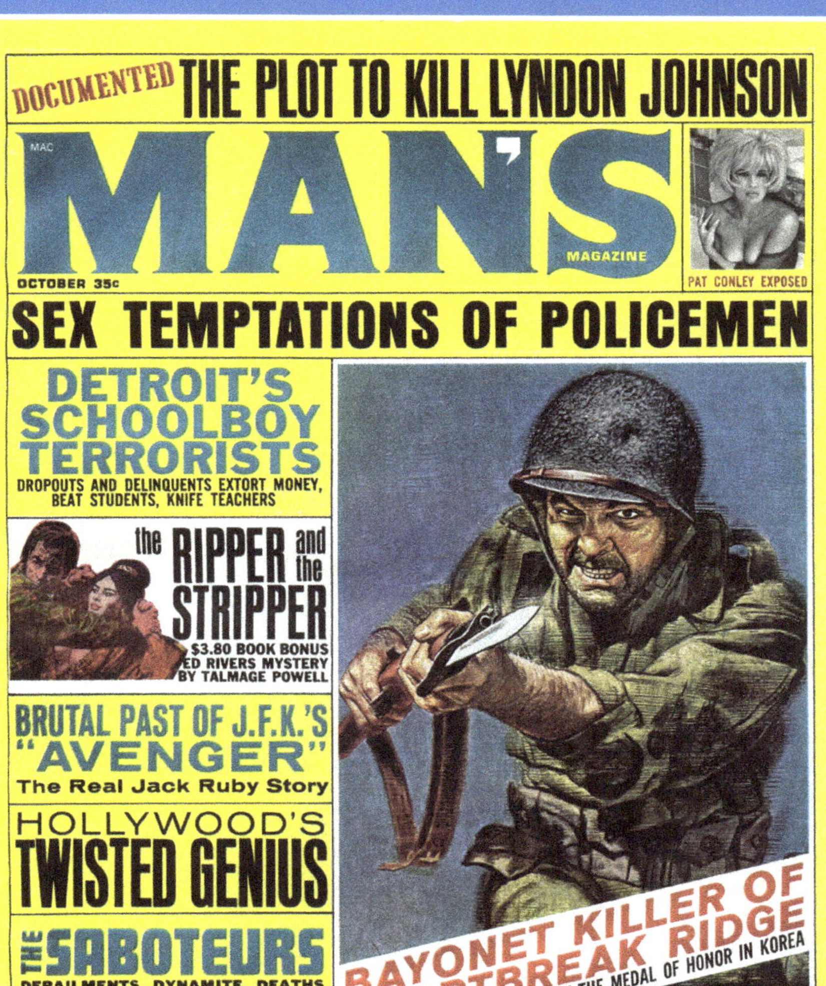


## "BAYONET KILLER OF HEARTBREAK RIDGE"

— ROBERT F. DORR —

*Man's Magazine*, October 1964

COVER ARTIST: MEL CRAIR

## Bayonet Killer

(Continued from page 19)

...gain, the sergeant was caught in the mid-...

...Amid the noise and mélee, Porter had ...

he headed back to the bunker again—seething with a new determination to hold it. The Chinese had been very close and very real, as vivid as the few inches which had separated his face from a Red bayonet seconds earlier, and he was beginning to think of Heartbreak's defense as a personal cause, something to be accomplished at any ...

In the glow of flares, Sgt. Porter's bayonet gleamed menacingly. Few GI's ...

...The error made by the enemy's own artillery, and the sheer brute force with which Porter had defended his position, ...d again repulsed China's best infantry-...en. Those Chinese closest to the bunker ... trench war of the kind which had been unknown since 1918. The conflict settled into a stalemate which, to the enemy's chagrin, would continue until its end. Porter's outfit dug in on Heartbreak Ridge at the east tip of the Iron Triangle, determined rea would ever again see **such madness, mayhem – and magnificence.**

LEAVING his three men behind, Sergeant Donn F. Porter groped downhill from the bunker he'd been ordered to defend. He hugged the Korean slope's powdery surface with his belly, staying low to keep from presenting a silhouette in the moonlight. Crawling on his elbows, he reached a point 40 feet downhill from the bunker when a faint whisper of sound—reminiscent of the one which had attracted him in the first place—repeated itself just below. Porter spot-guessed the location of the sound and lobbed three grenades at it.

# BAYONET KILLER OF HEARTBREAK RIDGE

**by ROBERT F. DORR**

Three blasts shattered the night silence, flashing in the darkness and throwing up dirt and rocks only feet below the sergeant. The harsh glare of the explosions illuminated half a dozen figures who'd been climbing uphill. The Chinese troops were close enough for Porter to see shock in their eyes, and streaks of lampblack on their jaws. They had the usual quilt uniforms, pile hats and automatic weapons—and Porter could see that the grenades had stunned them, knocking some down.

Raising his M-1, the sergeant

anked the keen hearing which had allowed him to pinpoint the Red patrol. While e Chinese were still groping through a shower of flying steel, he pumped off uick shots at them, aiming low, shooting to wound.

Behind Porter, the trio of GI's at the bunker opened up with carbines, sending murderous spray of bullets into the ranks of the stunned attackers. As darkness gain veiled their movements, the enemy troops replied with blinking weapons d frenzied screams. They were moving closer to where Porter held his ground, ming and firing at their muzzle flashes.

The Chinese were good. They struck fast. But in the noise and confusion of the arkened gun battle, they made a fatal error. Instead of storming the bunker—where killing stream of automatic fire poured at them—they attacked Porter.

continued on next page

17

**LEAVING** his three men behind, Sergeant Donn F. Porter groped downhill from the bunker he'd been ordered to defend. He hugged the Korean slope's powdery surface with his belly, staying low to keep from presenting a silhouette in the moonlight. Crawling on his elbows, he reached a point 40 feet downhill from the bunker when a faint whisper of sound—reminiscent of the one which had attracted him in the first place—repeated itself just below. Porter spot-guessed the location of the sound and lobbed three grenades at it.

Three blasts shattered the night silence, flashing in the darkness and throwing up dirt and rocks only feet below the sergeant. The harsh glare of the explosions illuminated half a dozen figures who'd been climbing uphill.

The Chinese troops were close enough for Porter to see shock in their eyes, and streaks of lampblack on their jaws. They had the usual quilt uniforms, pile hats and automatic weapons—and Porter could see that the grenades had stunned them, knocking some down.

Raising his M-1, the sergeant thanked the keen hearing which had allowed him to pinpoint the Red patrol. While the Chinese were still groping through a shower of flying steel, he pumped off quick shots at them, aiming low, shooting to wound.

Behind Porter, the trio of GIs at the bunker opened up with carbines, sending a murderous spray of bullets into the ranks of the stunned attackers. As darkness again veiled their movements, the enemy troops replied with blinking weapons and frenzied screams. They were moving closer to where Porter held his ground, aiming and firing at their muzzle flashes.

The Chinese were good. They struck fast. But in the noise and confusion of the darkened gun battle, they made a fatal error. Instead of storming the bunker—where a killing stream of automatic fire poured at them—they attacked Porter.

The lanky, six-foot sergeant was ramming a fresh clip into his M-1 when Red grenades chewed into earth only feet away, jarring his eardrums and shaking his tensed body. Dazed, he wriggled backward, wiping blood from his face with a quick handsweep. Then he rose, without cover, to shoot from a standing position.

A Chinese rifleman broke from the shadows below, rushing up at him from only feet away. Another quilt-jacketed Red soldier appeared behind the first-and then another.

Porter fell back a step and shot from his hip, gunning down the second and third men with quick bursts. The first attacker, a quick, wiry figure, was suddenly on top of him. Porter's rifle clicked empty.

*I've bought it*, Porter thought.

But he braced the M-1 firmly against his hip and reached forward with his bayonet, coming off his knees in a driving crouch to meet the attacker head-on.

Arriving at a dead run, the Chinese slammed into the knife and took the full impact of its razor-honed blade. It sank in—deep. His momentum knocked Porter backward, almost twisting the M-1 from the sergeant's hands.

The collision was brutal. A grunt of pain and shock halted in mid-breath as the Chinese lost his forward speed and began to crumple. His hands reached out blindly for Porter, flailing crazily in the night air.

The big sergeant raised a boot and kicked his assailant back off the blade. Then he cartwheeled the rifle in a quick arc and felt its buttplate strike against bone.

The Chinese tottered half-balanced on one foot, a mushy lump of blood marking the spot where his mouth had been. Porter turned the rifle again, lunged, and felt the blade sink to its hilt. This time he did not need to wrench it free, for the man fell away from it, collapsing like a pile of discarded laundry.

Porter regained his own balance, stood above the blood-spattered figure, and struck again with his buttplate—crushing the man's skull.

His nerves frozen to ice, the big sergeant spun around, ready for the next grenade or the next screaming figure to plunge out of the darkness. But the attack, launched so quickly, was over.

The Chinese patrol had failed in its attempt to overwhelm the bunker outpost, primarily because Porter's alert bearing had denied them the element of surprise.

The Red troops, veterans of General Chen Yi's Third Field Route Army, had been caught in a savage crossfire between the sergeant's M-1 and the bunker's carbines. They'd been cut to shreds and pushed back -repulsed so quickly that Porter hadn't found time to worry about seeking artillery or mortar support.

It was nine minutes past midnight, September 7, 1952. The firefight bad lasted exactly 43 seconds.

Reeling with shock and nausea, Sergeant Donn Porter bad little reason to be pleased with the results of the skirmish. He knew it was only the tough beginning of a long and terrible night....

WHEN IT came to soldiering, Porter was a stubborn man. He had a job to do, and that was it. Defending the bunker meant keeping someone posted just ahead of it in the darkness, to listen and look for the enemy. Porter, who was always thinking of his responsibilities as an NCO, intended to handle that risky job himself. His stubborn streak prevented him from worrying about his own safety and comfort. If the night ahead was going to be filled with risk, Porter was determined to face the danger squarely.

He could return to the bunker now, but he would soon have to leave it again to keep a vigil for the Chinese. He didn't make compromises when it came to being a good soldier, and he wouldn't tell his men to take any more chances than he was prepared to accept himself.

He reached for the sticky cut on his forehead and was relieved to find he'd only been grazed by flying shrapnel. Luck had been on his side, but he didn't want to think about how soon it might run out. Turning from the mangled corpse of the man he'd stabbed, he felt waves of dizziness creeping over him. It took 30 seconds to repress a strong urge to vomit.

When the urge passed, Porter crawled uphill to rejoin Corporal Ray Schwab, Corporal Paul Matichek and PFC Jerry Bachelor. At the fortification's entrance he paused to glance at the towering peak beyond. The hill—with its machine-gun nests, barbed-wire barricades and deep trenches—had been silent throughout the battle.

Now it seemed asleep, the moon a silvery disk at its crest. Porter quickly looked away, not wanting to remember all the men he knew who would never leave this dark slope.

Its name was Heartbreak Ridge.

Corporal Ray Schwab was a blurred figure in the darkness, bent over the bunker's sound-power telephone. An ex-farmhand from Struthers, Ohio, Schwab was a seasoned veteran with four months of combat behind him. He was good at sensing what the Chinese would do next, and he had a talent for explaining what they had already tried, so the phone was his responsibility. He knew when to use it.

"Regiment CP just called," Schwab whispered. "I talked to Major Eckhart. They heard the shooting and they have to know—was it just a patrol or the start of a big attack?"

Porter shrugged, still wiping blood from nicks at his temples.

He was remembering what a bayonet can do to the human body, and he still felt sick.

"They're really worried up there in the trenches."

"*They're* worried!" Porter half-grinned at Schwab. "How do they think we feel? What about it, Ray? What would you tell the major?"

"Well, we just got hit by a small patrol," Schwab said. "A very small one, in fact. Maybe six Chinks. But you know I can't answer the question about an attack. The Chinks didn't invite me to their last strategy conference."

"You, Paul?"

PAUL Matichek shook his head. He'd been co-owner of a gas station in Sharon Springs, Kansas at one time, but was now an "old man" on the line—another vet. Three days earlier, at another outpost on the flank of this ridge, he'd duplicated Porter's feat of slashing down a Chinese soldier with a bayonet.

"We can't tell Regiment beans," Matichek said slowly. "None of us learned a damned thing from that skirmish."

"That's it," PFC Bachelor whispered meekly.

"That *is* it," Porter concluded, glancing around the dark bunker. "We didn't learn a thing. Ray, tell the major we just don't know. We'll have to see what happens next—whether they hit us again, or go after one of the other bunkers. The Chinks may only be prowling around, or they may be getting ready to make a big try for the ridge. But we just don't know—"

Ray Schwab returned to the phone. Paul Matichek shifted uneasily. "If they do attack, it'll come before dawn. That means we've had it—"

Sergeant Porter nodded grimly and leaned back to reload his M-1. It was now 35 minutes past midnight....

Porter and his trio were at the center of a V-shaped gully which began at Heartbreak Ridge's peak, dropped a quarter-mile to this bunker, then plunged into the rice paddies below. The gully was the deepest groove in the slope of this looming ridge where the 25th Infantry Division's 14th Regiment had dug in to make a stand. Porter's "George" Company, commanded by Major Ronald Eckhart, of Monterey, California, was entrenched in the ditches along the top of the groove. The bunker stood in the middle. At the bottom—Chinese.

A real estate salesman wouldn't have given a bent penny for Heartbreak Ridge. The hill, four miles long and three wide, no longer had a single tree growing on its shell-blasted flanks. Its soil had been beaten into a fine, powdery dirt incapable of supporting the roots of even tough Korean *chonghwa* bushes. For all its commercial value, it might have been a sand dune in the Sahara.

But with the outcome of a great struggle at stake, Heartbreak Ridge was priceless in a way not measured in dollars and cents. It had become a showcase where the world could view and judge the determination of the opposing powers. The Communists needed a victory to parade before the watching world, to use as leverage in the Panmunjom truce talks, and they looked bad all over the globe simply because Porter's regiment hadn't given them anything to strut about for a long time.

Every GI on the ridge, from the regimental command post down to Porter's bunker, knew the American will to fight was on trial. The verdict could affect the balance of the entire Cold War. The Communists hoped to show the rest of the world that Americans couldn't and wouldn't fight, that freedom had become a forgotten word in our dictionary.


Today, 12 years later, it is difficult to remember how grim the situation was. But at the time the implications were clear: If the Reds could prove that Americans wouldn't defend a gnarled scab of a Korean hilltop, they would be one step closer to proving that Americans couldn't defend Denver or Chicago.

Heartbreak Ridge, held by determined men, was a toothpick in the enemy's throat. The 700-foot peak mocked Red propaganda and blocked

Red intentions. To save face, and to win concessions in the forthcoming cease-fire agreement, the Chinese desperately wanted to capture it and dislodge the toothpick.

But the attack would have to come uphill along the V, passing the bunker outpost where Porter and his men watched, waited, and sat on a telephone.

It was like sitting on dynamite.

Porter, Schwab, Matichek and Bachelor were all wondering if the Chinese would return in force. It seemed likely. Preparing for the worst, they talked little. Words would not help, and anything but a whisper might carry to Red artillery spotters in the valley below. At 12:38 Porter leaned close to Schwab and summed things up:

"I'm sure they'll be back," he whispered. "When they come, we stand firm and fight."

He'd put all his beliefs, all his determination to be a crack soldier, into a nutshell.

At 12:42 the Chinese swept aside all doubts. Their second assault came with blinding speed. The Reds screamed out of darkness at a dead sprint, a dozen abreast, their voices raised to a pitch and their weapons spitting fire. This was no patrol, no probe, no sneaky attempt to feel out Heartbreak's defenses. It was a major attack, accompanied by the nerve-

Elsewhere on the contested hill, GI's were dug in well, had heavy firepower.

grating shriek of bugles, the raw glow of exploding flares, and the deafening impact of howitzer shells falling just above the outpost.

Seconds earlier Porter had paused at the doorway of the outpost while Schwab tugged at his arm.

"I know somebody's got to go out there," Schwab whispered. "But you almost got sliced up. Why don't you let me take it this time?"

"You just stay on the phone," the sergeant snapped. "I'll handle point."

"But, dammit, no sense you taking all the chances—"

"I'm not. Things'll get hot enough right here. Besides—" he was already halfway outside when he finished "—that's what I get paid for."

Porter had again crawled downhill from the bunker and was crouched on the dirt behind his M-1 when the second attack started…

He began firing while the Red troops were still shrouded by far-off darkness and he continued tugging the trigger in quick, careful jerks as they came closer. He aimed low, again aiming to wound rather than kill—for the Chinese took care of their casualties and an injured man could tie up several others. He knew his bullets were striking men, but as the roar of gunfire boomed in his ears he felt his mind swimming, his senses going numb. He lost himself to the fleeting images in his gun sight, too absorbed in action to think clearly fighting by instinct.

In the bunker, Schwab struggled with the sound-power phone, cursing and having no luck in a desperate attempt to reach Major Eckhart—to tell him the size of the onslaught. Matichek and Bachelor were firing in mad, prolonged spasms, their faces twisted in shock as they burned their carbines and sprayed empty shells around the emplacement. Schwab gave up on the phone, grabbed his weapon, and joined the frenzied defense. Thirty seconds after launching the attack, the Chinese were within a few hundred feet….

Once again Porter stood squarely in the path of the onrushing Reds and once again screaming figures plunged out of darkness, reaching for him with chattering burp guns and flashing bayonets. The sergeant stood and battled, oblivious to the bullets flying all around him, too dazed to appreciate the miracle which prevented him from being cut down. In front of him the Chinese came within 50 feet—pointblank distance. Behind him, the exploding US artillery shells began to walk downhill. He was caught in the middle.

He was looking the other way, too busy shooting to notice, when "incoming mail" from Chinese guns finally punched into the bunker, crushing the left corner of the emplacement where Cpl. Matichek and PFC Bachelor crouched. He didn't even hear the blasts moving his way.

THE ROAR of the firefight had alerted Heartbreak's main trenches—something Schwab had been unable to do with the field phone. Yellow tracers lashed down from the hilltop, seeking the Chinese. Shimmering beads of return fire skipped up from the dark valley. Again, the sergeant was caught in the middle.

Amid the noise and melee, Porter had no time to think, or even to plan a split second ahead. He was fighting on reflex, trusting his eyesight and body to do what his mind had no time to order.

The first attacker reached him-a lean, panting figure of a Chinese coming on like a freight train-and Porter acted by instinct. He brought his bayonet around in a sliding vertical curve, aiming for the man's jugular.

He missed.

His M-1 stock slammed against the Chinese soldier's burp gun. The rifle flew from his hands. Then the man piled into him.

Porter fell to the ground and rolled, feeling his breath escaping in quick spasms as the Chinese bayonet followed him down, gouging into dirt only inches from his face.

He kicked out, feeling his boot glance off the attacker's shin. The Red soldier stood firm, towering above him and again raising the bayonet. Between the man's legs, Porter could see half a dozen more Chinese rushing his way. They were leveling their weapons to fire from the hip.

Still unaware of the approaching artillery blasts, Porter rolled again, trying to dodge the bayonet and at the same time to keep the first attacker as a shield between him and the others. Again the bayonet plunged into dirt beside him, and this time he lashed out with both feet, throwing all his strength into the kick.

One of his boots caught the towering Chinese in the groin and threw him backward, opening a gap for the others to shoot.

At the same instant, Red artillery gunners in the darkness far below made a classic blunder. In their frantic desire to wipe out Porter's emplacement, they pulled their shots too short. The reeling Chinese soldier, the other onrushing Red troops, the exploding shell—and Porter—all came together at once.

The sergeant's ears were deadened by the roar of earth being torn up around him. The Chinese troops were caught in cone-shaped geysers of flame, while he was sent hurtling in the other direction. He was scooped off the ground by a rush of searing hot air which lifted his whole body and sent him flying end-over-end like an acorn in a hurricane. He smashed into the bunker, fell, and tasted the warm saltiness of blood in his mouth.

"*Damn*—" he stammered.

Almost blindly, he groped upward on all fours and shook his head, struggling to catch his senses. He was hurt, but had no idea how badly. The barrage was lifting and he stood with his back against the wall of the outpost, expecting the attackers to finish him off within seconds.

No one came.

The error made by the enemy's own artillery, and the sheer brute force with which Porter had defended his position, had again repulsed China's best infantrymen. Those Chinese closest to the bunker had died horribly in the blasts of their own shells and now, once again, Heartbreak Ridge was silent.

Coming out of his daze, Porter fumbled downhill, stepped over shrapnel-pelleted Chinese bodies, and found his rifle.

He pictured a hapless Red artillery officer being chewed out for snarling the attack. But he also knew that the enemy troops would return as soon as they could rally.

Not even pausing to examine his wound, he headed back to the bunker again seething with a new determination to hold it. The Chinese had been very close and very real, as vivid as the few inches which had separated his face from a Red bayonet seconds earlier, and he was beginning to think of Heartbreak's defense as a personal cause, something to be accomplished at any price....

It was no accident that Porter was the man on the spot, seemingly picked by fate to make a stand along Heartbreak's most vulnerable approach. Barely 21, but a veteran of 13 months in combat, Porter had spent his whole career working toward this moment of truth—his decisive role in holding back the last great enemy effort of the Korean War.

The big sergeant, a former high school halfback, had worked hard to become a first-rate soldier and was proud of it. He might have fulfilled his service obligation by avoiding trouble, sticking to the rear, and winning easy promotions—but his keen sense of duty wouldn't permit it. Instead he won his three stripes in battle. He once told a buddy that "Soldiering is like playing football. You can sit on the bench or you can do what has to be done. If you're a soldier, your job is to kill your country's enemies."

If his country's enemies happened to be Red China's crack infantry

DEPARTMENT OF THE ARMY
WASHINGTON 25, D. C., 18 August 1955

GO

AWARD OF THE MEDAL OF HONOR

By direction of the President, under the act of Congress approved 9 July 1918 (WD Bul. 43, 1918), the Medal of Honor for conspicuous gallantry and intrepidity at the risk of life above and beyond the call of duty is awarded posthumously by the Department of the Army in the name of the Congress to the following-named enlisted man:

Sergeant Donn F. Porter (Service No. RA13376470), Infantry, United States Army, a member of Company G, 14th Infantry Regiment, 25th Infantry Division, distinguished himself by conspicuous gallantry and outstanding courage above and beyond the call of duty in action against the enemy near Mundung-ni, Korea, on 7 September 1952. Advancing under cover of intense mortar and artillery fire, two hostile platoons attacked a combat outpost commanded by Sergeant Porter, destroyed communications, and killed two of his three-man crew. Gallantly maintaining his position, Sergeant Porter poured deadly accurate fire into the ranks of the enemy, killing 15 and dispersing the remainder. After falling back under a hail of fire, the ...

Porter (above) posed for photo at paratroop training school. Medal of Honor citation is shown (left).

troops, Porter was going to kill them and kill them well.

Back in February, 1951 he'd gone with his father, Joseph D. Porter, into the Army recruiting office at Ruxton, Maryland equipped with a high school diploma, a serious look in his eyes, and a carefully thought-out desire to serve in combat. He was inducted at Fort Holabird, Maryland, and decided early in basic training to become more than just another number—RA13376470, the Army tagged him—so he volunteered for jump school.

Donn Porter was one of the first paratroops to jump from the C-U9 "Flying Boxcar" airplane at Pope AFB, South Carolina. While there he fired "expert" with the M-1, the carbine, and the grease-gun, but still wasn't satisfied. When orders were cut assigning him to the 101st Airborne then stateside—he asked that they be changed.

HE GOT what he wanted—shipping papers for Korea. He'd been in combat only a few days when, in August 1951, General James A. Van Fleet's 8th Army pulled one of the great reverses of modern warfare turning around the oncoming hordes of Chinese at the peak of their strength, pushing them back, and advancing into the sprawling ricebowl known as the Iron Triangle.

There the American and Chinese armies, each sharpened to the keenest possible edge of fighting strength, butted against each other like an irresistible force meeting an immovable object. Generals Van Fleet and Chen Yi found themselves directing a trench war of the kind which had been unknown since 1918. The conflict settled into a

stalemate which, to the enemy's chagrin, would continue until its end.
Porter's outfit dug in on Heartbreak Ridge at the east tip of the Iron
Triangle, determined to stand firm against constant heavy assault.

By this time Porter had made himself an expert with the Army's
oldest and most fearsome weapon-the bayonet. Ex-GI and war historian
Bruce Jacobs recalls that Porter was a "wild man" with the knife.
The sergeant spent his free time drilling newer troops on the use of
the blade, for he realized that neither radar-guided artillery nor jet-
propelled warplanes had replaced the need for cold, sharp steel.

He had no way of knowing it, but his skill with the bayonet would
win him a small paragraph in the history books.

AT 1:14 AM on the night of his brush with destiny, the big sergeant
again returned to the bunker. He ignored the fierce, driving pain in his
ribs. His mind was on other things.

Intuition told Porter that the Chinese attempt to overwhelm
Heartbreak was only moments away from its climax. He didn't know
whether the Reds had attacked other bunkers on the slope. He didn't
know if their artillery had sought out the main trenches. He didn't
know if a victory over the Chinese tonight would make Heartbreak
any safer tomorrow, the day after, or the night after that. None of
these things mattered. The generals could worry about tomorrow,
just as they could worry about White Horse Mountain to the east and
Bloody Nose Ridge to the west. Porter was worried about *now*. He was
concerned only with his personal role in the defense of Heartbreak on
this one, crucial night. And he knew the showdown was near.

The sight of destruction in the bunker stunned him, even in
the darkness, and he almost knocked over Ray Schwab, who stood
transfixed in awe.

"They banged hell out of this place," Schwab muttered.

"They almost walked over us," Porter admitted. "For a second I
guess I was on the brink of going crazy."

"Me too. I guess I'm okay now. Just shook up is all."

"The others—"

"Paul and Jerry… They got hacked—"

PORTER nodded grimly, glancing at the corner where a shell had
punched into the bunker's roof. For the first time he saw what had
happened to two of his men. Corporal Paul Matichek's arm protruded
straight up from beneath a pile of debris and rubble, his index finger
aiming at the sky, his body crushed. PFC Jerry Bachelor lay sprawled

in a broken heap, twisted grotesquely out of any recognizable shape, his blood caked in ugly brown pools on the floorboards. Matichek might have lived for a few, agonizing seconds. Jerry Bachelor had died instantly.

"I don't know how we stopped the bastards," Porter said, "except that our guys on the ridge helped a lot, and the Chinks' own shells dropped short. But they're probably on the way back now for the final try—"

"The phone's broken in a thousand pieces. I don't imagine either the Major or the Chinks think any of us are still alive. And we couldn't pull back to the ridge if we wanted to, because the Chink snipers would hit us like fish in a barrel." Schwab's expression suddenly changed and his eyes widened. *"Hey—"* he began. *"Hey, you're hurt!"*

Porter looked at his ribs for the first time. Shrapnel had torn through his jacket and shirt, leaving a hole more than two inches in diameter. A bone was exposed and he could see its sheeny white surface, splotched with a trickle of blood. To him the wound seemed no more important than the dreadful inadequacy of words at this moment when good men were dead—no more a reality than the strategy maps back in Tokyo.

He and Schwab had no time for normal things, such as treating the injury, discussing the situation, or worrying about their fate. Their future was unreal beyond the next few minutes. Hurt, sick, and exhausted—surrounded by the stench and decay of death—they had reached the point where anything but the present was meaningless. Nothing was important except the fight to hold this V-shaped gully.

Porter felt no bitterness about being there. Bunker warfare was a vital part of the larger scope of the war. He didn't blame Major Eckhart, or the generals in Tokyo, or anyone else for the fact that he and Schwab stood alone in the path of the Chinese. Ninety-nine nights out of a hundred, a bunker like this one would serve its intended purpose of keeping an eye on the enemy. Men at these listening posts rarely faced the danger of mass attack, and when they did it was simply a fluke of chance—nothing more.

"I'm all right," he lied. Avoiding further talk, he scoured the wreckage of the outpost to find every available grenade—10 in all— and stuffed them into his pockets. Ray Schwab, meanwhile, taped together new banana clips for his carbine. Then the two men were facing each other like ghosts, stiff and unreal, when flares exploded in the darkness above, bugles screeched in the valley below. and the enemy returned.

"It sounds like everybody in China is coming after us," Schwab whispered. "Like you said earlier, we stand firm and fight."

"This is it," Porter nodded. "Cover me."

MACHINE guns on the ridge and in the valley below already had begun exchanging fire. Artillery shells were flying in both directions. Automatic weapons crackled at other bunkers, to the left and right of Porter's position. But the vanguard of the Chinese assault force was coming up the V.

And they were coming much too recklessly.

Porter plunged outside. He knew the only chance was to try the unlikely—to attack. The only hope was to surprise the Reds and foul up their assault *before* they could guess the odds.

He could see from the way the Chinese emerged from the shadows, walking tall, coming fast, that they believed the bunker to be wiped out. Although they were still too far away for him to see their eyes, he knew they were watching the main trenches far above.

He had a little surprise for them—10 grenades. Leaning against the side of the outpost, he began pulling pins and lobbing the round projectiles. He threw like a pitcher in slow motion, carefully figuring his aim and trajectory.

When the first explosion jarred the oncoming Reds, Ray Schwab's carbine began chattering. When the last grenade left Porter's hand, the sergeant braced the M-1 on his hip and began walking forward, shooting on the move.

One after another, the exploding grenades tore into the Chinese—killing some instantly, knocking others flat, turning still others into dazed, senseless creatures with horrible wounds all over their bodies. Carbine and M-1 bullets rained into the survivors, scattering them and momentarily halting their advance.

The sign of resistance at the bunker drew quick support from GIs up at the main trenches. Machine-gun fire began to rake the scene of the blasts, and mortar shells dropped just behind the first wave of Red troops.

Porter continued walking forward. He moved like a man in a trance, heading straight for the Red soldiers, his M-1 spewing fire.

From behind the bunker's ledge, Ray Schwab placed his shots quickly and accurately. But he also watched Porter. Later he would recall that the sergeant looked like a sheriff in a Western movie, as if walking into a six-gun duel. However, Porter wasn't waiting for the enemy to draw. While the final grenade was still echoing, he cut down more stunned Reds with a hail of bullets.

In the glow of flares, a long and bright object stood gleaming at the front of his rifle—the bayonet.

The sergeant was moving into his final act with the weapon he'd learned to use so well.

Within seconds Schwab was forced to stop firing: Porter had merged with the first wave of Chinese.

In the noise, confusion and darkness, the sergeant struck hard. He rammed his bayonet into a Chinese soldier's stomach, squeezed off the last bullet in his clip to free it, and downed the man with a swipe of the rifle's barrel.

ANOTHER Red soldier, only feet away, emptied his burp-gun clip at Porter. For a long instant, the sergeant stood unmoving while the weapon flashed and chattered before him. Every bullet miraculously missed! Porter stepped forward again and bayoneted the man three times with quick stabs.

Several Chinese had jogged uphill from Porter and were now turning to gun him down from behind. Schwab was faster. Nailing them against the skyline, he fired at them like ducks in a shooting gallery.

But Schwab could do nothing more to help Donn F. Porter. The big man was now in the middle of several dozen enemy troops who fired, dodged, balked and probed after him with their own knives. He had an enormous advantage, for they couldn't shoot accurately without hitting each other, and he seized it. His rifle barrel turned one man's face into a blob of raspberry jam. His bayonet pinned another's neck against the soft dirt.

The sergeant's incredible display of courage had a strange, terrifying effect on the Chinese. Many who could have fought Porter turned instead to run. A few fled in such panic that they cast their weapons aside like dead wood. After moving a short distance, they became perfect targets for Schwab's carbine and the ridge's machine guns.

Porter fought like a madman. When his blade glanced off one Red soldier's arm he kicked the man, spun him around, and sank the bayonet into his back. Then he raised the M-1 to bring it down like a club, knocking a burp gun from another Chink's hands.

For more than a full minute the sergeant roved among the ranks of the Chinese—chopping, swinging, stabbing. The sporadic glow of flares sometimes made him visible to GIs far above, and few of them would ever witness such a sight again in their lives. It was mayhem and murder, madness and magnificence. It was probably the most amazing hand-to-hand battle ever fought by an American soldier anywhere, and no man who saw it would ever forget.

For weeks to follow, countless Chinese would wonder why they'd been too fear-stricken to stop this bayonet-slashing apparition of a man. In years to come, GIs from Wiesbaden to Manila would tell barracks lies about having been with Porter, about having seen blood on his knife from the trenches a quarter-mile above, or about having taught him to use the weapon.

But Porter himself didn't have any years to come. While he was bayoneting his sixth Chinese in 60 seconds, Red artillery again began seeking the bunker.

The artillery fire came too late to help the sputtering Oriental who backed away from Porter's knife with tissue and intestines gaping in his hands. It came too late to help the largest assault ever launched on Heartbreak Ridge, for the enemy advance had bogged down and fallen apart. But it came, sluggishly and inaccurately, striking earth a dozen yards uphill from the sergeant.

Suddenly Porter was alone. The Chinese had been routed, and only corpses at his feet kept him company. He was turning to rejoin Schwab when he heard the muffled cry of cheers from the ridge's peak—and then the voices were cut off by exploding shells.

Ray Schwab saw it happen. He had just begun to tell himself that the worst was over—that the sergeant's hand-to-hand struggle had turned the tide—when the bracket of shells landed. In one instant he saw Porter turning to walk uphill slowly, probably hampered by wounds, and in the next second, Cpl. Schwab saw the sergeant disappear.

There were only a few blasts. They came after Heartbreak Ridge's fate was already decided, and they had no effect on the battle or the war. Perhaps they would have come earlier had the enemy known the bunker was still manned, or perhaps they wouldn't have come at all a few minutes later.

Donn Porter, returning to rejoin his friend, was killed instantly. Schwab was at his side in seconds-but he was too late to help.

That was autumn of 1952. The following summer Ray Schwab was still on the line when the Korean War came to an end. After months of trying, the Chinese never succeeded in taking a single major ridge from stubborn UN defenders, and finally they gave up altogether.

Today few people remember those ridges at all, or what they stood for. Vegas, White Horse Mountain, Carson City, Bloody Nose Ridge and Little Bunker Hill are now only names in military textbooks. Perhaps a few of us remember Pork Chop Hill. But only Heartbreak Ridge still evokes a strange feeling of nostalgia, an emotion that reminds us of how much we stood to lose in that Asiatic war—and how we refused to do anything but win.

That summer was warm and sunny. Most Americans were at the beach when a Pentagon steno worked overtime to polish off General Orders No. 64, signed by Chief of Staff General Matthew B. Ridgway. Those orders officially awarded the Congressional Medal of Honor to Sergeant Donn F. Porter—the soldier with a keen sense of duty who became Heartbreak Ridge's boldest bayonet killer.  ///

# ABOUT BRUCE JAY FRIEDMAN

BRUCE *Jay Friedman (1930–2020) is often cited as the writer who coined modern-day Black Humor…who invented the Jewish Mother in fiction (*A Mother's Kisses, *1964) and wrote the first "Freudian novel" (*Stern, *1962)…who first introduced nudity and obscenity to the New York stage (*Scuba Duba, *1967)…and is one of the unsurpassed masters of the short story.*

*Before all this, he was a nine-to-five editor at Magazine Management in the 1950s. (See "Even the Rhinos Were Nymphos," pg. 417) Fresh out of the Air Force in his early 20s, BJF often carried a Rolleiflex camera with him. It was his most prized possession, as he leaned toward the burgeoning field of photo-journalism. During a casual trip to the zoo, he suddenly witnessed a moment that seemed like something out of a BJF short story: A tiger began to chew the leg off another tiger in the adjacent cage. As pandemonium broke out, he snapped several photos, one of which accompanied the story. He interviewed the zookeeper, then did a stylized take from the zookeeper's point of view ("Eat Her—Bones and All," *Male, *December 1954). The piece was long forgotten until editor Robert Deis discovered and included it here.*

*Not long after that incident, Friedman wrapped up his photographic ambitions. His exploits as a writer include the proverbial Hollywood chapter. He wrote the screenplays for* Splash *and* Stir Crazy, *as well as uncredited contributions to other Richard Pryor films.* The Heartbreak Kid *and* The Lonely Guy *were based on his stories. (Neil Simon, who scripted both, has said BJF is the only writer he adapts.) And to cap off his Hollywood career, he made cameo appearances in three Woody Allen films:* Another Woman, Husbands and Wives, *and* Celebrity.

*Bruce Jay Friedman's final publications were the literary memoir,* Lucky Bruce *(Biblioasis, 2011) and the collection 3.1* Plays *(Leaping Lion Books, 2012), which includes* Steambath *and* Scuba Duba.

—*Josh Alan Friedman*

## "EAT HER ... BONES AND ALL"

— BRUCE JAY FRIEDMAN —

*Male*, December 1954

COVER ARTIST: ROBERT E. SCHULZ

ZOMBIE HAD QUEEN'S LEG IN HIS MOUTH AND WAS SLOWLY CHEWING HIS WAY UP TO HER SHOULDER

as told to BRUCE J. FRIEDMAN

# EAT HER

# ... bones and all

▶ I've seen my best friend crazy on the ground swallowing dirt after a horse kicked him in the brains. . . . A jaguar once ripped a 14-stitch gash down my finger and across my wrist. . . . I've had an antelope in heat go out of his head and ram a jagged antler into the flesh of my buttocks. Twelve monkeys once ganged up on me and chewed the flesh off my legs until they looked like rotten sea barnacles. So I think I know animals. Or rather, I *thought* I knew animals until the day Zombie went off his rocker.

Let me say first, I work in a zoo; it doesn't matter where. What happened with Zombie was the zoo's fault.

I've got cats, 14 of them. Zombie is a tiger. He weighs 650 pounds, and he doesn't make friends. I can go over to my lion, for example, and say, "Jackie boy, Nyaaaa; Jackie boy, Nyaaa," and he lets me put my hand on his shoulder. Or my black leopard. She put a gash in my cheek, but now she sings to me. Yet if I come within two feet of Zombie, he rams 650 pounds against the bars and makes the whole street shake. We got that animal mean; he's mean now, and he's going to die mean. Somebody smacked him with a rock when he was young. He never forgot it.

Like I say, though, I *thought* I knew cats. I had this idea in my head you can make friends with any animal if you're nice to him. When they shipped us Zombie, they told me how mean he was, but he was the most beautiful cat I ever saw. I started talking to him through the cage, and I slipped him an extra steak every day. That was the time I figured I knew his secret—the way to make friends

**I'VE SEEN** my best friend crazy on the ground swallowing dirt after a horse kicked him in the brains.... A jaguar once ripped a 14-stitch gash down my finger and across my wrist.... I've had an antelope in heat go out of his head and ram a jagged antler into the flesh of my buttocks. Twelve monkeys once ganged up on me and chewed the flesh off my legs until they looked like rotten sea barnacles. So I think I know animals. Or rather, I *thought* I knew animals until the day Zombie went off his rocker.

Let me say first, I work in a zoo; it doesn't matter where. What happened with Zombie was the zoo's fault.

I've got cats, 14 of them. Zombie is a tiger. He weighs 650 pounds, and he doesn't make friends. I can go over to my lion, for example, and say, "Jackie boy, Nyaaaa; Jackie boy, Nyaaa," and he lets me put my hand on his shoulder. Or my black leopard. She put a gash in my cheek, but now she sings to me. Yet if I come within two feet of Zombie, he rams 650 pounds against the bars and makes the whole street shake. We got that animal mean; he's mean now, and he's going to die mean. Somebody smacked him with a rock when he was young. He never forgot it.

Like I say, though, I *thought* I knew cats. I had this idea in my head you can make friends with any animal if you're nice to him. When they shipped us Zombie, they told me how mean he was, but he was the most beautiful cat I ever saw. I started talking to him through the cage, and I slipped him an extra steak every day. That was the time I figured I knew his secret—the way to make friends with him. I noticed when I gave him the meat sloppy—I mean just curled it up and flipped it to him—he acted like a killer. But when I gave it to him nice, flattened it out and slipped it under his feet gently, he acted real nice. Every day, I saw it happen. When I fed him the meat nicelike, I could handle him like a baby.

THE DAY when we had all the trouble, I was working on the gorillas indoors. I remember, because my assistant was out sick and I had to handle the cats *and* the gorillas at the same time. While I was feeding bananas and fruit to the gorillas, I kept the big cats, including Zombie, outside. I know it sounds like I'm showing off, but I swear to God I knew something was wrong that day. For one thing, it was the hottest day I can ever remember for June. For another, that was the day we switched from beefsteak to horsemeat. The cats didn't like it. I gave some to Zombie and he just turned away from it real quietly. Maybe it was the way I gave it to him. Anyway, he was too quiet. In the next cage, I gave some horse steaks to the lady tiger, Queen. She left it there, too. Then I went inside.

Anyway, I'm feeding the gorillas. Even they're acting up. The big one is going *"Brmmmph, Brmmmph."* When he does that I don't want to be near the cage. I'm sweating like a crazy man when this snotty little guy comes in yelling at the top of his lungs, "A cat's eating a baby. A cat's eating a baby." He's breathing real hard, and he's all excited. But I know this guy. He's a queer duck who comes in every single day and talks to the cats. Then he asks me dumb questions about ocelots. Once when I wouldn't answer, he told me he was a taxpayer and I *had* to answer his ocelot questions. Anything's liable to come out of his mouth. So I don't pay any attention. There's a law, or a rule, that says when I'm feeding the animals I can't turn my back to talk. It's a good way to get your ears torn off.

So the little guy starts tugging at me, still yelling about a cat eating a baby. And I don't pay any attention. Then I heard a scream I'll never forget as long as I live. Scream is the wrong word. The cats scream at each other maybe four times a day, but this was different. It seemed to be wrung out from down deep inside some cat's belly.

I moved outside quickly. The guy stayed on my heels. There was a crowd standing in close around Queen's cage. They were standing stiffly, not making much noise, a few with their mouths open. It was a funny kind of quiet, like when people see an accident. I still wasn't too excited. I just walked a little faster and pushed through the crowd. The scream continued. I went right up to Queen's cage.

Inside was a terrible thrashing movement, then a blur. Zombie had leaned forward from the next cage, caught Queen's right front leg in his mouth through the bars, and lifted the female tiger three feet off the ground. Zombie was calmly eating his way up Queen's leg. The scream came from inside Queen's bowels. It turned into a high-pitched squawk. Queen's tail was frozen upward behind her into a frightened half moon, her striped head revolving slowly in a terrible circle of agony.

Someone in the crowd found a voice. "What are you standing there for?" the man yelled at me. Another shouted, "You want a keeper, and you can't get one. You get one, and he just stands there."

I realized then I hadn't moved. What paralyzed me was the scream. It stuck in my ears like some terrible, off-key symphony. I felt myself moving for the padlock in Queen's cage. I grabbed a feeding pole and went inside the trapped animal's cage.

Through the bars I poked at the killer cat in the next cage. It was like trying to fight a crazy bull with chiclets. Zombie didn't budge. He moved a little further up Queen's leg. Someone in the crowd yelled, "You're in the wrong cage, goofball. Get in that murderer's cage." Queen kept up the terrible tongueless squawk. With her free paw, she swiped feebly, almost playfully at the killer cat in the next cage. My uniform was soaked and my wrists were full of sweat.

I jumped out of the cage like a madman and ran for the monkey house. Where I got the idea, I don't know, but I grabbed a big net crate that we use for packing and shipping monkeys. Then I made my way back to Queen's cage. I went through the crowd, toward Queen back inside the cage.

Then I stopped. Zombie, in the next cage, was calmly moving further up on the leg, eating as he went. Where Queen's shoulder should have been, there was a swamp of the reddest blood I have ever seen. She was still frozen stuck to the bars. The screams had turned into a moan, low so you could hardly hear it, and her leg was coming off.

I came up close and the smell of animal blood rushed into my nose and turned my stomach over. I tried to scoop Queen up in the monkey crate, but every time I tried she shined her teeth at me and tore at my uniform. Then the leg came off. I had no way of telling for sure, except that all of a sudden there was a flash of white underneath the blood and then a jagged bone sticking out of a bloody, mangled shoulder.

In the next cage, Zombie was finishing off the leg with genteel skill, running his tongue politely over his four-inch teeth. Later, I didn't see a trace of the leg. Zombie ate it, bones, blood, gristle and claws.

The keepers came then. My buddy with the thick glasses who works the monkey house came with a thick pole and a razor on it and used it to force Zombie back into the indoor cage. Zombie must have still been hungry. He sank his teeth into the pole and bit it off.

I was still with Queen, but I could hear them outside, like idiots, yelling, "When are you going to gas that Zombie? ... Kill that cat."

Queen was still frozen stuck between the bars. I thought with her leg off it ought to be easy to pry her out of there, but she was still stuck. The boss came then. He had crowbars. He gave me one, and we squeezed what was left of the shoulder out from the bars. The animal spurted out into the monkey crate on three legs and fainted. A piece of shoulder fell into the center of the cage.

Later, as I was going home, I saw a kid point to the bloody shoulder and ask his mother what it was. "It's what they feed the animals, honey," she said.

ANYWAY, we killed Queen that day. It took the damned expert four shots to polish her off. A cat with three legs is no good to anyone.

You come to our zoo these days, and you'll see it's different now. We got solid black sheets of steel in between the cages, and nothing like what happened to Queen can happen anymore.

Zombie's still around. Those idiots who were yelling for us to kill him don't know what they're talking about. You can't blame an animal for being wild. He's just in there waiting for a chance to do something like that.

I'll tell you a secret though: I'm still trying to make friends with him. He's such a beautiful animal. Maybe I was wrong about the meat—giving it to him nice and everything. But I got a new way to get under his skin and make friends. I look right in his eyes, real loving-like, every day. I swear to God I'm going to make friends with that cat.  ///

# "I photograph the miracle of new hair growing on bald heads!"

"I am Von Smith of St. Helens, Oregon, and as the photographer who took these pictures I can verify that Roy Smith, Oiva Witikka and Eldon Beerbower have actually regrown hair, thanks to the Brandenfels Home System."

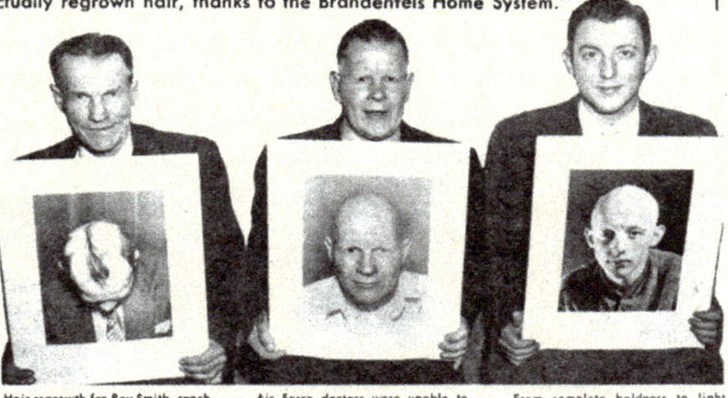

Hair regrowth for Roy Smith, rancher, was so marked after almost 20 years of near-baldness that friends could hardly believe what they saw.

Air Force doctors were unable to help Oiva Witikka when he lost all his hair, and he was bald when he was discharged. What a change!

From complete baldness to light fuzz in 8 weeks (picture he's holding). Eldon Beerbower's final reward was a full head of hair.

## Why You Can Order With Confidence

▶ All letters and testimonials quoted here are bona fide. Full addresses of any one gladly sent on request.

▶ All scalp pictures are just as photographed — never retouched.

▶ Against a common disbelief in hair regrowth Carl Brandenfels relies on the expert opinion of competent medical doctors and clinicians who conducted tests and made observations that showed hair regrowth while using Brandenfels Scalp and Hair Applications. The drawings below explain their considered opinions.

▶ In addition, more than 20,000 letters and reports telling of hair regrowth, relief from dandruff scale, less excessive hair fall and improved scalp conditions, have been audited and attested to by outside, impartial, licensed certified public accountants.

▶ There are Brandenfels users in every state in the Union, in Alaska, Hawaii, Puerto Rico, and in more than 80 foreign countries in the free world.

▶ Testimonials may be seen at St. Helens, Oregon, when permission has been given by the writers.

▶ References: U. S. National Bank, Bank of St. Helens, Chamber of Commerce—all of St. Helens, Oregon.

## Drawings Explain Miracle of Hair Regrowth

These drawings were made from photomicrographs of biopsies taken in a medical test to show what happens when hair successfully regrows while using Brandenfels Applications. This is an unproductive hair follicle (root). It is blunted and the opening plugged with sebaceous gum and scaly skin, the doctors diagnosed.

Now, during use of Brandenfels Applications and Dilative Massage, an improved condition of the follicle was noticed. The follicle is less distorted, the scaly skin layer is disappearing and there's actually regrowth of a tiny hair in the follicle.

Now the follicle is producing hair! These sketches were made from actual biopsies on a test group of people who volunteered to participate in this, the world's first sub-dermal research project, conducted by medical doctors and technicians. Here's positive proof hair roots may still be alive in a bald head!

"When I first started taking these pictures I felt mighty foolish at not recognizing the men, women and children who came in for 'after' pictures as the same people I had 'shot' when they were bald, or virtually so. "Now I'm glad when this happens! It means another happy man or woman —or child. Yes, regrowth of hair is an actual fact in many cases with the Brandenfels System. "In the Brandenfels offices I have seen files bulging with letters from men and women all over the world telling of one or more of these benefits:

✔ RENEWED HAIR GROWTH
✔ RELIEF FROM DANDRUFF SCALE
✔ LESS EXCESSIVE FALLING HAIR
✔ IMPROVED SCALP HEALTH

"I have seen how it is true that even on smooth, bald areas where no hair is visible the hair roots may still be alive and in many cases lack only the proper stimulation of the Brandenfels System to make them grow hair again."

### Pleasant to use at home — no expensive office calls.

If you have excessively falling hair, ugly dandruff scale, a tight, itching scalp, a rapidly receding hair line, or any unhealthy scalp condition which is not conducive to growing hair, DON'T WAIT! It may be possible for you to arrest these conditions RIGHT IN THE PRIVACY OF YOUR OWN HOME without expensive office calls. Carl Brandenfels does not guarantee to promote new hair growth, because not every user has grown new hair. He emphatically believes, however, that his formulas and unique pressure massage will bring about a more healthy condition of the scalp that in many cases helps nature grow hair. YOU OWE IT TO YOURSELF...YOUR BUSINESS ACQUAINTANCES...AND YOUR FAMILY to give the Brandenfels System a thorough trial. Brandenfels' wonderful formulas are non-sticky, with a "clean" aroma, and they will not rub off on bed linens or hat bands. The formulas and massage are pleasant and easy to use. Enclose $18.00 (includes Federal tax, postage and mailing). Use the handy coupon below. Send your order to Carl Brandenfels, St. Helens, Oregon.

### Baldness may begin 2 years before your friends notice — act now!

If you—or anyone in your family—have already become bald, or are losing hair rapidly, SEND TODAY, for a five-week supply of Brandenfels Scalp and Hair Applications and Massage, with complete easy-to-follow instructions on how to use. Send the coupon below RIGHT AWAY. Remember, every day you wait may make your problem more difficult. ACT NOW!

# ABOUT ROBERT SILVERBERG

ROBERT *Silverberg has been a professional writer since 1955. In the decades since then, he has written enough stories and books to fill several normal writing careers. In fact, in a way, he's had three separate writing careers. He started out and is best known as a writer of science fiction stories and novels, though he also wrote crime, mystery and western stories.*

*In the late 1950s, as many of the classic SF and fantasy pulp digest magazines went out of business, Silverberg's focus began to change. During that phase, which lasted until around 1970, he primarily wrote stories, articles and books outside the realm of science fiction. His work in those years ran the gamut from crime and mystery stories to non-fiction books about archeology, geography and history.*

*In addition, under various pseudonyms, he helped pay the bills by writing erotic novels for "sleaze paperback" publishers and racy stories for men's magazines.*

*Silverberg eventually went back to a focus on writing science fiction and fantasy again and is still at it. In that arena he is literally a Grand Master. In 2004, the Science Fiction and Fantasy Writers of America presented him with the Damon Knight Memorial Grand Master Award. That's on top of his multiple Hugo and Nebula awards, and his 1999 induction into the Science Fiction Hall of Fame.*

*In recent years, there has been a resurgence of interest in Silverberg's vintage erotic novels and stories. This anthology includes two examples of racy stories he wrote for men's adventure-style magazines.*

*The first, "Trapped by Mau Mau Terror," was one of nearly twenty he wrote for a short-lived men's adventure/girlie mag hybrid called* Exotic Adventures. *In fact, the majority of the stories in the six issues of* Exotic Adventures *published in 1958 and 1959 were written by Silverberg—under seventeen different pen names.*

*When I asked Bob what he recalled about writing for* Exotic Adventures, *here's what he told me:*

Well, let's see—how did *Exotic Adventures* go?

It was 1957. I was about a year and a half out of college, married, living in a nice apartment on the West Side of Manhattan, and supporting myself by writing stories at a terrific rate for the dozen or so science fiction magazines that existed at the time. Suddenly science fiction started to totter. (The US was heading into a recession in 1957, and everybody was depressed about the early Soviet successes with space satellites while we were getting nowhere, and didn't want to read science fiction, I guess.) I needed some other way to make a living, and started paying attention to the booming men's-magazine market. Somehow—probably my agent set up the meeting—I was introduced to a young editor named Monty Howard, maybe five or six years older than I was, who was running a couple of low-rent *Playboy* imitators called *Venus* and *Mermaid*, and was starting one of those man's-adventure mags, to be called *Exotic Adventures*. He needed a lot of copy fast. I sold Monty a few short stories for the fiction magazines, and then he asked me to do some tales of, well, exotic adventure for *Exotic Adventures.*

In those days "exotic" still meant "foreign," and had not yet become an illiterate synonym for "erotic." So the material needed to be about far-away places with strange-sounding names. I didn't really qualify as a world traveler, then—I had been to London and Paris, at least, and also Philadelphia and Cleveland, and a few other places about as interesting as Philadelphia and Cleveland, but Kenya and Zanzibar and Suriname and Guyana were still some years in my future. But I was a quick study and I had a lengthy file of *National Geographic.* So I began turning out articles for Monty Howard. The first issue of *Exotic Adventures* used only a piece of fiction by me—"Campus Hellcat" under the "David Challon" byline, which I had sold to *Venus* or *Mermaid* and had nothing exotic about it at all, but which, I suppose, Monty jammed into the new magazine to fill an empty space on the contents page. And I had nothing at all in the second issue. But, starting with issue three and continuing on to the sixth and final one, I had three, four, maybe even five articles an issue, each under a different pseudonym—I was practically writing the whole magazine, which made editing easy for Monty (I would show up every month or so with a package of pieces) and was profitable for me, too, since each piece took me about an hour and a half to write, and I could do two a day, one in the morning and one in the afternoon, time for research included. The pay was $75 apiece, very nice money indeed, when you figure that the 1957 dollar had at least ten times the purchasing power of today's currency, maybe more. (My handsome five-room apartment, with 24-hour doorman service, ran me $150 a month. The equivalent rent today in the same building would probably be $4000, if there were any five-room apartments left, but they were all cut up into studio jobs long ago.)

So off I went in my imagination to tell how I watched the secret sex rites of Uganda or was attacked by giant crabs in some tropical island or smuggled things into or out of Tangier, and those pleasant little checks came rolling in, and in the fullness of time the publishers looked at the circulation figures and discovered that exotic adventure didn't pay as well as it once did, and *Exotic Adventures* got the hook. So that was that, and I forgot about the magazine for the next 53 years, and then, lo and behold, all those articles have returned to existence on something called the Internet that was mere science fiction back when they were written. What fun to have written them—and what fun to have lived long enough to see them reappear in this fantastic new incarnation!

—Robert Deis

## UPDATE FOR THE NEW EDITION

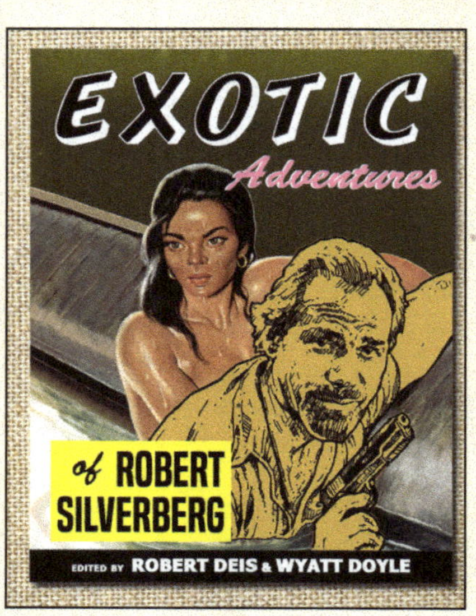


*Some years later, we were proud to release* Exotic Adventures of Robert Silverberg, *at last collecting all of Bob's pseudonymous stories for* Exotic Adventures *in facsimilie editions meant to replicate the experience of reading the original magazines back in the '50s. Silverberg contributes fresh insights in the book's introduction, and we address some of Silverberg's other work in MAMs as well. Available in softcover and as an expanded hardcover.*

—Wyatt Doyle

## "TRAPPED BY MAU MAU TERROR"

ROBERT SILVERBERG (AS NORMAN REYNOLDS)

*Exotic Adventnures*, 1959

COVER ARTIST: UNCREDITED

and came over here. Do you mind?"

"Don't be silly. I'm all alone too—
I'm graceful for your company. Care
for a drink?"

"Yes, please. Thanks ever so much."

I poured her a Martini and she sat
down opposite me in the big chair. I
had to

crashing in, with a short, stocky one
right behind him.

Never in my life did I disentangle
myself from a wench so fast. The big
bruiser came straight at me, with his
knife out in front of him. The other
took out toward Sally. The dogs came

by the sword. I didn't want to have
that happen to me.

But it might have, if the attack had
come twenty minutes later. As it was,
I was sitting there palming those heavy
breasts, and Sally was getting hotter

out. Sally had her gun out by this
time and she winged him in the
shoulder as he turned. He went
toppling forward, staggered for a second on the porch. Her second shot
blasted him back of the ear and he fell

appeared below the door.

"That'll take care of him," I said.

by

*Norman Reynolds*

EVERYONE in the British colony of Kenya knew that trouble was coming, because the Mau Mau were on the warpath and an epidemic of killings had broken out. Hardly a night went by without one of the white settlers meeting a bloody death at the hands of the enraged Kikuyu tribe, which had risen under the Mau Mau name to throw off the yoke of European domination.

My family has had land in Kenya for generations, but I had been living in America and England for most of my life. I had returned to Kenya in 1952, just after my thirtieth birthday, at the request of my uncle. He wanted me to manage a middle-sized farm near Nairobi. Having put in a spell in Korea, I was looking for some peace and quiet. What nobody told me was

(Continued on page 26)

# TRAPPED BY MAU MAU TERROR

They almost paid for their illicit love with their

lives the night her husband stayed away and the

dreaded Mau Mau decided to attack.

Without warning the black-skinned killers of the jungle were upon them. There was only one way out... a fight to the death!

5

**EVERYONE** in the British colony of Kenya knew that trouble was coming, because the Mau Mau were on the warpath and an epidemic of killings had broken out. Hardly a night went by without one of the white settlers meeting a bloody death at the hands of the enraged Kikuyu tribe, which had risen under the Mau Mau name to throw off the yoke of European domination.

My family has had land in Kenya for generations, but I had been living in America and England for most of my life. I had returned to Kenya in 1952, just after my thirtieth birthday, at the request of my uncle. He wanted me to manage a middle-sized farm near Nairobi. Having put in a spell in Korea, I was looking for some peace and quiet. What nobody told me was that Kenya was on the verge of a blood-bath that, for a while, threatened to make the Korean War look like a game of tiddlywinks between Oxford and Cambridge.

The night that the incident I am about to recount took place, I couldn't have been in a more vulnerable position. I was the only white man on the farm that night. My teenage cousin, who lived there with me, was out on a Mau Mau posse. We had drawn lots, and it had fallen to me to stay behind and guard the homestead. My only company that bloody night, aside from my two massive Great Danes, were three loyal natives: the cook, the houseboy, and a porter.

It had been a bad week. Just the other day, on Lower Kabete Road on the far side of Nairobi, a white man and his wife had been hacked to death. A couple of crusty old bachelor farmers had had their heads chopped off at dinner-time by their own houseboy. Chief Waruhiu, the loyal native leader known as "The African Winston Churchill," had been shot to death in his car by terrorists. A Kikuyu city councillor had been murdered. Over in Thomson's Falls, Commander Jock Mikkelson had been shredded by Mau Mau blades, and his wife horribly mutilated but not killed. And at Nanyuki an entire family, mother, father, seven-year-old daughter, six-year-old son, had been cut down. Only the girl survived, but her legs had been severed and she had been raped a dozen times. Not a pretty thing, this Mau Mau business. And if I told you of the oaths the Mau Mau took in the forest, while devouring entrails and eyeballs and genitals plucked from live goats, it would turn your stomach. Let's just say it was sheer deadly savagery, all the terror of Africa's black barbarism rolled into one.

And there I was, that night. Already more than a dozen white settlers had been murdered, and I don't know how many hundreds of loyal natives. Kenya was full of British soldiers, the jails were full of natives, settler posses roamed around in big bands looking for troublemakers, and still the killing went on. On Christmas Day a note was found pinned to the skin of a dead African, declaring perpetual war on the white man and his black supporters, and announcing that the Mau Mau would claim twelve heads before New Year's Day.

They went one over their quota. After each killing they left behind souvenirs, Mau Mau symbols—disemboweled chickens, strangled cats, cows whose udders had been hacked off, sheep whose eyes had been plucked out and impaled on thorns. They weren't content to murder settlers, they wiped out farm animals as well. It was a messy business. We figured that some 90% of the million and a quarter adult Kikuyus had gone Mau Mau. They came down from the mountains, killed and looted and burned, and ran back to their hiding places.

This night that I was alone, I had an inkling that there was going to be trouble. Our farm was pretty well isolated from the rest. Just down the road a couple of miles was the Brewster farm, but they were our only neighbors. There were two of them, Mike and Sally Brewster, who had come out to Kenya from England some time in the late '40s. Mike was a red-faced, beer-swilling English type, not very long on the brains department but extremely good-natured. So good-natured, in fact, that his wife Sally had cuckolded him a few dozen times, never with me unfortunately, and if he knew about it he didn't seem to mind. She was a girl of twenty-eight or so, with flaming red hair and enormous breasts and mocking come-hither eyes.

I had settled down for the evening. The wireless was bringing in the BBC, the fire was blazing—there wasn't any electricity or central heating inside the house—and on the porch a lantern was glowing, by command of the Kenya Police Reserve. The idea was that if the lantern went out, it would be a signal that something was wrong and the inhabitants of the farm needed help.

I had mixed up a pitcher-full of Martinis, a habit I developed in America, and I had a good book open. Just a comfortable evening at home, you might say. Except that I didn't ever know when a horde of black-skinned devils would come rushing in and hack me to pieces. I had a .45 strapped to my hip and there was a hunting rifle propped up, fully loaded, at every window. Just a quiet evening at home, you see.

My cousin Hal, out riding with the posse, was due to return home at midnight. I had to hold the fort until then. Everything was quiet until along about half past nine, when Sophocles, the bigger of my two Great Danes, suddenly fetched up from his place in front of the fire and started to prick up his ears and growl.

I was alert instantly, knowing the range of his hearing. My three supposedly loyal servants were in their quarters. But you never knew when a man loyal for twenty years would suddenly turn killer.

Going to the window, I peered out into the lantern-lit darkness. I was surprised to see a Jeep pulling up in front. A woman got out, looked around carefully in all directions, and sprinted toward my porch. As she passed the lantern, I could see her plainly. It was Sally Brewster. Her heavy breasts bobbed wildly as she ran.

I threw open the door, admitted her, and slammed it shut.

"Sally! What are you doing here? Has there been trouble up your way?"

"Not yet," she said, panting to get her breath. "But there's noise in the hills, as if they're going to come down to make a raid. And I was all alone—"

"Alone?" I repeated, astonished.

She nodded. "Mike's in Nairobi with some friends. He was supposed to be back at sundown. He might be dead, or—" her face hardened scornfully— "he might be lying drunk somewhere. Either way, I was alone except for our native boys, and I didn't like it. So I tacked up a note for him and came over here. Do you mind?"

"Don't be silly. I'm all alone too—I'm grateful for your company. Care for a drink?"

"Yes, please. Thanks ever so much."

I poured her a Martini and she sat down opposite me in the big chair. I had to admit she was a remarkably attractive woman. She wore jodhpurs that clung tightly to her hips and buttocks, and her breasts jutted forward from her white open-collar blouse. The red glory of her hair tumbled about her shoulders.

We had a couple of drinks, and she moved over next to me on the sofa, and I realized she was in an amorous mood. It was a devil of a situation. She kept getting closer and closer, and finally she took my hand and slipped it into the front of her blouse. She had no brassiere on, and I found myself holding one of her big breasts. The nipple, stiff and hard, pressed into my hand. She was beginning to pant. "It makes me feel relaxed when a man holds me there," she said. "With this Mau Mau thing I need to be relaxed."

Well, I didn't mind relaxing her, and I knew what would inevitably follow. But I didn't want to share the fate of that couple up near Limuru. They had been spending the evening together under similar circumstances, and there they were, naked as jaybirds, having each other on the floor, when the Wogs burst in. One of the Mau Mau boys pinned the couple together with his sword, driving the *simi* through the man, through the woman beneath him, and into the floor. That was the way they were found, dead, when the woman's husband and some friends of his came in. Man and woman were still locked together in the act of love, as well as by the sword. I didn't want to have that happen to me.

But it might have, if the attack had come twenty minutes later. As it was, I was sitting there palming those heavy breasts, and Sally was getting hotter and hotter, when suddenly the front door was smashed open and an immense native carrying a *simi* in one hand and a club in the other came crashing in, with a short, stocky one right behind him.

Never in my life did I disentangle myself from a wench so fast. The big bruiser came straight at me, with his knife out in front of him. The other took out toward Sally. The dogs came bounding up off the hearth and got into the general confusion.

My gun was in my hand and I put a bullet into the big fellow's chest at a range of about eight feet. A .45 packs quite a wallop at that distance, and the impact knocked him back against the door. A third native, coming in, tripped over his fallen comrade, and I shot the

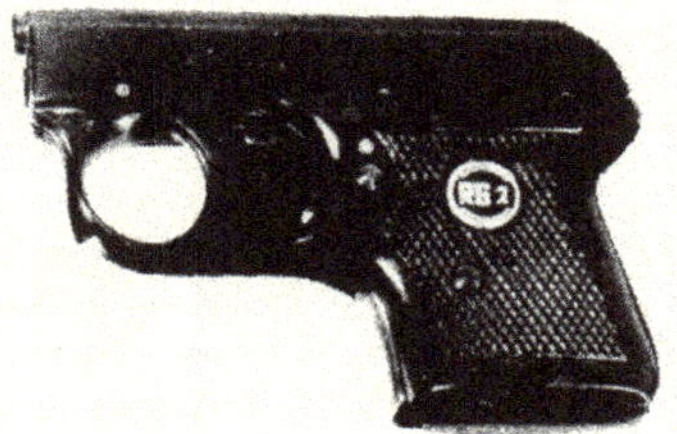

newcomer in the middle of his face.

Meanwhile Sally had gotten up out of her seat and was struggling with the short, stocky one. He was holding her tight with one hand and had the other in the air, about to slash her with the *simi*, when Euripides, the younger of the two Great Danes, went into action. He bounded across the room, a gray-violet blur, and took off like a gazelle, soaring through the air and opening his jaws wide. He got a grip on the native's sword arm just above the wrist, and I heard a horrible crunching sound. The sword went clattering to the floor.

For an instant I couldn't do anything, because the dog was hanging to the native's arm and I didn't want to shoot Euripides by mistake. But then the Mau Mau swung around, lifting the great beast completely off the floor but in the process presenting his back to me. I put a shot just above his shoulders and nearly severed his head with it.

Then a fourth one came in. He saw that we had the situation pretty well in hand, and he turned, trying to get out. Sally had her gun out by this time and she winged him in the shoulder as he turned. He went toppling forward, staggered for a second on the porch. Her second shot blasted him back of the ear and he fell forward into the rose garden.

For the first time since the attack began, we had a breather of perhaps thirty seconds. I heard the sound of scuffling behind the door to the left, and I knew there were more Mau Mau around somewhere, giving trouble to the houseboy and the cook and the porter.

At least that was what I thought. But I got out into the passageway just in time to see Kungo, our cook, pick up his meat cleaver and bury it in the skull of Wapaga, the houseboy. Brains went spurting. So Kungo had gone Mau Mau too! He was wrestling with the cleaver, trying to get it out of Wapaga's head, fixing to cut me in half next. I started to go for him with my gun, but just then old Sophocles came bounding out, saw what was going on, and leaped for Kungo's throat. The cleaver came around and ripped into the dog's neck. Furious, I pumped two shots into Kungo, and he lay dead over the corpse of my faithful dog.

I heard a shot from the other end of the house and hurried there. Sally had nipped someone skulking in the back yard. Euripides rushed out and got his fangs into a throat out there. We heard horrid guggling sounds, the sounds of a man's throat being ripped out.

Everything was very quiet, suddenly. Sally stood in the middle of the living room, her breasts heaving, the smoking gun at her side. Neither of us had been touched. There were Mau Mau bodies everywhere.

"Is that the last of them?" I asked.

She shook her head. "There's one more. I wounded him but he ran into the pantry and locked himself in."

"Come on," I said.

We went into the kitchen. The pantry door was bolted from within. I had installed the inner bolt myself, to make the little closet a good hiding place in case of attack. But I hadn't intended it to be used by our attackers.

"Give me your gun," I said.

I took Sally's weapon, since mine was all but empty and she had reloaded. Standing back, I fired a shot through the oak planking. There was a groan within. A trickle of blood appeared below the door.

"That'll take care of him," I said. "We'll give him a night to bleed to death. Then I guess we'll have to take the door off its hinges to get him out."

"Suppose he comes out by himself?"

I shrugged and fired again, aiming low. There was a second groan from within, and the sound of a body falling. "He won't come out," I said.

We walked back into the living room. The place was a bloody mess, corpses everywhere. Nahanga, our porter, the sole survivor of the three native servants, came out. His black skin was a fine shade of green.

"All over, *bwana*?" he quivered.

"All over," I said. "Where were you?"

"In the WC, *bwana*. Fighting frights me."

I made a mental note to get rid of him next chance I had. Cowards were no use around here. "Help me clean this carrion up," I ordered him.

We got together all the Mau Mau corpses, and piled them in the front yard. The police would be along in the morning to pick the bodies up and identify them. We took the dead houseboy around back, along with the dead dog. They were on our side, and we would bury them.

It was close to eleven by the time the job of piling up the dead and mopping up the blood was finished. I sent the cowardly Nahanga to his quarters. Then I turned to face Sally. Her blouse and face were smeared with Mau Mau blood. I remembered that we had been on the verge of making love, so long ago—was it really only an hour?—before the attack. But it seemed inappropriate, I thought, to try to take up where we had left off when interrupted.

But Sally had different ideas. Her eyes were glowing and by the dim light of our fire I saw the lust smoking in them.

"You were wonderful," she breathed. "You and that wonderful dog saved my life. And if I'd stayed at my farm they would have killed me."

"I'll drive back with you now," I said. "Perhaps your husband is home, and—"

"There's no rush." Her fingers went to the collar of her blouse. The bloodstained blouse came off in a moment, and before I could speak she had unzipped her jodhpurs and had stepped out of those. She was naked. Her body, stained with blood and beaded with sweat, was magnificent, a thing of sheer animal beauty. Her large round breasts rose and fell with the agitation of her desire. She rubbed her palms sensuously against her firm hips.

A thousand protests rose to my mind. The Mau Mau might return, her husband might come here to fetch her, my cousin Hal could come back, the police might arrive. But the glory of her body wiped out any thought of objecting. She pulled me to her and ripped the clothes from my body like an avenging fury. And there, on the floor, lying in a puddle of Mau Mau blood, we made love.

When it was over, we dressed silently. It had been a strange evening, an evening of killing and loving. I got into my Jeep and drove alongside hers all the way back to her farm, and then returned to my own. I learned later that her husband *had* been drunk in Nairobi that night, and did not return until morning.

Two months later there was another Mau Mau raid on our area, and Sally Brewster was killed. She died a horrible death—the attackers slit her belly open and dragged out her bowels while she still lived, and then they cut off those splendid breasts I had fondled that evening. Some time later, her husband confessed to me that she had been in the first months of pregnancy. I often wonder if it were my child she was bearing, conceived on that night of blood and lust. I shall never know, of course. But in the two years that followed no one was more dedicated to the ultimately successful task of wiping out Mau Mau than I, and I like to think that perhaps some of the natives I helped to kill were those who had so cruelly slain Sally. Certainly she was heroic that night the Mau Mau attacked, and certainly she was splendid in her lovemaking afterward. Nowadays, with Kenya as safe as it had been in the days before the Mau Mau terror, I think longingly of her, and wonder what might have happened between us if she had lived. **///**

"Gangway for America's Hell-Raising Nuclear Marines" by Walter Wager
*Men,* April 1962    Artist uncredited

# WALTER WAGER

## INTERVIEW BY JOSH ALAN FRIEDMAN

**BORN** *in 1924, Walter Wager's career took him from being a Fulbright Fellow at the Sorbonne in Paris to becoming diplomatic adviser to Israel's Director of Civil Aviation. He was also editor-in-chief of Broadway's* Playbill *in the '60s, and public relations director for ASCAP. Walter Wager wrote some 30 novels, a number of which became films, like* Die Hard 2 *(from his 58* Minutes*) and* Telefon. *He sometimes wrote under the pseudonym "John Tiger" at Mag. Management. Wager passed away in 2004.*

**What year did you join the club?**

I never worked there, I was a writer for them and wrote about a hundred pieces. In 1952 I started doing research memos for other writers to use for articles in their little news magazine, *Focus*. Then the memos got good enough for them to run. It was the beginning of a brilliant career writing fake true adventure stories. Later on, when I was working with Bruce [Jay Friedman], a whole genre of stories

**Male, April 1962**

**True Action, May 1959  Art by Charles Copeland**

developed in which Allied pilots or spies, in various parts of the world, were hidden by the underground in secret headquarters, which were always brothels, cathouses. Bruce said they were doing so well, let's do another. I said, "For God's sake, Bruce, we've done everything except an underwater cathouse."

He said, "I love it, do that."

Someone else ended up writing it: an underwater whorehouse which was used to train Italian scuba divers.

**Was this in a submarine?**

An underwater building. The Allies infiltrated the whorehouse and wiped out the scuba divers.

**Your staple was the spy-espionage story?**

Yes. I went to work at the United Nations as an editor for two years. When I came back in '56, I continued doing stuff for Magazine Management. I did some genteel sex stories, also. You found out what part of each city was the red light district, then you wrote a vigorously indignant article about the hookers. The first article I did for *Swank* in '56 was called "Build a Better Monster"—a picture story on Hollywood

monsters which advised readers on how to get ahead in life by building
one. *Swank* had a sense of humor. Then I did a piece of fiction for
*Swank* which was later reprinted in an Australian magazine, so *Swank*
was obviously being read around the world.

**Did you get paid for the reprint?**

I got a big $25 from the Australians. I would do an article every week
for Bruce. I would bring it in on Thursday and have a check in my
mailbox Saturday. The most attractive thing about *Swank* was the sort
of freewheeling atmosphere there. But it was a time of very cautious
writing about sex. *Swank* was the baby of all the men's magazines there.

**How do you mean?**

It never got as big as the others and it didn't live as long. [*Swank* ceased
publication several times.] It was always an experimental venture.
Martin Goodman's effort to compete with *Esquire*, but a little saucier.
It had the advantage of working on a modest budget, so it needed an
inventive editor.

**Do you recall a favorite story you wrote for *Swank*?**

A piece of fiction that preceded *The Stepford Wives*. A story about an
engineer whose wife dies, and he builds a new wife ["The Second Mrs.
Gilbert," August 1956]. Every night was perfect, he'd come home,
she'd be waiting with martinis, she never bothered him to have a baby.
Then he comes home one evening and can't find her. He goes down
to the basement and there she is in his workshop building a perfect
new husband.

**Were any of your Mag Management stories developed later into
novels?**

Oh, yes! I did a double-length piece of fiction for *Men* which developed
into the novel *Viper Three*, very successful here and abroad, and later
became the film *Twilight's Last Gleaming* [starring Burt Lancaster]. You
wanna hear something funny? Not only did it first appear in a Magazine
Management book, but after the novel was successful and the paperback
came out years later, Chip Goodman [heir to Martin Goodman's
empire] didn't know it had come from an original story in his father's
company—he bought the condensation rights again. **///**

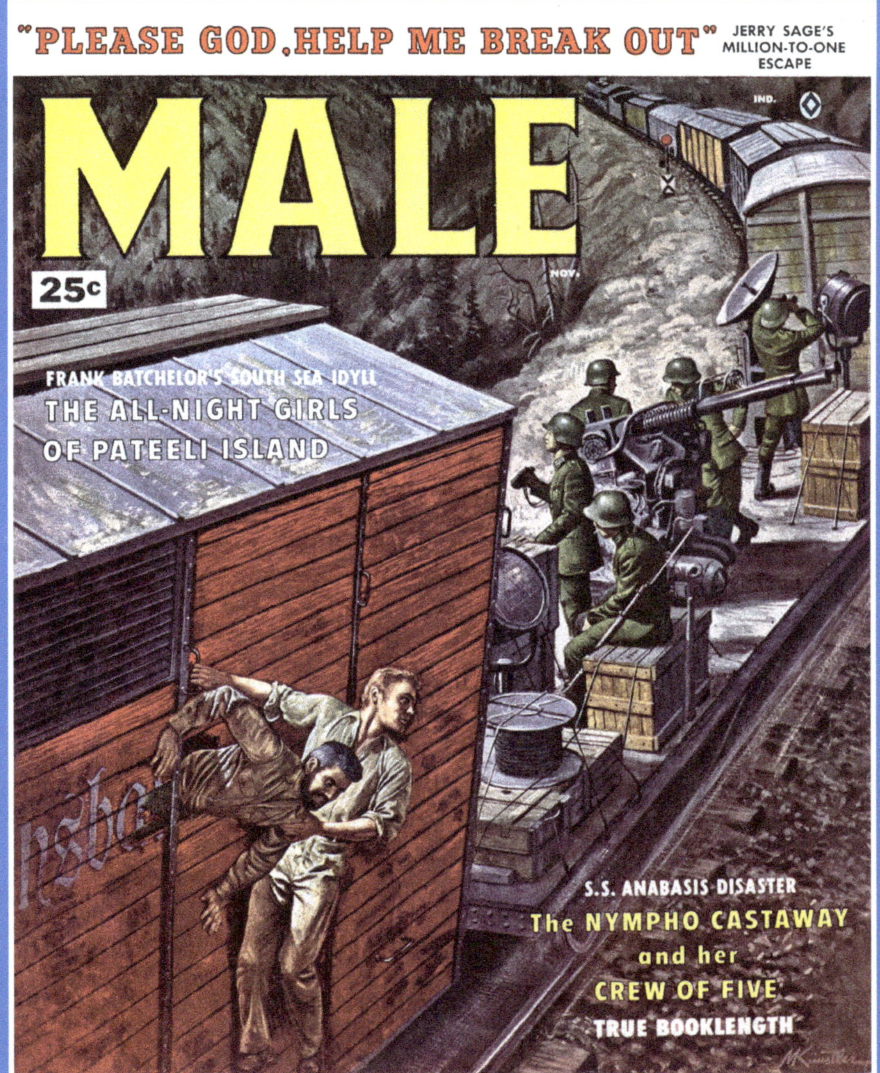


## "PLEASE GOD, HELP ME BREAK OUT"

— WALTER WAGER —

*Male,* November 1958

COVER ARTIST: MORT KÜNSTLER

Sage could have killed him with his bare hands, and they both knew it. He tossed a jocular  *Wiedersehen* over his shoulder and strolled into the woods. As soon as the trees screened him, Sage ran at full speed, branches whipping his face, thorns cutting his hands and his feet burning. When he couldn't go another step he crawled into a small culv...

but with a man this big and angry why take chances? They stopped the abuse. At noon, a *Wehrmacht* doctor arrived to fix the O.S.S. raider's raw and swollen feet so deftly that he could walk reasonably when the escorts arrived from Stalag III two hours later. Sage was still very hungry but he felt better.

"You've given us some chase, Giant," one...

"Get it straight? Two of us jump out and the third guy has to guess who's left."

...was the camp commandant, Colonel Von Lindeiner, with two members of his staff. The Prussian colonel was yowling with fury at the first man to break out of Stalag III since a recent Gestapo reproach about escape activities. He was half out of his mind as he pulled back the slide of his automatic and aimed it between the O.S.S. raider's eyes. One more attempted escape, the colonel...

# "PLEASE GOD, HELP ME BREAK OUT"

**COVER STORY**

The enemy called him "The Slippery Giant," watched him parlay a demolition knife and a deadly weapon called the "manure bomb" into WWII's most bizarre getaway

### By WALTER WAGER

▶ "Here they come," the tall blond major warned. The two sergeants sweating beside him in the thorny North African brush squinted into the sun, toward the vehicles swooping down the black asphalt strip. A minute later, the three Americans made out a German armored car leading three trucks jammed with *Wehrmacht* infantry. It was the convoy that this O.S.S. team had been expecting.

"Here we go again, boys," Sage announced with a laugh.

The dust-caked *leutnant* in the armored car scanned the road ahead and nodded. He was tired after two-and-a-half years in the *Afrika Korps*, and he was glad to know that he was a safe 12 miles behind his own lines. There was sand in his teeth, he was dank with perspiration, and the stink of camel and burro dung soiled the air. These Arabs certainly left the highway filthy with their primitive animal transport,

**AT THE TOP OF THEIR LUNGS the French prisoners sang the "Marseillaise" as Sage slipped out of the box-car**
Art by TOM RYAN

**Illustration by Tom Ryan**

**HERE THEY** come," the tall blond major warned. The two sergeants sweating beside him in the thorny North African brush squinted into the sun, toward the vehicles swooping down the black asphalt strip. A minute later, the three Americans made out a German armored car leading three trucks jammed with *Wehrmacht* infantry. It was the convoy that this OSS team had been expecting.

The dust-caked *leutnant* in the armored car scanned the road ahead and nodded. He was tired after two-and-a-half years in the *Afrika Korps*, and he was glad to know that he was a safe 12 miles behind his own lines. There was sand in his teeth, he was dank with perspiration, and the stink of camel and burro dung soiled the air. These Arabs certainly left the highway filthy with their primitive animal transport, and the German officer consoled himself with the thought that this disgusting trail of manure would never be tolerated on the autobahns of the Third Reich.

Then the whole road exploded.

A dozen blasts ripped open the armored car as if it were a milk carton, drenched one truck with flame and spun another over on its side like a toy. With 22 of their comrades dead a score of battered German infantry piled out and scattered in defensive formation—machine pistols ready to fight off the enemy.

There was no enemy.

The *leutnant* was a charred corpse, so a beefy sergeant took command and sent four men to search the road ahead for more mines. They inspected the black strip minutely for 300 yards before they reported the route was clear. The edgy *Wehrmacht* survivors scanned the landscape carefully before they climbed into the remaining truck to proceed to the next German post.

Half a minute later the last vehicle blew up. The convoy of four vehicles and 42 combat toughened troopers had been blasted into eight dazed and bleeding soldiers lying in the ditch, victims of Major Jerry Sage and his secret weapon. The invisible devices that clobbered the German convoy were manure mines, compact killers made by attaching pressure detonators to lumps of plastic explosive and covering the whole thing with a layer of the animal dung found on the Tunisian roads. Camouflaged as camel and burro droppings, the mines were a threat to every enemy vehicle on the road.

THE STRANGE but effective manure mines were typical of the ingenuity of Sage and his hard-bitten infiltration team the Office of Strategic Services code-named "Dagger." This special unit had been added to the US ground forces in North Africa in January, 1943, to spy and sabotage behind the German lines. The American divisions that landed in Algeria and French Morocco in November 1942 had already driven the Germans back, but here, in Tunisia, Rommel was putting up a stubborn defense.

Jerry Sage surpassed Hollywood's hokiest idea of a US spy; he was a strapping, blond giant who'd been a football star at Washington State College, where he picked up both an ROTC commission and a Phi Beta Kappa key. Not only was he an excellent shot and deadly with a knife, he was also skilled in the art of breaking backs and snapping necks without a sound. But Sage was no grim-faced butcher; he had a lively sense of humor and a fine singing voice. All these talents proved life-savers in one of the greatest adventures of World War II.

Sage's mission was to harass the retreating Nazis, to sneak through their outposts and rip up their supply and communications lines so they couldn't stop the Allied advance. By the end of January, the resourceful major had recruited anti-Fascist Arabs and Spanish Republican refugees who knew the terrain to guide the "Dagger" through the *Wehrmacht* defenses and blow up Kraut rail lines, fuel dumps and ammunition depots.

By mid-February, Sage had planted so many manure mines behind the enemy lines that every German convoy was preceded by a squad of nervous dung sweepers. He had also made such a name for infiltration that he was asked to scout the terrain selected for an important raid planned by the Derbyshire Yeomanry, the historic British armored reconnaissance team.

On February 23rd, Sage and four "Dagger" sergeants drove up to the most advanced British outpost with two Derbyshire officers. German howitzers were dug in on high ground on either side of the key pass; the only approach to the pass itself was across an open plain. This naked flatland was gashed by two wadis, dried-up river beds about five feet deep. The situation was complicated by British observers' reports that they thought the Nazis were planting a mine-field right in the pass.

"We can sneak up the wadis," Sage told the Derbyshire colonel,

COL. SAGE: "Broke backs, didn't make a sound"

CITATION FOR LEGION OF MERIT

JERRY M. SAGE, 0362876, Lieutenant Colonel, United States Army, Office of Strategic Services, for exceptionally meritorious conduct in the performance of outstanding services in the Mediterranean Theater of Operations from 1942 to March 1945. As one of the first instructors for the Office of Strategic Services, joining in 1942, Lieutenant Colonel Sage was sent to England and North Africa to study the subject of industrial sabotage. As a result of his knowledge of this type of operation, he was assigned to work with a detachment on the Tunisian front where he planned missions and infiltrated specially trained personnel to destroy German communication lines and destroy ammunition dumps. On 24 February 1943, Colonel Sage, while directing a sabotage group in activities near Feriana, was captured as he was endeavoring to rescue one of his men who had been wounded during a heavy enemy barrage. From that date until his escape just before the liberation of Poland, Colonel Sage was held prisoner. Throughout this entire period, he worked incessantly, organizing the other prisoners and leading them in repeated attempts to escape. because of his activities, he was repeatedly punished with solitary confinement and transferred from one camp to another. The exemplary manner in which Colonel Sage performed his assignments, his devotion to duty and to his fellowmen, regardless of the dangers of personal risk, the strenuous hardships which he underwent as a prisoner of war, his initiative and persistent ambitious (sic?) to fight the enemy through instruction and personal participation, his alertness to safeguard his own security and that of countless others while in enemy hands, reflect great credit upon himself and the Armed Forces of the United States.

AFRIKA KORPS: "Ripped by Sage manure bombs"

"but I don't enjoy the idea of trying to outrun Kraut armored vehicles if they spot us in the open. Can. you cover us?"

"I'll bring up two self-propelled 75s," the weather-beaten English commander promised.

While the half-tracks rumbled up into position, Major Sage and two of his men started along one wadi toward the bust-out pass. At the same time, a British captain and another "Dagger" NCO started down the other. It was 4:00 PM as the scouts walked, crawled and sprinted forward, taking advantage of every bit of natural cover afforded by the dry river bed. They were more than half-way to the pass when Jerry Sage heard the familiar howl of an invisible Arab, an eerie wail of alarm repeated by other unseen tribesmen as they signaled the presence of invaders back over a human telephone to the nearby Germans. Sage decided to finish his reconnaissance before the *Wehrmacht* could react, so he just plowed ahead and wondered what the hell he could do against a Tiger tank with a .45 and a demolition knife.

Exactly 25 minutes after he'd left the Derbyshire outpost, the tough major peered out at the pass from the end of the wadi. Through his binoculars, the ground looked as if somebody had been digging—the usual sign of a fresh mine field. Sage coolly resolved to walk out into the open to try to find a path through. Picking his way carefully, he advanced for 90 seconds before he heard the easily recognized whistle of "incoming mail." He waved his men down, and two loud booms shattered the quiet of the sunset an instant later as the infiltrators dropped flat on their faces. At this point, Sage expected the Yeomanry 75s to open up to create some kind of diversion. They never did.

"Here we go again, boys," Sage announced with a laugh.

As they jumped up, they heard the metallic roar of tanks grinding down the pass. "Let's move," Sage bellowed over the noise. They sprinted desperately for the cover of the wadi 150 yards away, but another salvo from two German howitzers stopped them cold. The first shell wounded one sergeant in the leg and head, and as Sage tried to help him, the second shell exploded so close that it sent the major flying. Hurt but determined to save his sergeant, the "Dagger" CO ignored the plea that he save himself and crawled over to bind up the NCO's bleeding wounds.

More enemy guns joined the party, ripping and pounding the entire plain with a mounting barrage. Sage took the precaution of sending the uninjured sergeant back with information about the mine field while he finished bandaging the wounded man. It was only when Jerry Sage tried to crawl back to the wadi himself that he realized how badly his own leg was damaged. But he hardly had a chance to think of this before he heard tanks moving up swiftly. They were so near he could hear the crews shouting to each other in German.

Sage grabbed at the only chance of escape. He rolled over on his face to play dead, hoping the Krauts would ignore the "corpse" and return to the safety of their lines. He pressed his face into the gritty sand and waited tensely.

It didn't take long.

"Get up," somebody ordered in a thick Bavarian accent.


SAGE stared up into the three *Schmeisser* machine pistols. Eager to get out of the mine-strewn No Man's Land, the Germans put the battered Yanks on one of their armored vehicles and headed back through the pass. These Nazi veterans knew the importance of fresh combat intelligence; they stopped a few minutes after they reached their own lines in a desolate place called Gafsa and began to interrogate the prisoners.

Then Jerry Sage got angry, for it was inhuman to ignore the NCO's serious wounds while they probed for military information. Harshly implying the Germans were beery bums and amateur soldiers who didn't know the rules of civilized warfare, the sizzling major so shook up the *Afrika Korps* officers that they immediately ordered a doctor for the bleeding sergeant. When the MD finished with the injured scout and began to patch up Sage, the Germans resumed their bombardment of questions. It was then—as he tersely stuck to the fundamentals of name, rank and serial number—that Jerry Sage swore a silent oath that they'd never keep him prisoner.

So started one of the great escape stories in military history.

Sage slept heavily that night in Gafsa in the bed of an absent *Wehrmacht* colonel, but the next morning he was loaded into a truck bound for the divisional HQ in Gabes, 80 miles away. En route the eight German guards paid little attention to him as he shammed extreme weakness by slumping against the side of the truck and keeping his eyes closed. They hardly bothered to watch him when they stopped for lunch on the road, 21 miles from Gabes. While the soldiers ate and joked on the tailboard, the "Dagger" leader peered into the truck cab. He saw the ignition switch marked *"Ein"* and *"Auf,"* which obviously meant "On" and "Off."

Sage jumped in behind the wheel, flicked the switch to *"Ein"* and pressed the starter.

There was a grinding whir as nothing happened.

When the outraged guards poured off the back to grab him, the Phi Beta Kappa learned his first lesson in German. *"Auf"* means "On."

Sage spent the night reflecting on his error in a POW cage at Gabes. He tried to crash out of there shortly before breakfast, but didn't quite get over the wire before he was caught. His third attempt began on the following day when he resolved to try stealth, the first step being to steal a German cap to build a disguise. By this time, the wary guards knew that Jerry Sage was an inventive type so they searched him again as a routine precaution. They became quite excited when they saw the cap.

THEY missed an even more interesting item that the major had concealed inside his paratroop boot—a razor-sharp demolition knife he was saving as a surprise. He was working on Escape Plan Four, when all the men in the Gabes cage were suddenly loaded into box-cars for a rail trip north, toward the Tunisian coast. As soon as the train started,

Sage pushed his way through the crowded car to study the metal covering that sealed the window. He saw that he had to cut away the metal without making so much noise that the Germans would hear him. In front of the rolling prison was a car with armed guards, and behind, a flat car moved an AA battery with full crew.

A practical fellow, Jerry Sage knew that it was a lot easier to cut wood than metal. He started to cut into the side of the boxcar to chop loose the fastening that held the cover in position. At the same time, he improvised a human noise machine to drown out the sounds of his work.

"Everybody's going to sing," he ordered confidently. Dozens of Americans burst into a rousing rendition of "I've Been Working on the Railroad," while patriotic Free French let loose with the "Marseillaise." Sage started to saw away purposefully, gouging deep into the wood until his arm was numb with fatigue. Then a US pilot and a South African airman spelled him, the three men taking turns with the demolition knife. After 5 ½ hours, the OSS major finally hacked loose the fastening.

They waited for darkness. When the sky was safely black, the fliers boosted Jerry Sage up to the hole and he began to wriggle through. Halfway out, the big-boned raider found himself jammed tight in the opening. For 10 terrible seconds he was wedged helplessly in the small window, staring out into the night as the train clattered north. He struggled grimly while the men behind him pushed. Finally, he pulled himself out. For a few seconds he clung to the top of the swaying box-car, and then, hand over hand, he moved away from the opening to let the aviators out.

Swaying and banging against the side of the train, Sage knew that they couldn't hang there very long. The German AA crew 10 yards away might get them or their clenched fingers might slip loose from the ledge. Their muscles were aching to relax when the bucking train slowed down to take a curve.

Sage nodded gratefully for this timely luck; the trio dropped off into the blackness. Using his parachute school savvy, the ex-gridder landed and rolled like a well-trained acrobat. Tired, panting, but feeling good, he was on his feet within seconds, searching for his comrades. He filled his lungs with the air of freedom as the train chugged away into the night.

Finding the others also unhurt, Jerry Sage set a course due-west by the stars and they started hiking. They had one knife, one canteen of water and one orange peel. With this equipment, the three men set out to cross 100 miles of enemy territory toward the Allied lines of Tunisia. They tramped along steadily for 11 hours. Dawn saw them at the edge of the desert where they hid in a cactus thicket. They didn't dare to move by day; enemy planes were a constant menace. The hours passed slowly as they tried to sleep under the burning sun, but they were too conscious of their hunger and thirst.

As soon as night fell the three tired men started west again. They gained some strength from the awareness that they were marching towards their own lines, but then they heard the long, echoing yowl of Arab betrayal. Again and again the weird wail sounded in every direction. Directly ahead, a dozen lights suddenly revealed a cluster of native tents.

There was nothing to do but run. As far and as fast as they could. They were near exhaustion, but they staggered and gasped for two hours until they fell. As they lay panting on the sand, a swift desert overcast abruptly blotted out every guiding star in the sky. Suddenly they were lost like a ship in a strange sea.

They started to pray. There was the tough "Dagger" CO down on his knees, repeating the same grim appeal for divine aid over and over.

"Please, God—dammit, give us a star to see by! Please, God!"

They heard distant artillery fire rumbling, so Sage knew that US forces were only 10 or 15 miles away. Again Sage prayed, but all the heavens gave him was a driving rain. Hungry, thirsty, bone-weary and drenched, the stubborn OSS officer led his tiny detachment on through the downpour towards the sound of the big guns. They slogged on silently, and after an hour of trudging through the rain Jerry Sage saw his miracle. It was a small lake. Jubilant and grinning, the parched trio stumbled forward into the water and gulped the wonderful life-saving liquid.

They spat it out immediately. It was bitter, alkaline water, unfit for human consumption.

The rain stopped, and 20 minutes later Jerry Sage led them into a small olive grove that promised fruit and water. But they weren't that lucky; two ragged Arabs spotted them and within minutes the fugitives were surrounded by hundreds of bellowing men, women and children. The noisy, evil-smelling mob waved guns, clubs and knives, yowling down Sage's attempt to pass his men off as the crew of a *Luftwaffe* plane forced down in the desert. When one ambitious Arab swished a rusty scythe at the escapees, Jerry Sage showed his demolition knife and the crowd of heroes fell back before the single blade. The OSS major held the mob at bay until an Italian armored car arrived.

Sage immediately produced Escape Plan Six. "Once we get in that car and roll a few miles, we'll jump the crew and boot them out," he whispered to the pilots. "Then we'll take off for our own lines in real style."

The idea wasn't as wild as it sounded, for Sage was superb at judo and "silent death." But two trucks of *Afrika Korps* infantry arrived, grabbed them and hauled them off to another POW cage in Tunis. Here they caught up on food and sleep.

WHEN Sage heard the next morning that the three of them were to be flown up to Naples for interrogation, he burst into song as he started figuring out Plan Seven. He was in excellent spirits as he explained his bold scheme. Once the JU-52 transport was over the Mediterranean, he'd wreck the guards in the rear of the ship while the two pilots took care of the crew. Then the Allied aviators would fly the plane to the nearest US air base. It was simple, brutal and logical.

Plan Seven was jolted by the German decision to fly Sage, whom they believed a USAAF major, up to Italy alone. All the way north, Jerry Sage cursed the Nazis' treachery in separating him from the two pilots, for while he was confident that he could clobber the three drowsy guards, he was bitterly aware that he couldn't fly the plane himself.

In Naples, the Nazis began their usual softening-up process for airmen by tossing the OSS operative into solitary, on sub-survival rations. Jerry Sage wouldn't talk. The Germans coldly refused to treat his infected wounds. Sage still wouldn't talk. The angry Krauts shipped him up to Rome for further questioning, and there German officers decided to put the sick man in a military hospital before he died on their hands.

The hospital was staffed with German and Italian nurses, and Jerry Sage was a good-looking fellow with a distinct way with women. In addition, he sang beautifully. For the Italian nurses, the major gave a passionate rendition of *"O Sole Mio"* with gestures. Less than 40 minutes later, he was filling his near-empty gut with bowl after bowl of thick minestrone soup, the first decent chow since he was captured. The German nurses were so moved by his tenderly sung *"Du, Du, liegst Mir im Herzen"* that they gave his shoulder special care.

This treatment was too good to last. On March 12th—17 days and 1500 miles from the advanced outposts of the Derbyshire Yeomanry— Major Sage arrived by train in Frankfort.

From Frankfort, Sage was shuttled to the German Air Force Interrogation Center called "Dulag Luft" where the softening-up began with 16 days in solitary.

More annoyed than depressed by the 16 days of isolation, Jerry Sage then spent three weeks "fencing" with the cunning questions of a German paratroop captain.

On April 3rd, the *Luftwaffe* intelligence team grudgingly concluded that it was rapidly getting nowhere with Major Sage. The next day he was exiled to Stalag Luft III, about 100 miles south-east of Berlin. He immediately began to study the security system for gaps, for the idea of busting out never left him for an hour. Finding the camp crowded with prisoners from a dozen Allied countries, Jerry Sage started picking up as much Polish, German, Czech and Hungarian as he could.

He had three big reasons. First, he had to talk to get every scrap of information about the guards, wire fences, watch towers. Second, he wanted to add a few foreign numbers to his repertoire of folk songs. Third, these languages would come in handy when he made his escape. He meant to get back to "Dagger" as soon as possible.

Sage's big break came some weeks later, when a sick American in his barracks reported that a resolute man might get away on the ambulance which traveled to the nearby hospital. In this hospital was the X-ray equipment for the area. Sage reasoned that he would have to feign some kind of disability—broken bones, say—that would require an X-ray. Then, once aboard the ambulance, he would have to force the rear-window bars. It was no use pretending to have a minor illness: that could be treated inside the camp.

The secret escape committee at Stalag III was dubious about the scheme, but agreed that if anyone could pull it off, that person was the one-man gang named Jerry Sage. The committee supplied the OSS major with map and compass. He had to arrange the broken bones for himself.

This was easy. Sage persuaded a big South African friend, a former soccer star, to kick his ribs in during a soccer game. Shortly before he went to see the German doctor in the camp, Sage cut his finger and held the blood back in his mouth. While the doctor was examining him, Sage coughed painfully and told the doctor it felt as if a broken rib had punctured his lung. With exquisite timing, Sage then spat a blob of blood.

*"Bestimmt,"* said the medico, "you have a hole in the lung. An X-ray you must take." And he sat down and wrote out the necessary paper.

One of Sage's Dutch POW buddies, another escape artist named Karl van der Stok, taped Sage's ribs with bandages stolen from the camp dispensary.

That night, Sage put on RAF pants, sweater and overcoat with all insignia razored off. He filled his pockets with D-ration chocolate and went over the plan for the twentieth time.

He must get the seat by the window so he could break open the grill and reach out to open the door as the ambulance rolled through 150 yards of trees. If he made his move too soon, he'd be spotted by guards in the machine gun tower at the edge of the camp. If he got out too late, he'd be shot down by troops drilling on the parade ground just beyond the woods. It was a matter of split-second timing.

The next morning when patients gathered in the infirmary to await the ambulance, Sage didn't dare discuss his plan. He barely had time to whisper "I've got to get the right rear seat by the window, boys." Then the German guard entered to lead the sick POWs out into the waiting vehicle. For an instant the whole escape plan jammed as an RAF officer with a broken leg in a cast took the right rear seat. He hadn't understood what Sage meant. The OSS major gently but firmly picked up the airman and moved him further in so he could occupy the escape position.

The guards locked the ambulance door and the white vehicle rolled out of Stalag Luft III.

An instant later two Yanks in on the plot deliberately blocked the view of the Germans up front by obstructing the peep-hole with their bodies while Sage immediately started wrecking the window. As the ambulance neared the wood, he had the metal grille loose—but he couldn't get the door unlocked by the outside handle. There was no time to fiddle with it. Jerry Sage took a deep breath and forced his way out the small window, head-first, landing and rolling in the dusty road a few seconds before his buddies flung his coat out after him.

His timing was six seconds off. The ambulance hadn't entered the trees, and he was out in the open. Guards in the corner sentry box sounded the screaming alarm as they opened fire, pouring a hail of slugs at the American sprinting into the woods.

But Jerry Sage was free again.

He had no childish illusions about his chances this deep in enemy territory, but he meant to do his damnedest to reach Allied or neutral territory. At least he was free now, and he was going to enjoy it.

He heard the siren howling and the police dogs barking over the gunfire as he ran. Now they were hunting him like a wild animal, with every Kraut in the area joining the pursuit. He'd gone 300 yards when two fat Home Guards bicycled by on paths less than 20 feet from where he crouched; they stopped ahead of him to beat the bushes for the missing POW. Sage passed up the chance to snap their necks because the corpses would point his route, so he crawled away on his belly through the thorny brush as he listened to the hounds barking and remembered the old chain-gang movies.

Then he rose to a crouch, looked around carefully to all sides—and started running.

He ran and crawled for almost five hours, pausing only briefly to catch his breath from time to time in his steady flight into the densest part of the forest. At last he had shaken the dogs. When all sounds of pursuit faded, he stopped beside a small green puddle of water to drink, shave off his beard and wash his burning feet. He had to take good care of them; they were his only transport over 1800 miles of Fascist territory. The water felt good. Now his beard was shaved off he had a chance of passing for an ordinary civilian. Sage always grew a four-square goatee in prison, and shaved it off on each escape.

He began to walk again, trying to figure out what he'd do if he met any German farmers. He'd fake a bad limp to explain why such a muscular young man was out of uniform, and he wouldn't loiter to discuss the question. He had to keep moving, to get as far as possible from Stalag III. He had to rejoin "Dagger."

He was miles from the prison camp, but many hundreds of miles from freedom. The nearest anti-Axis soldiers were 1000 miles east in Russia, and he wasn't going to try to march through the battle lines to join the Soviets. He headed southeast, toward Yugoslavia and the Chetniks. Half-an-hour later, Jerry Sage walked around a turn in the narrow road and faced 300 Germans. These villagers on their way to pick berries looked at the big blond stranger curiously, and a few smiled and nodded in such a friendly way that Sage answered with a pleasant *"Guten morgen"*—and walked on.

He'd done it again. Just as he felt safe, he suddenly heard a harsh voice behind him demand "Are you English?"

It must be the RAF clothing.

He paused, turned and answered in Hungarian, confident that few citizens of the Third Reich spoke that Magyar tongue. "I'm a Hungarian laborer here to help the New Germany," he explained glibly. The suspicious farmer was either baffled or satisfied, for he shrugged as Sage nodded again and went on his way.

Ten minutes later there was another crisis. A group of poorly clad workers stopped the OSS officer to demand in broken German, "Are you Russian?"

"No, are you?" Sage fired back. They told him that they and all other foreign laborers in this area were captured Russians, and when they learned he was a Yank they excitedly warned him to keep to the woods. "The towns are thick with Gestapo and MPs looking for draft dodgers and deserters," they urged, "so stay outside

the villages as much as you can."

Grateful for this warning, Jerry
Sage turned to head back for the denser
part of the forest. He'd hiked about 900
yards when he found the path blocked by
a horse-drawn wagon carrying a man,
a woman and half-a-dozen arrogant
teen-agers of the *Hitler Jugend*. Since he
couldn't pass, Sage wearily sat down by
the side of the road as if he were a tired
hiker pausing to rest in the shade.

This time the Hungarian act was
less than convincing, and the belligerent
Fascists challenged his story with a
bombardment of questions while one
boy ran off to town for the police. Sage
had neither the time nor the desire to
face the local law, so he stood up with a
harmless grin and started to walk away.

"Stop where you are!" the adult
leader of the *Jugend* shouted as he
picked up a club menacingly.

Sage paused, looked back. The
guards at Stalag III had nick-named
Jerry Sage "The Giant." The noisy
German with the club advanced. Then
stopped some yards away.

Sage could have killed him with his
bare hands, and they both knew it. He
tossed a jocular *"Auf Wiedersehen"* over
his shoulder and strolled into the woods.
As soon as the trees screened him, Sage
ran at full speed, branches whipping
his face, thorns cutting his hands and
his feet burning. When he couldn't go
another step he crawled into a small
culvert to hide until darkness.

In the dank culvert, be slept for
three hours before he awoke to eat. He
nibbled at the D-ration candy, chewed
on some forest berries and munched raw

spinach leaves. But he was still very hungry, and his feet were giving out. They hurt constantly now.

Jerry Sage crawled out of the culvert when the moon rose, and walked on all night. The limp was quite real by this time, but he plodded on. At 4 AM, he was so worn out that he lay down under a tree for a few minutes' rest—and fell into a deep sleep. Morning sunlight awakened him at 6:05. Sage pulled himself up and marched on. Shortly before 7 AM, he nodded good morning to a milkman in the suburbs of a small agricultural town. He had a sudden feeling of apprehension as he walked on, and at that instant he looked up to see a uniformed Gestapo man bicycling towards him. He watched the Nazi stop, get off and pull a huge Luger. Here we go again, Sage thought as he braced his sagging shoulders for the new challenge.

*"Was ist los?"* he asked as he limped past the pistol-packing patrolman.

The reply was short and loud. A slug whistled past the American's ear, and he stopped. Townsfolk poured out of nearby houses.

He'd failed again. Sage wearily produced his POW identity card, and was escorted at gunpoint to the local office of the secret police, where they phoned word of his capture to Stalag Luft III. While waiting for soldiers from the camp, the Gestapo heroes amused themselves by refusing Jerry Sage all food and water and slapping him around. After a few such blows, the burly major got to his feet.

"The next man who lays a hand on me will get a broken neck," he announced.

The Nazis pulled their guns to show him who was boss.

"I'll kill him," Sage repeated.

The Gestapo could see that this powerful American was serious. They had the Lugers, but with a man this big and angry why take chances? They stopped the abuse. At noon, a *Wehrmacht* doctor arrived to fix the OSS raider's raw and swollen feet so deftly that he could walk reasonably when the escorts arrived from Stalag III two hours later. Sage was still very hungry but he felt better.

"You've given us some chase, Giant," one of the guards confided as they boarded the train back to Stalag III.

"Anything to give my friends some sport," Sage answered cheerfully.

"We knew you were strong," another soldier admitted, "but we didn't realize you ran so good. To go 85 miles on foot in two days— that's something, *nicht wahr?"*

MAJOR Sage was welcomed back to Stalag III with a quick trip to solitary. He continued to starve there for four more hours until an RAF officer in the next cell managed to pass him the first decent food in three days.

While waiting for his feet to heal and toying with new ideas for busting out of Stalag III, Jerry Sage sat on the floor and sang away the hours. To cheer up the other prisoners in solitary Sage chanted special request numbers from his growing international repertoire of folk songs. This annoyed the German guards immensely; prisoners weren't supposed to enjoy solitary. They were supposed to suffer in silent misery. So they turned off Sage's cell light an hour before the normal time as a pointed hint to shut up and go to sleep. Sage retaliated by getting every English-speaking prisoner in solitary to join in an ear-splitting version of "Pack Up Your Troubles in Your Old Kit Bag, and SMILE! SMILE! SMILE!"

This defiance was no laughing matter to the Germans. Three angry guards yanked the smiling OSS man out of his cell and flapped their Lugers in his face. They were going to give this insulting Yank a beating he'd never forget.

That did it. "If anyone of you so much as touches me," Sage grated, "I'll break his stinking back."

The Germans should have laughed in his face. They should have spat in his eye.

There were three of them all armed facing one weary POW But they'd seen the way "Giant" Sage tossed men around in friendly wrestling demonstrations. Even if they all went for him Sage might get to one of them first, and do untold damage. Wisely, the guards shoved him back into his cell.

At 4 AM, the blond giant was awakened by a flashlight shining directly into his eyes. Major Sage had visitors—VIPs. It was the camp commandant, Colonel Von Lindeiner, with two members of his staff. The Prussian colonel was yowling with fury at the first man to break out of Stalag III since a recent Gestapo reproach about escape activities. He was half out of his mind as he pulled back the slide of his automatic and aimed it between the OSS raider's eyes. One more attempted escape, the colonel shouted, would mean death preceded by terrible torture.

Sage let the hysterical German foam for a minute or so, then he fixed him with his eyes and talked to him like a child. It was his duty as a VS officer, Sage explained, to escape.

"We'll teach you some German discipline, Herr Major," Von Lindeiner promised. He kept his word by locking Sage in solitary for many weeks, letting him broil in the small cell until mid August, when the "Dagger" CO was suddenly sent back to his barracks.

At this time, another escape route was being planned, and Sage served as "chief of disposal" for the 200,000 tons of sand dug out of the underground escape tunnel. After four months of this work, Sage was tossed back into solitary, for "having threatened three armed guards." The Germans saw nothing ludicrous in accusing a bare-handed prisoner of menacing a trio of armed men.

When Sage got out of solitary in Spring 1944, the senior VS officer in Stalag III had a special assignment for the singing spy. US and British forces had landed in Italy, and Allied air raids were taking such a terrible toll of German cities and war plants that there were rumors of a plan to massacre all captured aviators in retaliation. Sage's job was to train the toughest types in the camp in the fine points of judo and silent killing, a task he took to with such relish that there were soon 30 in "Sage's Storm Troopers" ready to kill the guards if the Germans tried any such mass murder. One of the Krauts accidentally stumbled on Sage's "training class," however, and four days later Jerry Sage was told to prepare for a trip. It had all the earmarks of an execution. The Escape Committee was sure that the adventurous Washingtonian was on his way to a firing squad, a notion that everyone but Major Sage shared.

The CO at the Stalag Luft in Bavaria wasn't smiling at all when the OSS operative arrived.

"Major Sage, I've studied your escape record and frankly don't want you here," he stated coldly. "Great—because I don't want to be here either. How about sending me home to Seattle?"

The Nazi colonel was not amused. He had enough problems without adding a burly escape artist with an odd sense of humor, so he shipped Sage off to Offlag 64 in Poland a fortnight later. There the "Dagger" commander started work on another scheme to get out, a project that was severely jolted in July 1944 when Allied HQ radioed orders that prisoners should defer escapes because liberation was probably near.

To add to Sage's frustration, the food rations were shrinking so steadily that the big-boned major who'd tipped the scales at 210 in North Africa was down to 150 pounds. He kept busy with plenty of exercise as captain of both the football and baseball teams. The whole camp was excited the afternoon he pitched the only perfect game in the grimy history of Offlag 64. No runs, no hits, no walks and nobody on base. Sage rejoiced like a kid when he walked off the field to resounding cheers.

Football halted at the end of November 1944. In January 1945, the commandant at Offlag 64 was getting increasingly jittery as the Red Army juggernaut rolled west, crushing everything in its way. On the afternoon of January 20th, he heard the Russians were only 35 miles away and ordered the entire camp evacuated within 24 hours. The next morning, Jerry Sage and hundreds of other prisoners trekked out of Offlag 64, heading west under the muzzles of 50 machine pistols. There was practically no food and no shelter in the ruined Polish countryside, a ravaged area criss-crossed with SS patrols.

Sage spent the night of the 21st with 40 other prisoners and a handful of guards in a Polish farmhouse, listening to the wind howl across the frozen plains. Just before dawn, he and an Army colonel hid and remained concealed until the column marched on out of sight. Hungry and cold, he and his new buddy waited for the Red Army.

At midnight he awoke to the grinding sound of tanks. They were Soviet spearheads, sweeping by in pursuit of the crumpling *Wehrmacht*.

*"Amerikanski! Amerikanski!"* he chanted. Then he yelled some of the Russian he'd learned from the janitor in solitary at Stalag III.

There was a long moment of silence.

Finally, the turret of the lead tank opened slowly and a Red Army captain stuck his head up into the pale winter sun. *"Amerikanski!"* he agreed with an ear-to-ear grin. Three escapes and 23 months to the day from his capture in North Africa, Jerry Sage was free.

By tank, foot, sledge and truck, he made his way east across Poland then hitch-hiked into Russia where he got a ride to the Black Sea in a box-car. The war wasn't over and Sage was determined to rejoin his outfit. He got aboard a freighter bound for Port Said, completing a six-week odyssey that returned him to active duty with a somewhat amazed Office of Strategic Services.

WHEN the OSS brass got over the idea that Sage was dead, they promoted him to Lt.-colonel and pointed him west towards Seattle. Jerry Sage felt pretty good in March 1945 as he boarded the plane for home. Sure, he had a bump on one rib from his Stalag III escape. But he'd hurt the *Afrika Korps* with his "Dagger" and he'd raised more hell in German prison camps than any other Yank. He'd kept his promise to escape, he'd learned some swell songs and he'd pitched a perfect game.

"Yes," the fabulous singing spy told himself as the C-54 circled over LaGuardia, "it's been a damned interesting war at that." ///

This dramatic portrait of "Commando-General" Paul D. Adams by Gil Cohen for the May 1962 *Men* accompanies a non-fiction story by Wager in that issue, "The Army's Fast, Tough, Elite Specialists in 'Instant Hell'."

At the time, General Adams was Commander-in-Chief of the United States Strike Command (STRICOM).

# ABOUT "CHEWED TO BITS..."

ALTHOUGH *"Weasels Ripped My Flesh" is the most famous killer creature story published in a MAM, I am even more partial to "Chewed to Bits by Giant Turtles" as a piece of pulp fiction.*

*Both stories were published in* Man's Life *and illustrated with fantastic cover paintings by artist Wil Hulsey. Both were written as a first person account under a probable pseudonym. Both feature a wild, bloody finale featuring a horde of vicious critters.*

*But "Chewed to Bits by Giant Turtles" adds a classic pulp sleaze element to its gonzo killer creature scenario, in the form of a flirtatious bombshell blonde. And the violence is even more hardcore.*

*The subhead used for the interior spread gives a hint of what's to come:*

> Steel-like jaws clacked away, each bite slashing flesh from my body—I used my knife and my hands, and when they were gone, my bloody stumps—and yet the turtles came—

*Like many of the subheads men's adventure editors wrote for the stories they published, that one stretches things a bit. But not enough so that you'll feel disappointed when you read "Chewed to Bits by Giant Turtles."*

*It's a ripping yarn…in several ways.*

*—Robert Deis*

## UPDATE FOR THE NEW EDITION

*JUST AS MAM readers couldn't seem to get enough of animal attack stories, we found modern Men's Adventure Library readers felt the same. So we launched our Men's Adventure Library Journal series with the killer creature anthology* I Watched Them Eat Me Alive *(or, as we refer to it in internal communications,* Eat Me*).*

*The collection is available in two editions. The softcover, intended as a budget-priced appetizer for the series, is a slim 106-page volume, while the expanded hardcover edition includes additional content, adding 20 pages.*

*Some thoughts on killer creature stories from my introduction to that book:*

While some scenarios seem laughable, the stories, taken on their own terms, are a different experience. Their horror is rooted in primal impulses, rational and irrational fears, and phobia of animals both large and small. The victims aren't usually bad guys; often they're simply in the wrong place at the wrong time. Even those who survive are left maimed and deeply scarred by their ordeal, physically and emotionally. Most stories end with the profoundly shaken narrator cataloging his missing body parts and describing the nightmares he still suffers. These sobering aspects of otherwise outrageous killer creature fiction take on unexpected resonance, considering MAM readership skewed heavily to veterans (then a significant percentage of the population) intimately familiar with comparable physical and emotional trauma acquired in real-world combat in World War II, Korea, and Vietnam.

—Wyatt Doyle

"CHEWED TO BITS BY GIANT TURTLES"

— VIC PATE —

*Man's Life,* May 1957

COVER ARTIST: WIL HULSEY

# Chewed to Bits by GIANT TURTLES

**Steel-like jaws clacked away, each bite slashing flesh from my body—I used my knife and my hands, and when they were gone, my bloody stumps—and yet the turtles came—**

## by VIC PATE

BETWEEN the blonde and the motor I was in one hell of a stew! The blonde had wanderlust and the motor wouldn't start. I was tucked in the skiff, sweat to the eyeballs, filing overly carboned points with the tip of my knife, and getting nowhere.

From a distance of 100 yards, the blonde shrilled, "Vic! Look at the baby turtle I've found—"

I looked. I got my head over the gunnel, briefly, staring at the svelte, full-bosomed, wide-hipped Mrs. John Williams of Shreveport, stooping over the thick green carapace of a snapping turtle. Even at that distance it sounded like castanets.

"That's a snapper, Gale!"

"Nuts!" Gale Williams snorted. "For God's sake, Pate, stop being a kill joy—"

*All right! I thought. Get your goddammned beautiful fingers torn off!* But I didn't say anything. I just wiped my face, focused again on the stooping figure,

[Continued from page 23]

**Illustration by Wil Hulsey**

**BETWEEN** the blonde and the motor I was in one hell of a stew! The blonde had wanderlust and the motor wouldn't start. I was tucked in the skiff, sweat to the eyeballs, filing overly carboned points with the tip of my knife, and getting nowhere.

From a distance of 100 yards, the blonde shrilled, "Vic! Look at the baby turtle I've found—"

I looked. I got my head over the gunnel, briefly, staring at the svelte, full-bosomed, wide-hipped Mrs. John Williams of Shreveport, stooping over the thick green carapace of a snapping turtle. Even at that distance it sounded like castanets.

"That's a snapper, Gale!"

"Nuts!" Gale Williams snorted. "For God's sake,

"Pate, stop being a killjoy—"

*All right!* I thought. *Get your goddamned beautiful fingers torn off!* But I didn't say anything. I just wiped my face, focused again on the stooping figure, shrugged and went back to my other thankless job.

I was still tinkering when the blonde took a header into the murky sluice and came up screaming. For a second I sat there, too startled to move. Then when I saw the wide dollop of blood run down her hand, I slammed out of the boat and began running.

"Vic!" she screamed. "For God's sake, Vic, they're tearing me to pieces—"

BLONDES and bogs weren't my racket, normally. But then things weren't exactly normal that July of '53 when, broke and my belly scraping bottom, I hit the Louisiana bayous and became a sort of assistant mate to a New Orleans gambler who had a yacht. One of those stories, common as hell. The blonde belonged to the gambler, or was about to when her divorce from one John Williams became final. Anyway, the blonde was on the yacht and the gambler was not, and the blonde wanted a slow skiff ride through the bayous. That's the gist of it.

My business was overland express but the recession killed it, and the trailer rig my brother and I bought after the war went back to the finance company. I took to hiking then. On the thumb. A guy hits some

of the damndest places
that way. Actually
my destination was
Houston, but I ended
up at Lake Charles,
LA, sitting in a greasy
spoon and reading a
free paper some guy
had thoughtfully left

behind. The ad read:

"Mate to work on yacht. $90 month, uniform and keep. Experience preferred..."

The address said something about a boat yard at Leesburg, so I got on my legs and started walking again. Three hours later a swarthy looking guy gave me the once over, rolled a cigar meditatively over his lips and said I passed inspection.

"What the hell do you know about boats?" the guy grunted, tossing me a set of keys.

"Spitkits in the Navy," I said. "Sub chasers, Yipees, that sort of thing."

"This ain't a spitkit, mister," he grinned. "I went for 125 Gs on this! Treat it kindly—"

THE GUY—he's alive and too important to give his square name—was all right. He handed me $20 against my salary, showed me around the boat and said the keys were for all compartments except the bridal suite, his. That was private, he said, and did I understand? And I said I did.

"She's all yours now, Pate," my new-found guardian angel puffed his cigar. "I'm due in New Orleans—unfinished business. Be back Friday. You've got three days to learn the boat. You—" he stared at me "—might give the bayou a whirl in the skiff. For some cockeyed reason my woman likes gloomy places."

"Okay, Mr. Selina," I nodded. "Thanks for everything." He winked affably. He was a snort, heavy set man about 50; coal black eyes, graying temples, thick hands. Thick but not soft. I shuffled around embarrassedly, jamming the $20 in my pockets, trying to say more.

"I'm a gambler," Selina said quietly. "I gamble on people, too. And usually I win."

I didn't see him after that for three days. There was a big black Caddy parked down the stringpiece and my boss gingerly took off for same. He saw me watching him, so he waved. I waved back. *There,* I thought, *is the last guy in the world I'll disappoint!* Then I headed about to inspect my 60 feet of glistening cruiser, and get squared away.

NINETY-SIX hours later, we were all chummy—Selina, his woman Gale Williams, and me. Selina wasn't aboard but for one meal when the wire came for him. Kid on a bike brought it down to the dock and Selina read it and said if that's the way things are, that's the way they are.

"Hell," he mumbled. "I wanted a weekend on the Calcasieu, Vic. Now it looks like I can't make it."

"Anything I can do?"

"I don't know. Maybe," he shoved the telegram in his, jacket. "Finish serving chow and I'll let you know later—"

Dinner, butlering, boat handling—it was all part of the $90 per. I didn't mind. And when the blonde came aboard, I took one long look and decided Selina could cut my pay in half and it'd still be okay. Not that I made any passes, nothing like that! She was just a beautiful, well-stacked broad. A lady, by another name.

"You're Vic," she smiled when Selina brought her aboard. "Hope you can run an outboard, Vic! I'm crazy about—" she smiled "—the bayou—"

Selina was behind her on the gangway and couldn't see her expression then. I did, and it said everything I saw, and more. Then I looked at my blissfully ignorant employer, and brought their bags to the bridal suite.

ABOUT dark, Selina rumbled out on deck saying he'd made up his mind. Casually, he said:

"Vic. I trust you with Mrs. Williams. I don't know you from a hole in the wall, but I trust you.

I've got to go back to town, and I don't think it's fair to bust up her weekend. You dig me?"

"Sure."

"Okay," Selina grunted emphatically, wrapping a cigar. "Thought you would. She's a barrel of fun—just don't let the fun get out of hand!"

"Naturally."

"When I lose a bet on a guy," Selina lit his stogie, "*the guy always pays, Vic.* I'd never want anything violent to happen to you. You're working out fine here. Next month I'll double your pay."

I got the whole message, the straight part quickly and deftly eased into the softener. I nodded, and that was the end of our discussion.

Selina left. Gale and I were alone.

I DIDN'T exactly care for the setup and apparently Gale Williams didn't either. I told her her room was made up and we politely said good night. That part was tough, but the next morning was even tougher. She came out on deck in a bikini and I almost blew up the galley range. Later, about noon, we took a walk into town. She got some hairpins, something like that. Not in the bikini, naturally, but in another of those tight things with a flared skirt that was virtually transparent when the light caught her right.

Then, about mid-afternoon she rapped on my cabin door, opened it, leaned in and said how about a ride into the bayou. Without any more buildup, the thing about Williams I then decided, was a simple case of tease. And I wasn't buying. Without putting it into words, Gale got the word. She lapsed into a long, frosty silence as we pushed away from the yacht, working slowly into the myriad webwork of canals to the deep, overhanging moss country.

THE OUTBOARD broke down about eight miles later. I nosed the skiff into a mudbank and held out a hand for the lady. It was still quite hot, but Gale didn't mind it particularly. The top three buttons of her tight white blouse came open and she smiled and jumped into my arms. I offered no resistance at all.

"You're strong, Vic!" the blonde whispered. "I'll bet you pulled the oldest gag in the world deliberately."

"I might have," I said, lowering her slowly, "but you're somebody else's woman—"

"My! How noble!

Selina didn't tell me that was one of your virtues too—"

"Listen," I grimaced, "I've got as much hot blood as the next guy. Only this isn't my kind of setup, Mrs. Williams. Let me fix this damned boat so we can get back before midnight."

The blonde laughed huskily, reached up and a soft white hand brushed my mouth lightly.

"Fix the boat," she said quietly, studying me. "I'll bet you can fix *anything*, Vic."

I watched her slowly back away, then sit under a moss tree, staring at me. I beached the skiff high, pulled in the motor and started looking. The blonde got up and started walking along the bank. Sweat spanked out from my temples to my toes, but I stayed right there messing with my other trouble. Between the blonde and the motor I was in one hell of a stew!

I WAS up to my eyeballs in motor, filing the points with my knife when the blonde squealed delightedly:

"Vic! Look at the baby turtle!"

"That's a snapper, Gale!"

Even at 100 yards, I could hear it clacking away. I assumed the blonde had brains enough to let it alone, so I ducked down, let her rant and went back to my filing. And seconds later, still fussing in the shallow sluice, chasing a turtle, the blonde took a header and came up turtle bait.

I saw the wide dollop of blood staining fast on her hand and I slammed out of the boat, running like a madman.

"Vic!" the blonde screamed. "For God's sake, they're tearing me
to pieces—"

I got 10 yards when my right leg munched into a sump, deep,
spilling me flat. A jagged race of pain shot up from the kneecap and my
mouth flew open involuntarily, and I swallowed the brackish sluicewater
down the wrong pipe. I came up gasping, wincing as my leg blew up like
an erratic grenade. Ahead, the screeching blonde pawed her clothing
and the gruesome sound of clacking beaks began its obligato of death.

GALE was trying to run, shrieking, her face contorted in frenzy as she
ripped away the bulky thing crawling up her right leg. And I couldn't
help her; I couldn't move! I slumped there dizzily, shaking my head,
praying, hearing the spine-chilling shrieks wafting over the shallows for
an eternity before I realized that I was now crawling.

Then only the pain remained as I hobbled up, grabbing the bank,
falling again, the knife dropping from my grasp. Frantically, I ducked
under, raking the soft mire, staying under until the pounding in my
chest lurched bile to my mouth. I was halfway to her, wincing as I could
count them suddenly. Big—big as a man's forearm—their beaks and
talon claws impaled the blonde's lower torso—there were six then,
and more swimming around beneath her, climbing on, pyramiding,
scratching the skirt and then digging in.

Blood spurted from her back as she suddenly whirled, screaming,
trying to detach a fast moving snapper that raced up her buttocks. The
beak, offered the beautiful hand of Gale Williams, struck, locking on
her palm and she crumpled back sobbing "Vic! I'm bleeding to death—"

I CHARGED ahead, desperately, busting water in wild, sleeting spray.
The knife was vised in my fist and I kept screaming to get up! To roll
over! It was so much gargle in my throat because she couldn't, and the
whole crawling army of snapping turtles, hissing, beady-eyed red, were
deluging the blonde as she thrashed insanely in the shallows.

My leg buckled under me then, again, and I went down like some
sloughed timber, rolling, desperately trying to hold the knife. When I
came up the water around me was a boil of crimson, and I felt the first
searing jolt of pain as a shell hard beak sliced through my trousers.
The calf of my right leg felt heavy enough to weight me, but I didn't
go down. Hot waves of pain and blackness raced across my eyes, but I
didn't go down.

I was a yard from the half submerged, half-shredded blonde who
whimpered like a demented animal, thrashing in bloody paroxysms.

The more she shook, the deeper their bites, the more hideous the angry clacking.

My knife slashed down, raking the hard shell, spilling away. I saw the beak bunched on my trousers and I cut my own flesh in order to clear it. Then I did a header, grabbing the blonde as she started to drown.

"Hold on, Gale!" I groaned, pulling her to her feet. "Just hold on—don't pass out, *please!*"

My leg felt like all the blood was running out of that flesh wound. It hurt, it scared me, it made me lunge howlingly at the thick carapace on Gale's leg. I slammed the knife in the lighter belly and flung one off. The abrupt movement of my knife frightened a turtle clinging to her arm. Its serpentine head withdrew, but when an instant later it came out, I jabbed the blade upward, in, pulling at the same time. The head came off, biting the knife blade and Gale Williams slumped at my feet.

Frantically, I reached down, grabbing her around the chest, trying to pull her away from the massed surge of turtles beneath us. I went back a few yards, flobbed backward, shouting and hacking the busting water, sitting there trying to keep her head out.

My knife arched in hard, the sound like graham crackers, like autumn leaves as the blade begged into shell. But I left it too long in one twenty-pounder.

Suddenly my own back was alive with fire, insane crawling, pulling me under. I screamed trying to shove the knife down over my shoulder, missing, stabbing myself. I could feel the hotness dribble through my lips running down my chin like lava. The blade came away wet for three inches.

"Gale!" I moaned. "Gale, help me crawl!"

THE BLONDE'S face was frozen, slumped on my chest, with three turtles fighting for her shoulder. Her eyes opened once, starkly, but no sound escaped her from her lips. Long, pink strips of flesh ripped away with the white blouse as the three turtles backwatered. Instinctively I grabbed, my hand digging the knife and pulling back in a blur of panic. I felt pressure on my left side and as I probed with the knife the crawling raced to my head. My ear. I could feel my ear coming off!

My knife brushed again, feeling for the softer underpinning but two fingers got in the way and I lost them. I was beyond pain now; I could feel the waves of blackness laying down a soft velvetness and the fact that two of my fingers were swimming away before me, seemed more a curious monstrosity than anything. I coughed great wads of blood and again began backing.

I backed as far as the shore, pulling Gale and an assortment of feeding turtles. It was wasted effort. Coronary. She died of fright in my arms, her beautiful body like some degraded relic of a beautiful thing. Even as I put her in the skiff, I hacked six turtles trying to climb in after her. Then I looked at the bloody maw that was me and passed out.

I TOOK a lot of healing in New Orleans—that's where Selina had the body shipped. Mine, I mean. Gale Williams was buried in Tennessee, what was left of her. Her father claimed the remains. Today I have one of those artificial hands, three and a half fingers of it, anyway. And a calfless right leg. And all kinds of catgut from one end of me to the other. To be exact, from my toes to my ear—the turtles got that too. Selina heard the story in dribs and drabs, but I didn't like hurting his feelings. I said it was all legit; no passes. But inside I detest myself; I keep thinking if I'd made a pass she never would have gone off mad, turtle-picking mad. Still, I never told Selina that part. He'd have figured he bet on a loser—which he did anyway, damn it.  ///

# SADISTIC NAZI STORIES

VINTAGE MAMs *are sometimes referred to as "sweat magazines." One theory why suggests the name reflects the frequent images of sweaty males in scenes shown in the cover and interior illustrations. Another is that the images of bound, scantily-clad women in the magazines made readers all hot and sweaty.*

*I use the term "sweat magazines" to refer to a specific subgenre of MAMs: those that primarily featured artwork and stories in which attractive, usually American-looking women or men are tortured and abused by evil Nazis, Japs, Commies, natives, Satanists or some other fiends. Sweat mags with cover paintings showing Nazis tormenting barely-clothed babes are the most notorious. They're also the most sought after by collectors.*

*The most prized issues feature Nazi B&T (bondage and torture) cover paintings by some of the great illustration artists who worked for MAMs, such as Norm Eastman, Norman Saunders, John Duillo, Basil Gogos, Syd Shores and Vic Prezio.*

*Their artwork is a good reflection of what the stories in sweat magazines are like. They are spiced up with a bit of sex and violence. And, some of the torture scenes are creatively horrific. However, like the cover paintings, the stories aren't really explicit by today's standards. As movies they'd be R-rated or even PG, not X-rated.*

*There is a notable absence of "obscene" words. Sex and body parts are described using words and metaphors that would avoid the wrath of censors. The gore factor is generally lower than what is now common in modern crime novels, movies and even TV shows. And there is never, ever any kiddie porn (the truly despicable form of pornography that is all too common today).*

*It should also be noted sweat mag stories are not about consenting adults engaging in BDSM sex games, as in the recent bestseller* Fifty Shades of Grey. *The women and men who are tortured and abused don't enjoy the pain. And, the characters doing the torturing and abusing are typically portrayed as demented fiends who usually get their just desserts in the end.*

*"Grisly Rites of Hitler's Monster Flesh Stripper" is a classic example. It was the featured cover story in the March 1965 issue of* Man's Story, *one of the longest-running men's sweat magazines. The jaw-dropping cover painting was done by Norm Eastman. The equally creative story is credited to Jim McDonald, which is almost certainly a pseudonym for a pulp writer whose real name remains unknown.*

——*Robert Deis*

— JIM MCDONALD —

*Man's Story*, March 1965
COVER ARTIST: NORM EASTMAN

# GRISLY RITES OF HITLER'S

### Only a maniac could have concocted so bestial a scheme for exacting the last bit of torment and degradation from his cruelly chained sin slaves.

#### By JIM McDONALD

THE sky vomitted yellow and red flame. Mortar shells shook the very foundations of the great stone building which stood commanding the valley below. Billowing clouds of smoke obscured the dense woods which surrounded the castle.

Below, a sergeant of the famed American Thunderbird Division squinted through his field glasses. "Kraut castle up there," he spoke into his walkie talkie. "Range 0063. Bearing 298. Commence! Commence! Commence!"

The urgent request was heard at C. P. Corrections were made. The shells pocked ever closer to the thick walls.

In the ghostly light of the artillery barrage everything had a sense of an opium-induced nightmare. It caused terror to twist at Sharon Walker's soft belly. Once again she struggled with the huge brass knob of her locked door. Sweat ran clammy over her spine. The breath in her lungs was an instrument of torment. Her arms and legs corded with the strain of her effort. But the door would not give.

In fatigue she let her body slump against the wooden dresser. Her hand brushed against the lone item which stood there. She recoiled in repugnance.

The eyeless sockets stared back into her face. The even white teeth grinned in derision. The smooth skull seemed to take on life, seemed to find satanic glee in her situation.

It was as if the lipless mouth was forming the words of her death oration. As if it were saying, "They have come too late for you. They will find nothing of you here but what they find of me. You and I will spend eternity together in an unmarked grave. But first you will know the sensations of damnation. Colonel General Von Tanzer will see to that."

Sharon covered her face with her shaking hands. Almost drunkedly she reeled back to the bed which was the only other item of furniture in the small room.

"I'm going mad," she whispered into the sound filled night. The roar of gunfire drowned out her words. "I've come all this way only to lose my mind at the last."

An extremely close concussion sent a draft of air through the room. It swirled around Sharon, plucking at the skirt of her dress, peeling it back over the smoothness of her plump thigh. The coolness was welcome. Slowly her back stiffened. She would not go mad. If she must die, she would die with dignity. She would not crawl to Von Tanzer. She would not cajole nor plead. She would accept her fate, no matter how hideous.

She found now that she could look back at the grinning skull. She was prepared. The grisly thing no longer had the ability to strike her numb. Sharon moved to the window. She stood, steadying herself against the sill counting the muzzle flashes below.

"I die so that you can come this far," she murmured and the thought made it all worth while. "I die so that millions of others may live."

She wondered about those who would live. Would Jack Standlee be one of them? The faint hope caused a small smile to break over her lips.

SHE remembered the nights in the London flat while the buzz bombs rocked the city. She recalled how it had been between them. Had it really been love? Or had it been the kind of thing that the closeness of death brings on? She couldn't quite be sure.

Yet her mind's eye turned back to the handsome American O.S.S. man as he stood in the middle of the room. "Scotch!" she'd cried in delight. "You're an unconscionable blighter. Nobody but a thief and a swindler can find a bottle of scotch in England."

Standlee had laughed deeply. "If this offends your sense of honor, I'll just drink it all by myself," he said.

Now she remembered hurling herself across the room at him, her stockinged feet sliding on the wooden floor. She remembered him falling to the bed under her pressing weight. She remembered the faint odor of soap and tobacco and the strong sinews of his arms closing around the small of her back. She remembered the palms moving downward over the ungirdled softness of her hips and thighs.

She recalled cupping his cheeks in her soft hands, drawing his head upward. Her lips had been soft on his. She'd felt the lithe muscles coming alive in him. Her body had clung desperately to his as he had worked at the (Continued on page 68)

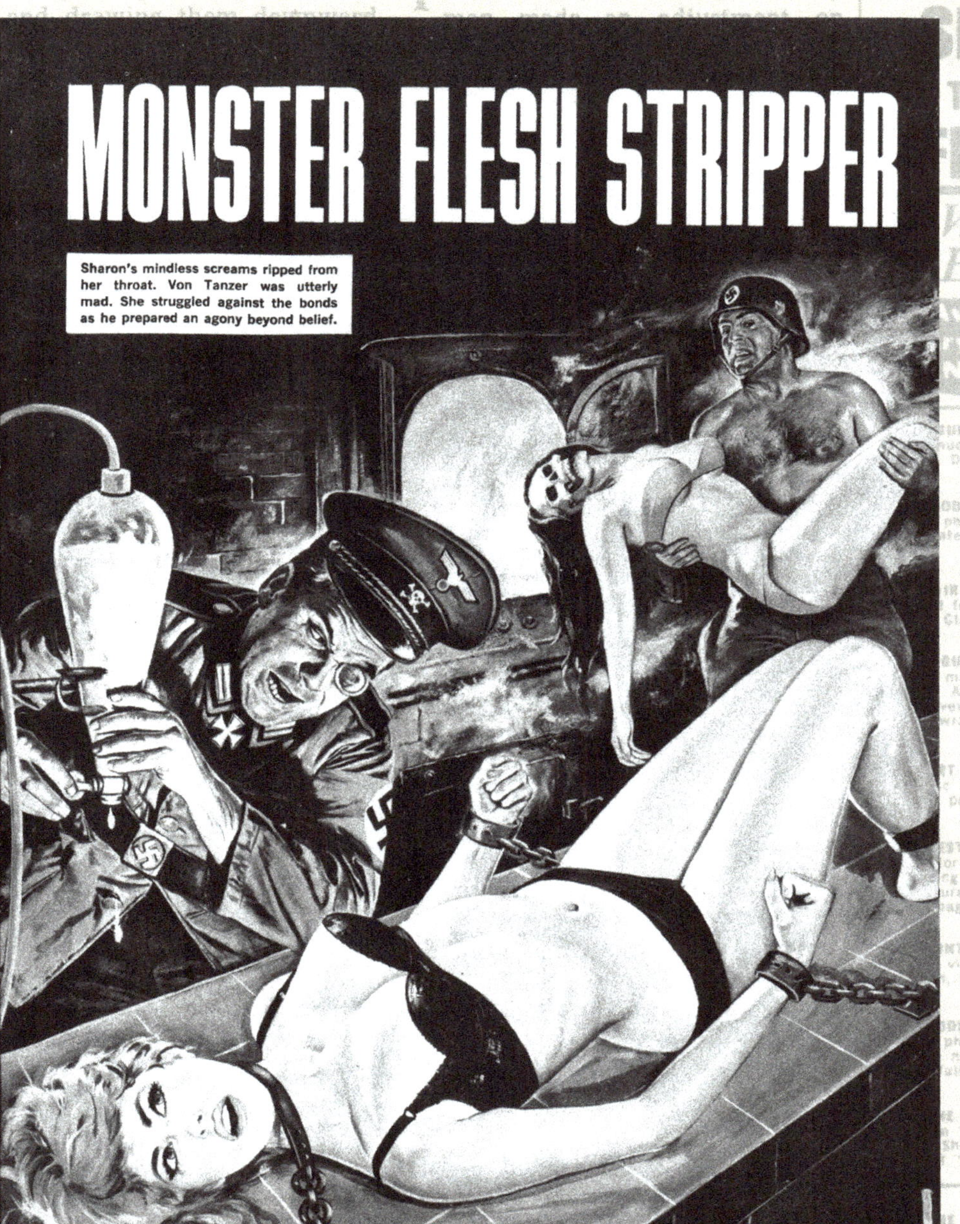


**Illustration by Norm Eastman**

**THE SKY** vomited yellow and red flame. Mortar shells shook the very foundations of the great stone building which stood commanding the valley below. Billowing clouds of smoke obscured the dense woods which surrounded the castle.

Below, a sergeant of the famed American Thunderbird Division squinted through his field glasses. "Kraut castle up there," he spoke into his walkie talkie. "Range 0063. Bearing 298. Commence! Commence! Commence!"

The urgent request was heard at CP. Corrections were made. The shells pocked ever closer to the thick walls.

In the ghostly light of the artillery barrage everything had a sense of an opium-induced nightmare. It caused terror to twist at Sharon Walker's soft belly. Once again she struggled with the huge brass knob of her locked door. Sweat ran clammy over her spine. The breath in her lungs was an instrument of torment. Her arms and legs corded with the strain of her effort. But the door would not give.

In fatigue she let her body slump against the wooden dresser. Her hand brushed against the lone item which stood there. She recoiled in repugnance.

The eyeless sockets stared back into her face. The even white teeth grinned in derision. The smooth skull seemed to take on life, seemed to find satanic glee in her situation.

It was as if the lipless mouth was forming the words of her death oration. As if it were saying, "They have come too late for you. They will find nothing of you here but what they find of me. You and I will spend eternity together in an unmarked grave. But first you will know the sensations of damnation. Colonel General Von Tanzer will see to that."

Sharon covered her face with her shaking hands. Almost drunkedly she reeled back to the bed which was the only other item of furniture in the small room.

"I'm going mad," she whispered into the sound filled night. The roar of gunfire drowned out her words. "I've come all this way only to lose my mind at the last."

An extremely close concussion sent a draft of air through the room. It swirled around Sharon, plucking at the skirt of her dress, peeling it back over the smoothness of her plump thigh. The coolness was welcome. Slowly her back stiffened. She would not go mad. If she must die, she would die with dignity. She would not crawl to Von Tanzer. She would not cajole nor plead. She would accept her fate, no matter how hideous.

She found now that she could look back at the grinning skull. She was prepared. The grisly thing no longer had the ability to strike her numb. Sharon moved to the window. She stood, steadying herself against the sill counting the muzzle flashes below.

"I die so that you can come this far," she murmured and the thought made it all worth while. "I die so that millions of others may live."

She wondered about those who would live. Would Jack Standlee be one of them? The faint hope caused a small smile to break over her lips.

SHE REMEMBERED the nights in the London flat while the buzz bombs rocked the city. She recalled how it had been between them. Had it really been love? Or had it been the kind of thing that the closeness of death brings on? She couldn't quite be sure.

Yet her mind's eye turned back to the handsome American OSS man as he stood in the middle of the room. "Scotch!" she'd cried in delight. "You're an unconscionable blighter. Nobody but a thief and a swindler can find a bottle of scotch in England."

Standlee had laughed deeply. "If this offends your sense of honor, I'll just drink it all by myself," he said.

Now she remembered hurling herself across the room at him, her stockinged feet sliding on the wooden floor. She remembered him falling to the bed under her pressing weight. She remembered the faint odor of soap and tobacco and the strong sinews of his arms closing around the small of her back. She remembered the palms moving downward over the ungirdled softness of her hips and thighs.

She recalled cupping his cheeks in her soft hands, drawing his head upward. Her lips had been soft on his. She'd felt the lithe muscles coming alive in him. Her body had clung desperately to his as he had worked at the fasteners of her blue Wrens uniform.

There had been no false modesty, no shying away from the moment of surrender. There couldn't be while the British ack-ack hurled their defiance at the marauding buzz bombs.

Her blouse and skirt had slid to the floor. The heat of her body had come through to him under the fragile covering of panties and bra.

Their bodies had blended together in one straining arc of passion.

Much later they had lain side by side, mindless of their nakedness. His hand had rested lightly on her belly. She had touched his fingers, drawn them to her cheek. Though neither of them had spoken, each counted the explosions in the night. Each wondered if the explosions would end their stolen moment.

Little fragments of Sharon's life came back to her now as she waited. Once again she was standing poised in the bomb bay of the Lancaster. Once again she was hurtling downward into the sky over France. Once again she was moving with the Maquis. Once again the group was surrounded in its Grenoble headquarters. Once again she was stumbling out of the cave, her hands clasped above her head.

That had been the moment of the beginning of her death. When she had joined the Office of Executive Service she had realized that capture, torture and martyrdom were possible side issues in the underground intelligence war. But realizing the potential and coming face to face with the Nazis themselves had been two different things.

Now as she stood in the window she recalled the first night in the Nazi cell.

She remembered the Gestapo interrogation, remembered how they had stripped her clothes from her and strapped her to a chair. Even now the excrutiating sensation of the wire loop being slowly tightened around her head came back. Even now she could not escape the sensations she had felt when they had bound her wrists behind her back and forced her to lie on her stomach on a hard wood table. She still felt their hands pawing her nakedness as they pushed her head into the bucket filled with filthy water.

The Gestapo had had their fun with her and then she had been shipped east in a locked railroad car. Others had replaced the Gestapo. These were SD who were charged with running the prisoner camps. The treatment had been much the same.

Then Von Tanzer had come on an inspection trip. He had swaggered past the line of young girls who stood rigidly at attention, their eyes straight ahead. He had prodded their flesh, subjected them to gross indecencies before their captors, and barked orders to a kapo who followed him.

It hadn't registered on Sharon Walker then. But only the most beautiful and the healthiest of the young women had been selected. For what purpose she had not been told. Yet she had been issued a ration of clothing, clothing which was unknown in the compound. The silk had been luxurious on her body. The moment of self-indulgence as she'd donned the costly lingerie and frock had evaporated quickly. The Nazis had a purpose for everything they did.

The significance was in the aberrations of Von Tanzer. It had been registered in the sounds which came to her from the bowels of the Rhine castle. Sounds that went on for days and nights at a time. Sounds which could only have been spawned in hell itself.


THEY had brought Sharon Walker to the castle alone. She had been driven in a sleek Mercedes Benz, the window curtains tightly drawn, an armed sergeant sitting beside her. They had locked her in the room and there she had stayed. Her meals had been served to her by an ugly brute who mumbled obscenities at her but made no other attempt to harm her. There she had remained until Von Tanzer had come to her.

He strode into the room without saying a word. The skull had been held under one arm. Its teeth were tightly clenched together. In the flickering light of the room, the skull appeared to be possessed by some demoniac life.

Von Tanzer had placed the gruesome thing on the dresser. He had turned to Sharon. "This was one of your countrywomen," he announced. His manner was that of a senior officer addressing his troops on a parade ground. "The owner of the skull was very much alive an hour ago. However, let us say she outlived her usefulness. You too will live until you are no longer of interest to me."

Von Tanzer's face had become distorted and bloated. The piggish eyes had squinted at Sharon. She felt as if the very flesh were being melted away from her soul, as if he could view the deepest portions of her being.

At that very moment a muted shriek had filtered through the narrow corridors from below. The sound, accompanied by the grisly sight before her, had struck Sharon Walker a savage emotional blow from which she had never quite recovered.

Von Tanzer had moved on her. His hands clawed out before him. The bone-crushing grip on her shoulders had sent tendrils of pain to the nerve centers of her brain.

Her body had bowed to his. His fat belly ground against the flatness of hers. Her firm breasts had mashed against the coarseness of his uniform. There was the stench of decay about Von Tanzer as she remained locked in his degrading embrace. His lips slobbered at Sharon's throat, the drool running down over her skin. When at last she had steped back, he had clawed the dress from her shoulder.

Instinct had told her to try to cover herself from his lascivious gaze. But there was another sensation, that of self preservation which told her she must remain standing statue-like as he systematically stripped the clothes from her.

Von Tanzer had drawn the degradation out to its ultimate. Inch by inch he had shredded her dress down the front. His clawing fingers had toyed with her bra, leaving their filthy imprints on her. At last he had denuded her breasts with one savage thrust. Then he had slid his thumbs under the waist band of her brief silk panties.

AFTER that he had come to her room many times. But there were other times—days and nights on end—when she had been left completely alone. At those times a guard would come to her with her food and shout his obscenities at her. And she would hear the hideous mewling from below, mewling that built up to a crescendo of horror and then subsided, only to begin once again.

She wondered how many rooms had been turned into cells, how many young and beautiful woman like herself were locked behind the doors waiting for the fearful sound of Von Tanzer's tread on the corridor stones.

Then another sound had entered her life. It had come as the distant rumble of a summer thunder storm. It had been faint at first. Then it had grown in intensity so that it almost blotted out the fearful shrieks from the subterranean dungeons. A nicker of hope had sparked in her tormented bosom. There could be no mistaking the concussion of gunfire. It wasn't the crackling of small arms, but the deep throated roar of massed artillery.

As it had grown closer, Von Tanzer had become more vicious. He seemed to recognize that the war for him was fast approaching its climax. Von Tanzer responded to this fact with increased bestiality. His demands of Sharon Walker can barely be hinted at.

Once in a moment of rage he had listened to the booming guns. He had gripped Sharon by the throat almost strangling her with his bare hands.

"You think they will save you?" he roared. "They will not. Your time will come before mine. I guarantee you that." He had thrust her from him and had run naked from her room.

Now she watched the muzzle flashes and waited. She was still standing poised at the window when the door slid open behind her. She felt herself being lifted from the ground. The crushing grip around her waist made her cry out in pain. The guard's derisive giggle came to her as she struggled in his grasp.

"The colonel general is waiting," the guard hissed. "He has things to show you. You'll enjoy them." The hands roved over her straining body, pinching and clawing at her hips. Her head hung down over the Nazi's shoulder. The moment of diabolical barbarism was at hand.

For weeks Sharon had known her time must come. She had tried to prepare herself for it. But no amount of preparation could have steeled her for the sight which now greeted her panic stricken eyes.

The first thing she was aware of was the blistering heat of a roaring fire. The flames danced blue and yellow through the open iron furnace door. The second sight tore at the fiber of her sanity. It was a low slung metal table to which a young woman had been chained. The body still glistened with sweat. The muscles were still corded in the arms and legs. Trickles of blood flowed from the wrists and ankles where the lovely victim had tried to tear free of the grip of the gyves which held them.

Almost swooning, choking on the nausea which clawed at her throat, Sharon Walker was forced to stand at the head of the table. She was almost hypnotized by the grisly picture. Where the woman's face had been, there was nothing but the naked, white, glistening skull bones. They had been stripped bare of all flesh.

The long dark hair made a gruesome frame for the faceless gargoyle. The huge beaker at the head of the table still spewed forth its tiny drops of fluid. The room stank of rotten eggs. Where the drops splattered, they raised little geysers of yellowish steam. There was a constant hissing sound.

Von Tanzer crushed Sharon's body to him. He held her immobile while the guard stripped the chains from the corpse. The woman's body was unceremoniously shoved to the floor. Still twitching it rolled over on its back, staring at the ceiling through its empty sockets.

Seconds later, the cruel metal, still wet and slime covered, bit into Sharon's back. She felt the heavy chain pinning her neck to its dank surface. Wildy she struggled. Von Tanzer leered down at her. He gripped her wrist. Savagely he drew it down to the table top. A chain rattled. Its cruel embrace due into her tender wrist. Sharon threw herself wildly from side to side. The guard watched her, savoring the action which caused her skirt to ride up around her hips. He fingered her thighs, capturing her legs with one arm and drawing them downward to meet the fearful touch of the waiting leg irons.

When they had secured her other wrist so that she was spreadeagled, helpless before them, the two Nazis began the orgiastic ritual of stripping her. She felt the fabric of her dress bunching around the swell of her breasts. Then there was no more pressure. The gossamer of her bra and panties reflected the fire light.

Von Tanzer muttered something in German. The guard kicked at the corpse. He squatted beside it. With a grunt he lifted the thing which had been a woman in his arms. Slowly he made his way to the open furnace

door. There was a shower of sparks and the fire burned with even greater intensity before the door slammed shut on its macabre contents.

Von Tanzer paid no heed to what was going on behind him. He busied himself adjusting the bracket which held the beaker. His action caused a few drops to spill out of the vial. It splattered onto the naked flesh of Sharon's shoulder. For a second she felt nothing but the coolness of the liquid. Then it came with the force of a branding iron, burning deeper, ever deeper into her flesh.

Sharon's lithe young body convulsed. Her struggles against the chains which held her made the whole table rattle. To the torment of the sulphuric acid burn was added the unendurable agony of irons scraping away the tender skin.

"You will stay alive for hours. You will die by drops. I will control the flow until you believe you have entered into an eternity of damnation. I will make you personally responsible for all of the English criminals who think they can smash the Reich. I have saved you for the last because you will be my masterpiece of torment. Scream! Beg! Whimper! It will do you no good."

Von Tanzer took a glass rod and placed it into the beaker. Dripping with the acid, he held it suspended over Sharon's naked belly. The drops ran off the end. They hung suspended in the air. Then they fell onto her flesh. Sharon stared up at the maniacal torturer who intended to burn her alive with acid. Her own torment would be drawn out far longer even than the girl she had replaced—the girl whose dead flesh now sputtered and sparked as it was turned to liquid fat by the furnace.

In the valley below an artillery man made an adjustment on a 105 howitzer. A shell slammed into the breech. The muzzle flashed. The Thunderbird artilleryman grunted with satisfaction. The forward observer squinted through his field glasses. He saw a corner of the crenelated wall of the castle tumble inward.

The Nazi colonel general's scream of mortal agony blotted out Sharon's whimper. His body slumped forward over hers, its weight almost crushing her. A drop of acid spilled onto the back of his neck raising a geyser of steam.

The Nazi guard looked up at the shuddering walls. Terror twisted his face into a gargoyle. He ran blindly through the corridors. He could not run fast enough.

At 0538 hours on 6 March, 1945, a reconnaissance patrol moved into the rubble of the castle. Strange sounds, like a kitten whimpering in pain, greeted their ears. A PFC lowered himself into the cellar dungeon. He shone his torch on the battered walls and stared in disbelief.

The acid had eaten away every bit of flesh on Von Tanzer's skull. And under his grisly remains, Sharon Walker cried out in pain.

"Medic!" the soldier managed to shout. "It's all right, Miss," the PFC comforted. But Sharon Walker was beyond reply. She never felt the litter bearers lifting her tenderly and placing her on a stretcher. She never knew of the act of decency with which the medic covered her with a poncho. She did not remember the trip back to England.

Psychiatrists say that if a person is normal and healthy they may survive the most hideous experience. In time they will regain all of their faculties. This was true of Sharon Walker. Today she lives in Summit, England. The only time she remembers is when she looks at the little white marks on her naked belly. Then for that moment, the madness closes in around her again. ///

# ABOUT "CALYPSO..."

GUSTO *was a short-lived MAM published in 1957 and 1958 by Arnold Magazines, Inc., one of several publishing companies founded by comic book pioneer Everett M. "Busy" Arnold (1899-1974).*

*In the 1940s and early 1950s, his Quality Comics company published many great "Golden Age" comics, like Will Eisner's* The Spirit *and Bill Ward's* Torchy.

*Gusto,* December 1957
Cover by Clarence Doore

*Then in 1954, Dr. Fredric Wertham's book* Seduction of the Innocent *dropped like an H-bomb on the US comics industry.*

*Wertham claimed that the violent images and "sexual content" in comic books was perverting the precious minds of America's youth (and no doubt their precious bodily fluids as well).*

*The resulting hysteria led to McCarthy-esque Congressional hearings and the mid-1950s "Comics Code," which essentially banned images or plots involving violence, sexy-looking women and any illegal or "immoral" activities.*

*Until then, young adult males had been regular readers of many comic books. When the comics were sanitized, emasculated and purged of busty female characters, several major comics publishers and many former comic books fans moved on together into the growing realm of men's magazines.*

*In 1956, Busy Arnold sold his comic book properties to DC Comics and focused on publishing more male-oriented periodicals. These included "true crime" and detective magazines, "cheesecake" photo and risqué humor magazines, and men's pulp adventure magazines like* Gusto.

*Unfortunately,* Gusto *didn't last long. Only three issues were published, in October and December of 1957 and February 1958. It was put out of business by another '50s censorship hurdle.*

*By today's standards, the action and adventure stories, exposés and glamour girl photos in* Gusto *are quite mild. But, based on the standards of the time, the US Postal Service decided* Gusto's *contents were "dominated by material of an obscene, lewd, lascivious, indecent or filthy nature"—and yanked the magazine's mailing permit.*

*One of the examples noted by the USPS bureaucrat who wrote the official written decision is this article about Calypso music from the October 1957 issue.*

*This partly tongue-in-cheek exposé discussed the shocking fact that some Calypso lyrics were even more sexually suggestive than those in the rock 'n' roll music that Elvis Presley sang!*

*Ironically, the diligent bureaucrat who investigated* Gusto *for the Postal Service concluded that the article itself violated USPS obscenity regulations. Why? Because it quoted some of those lyrics, such as the chorus of the popular Calypso classic "The Big Bamboo."*

*So… If you're not scared of "obscenity"—or "The Big Bamboo"—read on….*

—Robert Deis

"CALYPSO: IS IT PORNOGRAPHY IN HI-FI?"

— GEORGE MAJARI —

*Gusto*, October 1957
COVER ARTIST: CLARENCE DOORE

Now, perhaps, you understand why the boys in our second *piroga* — the one that was to catch up with us when we stopped for lunch — found me hysterical and delirious.

They found me in the *piroga*, which had floated into shore. I was sitting in the stern — seeing nothing, they told me later, and babbling coherently.

It didn't matter, though. Nothing mattered — except that I was alive. God knows how or why — but I was still alive.

'That was the miracle — and the only one that counted!

by GEORGE MAJARI

# CALYPSO: IS IT

...they throw is come with special delivery.
The fireman oh they carry a tremendous hose.
Policeman have big sticks everybody knows.
The milkman have de bottle which is long and cute...

...does a few basic tunes over and... or it borrows from tunes already popular. The calypso style is... It can adapt itself to a waltz, a rhumba, a fox trot or a march.

One of the recently popular calypso songs rode high on the crest...

# PORNOGRAPHY IN HI-FI?

Harry Belafonte is a top-notch performer who turned to calypso because of an interest in folk music. It was another kind of interest entirely that brought other performers to it

**Calypso comes from Africa by way of Trinidad, where it was once an art. An expert analyzes what it is today**

IMMORAL MUSIC? Listen. You may get a surprise. A yowling, screeching riot was kicked up by teen-agers of Little Rock, Arkansas, when a P.T.A. group in that town decided to brand singer Elvis Presley immoral.

You can say Elvis is a moron and a lout and get away with it. The teen crowd will shrug indifference if you say those unwashed hair-fenders next to Presley's ears turn your stomach. Complain that Elvis' slow, "sweet" notes sound like a cow that's eaten gassy clover and the kids may agree with you.

But you stick a nerve when you say Elvis has a dirty mind.

We'll never sell the younger generation on the notion that Elvis Presley is some kind of moral bubonic plague.

After all, the kids have eyes and ears. They've seen us do the mambo, the cha-cha-cha and the meringue. After those parties were over the kids put the calypso records back on the player and listened closely to the words.

How can the teeners believe we're serious about Elvis Presley when the same hands that slap Presley clap for calypso?

Calypso out-pelvises Presley by a country mile — and then some.

*"You're Nothing But a Houn'-Dog"* is a gentle lullaby next to *"Mama Put Out De Light and Give Me What You Gave My Daddy Last Night."*

*"Get Off My Blue Suede Shoes"* is a modest request compared with a song like *"Don't Touch Me Tomato:"*

> Touch me dis
> An' you touch me dat;
> Touch me everything I got;
> Feel me plums
> An' me apples too,
> But here's one ting you no can do."

Harry Belafonte is the only big-name calypso singer who doesn't have to be edited, rinsed off and inspected before being let into our home parlors. Harry sings a clean song. His *"Matilda,"* *"Banana Boat,"* and *"Marianne"* have stepped above the top rungs of every national hit tune survey.

Belafonte deserves his success. He's a gifted actor, dancer and singer who's plugged away for years at his craft and profession.

Another credit for Belafonte is that his enunciation is clear. He flavors his words with an accent so that we'll never mistake him for Frank Sinatra or some other heart-throb type. We hear distinctly every word he's singing. The kids hear them clearly too, but we'll never be embarrassed if they start singing them at Sunday School.

But you have to lay your ear in the speaker to understand what some calypso singers are talking about. Your ear will get shock-red when you do.

(Continued on page 52)

**IMMORAL** music? Listen. You may get a surprise. A yowling, screeching riot was kicked up by teenagers of Little Rock, Arkansas, when a PTA group in that town decided to brand singer Elvis Presley immoral.

You can say Elvis is a moron and a lout and get away with it. The teen crowd will shrug indifference if you say those unwashed hair-fenders next to Presley's ears turn your stomach. Complain that Elvis' slow, "sweet" notes sound like a cow that's eaten gassy clover and the kids may agree with you.

But you stick a nerve when you say Elvis has a dirty mind.

We'll never sell the younger generation on the notion that Elvis Presley is some kind of moral bubonic plague.

After all, the kids have eyes and ears. They've seen us do the mambo, the cha-cha-cha and the meringue. After those parties were over the kids put the calypso records back on the player and listened closely to the words.

How can the teeners believe we're serious about Elvis Presley when the same hands that slap Presley clap for calypso?

Calypso out-pelvises Presley by a country mile—and then some.

"You're Nothing But a Houn'-Dog" is a gentle lullaby next to "Mama Put Out De Light" and "Give Me What You Gave My Daddy Last Night."

"Get Off My Blue Suede Shoes" is a modest request compared with a song like "Don't Touch Me Tomato":

> *Touch me dis*
> *An' you touch me dat;*
> *Touch me everything I got;*
> *Feel me plums*
> *An' me apples too,*
> *But here's one ting you no can do.*

Harry Belafonte is the only big-name calypso singer who doesn't have to be edited, rinsed off and inspected before being let into our home parlors. Harry sings a clean song. His "Matilda," "Banana Boat," and "Marianne" have stepped above the top rungs of every national hit tune survey.

Belafonte deserves his success. He's a gifted actor, dancer and singer who's plugged away for years at his craft and profession.

Another credit for Belafonte is that his enunciation is clear. He flavors his words with an accent so that we'll never mistake him for Frank Sinatra or some other heart-throb type. We hear distinctly every word he's singing. The kids hear them clearly too, but we'll never be embarrassed if they start singing them at Sunday School.

But you have to lay your ear in the speaker to understand what some calypso singers are talking about. Your ear will get shock-red when you do.

Calypso music is the Negro music of Trinidad. It originally came from Africa and was popular among the people of their islands during the earlier colonial and slave days.

The calypso *patois* is a dialect similar to Haitian *creole*, but where the natives of Haiti mix French, Spanish, Carib and West African words together, calypso singers mix English words with African and Spanish words.

The English words are squeezed and wrung in such a way that we just barely know what's going on. One popular calypso number titled "The Postman" might send grandma away from the nice record player whistling the melody and thinking it's the national anthem for letter carriers. But if grandma ever turned up her hearing aid, she'd see this postman never worried about sleet or snow or gloom of night. Here are a few of the lines:

> *At 9 o'clock each morning all*
> *the women sing.*
> *They know the postman bringin'*
> *them the Same good thing.*
> *An' when he's at the door the*
> *women shout with glee*
> *Because they know he come*
> *with special delivery.*
> *The fireman oh they carry a*
> *tremendous hose.*
> *Policeman have big sticks*
> *everybody knows.*
> *The. milkman have de bottle*

> *which is long and cute.*
> *But all agree the postman have*
> *the longest route.*

Slaves in the Caribbean Islands used to record the big and little events that happened around them: wars, battles, family fights, hurricanes, visits of royalty. During island revolutions, calypso was used to carry secret information: Slaves used it also to carry information about their masters.

After slavery was abolished, calypso stayed on. It was circulated among the islands as a kind of newsletter.

Calypso singers became singing Winchells. Some of them specialized in politics; some in romance and adventure, some in sheer

gossip. They took fancy names like Lord Invader, Duke of Iron, Lord Invincible, Attila the Hun, The Growler, King Radio, and The Lion.

It took the American Tourist to lift the calypso singer to his present state of fame—or notoriety. The shrewd islanders found they could pick up more Yankee dollars by singing songs of American goings-on. The clever calypso artists took to reading American newspapers and movie magazines. By bending big scandals into the few basic calypso frames, he could grab up a sidewalkfull of shiny quarters and half dollars.

One Hollywood divorce case gave birth to a song about the stellar husband titled: "He Need a Bigger Muscle." A Hollywood star who was sent back from the Korean front for overexposing herself before GI photographers was immortalized on the islands with a song, "What I Wanna Know Is, Is You Blonde or Is You Brunette?"

Books came in for their share of calypso too: "I Just Read *Forever Amber* and I Am So Tired Out." *From Here to Eternity* inspired "The Officer's Wife."

Calypso is a kind of scavenger. It uses a few basic tunes over and over, or it borrows from tunes already popular. The calypso style is loose. It can adapt itself to a waltz, a rhumba, a fox trot or a march.

One of the recently popular calypso songs rode high on the crest of *Bridey Murphy* fame. It was called "Reincarnation":

> *Yes, I heard when you die,*
> *    after burial*
> *You got to come back as some*
> *    insect or animal.*
> *Well, if it's so, I don't want to*
> *    be a monkey,*
> *Neither a sheep, a goat or*
> *    donkey.*
> *My brother said he wants to*
> *    come back a hog.*
> *But not Invader, I want to be*
> *    a bed-bug.*
> *Just because I want to bite them*
> *    young ladies, partner,*
> *Like a hot-dog or a hamburger.*
> *If you know you're thin, don't*
> *    be in a fright,*
> *It's only big fat women I want*
> *    to bite.*

> *When you turn a horse, you got*
> *to carry people's loads,*
> *And get licks from your boss.*
> *And like a wood-ant wood is*
> *all you have to eat;*
> *But as a bed-bug I can bite*
> *the human meat.*

From "Reincarnation" it was an easy step to "Murial And De Bedbug." The entire song is devoted to the story of a bedbug who hid itself someplace in Murial:

> *That bug was really clever*
> *To find its way into Murial's*
> *treasure.*

The money-smart natives found that sex earned silver. More and more of their songs discussed fallen women, illicit love, private parts and scandal:

> *The big bamboo grows good*
> *and long.*
> *The big bamboo it grows*
> *always strong.*
> *The big bamboo grows*
> *straight and tall.*
> *And the big bamboo pleases*
> *one and all.*

The great, cold northerners put on a show of shock and disgust and, no doubt, some of them were sincere. They went back to their homes in New York and Ohio and told how naughty the natives were on the islands. Oddly, they seemed to remember almost as many songs as the calypso singers.

Gradually more and more curious north people dropped in on the Islands to see for themselves how bad these people were. They were not disappointed. Calypso singers were piling up a wealth of material raked up by Kefauver, the Hollywood Codes and other guardians of conscience and morals.

Mickey Jelke's famous trial alone gave them enough ideas to last them a generation.

Then one day a strange man from the north unpacked a box and set it in front of a calypso singer. "Sing to it," he invited, and held out some money. The calypso singer sang, a bit nervously because he learned that the box would swallow his song and sing it back to him later. That's what it did. Little by little the calypso artist overcame his fear of feeding the box with songs. Like most tourists, he found, it liked songs about sex. He even sang a song about the box itself. "The Tape Recorder He Like To Eat."

Actually, the first recordings taken out of the islands were documentary in nature. Sociologists and anthropologists found the recorder a perfect tool for taking notes.

Later came commercial ventures. They were less wholesome. Today, many island calypso singers are force-fed with ideas designed to tickle thrill-mad Americans. Almost half of the records ground out have to be sold under the counter. Calypso of this kind is nothing more than hi-fi pornography.

True calypso artists are as inventive as ever, but instead of being the pungent critics they once were, many of them keep· their ears aimed at the clink of the dollar. They sing what they can sell. Their records are jolting little spurts of life into parties all over the States.

Invariably, where police raid a house for pornographic film they also pick up a stack of calypso platters.

One veteran calypso singer, when asked about the condition of his beloved art confessed he felt sad about it and was soon going to retire. Then he laughed and broke into song:

> *I kiss her hand,*
> *I kiss her lips*
> *And I live her behind—*
> *For you.*

# "LOVE SLAVE" STORIES

*ALTHOUGH MAMs often claimed to feature "real stories," by now it should be clear that most were pulp fantasy. I note this because our next tale is set in one of the magazines' most popular sub-genres: "love slave" stories.*

*For the record, just like any sane person, I agree that a real-life situation in which someone is held against their will and forced to be a sex slave is horribly wrong. Of course, that doesn't mean I can't chuckle at the campy "love slave" fantasy stories in old men's pulp mags and admire the artwork used for them.*

*These aren't true crime-style stories involving convicted psychos, which were occasionally published in MAMs. I'm talking about erotic pulp fiction yarns. In general, these stories are mild by today's standards. But they were pretty wild for their day.*

*Stories about "love slaves"—male and female—were a staple of post-World War II men's pulp adventure magazines, with variations in tone depending on the story's setting and the protagonist's gender. In some of these stories, men are held captive and ravished by evil—but gorgeous—women. In other stories, women are the "love slaves." Naturally, they are beautiful women, and the evil men who hold them captive are ugly or otherwise abhorrent. Typically, in those stories, there are good-looking, manly heroes who help the damsels in distress escape.*

*The second story by Robert Silverberg in this anthology is a tongue-in-cheek example of a male "love slave" story. It first appeared in the November 1959 issue of* Sir!, *a long-running men's periodical published from 1951 to 1984. Up until about 1964,* Sir! *was as much or more a men's pulp mag as it was a girlie magazine. But from the mid-'60s on, it became more and more like* Playboy—*then more and more like* Hustler.

*Silverberg wrote "50 Days as an Amazon Love Slave" under his pseudonym David Challon, a name he used for several other men's adventure yarns and three of the classic "sleaze paperbacks" he cranked out in 1959:* French Sin Port, Suburban Sin Club, *and* Thirst for Love.

*—Robert Deis*

**"MATTERN'S 50 DAYS AS AN AMAZON LOVE SLAVE"**

ROBERT SILVERBERG (AS DAVID CHALLON)

*Sir!*, November 1959

COVER ARTIST: UNCREDITED

[Continued from page 12]



# MATTERN'S 50 DAYS AS AN AMAZON LOVE SLAVE

*Stateside, Mike Mattern Had Thought He Was Quite a Lover. But When He Landed in a Polynesian Version of a Female ROTC Camp—with 100 Sex-Starved Gals Clamoring for His Attentions—He Found out You Can Have Too Much of a Good Thing*

**By DAVID CHALLON**

● ● Soaked to the skin with sweat and salt water, his clothes cut to tatters, his body drained of energy and his mind almost numb with shock, Mike Mattern sprawled limply on the ground. He heard voices above him, female voices, but he didn't have the strength to look up. He lay there, just getting used to the idea that he had survived the crash.

He wondered where he was; there hadn't been time to check the maps. He knew he was somewhere not very far north of Samoa; maybe on one of the Tokelau Islands, or possibly one of the Phoenix Group, though he didn't think he was that far north. The storm had come up so quickly. And now his two passengers and his sleek little twin-engine plane were on the bottom of the Pacific, and he himself lay stranded on some forsaken bit of coral a hundred miles north of nowhere.

Losing the plane was a crusher. It was his sole capital, his only stock-in-trade, and he was still $5000 in debt on it. He let his breath out slowly, sadly. It had been swell while it lasted, the private airline business. But now it was over. If he ever got back to civilization, he would be up to his elbows in debts. He'd have to go back to working for other people again.

Right now, though, there wasn't much point in worrying about what would happen when he got back to civilization. He couldn't hitchhike back to Samoa. For all he knew, he might have landed on an island of cannibals.

At that moment something surprisingly like a bull whip exploded a couple of inches from his ear. He had been listening to the sounds of the conversation going on above him without bothering to listen for the meaning. He had been too tired out to care who might be holding a conversation over his half-drowned body. But the whip-crack startled him into caring.

He looked up. Four *(Continued on page 76)*

Dazed, Mattern looked up into beautiful face of a Polynesian girl brandishing a bull whip. Three other girls stood guard.

ooked to supple, girl who apalacas inted at ess be-

Tasman Sea to New Zealand, where he flew for a private fleet of freight planes.

In the summer of 1951—and summer-time means December in New Zealand—he decided he had worked for other people long enough. He had a few thousand dollars saved up, he had plenty of professional contacts, and he was widely re-

Suva to Honolulu, with no guarantees as to how long it would hold up.

Mattern made his decision. However, as he roared northward into the night a short while later, he felt grave misgivings. The plane was heavy, burdened to capacity with fuel. That would hurt its maneuverability. In case of trouble there was no

e of the le "taxi" ie South a plane although en, they

people to their destination on time. If, in his estimation, the weather was too bad he could insist on a layover.

Privately, though, he was anxious to go on. He had built something of a reputation for getting his people where they wanted to go.

He spent half an hour studying the

"I'm going to bring her down," Mattern said. "The instant she hits that door open and get yourselves out."

He had crashed before, during the war. He knew what to do. There was the stunning moment of impact and he realized it hadn't been a good landing. They had come in nose first. Within seconds the hull

**SOAKED** to the skin with sweat and salt water, his clothes cut to tatters, his body drained of energy and his mind almost numb with shock, Mike Mattern sprawled limply on the ground. He heard voices above him, female voices, but he didn't have the strength to look up. He lay there, just getting used to the idea that he had survived the crash.

He wondered where he was; there hadn't been time to check the maps. He knew he was somewhere not very far north of Sampa; maybe on one of the Tokelau Islands, or possibly one of the Phoenix Croup, though he didn't think he was that far north. The storm had come up so quickly. And now his two passengers and his sleek little twin-engine plane were on the bottom of the Pacific, and he himself lay stranded on some forsaken bit of coral a hundred miles north of nowhere.

Losing the plane was a crusher. It was his sole capital, his only stock-in-trade, and he was still $5000 in debt on it. He let his breath out slowly, sadly. It had been swell while it lasted, the private airline business. But now it was over. If he ever got back to civilization, he would be up to his elbows in debts. He'd have to go back to working for other people again.

Right now, though, there wasn't much point in worrying about what would happen when he got back to civilization. He couldn't hitchhike back to Samoa. For all he knew, he might have landed on an island of cannibals.

At that moment something surprisingly like a bullwhip exploded a couple of inches from his ear. He had been listening to the sounds of the conversation going on above him without bothering to listen for the meaning.

He had been too tired out to care who might be holding a conversation over his half-drowned body. But the whipcrack startled him into caring.

He looked up. Four Polynesian faces hovered above him, four unfriendly faces.

They were girls, and the oldest looked to be about 20. All four had the supple, graceful beauty of the Polynesian girl who has not yet borne children. Bright *lavalavas* covered their slim bodies but hinted at lean, agile, high-breasted loveliness beneath.

The three younger girls were carrying murderous-looking spears. The older girl gripped the thick knob of a bullwhip. She cracked it again, exploding its thunder just in front of Mattern's nose.

"Get up," she said coldly.

Mattern elbowed himself unsteadily to a sitting position and shrugged apologetically. "Believe me, I'd love to get up. But my leg—" He indicated the ugly swelling where he had wrenched his knee coming ashore. "I can't stand."

The whip-wielder glanced at her three younger comrades. Reaching out to take the spears from them, she said crisply: "The *mana'ia* is unable to walk. Carry him."

Together they managed to boost Mattern to a one-legged standing position. Then, effortlessly, they held him upright while two of the girls clasped wrists interlockingly to form a chair with their arms. He weighed 180 pounds, but the lithe brown-skinned girls carried him without apparent strain.

They started inland, the whip-wielder leading the way. As they moved slowly along Mattern wondered about the title they had given him—*mana'ia*. It meant white skin. But it had a connotation that puzzled him: god-with-white-skin.

He had heard of islands where white castaways were worshiped virtually as gods. He had heard of islands where the god was sacrificed at the end of a year to bring continued fertility to the island.

Mattern let himself be carried along. Even with two good legs he wouldn't have tried to argue with those spears. He had no choice but to be patient, to wait and see.

The day before, which had been the 27th of September, 1952, Mattern had left Auckland, New Zealand, in his plane. His passengers had been two executives of a pineapple company who had been vacationing near Lake Waikaremoana when they received a call to hurry back to Honolulu for an important business conference.

Auckland to Honolulu is a long hop and the commercial air lines don't have hourly planes making it. The men had two choices: they could take a plane across to Australia and transfer to a Hawaii-bound plane there, or they could hire one of the many free-lance pilots who provide "taxi" service over the vast stretches of the South Pacific.

They chose to hire their own plane. They chose Mike Mattern and, although they had no way of knowing it then, they were choosing death.

Mattern was 33, an American-born airman who had simply never returned to the United States after finishing his World War II stint. The war made him an experienced pilot. After mustering out in 1946 he drifted to Australia and took a job with a commercial airline. He spent two years working there, then moved across the Tasman Sea to New Zealand, where he flew for a private fleet of freight planes.

In the summer of 1951—and summertime means December in New Zealand—he decided he had worked for other people long enough. He had a few thousand dollars saved up, he had plenty of professional contacts, and he was widely respected as a capable flier. With these as his assets, he made a down payment on a two-engine plane of wartime vintage and set himself up in business.

During the nine months that followed Mattern had more business than he could handle. The Pacific is crisscrossed with air routes, but there are always plenty of people who can't wait for commercial schedules, or who want to go someplace the big lines can't or won't go. He agreed on one day's notice to take the pineapple executives back to Hawaii.

From Auckland to Honolulu is close to 4000 air miles. Mattern wasn't equipped to make a nonstop jaunt of such length. The best he could offer his impatient clients was a two-hop journey—1150 miles from Auckland to Suva, in the Fiji Islands; then, after a brief stopover for refueling, straight on from Suva to Honolulu and he canned the navigator, added fuel tanks.

Mattern wasn't happy about making that 2800-mile nonstop leg from Suva to Honolulu, but there wasn't much choice. By refueling in Samoa instead of Suva, he could cut the last leg down to 2200 miles, but the weather reports for Samoa and points east were rotten, and Mattern wanted to stay clear of the reported squalls.

He took off from Auckland at 5:30 local time, while it was still light. At midnight, when he landed at Suva, the ground crew had bad news.

"Squalls moving in from all sides, Mike," they told him. "Hell of a big thunderhead pushing in from the east, and now there's some new stuff kicking down out of the Philippines. You'd better layover tonight and go on into Honolulu tomorrow."

Mattern shrugged. "I'll talk it over with my passengers. But they're in a big hurry to get to Hawaii."

"It's better to get there a day late than never," one of the men said, grinning mirthlessly.

Mattern's passengers didn't agree. They had to get to Honolulu by tomorrow afternoon, and if Mattern didn't get them there as agreed, they were going to sue.

Mattern kept his temper. With great self-control he refrained from telling them there was nothing in his charter requiring him to fly suicide missions in an attempt to get people to their destination on time. If, in his estimation, the weather was too bad, he could insist on a layover.

Privately, though, he was anxious to go on. He had built something of a reputation for getting his people where they wanted to go.

He spent half an hour studying the weather charts and listening to the reports coming in from the checkpoints—Apia Airport at Samoa, Canton Island, Guam, Manila. The general word was that bad storms were sweeping in from the east, and worse storms were moving in from the west. There was still a slice of clear sky on the direct northeast route from Suva to Honolulu, with no guarantees as to how long it would hold up.

Mattern made his decision. However, as he roared northward into the night a short while later, he felt grave misgivings. The plane was heavy, burdened to capacity with fuel. That would hurt its maneuverability. In case of trouble there was no place en route to land except Canton Island, and there was 1500 miles of empty sea between Canton Island and Oahu.

The first hint of a storm came an hour out of Suva. Air currents began getting violent on the westward. The sleeping pineapple executives woke up and wanted to know what the matter was.

"Just a couple of bumps," Mattern told them. "Go back to sleep."

The bumps grew worse. Mattern veered sharply eastward toward Samoa, figuring he could make an emergency landing at Apia if things got really bad. But when he had gone 50 miles off course, he felt another storm come riding in out of the east.

He was sandwiched between the storms—and in trouble.

The passengers were up. The plane was being tossed like a straw in the winds.

"Get your life preservers on," Mattern said brusquely.

"Are we going to crash?" they asked.

"I'm not putting any bets either way. Just sit tight."

It was too late for the landing at Apia; Mattern computed they had already passed somewhere north of Samoa. In any event, the storm was too powerful to the east. The radio brought in nothing but static, and the framework of the old plane creaked and groaned.

The breakup came four hours out from Suva. An engine quit, rebelling at the workload Mattern was forced to impose on it. The other engine sputtered and the plane wobbled. They were in the middle of the storm now and darkness cloaked the ocean. A lightning flash gave Mattern a view of a tiny atoll a few miles, to the east. He figured on chancing a belly-landing, swimming ashore, and waiting to be rescued. It would probably mean the loss of the ship, and it would certainly mean that the pineapple executives were going to miss .their conference, but there was nothing else to be done. The twin pincers of the storm had closed in too fast.

The plane limped toward the atoll. Mattern was still more than a mile away when he saw that the end had come. They had lost altitude and the waves were just a hundred feet below. The white-faced passengers looked sick.

"I'm going to bring her down," Mattern said. "The instant she hits, get that door open and get yourselves out."

He had crashed before, during the war. He knew what to do. There was the stunning moment of impact and he realized it hadn't been a good landing. They had come in nose first. Within seconds the hull would have a thousand leaks.

The water came pouring in. Mattern found his escape hatch and looked back at the passengers, who were pulling open their door in the rear. Mattern breathed a sigh of relief; they would get out in time, safe and sound.

At least that was the way it looked. He vaulted through the hatch, found himself a few feet under the surface, and breast-stroked upward until his head broke water. He bobbed, looking around.

Where was the plane? Where were his passengers?

Mattern felt a sharp, stunning pang of shock. The plane had gone down like a stone seconds after he had abandoned it. And somehow the two numb-witted pineapple men had managed to remain inside. It was the only explanation. He waited, hoping to see two heads pop up above the waves. He was alone.

He felt sick with guilt, knowing that he should have remained aboard until he saw them safely out. But they had had the door open; all they had to do was launch themselves out. Had they been afraid to leave the plane? Had they quarreled over who would be the first to leave? Had they both had fainting fits?

For one reason or another, they had been trapped at the very moment of escape. And they were gone.

Passengers gone, plane gone. There was no way to call back this night, no way to reel back the strands of time, no way to stay in Suva. Mattern had made his choice, and he had lost everything but his life.

He swung around and struck out for shore. They had come down only a few hundred yards from the beach. He swam quickly but he hit trouble twenty yards off shore. A powerful undertow hurled him back to sea; he felt himself being dragged down and he had to swim wildly, madly just to stay where he was. He forced his way to shore with sheer brute effort, stumbled out onto the beach, was washed back, came up again. This time his left leg became wedged between two rocks. He pulled himself loose, feeling savage pains shoot thigh-high. Had he come this far only to meet with a fluke accident at the last moment? His knee throbbed agonizingly and it was beginning to swell.

Hobbling ashore, Mattern sagged to the white sand and lay there a few minutes getting his breath. Dawn was beginning to break. He knew it wasn't safe to remain here, exposed to the mercy of the tides. Like a giant turtle crawling ponderously inland to lay eggs, Mattern dragged himself up the 100-yard-wide strip of beach into the jungle region just beyond. The effort of pulling himself along was hellish. His left leg seemed to be on fire. He reached a clearing in the thickly wooded region and could go no further.

The next thing he knew, the sun was high in the sky and a bullwhip was exploding in his face.

THE FOUR girls who found Mattern brought him to a small village not far inland. He was growing dizzy from the combined effects of shock, exposure and the pain of his wrenched knee. But he knew he was still rational enough to trust the evidence of his eyes, and his eyes told him he had been cast ashore on an island of beautiful young women. Dozens of them came crowding up to see him. Some wore floral-printed *lavalavas* that covered them from breasts to mid-thighs. Others, more casual, wore only a brief twist of bright cloth or woven pandanus fiber around their waists. Mattern felt he had arrived in paradise, surrounded as he was by so many half-nude and near-nude girls.

They carried him into the *popui*, the large thatched meeting hut that is the hub of any Polynesian village, and bedded him down on pandanus mats. He was dimly aware that they were ripping away his tattered trousers to inspect his swollen knee. There was much muttered comment of sympathy above him. His clothes were waterlogged and salty and he made no resistance as they stripped him completely and wound a strip of their own cloth around his middle. With infinite gentleness one of the girls bound his throbbing leg with a cool poultice made from palm leaves. They swabbed his sunburned chest and shoulders with a soothing liquid.

He slept. He had no idea just how long he was unconscious, but he later thought he was delirious and fever-wracked for two or three days. When he became fully aware of his surroundings, the swelling in his knee had gone down, his skin no longer felt parboiled from his hours of lying in the sun, and his brain was clear.

A girl squatted by his side, holding out a mug of fermented coconut milk. "Drink this."

He took it without discussion and drained it. Handing back the empty mug, he smiled his gratitude. She was 16 or 17, no more. She wore only a loincloth and her young breasts, high and round, showed none of the loss of shape that Polynesian girls often suffer after bearing children.

"You are well now, *mana'ia?*"

"I'm a lot better. How about some more *kava?*"

She refilled the mug with the coconut milk. "We saw your sky bird fall just before the sunrise. But it was many hours before we could find you."

"Why did you greet me with spears and a whip?" Mattern asked. "Were you expecting trouble?"

The girl laughed. "We are warriors, *mana'ia*. We would not go unarmed."

Mattern spent the next fifteen minutes talking to the girl, who was named Tafanuii. He learned he was on an atoll in the Tokelau Group, a bit of coral called Nukutapu. It was located a couple of miles northeast of Atafu, where all these girls were from. Nukutapu itself was uninhabited, but once each year all the young unmarried women of Atafu came over by outrigger for an eight-week period of warrior training. Mattern smiled when he heard that. He realized he had stumbled into the Polynesian equivalent of a female ROTC camp!

Tafanuii went on to explain that the unmarried women of the island were expected to serve as a militia corps, the island having a considerable surplus of women. So each year they went away for drills and maneuvers without the distraction of having the menfolk around.

"If that's the case," Mattern said, "I'll have to leave, won't I?"

"Oh, no," Tafanuii said hastily. "You are the *mana'ia!* Your presence here will be a blessing to us all!"

She would not elaborate on that. Left alone, Mattern wondered just what she meant.

He was treated with loving care for the next few days, until he was strong enough to walk about. They stuffed him with yams, fish, breadfruit and pepper-root pulp until he had to throw up his hands in protest. By his sixth day on Nukutapu Mattern was able to hobble around with the aid of a stout wooden staff.

Leaving the *popui* for the first time, he hobbled out to have a look at the atoll in broad daylight. It was tiny, he saw, perhaps half a mile wide, three or four miles long, ringing a clear lagoon. It was horseshoe-shaped and the native village was near the lower prong of one side. Directly across the lagoon, at the other side of the atoll, the land rose steeply to form a hill perhaps 600 feet high. The geography of the atoll was far from unusual. But the maneuvers taking place that morning decidedly were.

FROM his vantage point in front of the *popui*, Mattern could see eighty or ninety girls divided up into several groups, each under the supervision of an older woman who wielded a bullwhip, apparently as a symbol of authority. To Mattern's right, a dozen nude girls were practicing the technique of the spear, using the carcass of a pig for a dummy. Their lady drill sergeant peppered her lesson with lively Polynesian invective.

To the left, a wrestling demonstration seemed to be taking place. Eight or ten girls sat cross-legged in a circle, watching two nude instructors. Their bodies, oiled with animal fat, glistened magnificently in the hot sun. Mattern watched them awhile, fascinated by the rippling play of muscles in their thighs and lean buttocks. No one appeared to pay any attention to him.

Wandering further from the *popui*, he looked down toward the lagoon and saw twenty girls in outrigger canoes. A race seemed to be in progress, across to the other prong of the horseshoe and back. One squadron was undergoing training in the use of the murderous double-edged islander blade.

Mattern was astounded by the efficiency of the organization. Perhaps these were simple island people, but they certainly had this training program worked out with skill and organizational know-how.

Taking a seat on a rock in front of the *popui*, Mattern waited for morning maneuvers to end. The wrestling session broke up first. Modestly donning their loincloths and lava lavas, they left the rough mats of the wrestling area and came running over, like so many gay, giggly schoolgirls, to cluster about Mattern.

One of the whip-wielders stepped forward. She was lean, with small breasts and thick muscle-corded arms.

"You have regained your strength, *mana'ia*," she said in a cold, quiet way. "I am A'aunia. I lead here."

Mattern made a gesture of respect.

A'aunia returned the gesture unsmilingly. "You have blessed us with your coming. And you shall bless us further, mana'ia. You shall give us many god-children and our tribe shall grow strong."

Mattern's jaw dropped. He repeated A'aunia's words to himself, wondering if he had translated wrongly. No, she had definitely said, "You shall give us many god-children."

Suddenly he realized why he had been nursed so carefully on an island where no man of the tribe was permitted to set foot. His white skin had aroused admiration among the warrior women, for white men were still rare on many islands in this area. These gals had a definite use for him—as a stud!

It was incredible, Mattern thought. There were about a hundred girls. Did they expect him to make love to all of them?

He had heard legends of this sort before, of islands in the South Pacific where the male population was dying out, whether through disease or accidents of genetics or simply the temptation to roam.

Mattern's shoulders drooped. He was as virile as the next man, and he had the typical free-and-easy South Pacific attitude about taking sex where it could be found. But there was a difference between a bit of casual romance with a willing girl and serving as a stud for a whole militia of young women. He didn't think his constitution would stand up to it.

He was right.

The island women had simply been waiting for him to regain his strength. Now that he was up and around they weren't going to let any more time go to waste.

That night after sundown a girl came to his hut. She was shy and skittish but far from backward about the reason for her visit. Mattern decided there was no point in trying to fight it. As long as he remained on the island, he was going to be in demand.

That first nocturnal encounter was pleasant.

But four hours after the first girl had left, he was awakened by a second. She stood over him, her lithe brown body gleaming in the moonlight that poured through the opening in the hut. She could hardly have been as old as 16. Grinning to display perfect white teeth, she slipped her hands to her narrow waist and undid the knot of her *lavalava*. Mattern felt her warm body pressing urgently up against his own.

"Give me a child, *mana'ia*. Give me a son who will be a chief someday and fly a sky bird!" she implored.

As the days—and nights—passed, a definite routine was established. Mattern received the kind of treatment that a prize stallion merits. During the day he was waited on hand and foot. There were girls waiting with breakfast for him when he awoke. When he was finished he would go down to the lagoon, strip and swim in the crystal-clear water for half an hour or so, then come ashore and lie in the sun. Maneuvers would have been underway for some time. They began at sunrise each day, with every girl up and down to the lagoon for a brisk swim covering two miles or more.

During the day, while Mattern loafed, the girls drilled with incredible vitality—knife play, wrestling, canoeing, spear-thrusting. At midday they would stop, take a brief dip to cool off, and eat. Once again Mattern would be gorged to the brim, the idea apparently being that the more he was fed, the more virile he would be.

In the afternoon it was more of the same. Then in the evening, just before sundown, there would be a *luau* at the beach. The island was full of small wild pigs, and a hunting detail would bring several of these in every day. The girls cooked the pigs and wrapped the meat in green banana leaves. There was hula dancing, singing, and plenty of fermented coconut milk to drink.

During the hula each girl moved with greater frenzy in an attempt to outshine the others, until Mattern was half-dazed by the profusion of swaying bosoms and undulating hips that surrounded him.

Then night would fall. It was a time of rest for the warrior girls, but not for Mattern. Twice and sometimes three times a night he would be visited in his hut at the edge of the clearing. Since it was dark it was difficult to tell whether any of the girls were coming more than once. But he was pretty certain that a group as rigidly disciplined as this one would make sure that each girl had her turn with the *mana'ia* before the cycle began again.

Mattern found his virility holding up surprisingly well. The perfect weather and the abundance of food had an aphrodisiac effect on him, stimulating his desires to an abnormal pitch. And the long hours of idleness each day left him more than adequately rested for his nightly tasks.

Still, he felt humiliated at being used in this way. He realized quite clearly that, regarded as a god or not, he was nothing but a prisoner, a slave. These girls had no desire for him; they simply wanted him to father children for them.

From A'aunia he learned a little more about the girls' tribe. There was such a surplus of women that most of the girls had no hope whatever of marrying. Mattern, then, was probably the only man many would ever give themselves to. They also believed that bearing a white man's child would greatly strengthen the tribe. Weren't the white men masters of the world? Didn't they fly glittering birds through the heavens? Didn't they devise weapons that could kill at hundreds of feet?

In the eyes of these people the white men were superior beings. And now they had one such superior being right where they wanted him—far from his fellow white men.

The routine went on for more than a month, while Mattern plotted ways of getting himself out of the clutches of these man-hungry Amazons. He had nothing against the girls. He was full of admiration for the way these superfluous spinsters had turned themselves into a formidable little army, and he had nothing but sympathy for their manless plight. But the stud routine was exhausting him. He was rapidly losing all interest in sex. It was a strange attitude for a healthy bachelor to have, but making love was rapidly becoming a dreaded chore for Mattern. He was now totally oblivious to the casual nudity that surrounded him. The sight of shapely breasts and curving hips no longer moved him.

Thinking things over, Mattern decided that the only hope was to plan for a rescue. There was no place for him to escape to except the home island of these women, and he would probably be kept there indefinitely. So escape on his own power was impossible. On the other hand, it was likely that any planes flying this route would have orders to keep an eye out for survivors of the crash. If he could manage to attract some attention—

That day, while the girls drilled, Mattern took a hike around the atoll. He estimated it was about three miles from the native village on this side of the horseshoe to the coral hill on the other. The quickest way to get there, of course, was by outrigger straight across the lagoon, but he didn't want to call that much attention to his activities. Instead, he slipped off quietly on foot, taking the long way.

The atoll was heavily vegetated, but by keeping to the beachward side Mattern was able to avoid the thickest brush. He walked slowly, favoring his leg, and it took him almost an hour to reach the hill. On the way he gathered fallen coconuts. The coral hill, luckily, had a gradual approach. He made his way up and found himself on a sandy plateau about 100 yards wide and close to 500 yards long. Looking down across the lagoon, he could see the girls vigorously going through their morning drills. He hoped they wouldn't look up.

Quickly Mattern dumped his burden of coconuts down in the sand and began to arrange them in the pattern of an SOS signal. They stood out clear and dark against the fine white sand.

Mattern didn't want to remain on the hill too long for fear of detection, so he left the design half-finished and returned to the village. It was almost time for the noon meal when he casually sauntered back. No one asked him where he had been.

For the next five days Mattern slipped off to the coral plateau every morning. Now three rows of SOS signals had been laid out, covering almost the entire area of the plateau. It was a natural billboard. Any plane passing overhead would spot the signal instantly—if anyone happened to look, and if any plane happened to pass overhead in the first place.

Mattern knew there was nothing he could do but wait. He had done all he could do to help himself. The rest was up to luck.

By this time he knew a number of the girls by name, and his knowledge of the dialect had improved until he understood practically everything that was being said. His special favorite among the little band of teen-age warrior girls was Tafanuii.

At meal times he found a way to sit next to Tafanuii more often than not. And during those hours of the day when the warriors were allowed to rest, she would contrive to spend time with him.

She was 17, and until Mattern had come to the island, she had never known a man. She had been one of the first to share his sleeping mat when the stud routine began.

"I bear your child within me now," she told him, grinning devilishly. "I am sure of it, *mana'ia*. I feel him stirring. He will be a mighty warrior. His skin will be white and he will stand as high as a palm tree, *mana'ia*."

Mattern smiled. It was altogether possible that he had impregnated a number of these girls. But he knew enough about the female body to know that what Tafanuii was saying simply was not true. He had been on the island a little more than a month. Even if she were pregnant, she certainly wouldn't feel the child kicking for several more months. He said nothing because he didn't want to disillusion her.

She told him: "Until you came, *mana'ia*, I thought I would never have a child. I thought I would come to be like A'aunia and the others— tough and ugly and hard. But now you have given me what I desire!"

"How is it a pretty girl like you couldn't get herself a man on Atafu?" Mattern asked.

Tafanuii shrugged. "For each man there are two or more of us. Many girls more beautiful than I am must die unmarried. My family is poor. The men choose the girl with the biggest dowry."

Mattern stared off in the distance, thinking that it must be paradise indeed for the few remaining men of Atafu if they could toss girls like Tafanuii into the discard heap of spinsterhood. But island life must be miserable for the girls.

"Tell me," he said. 'All this drilling you do, these military exercises—is your island frequently attacked by enemies?"

Tafanuii said innocently, "Oh, no. We have not been attacked since the days of my grandfather's father."

"But you keep drilling as if you expect war next week."

"We must have something to do with our lives, *mana'ia*. If an enemy ever comes, we will be prepared."

Mattern understood. The purpose of the maneuvers was only incidentally to develop military skills. The real reason for all this violent expenditure of energy was to give the girls an outlet for their bottled-up vitality. Unable to become wives and mothers, they could at least become experts with the spear and outrigger.

He asked the girl why, if there was such a surplus of women on the island, some of the extras didn't migrate elsewhere. There were many islands in the South Pacific where women were in demand. Tafanuii merely shook her head and replied that it was sinful for a woman to leave her island home. Men might wander, but a woman was bound by spiritual chains to her island. If the women left, the strength of the tribe would be lost.

Mattern didn't try to argue the point. If some deep spiritual compulsion made these girls stay on an island where they outnumbered the men more than two to one, no calmly reasoned argument was going to alter the situation.

A WEEK after Mattern had completed his SOS pattern across the plateau, he decided to revisit the area and make sure that the shifting sand hadn't covered his markers.

The day before he had received the news from A'aunia that the maneuvers would be extended indefinitely. He had been expecting something like that. After all, nobody needed the women back on Atafu, and if they remained here, eventually all of them might become pregnant by the *mana'ia.*

He thought with a trace of amusement that it would certainly startle the men of Atafu when their surplus females came back from maneuvers pregnant *en masse.* Not that a hundred fatherless children would greatly upset the economy of the island. When lunch dangled from the nearest palm tree and supper could be had by snaring a pig, there weren't any real social problems involved in raising illegitimate children, especially when these children would be the offspring of a *mana'ia,* with powerful white man's blood in their veins.

All the same, Mattern knew he couldn't take the pace much longer. The girls showed no mercy. It was an endless stream. He couldn't blame them for taking advantage of the only opportunity they would probably ever get; still, he longed for just one night of unbroken rest.

That night would not come until he was rescued from their clutches.

He was pleased to see that the wind had not obliterated his markers. Stooping, Mattern adjusted the position of a few of the coconuts. As he rose he heard a sound behind him and turned to see Tafanuii standing at the edge of the plateau, looking frightened.

"What are you doing here?" Mattern asked, startled.

"I—I saw you go away. I followed you. I wanted to know where you were going."

"You mean A'aunia sent you to spy on me, don't you?" Mattern's shoulders slumped. Now they would get rid of his markers and he would never escape.

Tafanuii shook her head. "No one sent me. I came because I wished to be with you." Staring down at the sand, she dug her bare toes in. "You have come here many times. Each morning I saw you leave and wondered where you went." Her eyes glittered with sudden shrewdness. "You have been making a design in the sand. You hope other white men's sky birds will fly overhead and see it!"

"I want to return to my own people, Tafanuii," Mattern said quietly.

"You will leave us."

"I've been here a long time. Now I want to be with my own people again."

"I hoped you would not leave," she said sadly.

Mattern glanced at her uneasily. A word to A'aunia and everything was ruined. They would probably keep him under guard in the hut while he performed his stud duties.

He clenched his fists. "Tafanuii— will you tell A'aunia what I have done?"

"It is my duty. She is my leader. But—" She shook her head. "It is not fair to those who have not had their chance to bear your children, *mana'ia*. But I myself, having known you—I would wish that you could return to your people if it would make you happy."

"It would make me very happy."

She brightened. "Then I will say nothing to A'aunia."

Mattern wondered what the decision had cost her in internal conflict. She had already broken discipline by following him here. And now, by failing to report his signaling attempts—

Suddenly she shaded her eyes and pointed at the bright blue sky. "Look, *mana'ia!* The sky bird!"

Mattern looked up. A moment later he heard the familiar, wonderful drone of engines and there was the plane, a silvery dart glinting in the sun and heading toward Nukutapu.

"They are coming for you!" the girl cried excitedly. "Your people have come!"

The plane was no more than a mile south of the atoll now. Mattern hesitated a moment; then, running to the middle of the plateau, he threw up his arms and waved wildly. It didn't matter now if A'aunia or the others spotted him up here. This was his chance and if he didn't grab it, he was finished.

Suddenly Tafanuii was at his side. With complete innocence she wriggled out of the *lavalava* that was her single garment and began to wave the brightly-colored cloth high above her head.

THE PLANE was directly overhead now. Mattern kept waving until his arms felt as if they would drop from their sockets. At his side the lithe, nude girl continued her efforts in his behalf.

"They see us!" Mattern cried. "They're circling. They're circling!"

Indeed the small plane was dipping down, swinging around the atoll at an altitude of no more than 1500 feet. Mattern could almost make out the faces of the men in the cockpit. They buzzed the island three times and then, straightening out, streaked off in the direction from which they had come.

"They are not coming," Tafanuii said sadly.

"But they saw us," Mattern cried. "There's no place for them to land here, but they've gone back to their base for a helicopter." He did a little dance of joy.

Tafanuii stood dejectedly, her *lavalava* drooping from her hand. Tears were beginning to glisten in the comers of her eyes. Mattern looked at her as she stood there, knowing that she was both happy and sad. And for the first time in more than a month he felt genuine desire for a woman. He folded her in his arms, pressing her warmth to him, tingling from the contact with her slim nudity.

They made love on the sand, under the blazing morning sun. It was one of the strangest moments in Mattern's life, a shimmering, trembling instant in which he felt something quite close to love for the girl. Then the moment passed.

"Come," Mattern said hoarsely. "Let's go back."

They returned together, reaching the village more than an hour later. A'aunia herself came striding up to meet them. She was carrying her whip and she looked furious. She lifted the whip as if to strike Tafanuii.

"No!" Mattern roared. "Don't hit her!"

It was the first time since his arrival that he had attempted to assert any authority. A'aunia was so stunned by his tone of voice that she lowered the whip.

Mattern said sternly: "Tafanuii is the loved one of the *mana'ia*. She must not be harmed."

"As you wish," A'aunia said.

Mattern went on: "You saw the sky bird overhead. My people are coming to take me away. I have given many of you children. Now you must let me go."

Somewhat to his own surprise, Mattern discovered he had cowed the formidable A'aunia. Perhaps the sight of the plane had reminded the girls that they had better not fool around with a *mana'ia*.

Obediently, though with obvious reluctance, they yielded to him. A last meal was prepared. Mattern saw plenty of tears.

One of the weepers really surprised him. It was A'aunia herself, the hard-as-nails commander. She turned away from him to hide her overflowing eyes. Like a good leader, she had not gone to Mattern herself, preferring to wait until the younger girls had had their chance. And now A'aunia's opportunity was gone forever. Tough, stringy-bodied, she had no chance of getting a man and she knew it. She was destined for a permanent career as a military woman.

Mattern felt a pang of pity for her. He even toyed with the idea of inviting her to go off with him before the rescuers arrived. But he knew her proud nature would never permit her to accept the indignity of a last-ditch act like that.

Several hours later a US Army helicopter operating out of Apia, Samoa, landed on the beach. A grinning, tanned Mike Mattern clambered aboard, pausing to turn back and wave to 100 half-nude girls who gazed mournfully after him.

"I'm Mike Mattern," he said, getting down into a bucket seat as the copter spiraled upward. "Private pilot operating out of Auckland. My plane cracked up here about seven weeks ago."

"You had the pineapple people aboard?" one of the Army men asked.

Mattern nodded. "They got tangled up and couldn't get out of the ship. I've been stranded here all by myself."

"All by yourself except for a hundred girls! The guys who saw your SOS told us you were all alone on a plateau with some beautiful babe who was using her sarong to wave with—and she didn't have another stitch on. What a life!"

Mattern Sighed. He wanted to tell them it had been anything but paradise. But try telling a couple of girl-hungry GIs that it's not great to be stranded on a desolate atoll with a horde of eager Polynesian belles!

He shrugged. "It was okay," he said. "But you can have too much of a good thing, get me?"

Mike Mattern returned to New Zealand in December of 1952. After several years of working for a commercial airline he was once again able to go into business for himself. He's still out there, plying the airlanes of the South Pacific. His life has been pretty uneventful—no more crashes, no more harems.

But, he told us, he's getting the itch to pay a visit to the island of Atafu. He's curious to see just how many little half-breeds of about 6 years are running around there. After all these years he wants to take a look-see and meet his family. **///**

"The Godfather" by Mario Puzo
*Male*, August 1969    Cover by Mort Künstler

## MARIO PUZO

— INTERVIEW BY JOSH ALAN FRIEDMAN —

**THE ENTIRE** *genre of the Mafia in books, movies and its countless cultural spinoffs, from video games to pizza chains, originated from the powerful imagination of Mario Puzo. Puzo (1920-1999) gave few interviews, preferring to represent himself from behind the typewriter. A World War II vet, MP's novels include* The Dark Arena, The Fortunate Pilgrim, The Godfather *and* Fools Die; *non-fiction books include* The Godfather Papers *and* Inside Las Vegas; *screenplays include the three* Godfather *films,* Earthquake *and* Superman. *The following interview was conducted in 1984.*

**When did you arrive and which titles did you work on?**

When I got to Magazine Management, I think it was '60. I worked on *Male* and *Men.*

**Did you save any of your issues?**

I had some, but I don't know where the hell they are now.

**Did you ever meet any authentic readers of the magazines back then?**

Naw. But I got letters, the magazines got letters. They would correct factual details, which was very funny, 'cause the whole piece was usually made up.

**How did it feel when you ran out of real battles and started making up new World War II battles?**

Oh, it was a lot of fun. I wrote "A Bridge Too Far," that story of the Arnhem invasion. After you got through reading *my* story, you thought the Allies won the battle, not the Germans.

**Weren't there any letters doubting this version?**

Never. I got the airborne division wrong and received a letter about that. The funniest time was when the FBI came up to investigate

**Mario Puzo *(left)* at a Magazine Management party with friend and editor Bruce Jay Friedman *(right)*, 1966**

us on a story made up about Russia. We printed some photos from Russia of people on the beach, and identified them as a group from the underground, or one of those bullshit things, and the FBI came up to ask us to really identify them. They talked mostly to [associate editor] Bernie Garfinkel, but he wouldn't spill the beans. Finally, just to get rid of them, he told 'em, hey, the story was all made up.

**Did you use any of your own World War II experiences in those stories?**

I used to love to do research—like when I wrote an adventure story about the Arctic, I would read all the Arctic books. I became an expert on the Arctic. Then I did an article on sharks, which was fascinating. It never occurred to me that sharks would make a novel or a movie. Doing research, I came across the story of *The Sting* in an old book, which I remember because it was such a good scam. But again, it never occurred to me it would make a movie.

**You used to have a lot of books around your desk.**

Yeah, well remember, I had to turn out three stories a month, and by doing all that research, it wasn't that hard. I'll tell ya, sometimes I would read 10 or 20 books to do one article. I'd go to the library and get 'em. I loved to read and I'm a very fast reader. I could read two books a day, so I just used to eat 'em up. I used to read them on company time and at home. We were always looking for stuff we could take off on, so part of our job was reading a lot.

**In recent years they've been digging out your old Mag Management stories and making what seem to be illegitimate movies out of them.**

Yeah, well the book bonuses, which were long stories, were very much like movie scripts. When I came to do movie scripts, essentially what I did was write a book bonus, which was broken up into dialog and description of scenes. You had to be economical, you had to cram as much action and plot as possible into a short space.

**Did you sense 25 years ago that it was so close to writing a movie script?**

No, because at that time, I was never interested in writing for the movies. It never occurred to me that someday I would be a guy who wrote movies. I didn't think of those stories in movie terms.

*Male,* November 1965
Illustration by Gil Cohen

**I remember a paperback with the "Mario Cleri" pseudonym.**

That was called "Six Graves to Munich" in the magazine. Then I wrote it as a movie script, *Six Graves for Rogan*. I made a lot of money on it, because I had it optioned about four times, and then finally it was made into a terrible movie. I had my name taken off the screenplay, but I got credit, you know, story by Mario Puzo. [*The film was released in 1982 as A Time to Die.*]

**Don't you have to keep a close eye on that today, if producers go scouring through old magazines for stories with your pen name?**

Yeah, but they're so similar. Like, *The A-Team* on TV today. I wrote a story called "The Lorch Team." I turned that into a movie script that's been optioned. But they got the idea, I think, from that story I wrote.

**When did these stories start to get optioned?**

After *The Godfather*.

**Did you ever write a story at Magazine Management which was a direct predecessor to *The Godfather*?**

The funny thing is, I don't think I ever wrote anything about gangsters. They were usually pure adventure stories dealing with the war or some exotic locale. The magazines didn't print gangster stuff, that wasn't part of our repertoire, as they say.[1]

**Banner Books, 1967**
**#B50-112**

---

1        Puzo misspeaks here. Mob stories did appear in MAMs, and Puzo himself penned at least one, under his Mario Cleri pseudonym. This book's co-editor Bob Deis unearthed "Girls of Pleasure Penthouse," a gangster story set in Hawaii, in the May 1968 issue of *Male*. The story was subsequently reprinted as "The Syndicate Killers" in the 1970 *Stag Annual*, No. 9.

(Cont'd on pg. 238)

**Male,** August 1969
Illustration by Earl Norem

Though organized crime didn't figure into most stories Mario Puzo wrote during his years at Magazine Management, Puzo *did* sell serial rights to *The Godfather* to MM flagship *Male* in 1969, just as the book was settling in for its lengthy stay at the top of the bestseller list. *Male*'s high-octane *Godfather* illustrations, by pulp art masters Mort Künstler (cover, pg. 231)

AMERIGO Bonasera sat in New York Criminal Court Number 3 and waited for justice; vengeance on the men who had so cruelly hurt his daughter, who had tried to dishonor her.

The judge, a formidably heavy-featured man, rolled up the sleeves of his black robe as if to physically chastise the two young men standing before the bench. His face was cold with majestic contempt. But there was something false in all this that Amerigo Bonasera sensed but did not yet understand.

"You acted like the worst kind of degenerates," the judge said harshly. Yes, yes, thought Amerigo Bonasera. Animals. Animals. The two young men, glossy hair crew cut, scrubbed clean-cut faces composed into humble contrition, bowed their heads in submission.

He was "the Don," the most hated and feared Mafia chieftain in the country. And trying to kill him guaranteed a vengeance bloodbath . . .

By **MARIO PUZO**
ART BY EARL NOREM

# THE GODFATHER

## Exclusive $6.95 Bestseller

Reprinted by permission of G.P. Putnam's Sons from THE GOD-FATHER by Mario Puzo. Copyright © 1969 by Mario Puzo.

and Earl Norem (interiors, above and pg. 238), speak volumes about how the look, mood, and *texture* of the 1972 film adaptation would soon transform visual perceptions of the Italian mafia, sending once-ubiqutious pinstripe suits, Borsalinos, and pugilist faces to sleep with the fishes.

—*Wyatt Doyle*

**Male,** November 1965
Illustration by Samson Pollen

*(Cont'd from pg. 235)*

## Did you ever write a story on Vietnam?

Yeah, I did one or two, but they were absolute poison. The readers
didn't like to read about it. That was very early on in Vietnam. We used
to emphasize that Vietnam only had poison sticks. "How the Poison
Stick Army Beat America's Ultra-Modern Weapons," shit like that.

## But it never went over?

Nah, they hated it. Also we weren't the heroes. Just like the Korean
War—we used to call that The No Fun War. World War II was The
Fun War. And you could get some mileage out of the Civil War and
World War I. World War II was a bonanza. But Korea and Vietnam
were losers.

## Did you ever write a story about animals nibbling people apart?

No, that wasn't part of my repertoire. Just a shark story. We had
specialists. I was the big specialist for adventure and war stories.
John Bowers was the specialist on hot love stories, another guy was a
factual reporter.

*"The Godfather"*
***Male,*** **August 1969**
**Illustration by Earl Norem**

**How about the legendary, though untraceable, Walter Kaylin?**
**[*Walter Kaylin has since been located; see pg. 58 and pg. 242*]**

He was great! He wrote these great adventures, but he couldn't turn them out that fast. He was outrageous, he just carried it off. He'd have this one guy killing a thousand other guys. Then they beat him into the ground, you think he's dead, but he rises up again and kills another thousand guys.

**Remember the illustrations of huge armies that accompanied your stories?**

Bruce used to scare me to death and say we got the illos, and I hadn't even started the story yet. Sometimes you had to write a story because they had a good illustration, you'd build a story around it. You'd stray off a bit, but you wrote a scene that would correspond exactly with the action in the illo.

**They never ran abstract illustrations?**

They were literal. Bruce showed me an illo of American paratroopers dropping on the roof of a German prison camp. I wrote that scene, and worked the rest of the story around it.

**How many pages of a book bonus could you write in a typical day?**

I used to do a book bonus on the weekends, which was at least 60 pages. I never could write in the office, I had to work at home. When I was working on *The Godfather*, I was doing three stories a month, I was writing book reviews for *The New York Times*, *Book World*, *Time* magazine, and I wrote a children's book [*The Runaway Summer of Davie Shaw*]. All at one time. And I was publishing other articles. I had four years where I must have knocked out millions of words.

I tell ya, it's absolutely the best training a writer could get, to work on those magazines. You did everything.

**There's no equivalent today.**

It's a shame. If I had a son who wanted to be a writer, I wouldn't even bother to send him to college. I'd get him a job up there as an assistant editor, leave him there for five years and he'd know everything. You've got to turn out a lot of copy.

**Now that men's magazines have all gone the route of pornography, when you look back, do the Magazine Management books seem more special?**

They were innocent in a funny kind of way. We had cheesecake and the stories themselves were innocent. They were like *Doc Savage* and *The Shadow* brought up to date.

**Like comic books for grown-ups?**

Right… Walter Kaylin, come back! **///**

# The "Body Beautiful" Personal Vibrator for massaging you delightfully all over

## From Larry Mathews, famous Beauty and Health Consultant to the stars

### Complete with three versatile accessories, for massaging face and body, for muscle aches and for deep-down tensions

Here's the personal vibrator every woman can use in so many wonderful ways that it's like having your own Swedish masseuse always ready when you need her. Yes, aching muscles, tensions, minor pains due to over-exertion, all seem to melt away after just a few delightful moments with the Larry Mathews "Body Beautiful" personal massager. Its unique shape and smooth contours were specially designed to concentrate helpful, penetrating massage right *where* you need it, *when* you need it, the way ordinary massagers can't. Soon you feel good again.

Battery operated and portable, the "Body Beautiful" personal massager is 7½" long and 1⅜" in diameter, the perfect size for home use and for traveling. You'll be amazed at how regular toning sessions in the privacy of your own home can become a delightful part of your life.

So don't put up for a single day longer with those nagging aches and tensions that the "Body Beautiful" personal massager designed to relieve so well. Delightfully feminine in its sleek black housing with gleaming golden inset, the "Body Beautiful" personal vibrator comes complete with foam pad for massaging in face and body creams, a cup accessory for deep-down aches and a special accessory for concentrated massage where you need it. Yet all it costs, complete with batteries, is just $8.95. What a small price to pay for years of invigorating, stimulating, relaxing pleasure. Satisfaction guaranteed or your money back.

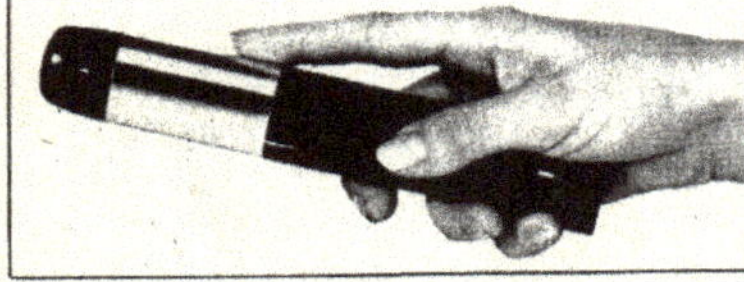

INVIGORATING!
STIMULATING!
RELAXING!

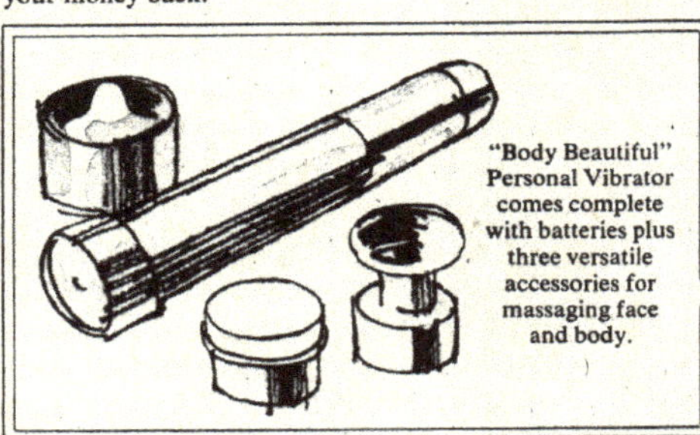

"Body Beautiful" Personal Vibrator comes complete with batteries plus three versatile accessories for massaging face and body.

# ABOUT KAYLIN'S "'CALL GIRL SLAVE' RING"

WHAT MORE *fitting way to drive home what an asset Walter Kaylin was to Magazine Management Company (and the wider realm of MAMs and MAM fiction) than to go another round with the great one?*

*And if you're interested in MAMs, you'll want to go another round. Then another. And another. You'll want to follow his shifting voices and try to keep pace with his relentless momentum, as he stacks up those uniquely Kaylin-esque plot complications in every MAM genre—Westerns, bizarre exotica, crime stories, war tales, animal attacks, you name it—all of it. Because he wrote all of it.*

*Obviously, we're fans. We took our admiration of Kaylin's stories further following* Weasels' *initial publication, assembling* He-Men, Bag Men, & Nymphos *as the second release from The Men's Adventure Library, and the first-ever collection of Walter Kaylin's MAM stories.*

*We said farewell to Walter in 2017, but he lived to see* Nymphos, *and we're glad he was celebrated while he was here to enjoy it.*

*This selection is also an opportunity to note how MAMs drew inspiration not only from history and headlines, but from ripples in the culture: Our second story by Kaylin comes from the days when airline flight attendants were mostly*

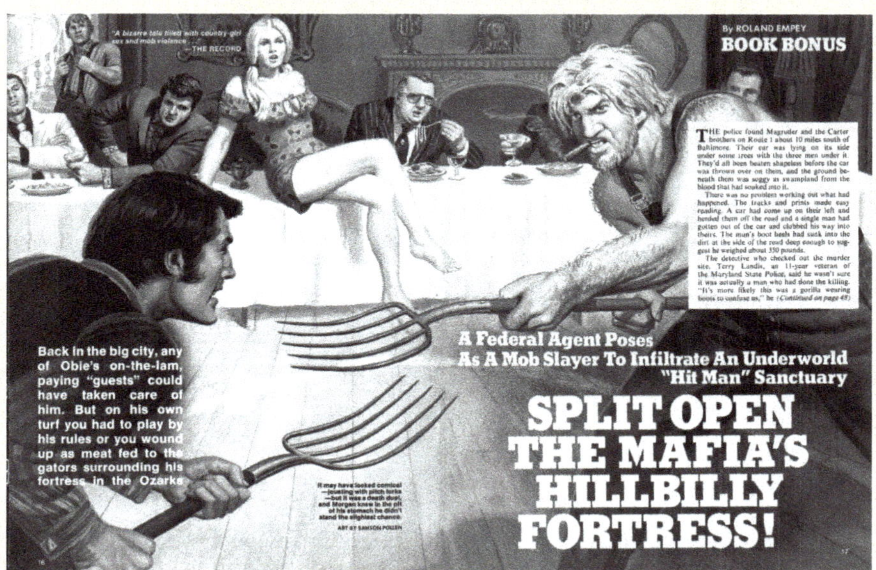


**For Men Only**, October 1973
Illustration by Samson Pollen

**In which Kaylin (as Roland Empey) delivers a Mafia-supported hillbilly pitchfork fight.**

good-looking women and were called stewardesses.

The private lives of "stews" would inspire a slew of racy stories and books following the success of the sexy bestseller Coffee, Tea or Me? An international publishing sensation, it embedded a catchphrase into the English language, but was later revealed to be a hoax, authored by veteran paperback ghostwriter Donald Bain. It was MAM-style hyperbole and hyper-sexualization in slightly (but only slightly) more upmarket dress.

So, a cultural phenomenon built around the idea that good-looking uniformed women in a service profession are quietly (but wildly) promiscuous and lead hidden lives of erotic adventure beyond one's wildest imaginings? And the whole thing is completely made up anyway?

Kaylin to the copy desk!

A hoax built upon a hoax, Kaylin's "The Stewardess Call Girl Slave Ring" was published in the December 1971 issue of For Men Only under his frequent pen name Roland Empey. It was touted as a "Sensational True Book Bonus," but in fact, there was no book. Nor is there any truth to it.

But it is sensational.

Taking a distinctly different tone than his sweat-and-lust-drenched

*"Congo noir" featured earlier in this collection ("Bar Room Girl Who Touched Off a Tribal War," pg. 59), Kaylin here delivers a shaggy-dog detective story that only gets shaggier as it unfolds. This is the kind of bursting-at-the-seams storytelling that consistently left his editors and peers—not to mention his readers—with jaws agape.*

*With the then-topical subject of sexually liberated flight attendants as a springboard, Kaylin goes into pulp fiction overdrive, top-loading his tale with not one but several popular MAM tropes. Part hard-boiled detective story, part hookers-help-the-hero adventure, with an entirely fabricated "scratch the surface" sexposé worked in for good measure, Kaylin even manages to fold in seemingly sympathetic nods to the hippie movement, and take a few well-deserved jabs at the hypocrisy of small town holier-than-thou types. And despite the bulk of the story's action taking place in sunny (albeit fictionalized) Valencia Hills, California, the sheriff's station is peopled with seedy lawmen who are as redneck as backyard wrestling.*

*From the resourceful, tough-talking PI willing to accept an orgy in lieu of payment, to an entire airline's flight staff happily sidelining in the world's oldest profession, the story is a blast.*

*The use of stock photos as illustrations is clearly a cost-saving move by the publisher, and adds yet another wacky dimension to the ramshackle silliness. In an effort to add menace to a staid portrait of a mountain hotel, the caption reads, "Photo shows building* similar to one *where white slavers held girls captive." (Emphasis added.)* Similar *to one, you say? Duly noted.*

*At least the lodge roughly matches the story's requirements; a grainy shot of a bikini babe being loaded into a small seaplane (black bars across the eyes,* True Detective-*style, to preserve the victim's anonymity) tacks on an entirely new angle to a story already stretched to the limits of plausibility—and which, it should be mentioned, features neither bikinis nor seaplanes. Per the caption: "Members of ring sometimes had to ferry 'drugged' girls down to warmer resort areas to accommodate calls from 'special' clients who didn't want to make trip." Perhaps Kaylin was saving that revelation for the sequel.*

*By 1971, when this story saw print, MAMs as the reading public had long known them were already fading from the publishing landscape. Kaylin's sex-heavy, over-the-top kidnap yarn serves both as a fitting epitaph for the heightened style of storytelling the mags perfected, and as a twilight fireworks display by one of the very best in the field.*

*— Wyatt Doyle & Robert Deis*

**"THE STEWARDESS 'CALL GIRL SLAVE' RING"**

WALTER KAYLIN (AS ROLAND EMPEY)

*For Men Only*, December 1971

**Sensational
True Book Bonus**

# They Kidnapped And Rented Them Out To High-Paying "Johns"

# THE STEWARDESS "CALL GIRL SLAVE" RING

**By ROLAND EMPEY**

Girls (like at left) were told to wear uniform for "hostess" duty and then were abducted.

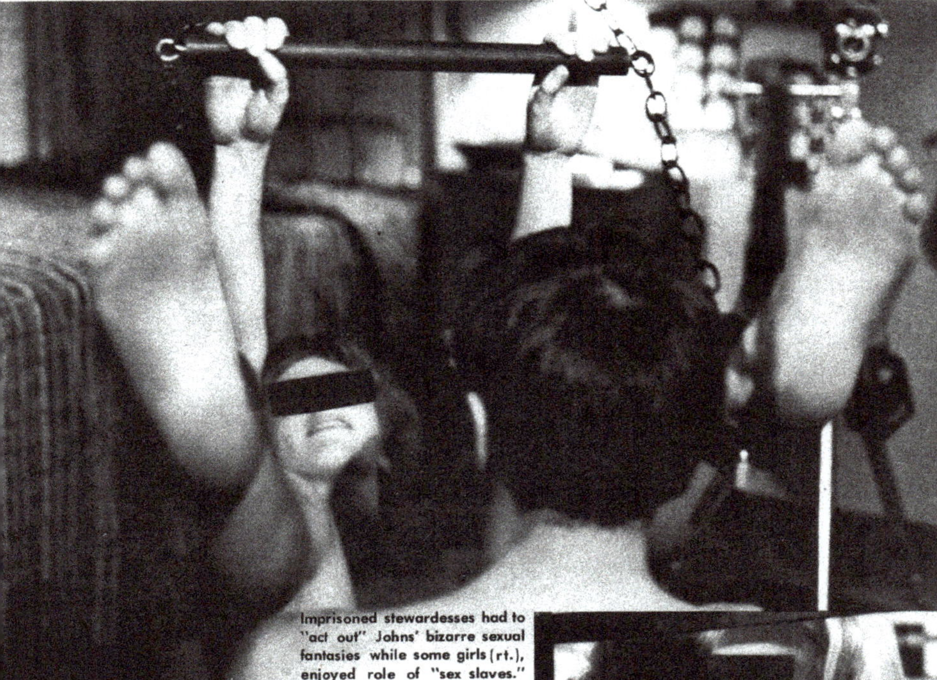

Imprisoned stewardesses had to "act out" Johns' bizarre sexual fantasies while some girls (rt.), enjoyed role of "sex slaves."

## It started out as just a routine search for a missing call girl. But before he was finished Franklin had uncovered the hideout of a ruthless gang of cut-throats that kept a harem of drugged girls for the pleasure of lust-crazed men

*Valencia Hills, California, July 26, 1971*—I was the only one that got off the train. The only one on the platform was the town marshall. He clanked toward me looking like Wild Bill Hickok in his chaps, spurs and 10-gallon hat. He had to have a gun of some sort on him somewhere, but I couldn't locate. His face as straight up and down as a red brick and his eyes looked like black raisins poked into it.

"Got business in Valencia Hills?"

"Yeah, I'm looking for a girl," I said, taking Adele Hopkins' picture from my pocket "This girl."

She was wearing her Mountain-Atlantic Airlines uniform. It was a black-and-white shot so you couldn't see he had red hair

41

**VALENCIA** *Hills, California, July 26, 1971*—I was the only one that got off the train. The only one on the platform was the town marshal. He clanked toward me looking like Wild Bill Hickok in his chaps, spurs and 10-gallon hat. He had to have a gun of some sort on him somewhere, but I couldn't locate it. His face was straight up and down as a red brick and his eyes looked like black raisins poked into it.

"Got business in Valencia Hills?"

"Yeah, I'm looking for a girl," I said, taking Adele Hopkins' picture from my pocket. "This girl."

She was wearing her Mountain-Atlantic Airlines uniform. It was a black-and-white shot so you couldn't see she had red hair. But you had no trouble seeing she was all doll anyway. The marshal said, "We got a few of them down at Comanche Street. You can come take a look if you want."

Comanche Street turned out to be the name of the town jail. He drove me over in his Jeep. It took us through the neatest cleanest streets I'd ever seen. The few people we passed were neat and clean, too, and the closest thing I saw to a hot spot was a movie theatre showing *The Sound of Music.* As we drove he told me his name was Jesse Thomas and then he gave me his philosophy of life.

"Drugs is sapping the life blood of America. Long hair and homosexuals and all this other freak stuff is making us easy prey for the Red overthrow. We don't hold with any of that pervert crap in Valencia Hills. Anyone wants to come and live the clean life with us, we're glad to have him. But anyone that's into drugs and using his body for dirty purposes…he ain't welcome here and we got ways of letting him know it."

I said: "I'm not figuring on staying here long enough to test any of the local ordinances. All I want to do is find this girl and bring her back to New York. If I can do that, I won't even be here long enough to get one of your streets dirty by spitting in it."

"She is a relative?"

"No, she's a missing person and I've been hired to find her. I'm a private detective. Harry Franklin."

"She running away from her family?"

"No, she met a guy on one of her flights and they shacked up in a hotel in New York that night. The next morning they were gone without her telling her friends anything about it and she hasn't been seen since. That was six days ago. It's her friends that are paying me to find her."

"Why're you looking for her out here?" he asked. "What makes you think she's out here in Valencia Hills?"

"I told you she met the guy on one of her flights. Well, I checked the passenger list and his name is Leon Appleton and his permanent residence is listed as Valencia Hills. The girl must have been with him."

"We don't have no Leon Appleton here," Thomas said positively. "I know everyone in this town to talk to personally and we don't have no Leon Appleton."

We were at the Comanche Street jail by then, a squat, square building, old-fashioned but clean. Beyond it were the slopes of the Sierra Nevada Mountains with snow gleaming white on the peaks. We went inside and a beefy deputy, wearing his own cowboy get-up, came out saying, "That you, Jesse?"

"Take this man downstairs and show him what we got there. He's looking for a missing woman. I'll be in the office seeing if I can find anything that'll help him."

I followed the deputy down a flight of stone steps to the basement. At the bottom he shouted, "All right, up on your feet and under the light, you pervert queers. This man wants to take a look at you."

There were about seven or eight hippies in a wire cell. They were a pretty scruffy lot—clothes ripped up and dirty and most of them bruised up around the face. There were three or four girls in with them and even without their getting under the naked light bulb, I could see none of them was Adele Hopkins.

I said, "She's not there," but the deputy was getting himself all steamed up because they hadn't gotten up the way he'd told them to. "I told you queers to get up on your feet," he shouted. When they didn't move, he ran to a window opening out onto an alley and began reeling in a heavy hose. He reached outside to turn a faucet and sent a high-pressure stream of water blasting into the cell, knocking the prisoners around like tenpins, banging them up against the bars, scuttling them around for places to hide even though there weren't any there. I could hear them shouting for him to turn it off, but he was having too much fun. "A little water won't hurt you…get some of that dirt off of you."

I got up next to him and put my mouth to his face. It caught

him off balance and swung him around over the back of a chair and
I grabbed the hose out of his hands and directed it into the seat of
his pants.

When he stopped hopping he tumbled into a corner of the room,
hollering for me to let up on him. I played the hose all over him from a
foot or so away, and when he looked like he was going to drown, gasping
and spluttering. I turned the hose off and began wrapping it around his
neck. I was in the process of putting a knot in it when Thomas came
downstairs. "What's the trouble, what's going on here?" he exploded.

"What," I asked, "do you get around here for interfering with an
officer in the lawful performance of his duty? Ten bucks? All right, here
it is." I took a ten dollar bill out of my pocket and handed it over.

Thomas didn't in the end seem particularly bothered by what happened.
You look like a fool.

"I've got some pictures upstairs," he said to me, "of everyone
we've had in here. I didn't see anyone that looks like the woman in that
picture, but you can take a look yourself if you want."

As I started out after him, one of the girls spoke from the cell.

"They'll beat the hell out of us as soon as you're gone, mister. That
big horse you tied up in the hose can't wait to start stomping us."

"What are they in here for?" I asked Thomas.

"Vagrancy. No visible means of support."

"How much?"

"Heck! We don't want to make any money out of them. We just
want them out of town. Give me a hundred and you can have 'em."

I handed him over a fifty, two twenties and a ten and he motioned
for the deputy to unlock the cell. As we went upstairs they came
along behind us and as I went into Thomas's office with him. The
prisoners filed outside the building. Thomas gave me a book of prisoner
snapshots and sat swiveling in his chair behind the desk until I'd
finished looking through it. "Looks like she's never been here, don't it?
I guess maybe you came out here on a wild goose chase. What are you
going to do now?"

I shrugged and got up to go.

I went out of the building and was surprised to see the hippies
sitting on the steps outside waiting for me. The girl who had talked
to me from the cell was waiting to talk to me. She stood up as I came
toward them and said, "That was nice of you. They would have stomped
us alright. Did I hear you say you're trying to find someone?"

I showed her the picture. "This girl."

She looked at it and handed it back to me, shaking her head. "I never saw her, but that doesn't mean anything. The day we got here, two ugly, little men asked me if I wanted a job as a hostess at a fabulous ski resort. The work would be easy and the tips would be great because our clients would be well-heeled businessmen. Maybe the girl you're looking for got into that some way or other."

I asked if she remembered the name of the resort and she said she didn't because she wasn't interested in the job.

"How about Sierra Vista? Does that ring a bell?"

"Yes," she said, "That's the name they gave me."

"Well, maybe we're finally getting somewhere...."


IT HAD been just a week earlier that nine stewardesses from Mountain-Atlantic Airways came to my office on East 54th St. in New York City. They were wearing their neat blue MAA uniforms with silver wings on their caps and collars. They added up to three blondes, three brunettes, two black girls and an Oriental.

"We'll come right to the point, Mr. Franklin." Betty Harrison, a blonde girl with long, tapering legs had been appointed to do their talking. "We're all stewardesses with MAA, but we have a private business of our own, too."

I said, "Give me three guesses what it is. One, you've got a little call-girl operation going. Two, you've got a little call-girl operation going. And, three, you've got a little call-girl operation going."

"My, aren't you clever," she said. "Yes, we've got a little call-girl operation going and one of our little call girls is missing."

"Tell me about it."

She said she and another stewardess, Adele Hopkins, had been handling an MAA flight from San Francisco to New York five days earlier. They had made a contact with two prosperous looking men on the plane, businessmen types, and gone with them to a luxurious suite in the Hotel Gascar on Fifth Ave. Adele Hopkins' date had given his name as Leon Appleton and he had taken charge of the party, getting a fine meal along with the best champagnes sent up to their suite. The four of them had eaten together, but then they had split up into couples and each of them had taken one of the bedrooms. The next morning, Betty and her date had knocked on the door of the other bedroom. There was no answer. When they went in, they found it deserted.

"That was four days ago and we haven't seen or heard from Adele since."

"Isn't it possible this Appleton offered her a good deal of some sort and she just went off with him?" I asked.

"Not a chance," she said. Several of the others nodded agreement.

"Oh, he kept telling her she ought to quit MAA and take a job as a

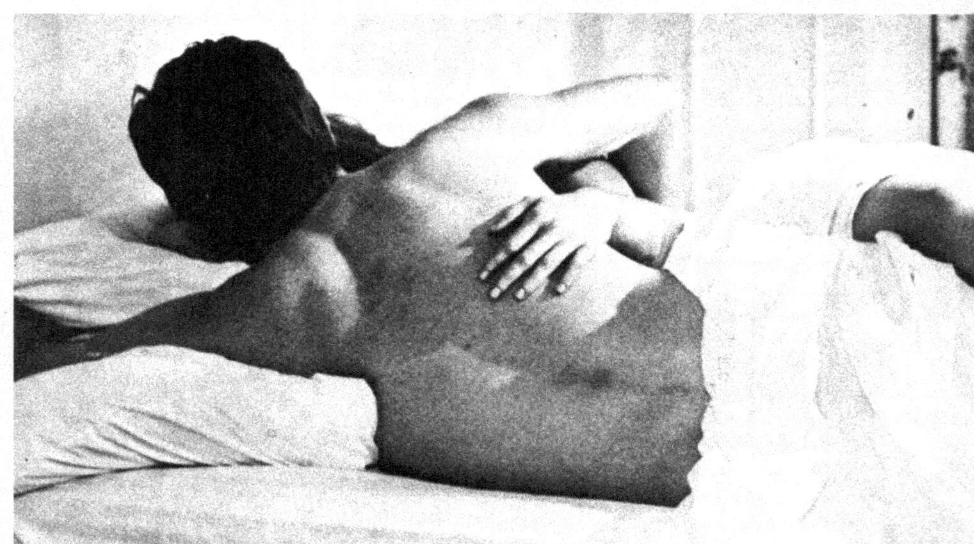

# "CALL GIRL SLAVE RING"

hostess with a new ski resort he was interested in, called Sierra Vista. But Adele just laughed and said he shouldn't hold his breath that long."

"Tell me something about the two guys. Were they friends? Were they together on the plane?"

"No, they didn't seem to know each other at all. They only went into the date together because they could see Adele and I were sort of a team. My date was a kind of quiet dude, the paper-on-the-wall type, but Appleton was full of jokes and had a lot of personality."

"WHAT about the condition of the room Adele and Appleton were in? What was it like when you went in the next morning? Any signs of a struggle or of violence?"

"No, just the unmade bed and Adele's little valise." She thought for a minute. "But I remember there was kind of a medicine smell and someone had vomited in the sink."

"You didn't talk to any of the personnel in the hotel? You didn't ask if anyone had seen them leave?"

"In this line of work, the one thing you don't do is make waves with hotel personnel. You need them too much for getting you rooms and for warning you if you're going to be broken in on or anything

"My roommate met a guy on one of her flights, and, well, they shacked up and the next thing you know they were gone without her telling her friends anything about it and she hasn't been seen since . . ."

Many customers (top left) enjoyed girls' favors unaware that they were being held at the lodge against their will.

Members of ring sometimes had to ferry "drugged" girls down to warmer resort areas to accommodate calls from "special" clients who didn't want to make trip.

like that."

I thought a few minutes, trying to get the feel of the thing in my
mind. I'd had to bring in some chairs from other offices to accommodate
them all and everywhere you looked you saw another pair of great legs,
crossed, with those little MAA skirts giving you a good view of thigh.
They sat quietly watching me for the most part, but the Oriental, Toni
Webster, was filing her nails. Actually, I could see she was a good deal
of a mixture, taller and longer legged than most Orientals and with no
trace of an accent in her raspy voice.

"Well!" I said. "There's enough to get started on. Now, of course,
the question of money comes in here, my fee and my expenses. I won't
be able to itemize it until the job's done, but I figure 5000 if the job
takes a month or less, 2500 now and another 2500 in two weeks."

They went into a huddle to talk it over and decided to accept. But
when I saw Betty Harrison start writing a check, I said, "It's got to be
cash, ladies. It's a kind of paranoia I have. Checks make me nervous."

So they got around my desk and started pulling money out of their
bags. It came out in tens and twenties and started adding up to a pretty
good pile, but when they'd put out everything they had, they were still
300 short. So they went into another huddle and when they came out of
it, Betty Harrison had a solution.

"WE CAN'T help noticing that you're built like a bull elephant," she
said. "And we've also noticed that you've been looking at our legs and
other conspicuous features ever since we got here. For the 300 we owe
you, how would you like to try taking on eight of us at one time? Toni
doesn't go in for group frolics, but the rest of us can see to it that you
get your money's worth."

There's no power on earth that could have gotten me to turn
down that proposition. "Ladies, what a sensible idea," I said and began
unbuttoning my shirt. In a moment they were all peeling off their
clothes. All except Toni who continued to work on her nails as though
we weren't even there. The rest of them were like kids getting ready for
a nude swim, giggling and prancing around the room.

Then they came at me. "History is made on East 54th Street," I
roared, throwing my arms wide. Then they were all over me and we
were tumbling onto the office daybed and I was grabbing and kissing
everything in sight.

"Let's see if he's got any Italian in him," one of the black girls
screamed. "Italians are wild about having their bellies kissed." And she
pushed her head in to the crush all over me, kissing me noisily all over

the area below the chest.

But almost immediately one of the blondes had another idea. "I think he's got some French in him. Frenchmen have this great thing about thighs." And she grabbed me by the ears, wrapping her legs around my head so I could kiss her thighs.

They swarmed on me, grabbed at me, flung their arms and legs around me. And I surged back against them, spilling myself into their warm, tensing canals, grunting in satisfaction as I moved from one to the next. I had a quick look at Toni Webster at one point, still filing her nails. Busy as I was, piling my way through that mound of soft bellies and outthrust breasts, I still found myself wishing she'd tear her clothes off and join in. That's what you call an obsession, and I've always had it where women are concerned. Once I get started, I don't know how to stop.

"Bull elephant is right," one of them gasped at last. "He comes at you like he's bucking and lunging in the tall grass."

A few minutes later, they began untangling themselves and getting back into their clothes. Betty Harrison said, "All right, there's your fee. Now, suppose you start earning it."

I HAD no trouble finding out how Adele and Appleton had left the hotel. One of the elevator operators remembered it. "The woman was shivering even though it was warm out," he said. "The man had his arm around her as though she might faint and he had to help her out to the cab. I would say that was about 5:30 AM." I asked if Adele had said anything in the car going down and he said she hadn't. "She was in a daze and didn't even seem to know where she was."

My next step would normally have been to try to find the cab that had picked them up outside the hotel. But by that time I had already looked over the MAA passenger list and noticed that Leon Appleton had given Valencia Hills as his "place of permanent residence." On that basis it seemed a good idea to check out all the airlines before bothering with cabs. My check of the major airlines didn't turn up anything. But a small outfit named Earth Ocean had sold two tickets for a flight to San Francisco to a Mr. and Mrs. Tom Cunningham, and the clerk who had made the sale recognized Adele Hopkins as "Mrs. Cunningham" from the picture of her the other girls had given me.

"Yes, that's the girl, all right," he said positively. "But she didn't look that good, I can tell you that. She was having trouble picking up her feet, and she was panting and shivering. Her husband was being very nice to her. You couldn't help noticing that."

So Appleton and Adele Hopkins were flying as man and wife.

"Wouldn't the fact that she seemed to be sick make you think twice about taking her aboard?"

"We're a non-sked airline and we're hurting for passengers. We'll sell a seat to anyone that's breathing—and if they're not, we'll sell them a box to lie down in."

By then it seemed obvious enough that Appleton had given Adele Hopkins a tranquilizing drug (which would explain her being cold and shivering), so he could get her to where he wanted to without her fussing. A look at the map showed me that Valencia Hills was less than 40 miles from San Francisco and chances were looking better and better that that's where he was taking her. I met with my clients, the nine MAA stewardesses, in their duplex apartment on Fifth Avenue to give them a progress report.

"It looks to me as though there's a kidnapping aspect to this thing," I said. "She doesn't come from wealthy people, does she? I mean it's not likely that anyone's holding her for ransom, is it?"

They said no, there was no chance of that.

"In that case, it's got to be something involving sex. There's always a certain amount of that going on, girls getting themselves recruited by spotters for different rings, and it's possible that's what's happening to Adele. I'd better get out to San Francisco and see if I can pick up their trail there."

The girls agreed and I was on a Pan-Am flight a few hours later. As soon as we put down, I checked at the Earth Ocean counter and found that a Mr. and Mrs. Tom Cunningham had gotten off there. The clerk remembered them well. "The woman was shivering violently and she didn't seem to know where she was. Her husband was being very kind and attentive to her."

I asked if he had any idea where they'd gone after they left the airport. He said because of the woman's condition and the fact that she was so great looking, he had watched as they left and seen them get into a car that had apparently been waiting for them. "It was sort of a resort station wagon with five or six seats going across. Two men were in the front seat." I asked if he'd seen in which direction they'd driven off, but he hadn't. It made sense to me to try Valencia Hills anyway, so I asked around and found the way to get there was by railroad.

A little less than two hours later I was getting out onto the station platform of the neatest, cleanest town I'd ever seen in my life and Jesse Thomas was walking toward me looking like Wild Bill Hickok and saying, "Got business in Valencia Hills?"

AFTER I finished talking to the hippies, I went back to the jail. Thomas was talking to someone on the telephone. When he saw me, he said: "I'll have to call you back," and clanked the phone down hard. Then he nodded at it. "That was Mrs. Hollis over at the church. She wanted to remind me about the picnic and bake sale they're having there this Sunday. What's on your mind?"

"I think maybe I'm going to stick around here for a few days. There are some loose ends on this thing I'm working on. And besides the clean life you live here might do me some good. What do you have in the line of hotels for me to stay at?"

"We got the Cherry Arms on Cedar Street"

There was a clomping of feet on the stairs from the floor below and the deputy, Vernon, came in looking soggy from the hosing I'd given him.

"You really gave me a bad time down there, fellow."

"Except for a little water leaking out of your nose and ears, it doesn't seem to have bothered you much."

"You mean cause I ain't sore? Shucks, what kind of a man would I be to hold a grudge for a little thing like that?"

He went out and I said to Thomas, "I'm feeling a better man already just being in this healthy atmosphere you've got here. How do I get to the Cherry Arms on Cedar Street?"

He said it was five blocks away, close enough to walk, and told me the direction. I told him thanks and started walking and 10 minutes later I was in the lobby of the hotel, a four-story building probably built around the turn of the century, but clean and well kept, with a blue-eyed, pink-cheeked, middle-aged man, beaming at me from behind the desk.

"Welcome, stranger! What can we do for you?"

I said I wanted a room and he looked over his register and said, "You can have 318." I said that would be all right. "Incidentally," I added, "I'm a man of strong needs. Where do I go to get a broad around here?"

He looked as though I'd hit him over the head with a shovel, so I said, "Oh! Sorry. I keep forgetting what a saintly set-up you've got here. All right, since you don't have any local talent working here, I'll have to see what I can come up with on my own."

HE WANTED to carry my bag upstairs for me, but I said it wasn't necessary. Being the suspicious type, I'd been wondering if there was a bug in my room, so I began hunting around for it as soon as I was inside. It took me five minutes to locate it on the underside of the bureau. But I didn't disturb it or say anything to let on I knew it was there. They probably had one in every room in the place, so there was no point in fussing about it. I just unpacked, put my things in bureau drawers, and went outside.

I found an outdoor public telephone a few blocks from the hotel and called my clients in New York. Betty Harrison answered the phone. I said: "I'm not sure, but I think I'm getting close to something here. I'm going to need a girl for bait, though. Any of you feel like taking it on?

"Whoever does it, though, she'd have to be able to put on a pretty good act. I've got a room in the Cherry Arms Hotel and she'd come out to stay with me, but then we'd have a fight and she'd cut out on me. The room's bugged, so we'd be listened in on, and if I'm figuring this right, as soon as she leaves me, she'll be approached by whoever it is that's got Adele and asked if she'd like to be a hostess in a ski resort."

"Just a second, I'll see," Betty said. I could hear her talking to some of the others in the room and then she came back on the line. "Toni says she'll do it."

I said, "All tight, let me talk to her to be sure she knows what to do."

Toni arrived early the next evening. There were eight or nine people in the lobby when she arrived, a couple playing checkers and the rest singing "Nearer My God to Thee" around the piano. Every one of them stopped what he was doing to stare at her. She was wearing pink slacks and open-toed pink shoes with heels like 6-inch needles and a leopard-skin cape, and her black hair was hanging loose and thick to her shoulders, framing her face with its Oriental features, her black eyes roving the room.

"Good to see you, honey. I'd have gone out of my skull if you couldn't make it." We kissed and you could feel them tightening their lips at us in disapproval, and then I put one arm around her waist and picked up her bag in the other hand and we went upstairs without a sound in the lobby behind us. As we entered the room, I put my fingers to my lips and then pointed to the bottom of the bureau, and she nodded to show she knew what I was getting at.

"They've got a funny thing about sex out here, honey. They don't believe in it."

"Well, you were smart to send for me, but why did you pick a dump like this for us to stay in."

I nodded to tell her she was on the right track. "They've got a good room rate here, honey, but I'm kind of light on dough."

"Light on dough?" she screeched. "I travel 2500 miles to get out here and you tell me you're light on dough. What am I getting for this junket?"

"I don't think I can do a lot better than pay for your plane fare, honey. Maybe I can throw in a couple of bucks—"

"You can't do any better than pay my plane fare? You'll throw in a couple of bucks? You son of a bitch, I was counting on at least 1500 and that's aside from the plane fare and anything else."

"I'm broke. I'm flat broke. What do a couple of bucks matter when you're flat broke?"

"You'll wake up the neighbors with all that screaming, honey!" I got my mouth against hers, pushing her down on the bed and lying partly across her. Her mouth was active under mine, her tongue all sweet and feathery, and I had to say "no, no" in my head to keep from piling into her. But I thought I'd probably need all the strength I had for whatever lay ahead, so I rolled off her and nodded at her to do some more screaming.

Then I left, with her still screaming. "If I had the plane fare back to

New York, I'd walk right out on you and let you make out the best you can with these Mother Hubbards out here."

I went down through the lobby, picking up all the shame-on-you looks again, and out into the street. I had rented a car the day before and had it parked across from the hotel. I wasn't interested in a drink, but I wanted to put something on the bug that would justify my going away and leaving Toni alone a while so the recruiters could make their pitch. So I drove around for about 45 minutes, which takes some doing in Valencia Hills since the same Route 51 takes you in and out of town and there isn't much more to it than that—and then I drove back to the Cherry Arms.

The same parking place was waiting for me, but the one in front of it had been taken by a big station wagon set up like a bus with half a dozen seats running across it. That figured to be the recruiters. The vehicle fitted the description of the one that had picked Adele up at the airport in San Francisco. I memorized the license number and then went up to the room, hearing voices from outside before I pushed the door open and went in.

"Well look who's here!" Toni jeered. "The fastest buck in the East. The last of the big-time spenders!"

There were three of them. A pair of stocky, frozen-faced men, both of them obviously gunners, and a big man with a wet-looking, smiling face. I had no doubt he was Appleton, Adele Hopkins' date at the Hotel Gascar, the man who had drugged her and brought her out to Valencia Hills.

"What's going on here? Who are these jokers?"

"They could be the Unholy Three for all I care. Whoever they are they've got a great paying job for me as a hostess in a ski resort and since I'm all hung up here without any money, I'm going to take it."

"Now, wait a minute," I said, playing my role to a T. "I brought you out here because I need you. You can't just cut out on me that way."

"Oh, you'll be all right! Just ask her nice and maybe one of those Mother Hubbards singing the hymn will take you on."

Appleton laughed. I took a step forward as though to grab her to stop her from going. The two gunners jumped their hands to their jacket pockets and I held it. They were quick, all right, and they were jumpy, too. Appleton laughed again and took Toni by the elbow to steer her to the door, which he opened and said, "What the hell, you can't win them all."

I WENT to stand beside the window. Toni and the three recruiters came out and got into the station wagon. The vehicle was in good shape, well kept up and shiny. The two gunmen got into the front seat and she got in behind them with Appleton. The wagon started forward, traveling a block and turning westward through a stretch of forest and brush-covered hills. That was as much as I needed to know. I'm a shark with a car and knew I could follow them without putting my lights on, the few stars that were out giving me enough to work with. But just as I was about to open the door, it was pushed in from out in the hall and Jesse Thomas stepped into the room wearing his badge, his sombrero, a gun in a holster, the works.

"I've got a complaint against you, Franklin," he said. "You brought a female person that's not your wife into your room here, didn't you?"

I spoke quickly. "Yeah, I did, but it was just a gimmick to help me track down Adele Hopkins. It's going to come as a shock to you, Thomas, but you've got some kind of prostitution ring operating here. They've got Adele Hopkins and God knows how many others."

His red face went dark: "We don't have no prostitution ring in Valencia Hills, Franklin."

"Look! Their recruiters travel around in a big station wagon and they've got that female person that was visiting me in it right now. All we've got to do is trail that wagon."

"You got its license number?"

I gave it to him. He said: "I think you're off your head, Franklin. But we'll go down to the jail and check out that number. If there's anything suspicious about it, I can get that vehicle picked up in five minutes just by making a few calls. It don't take a New York cop to do a thing like that."

I thought about arguing, but decided it would just be a waste of time. Not only that, but maybe what he was doing would be the best thing to do anyway. "All right, but let's move fast!"

"Don't tell me how to do my job, Franklin. We get a different kind of problem here than you get in your big cities."

WE WENT downstairs and started through the lobby and the hymn singers at the piano stopped singing again to watch us. An old lady said, "You going to run him out of town, Jesse?"

"I'll let you know as soon as I decide, Martha." He said to me as we went out into the street, "This ain't New York, Franklin. You want to have doings with a woman that ain't your wife, you don't do it in Valencia Hills."

He had his police jeep outside. We got in and drove over to the jail.

There was nobody in his office, but he opened the door leading down to the basement and his deputy, Vernon, called, "That you, Jesse?"

"Mister Franklin's here again, Vernon. See that he don't get you all wet like last time."

Then before I realized what he was doing, he had that gun of his up against the side of my head and a second later I was stumbling down the stairs with Thomas right behind me rapping his gun against my skull every step of the way and Vernon meeting me at the bottom and joining in with a gun of his own. It was all business with Thomas. But Vernon was having a good time. He giggled and said, "Do I see you turning the other cheek, Mr. Franklin?" and finally Thomas had to pull him off me and throw me in the cage.

Then he said, "I got to go pick up our customers, Vernon. They'll be coming in less than an hour. You be sure and get this girl out to the lodge. We got a man coming that says he wants to do a few private things to a hippy, and for thirty five hundred dollars he's entitled to get what he wants."

"What about Franklin?"

"We'll have to keep him here until I can figure out how many charges we got against him. That might take a couple of months. There's fighting with a policeman and there's bringing a female person that's not his wife into his room, and there's about seven or eight others. Give him something to eat so he don't bring no police-brutality charges against us, and see that he don't tie you up in the hose again."

Vernon grinned and said, "Don't worry." He followed Thomas upstairs into the office. I wiped blood out of my eyes and saw the hippy girl from a couple of days earlier kneeling in front of me, staring at me and biting her lips. She said, "Are you okay?"

My head felt like a warm, wet sponge. Blood was pouring out of it in thick streams, soaking my shirt and pants. "It wasn't exactly fun, but it wasn't as bad as it looked, either. What are you doing here?"

She took a sweater off for me to mop my head. "Didn't you hear them? They're bringing in a group of customers for their whorehouse and one of them said he wanted a hippy to do crazy things with. I was way outside the city limits with my friends, but they just came and took me anyway. It was the same two that asked me if I wanted to be a hostess a few days ago, only this time they said they were special deputies, so I guess it's all the same deal.

"I said I'll kill myself before I let anybody do crazy things with me that way,"

"Well, let's fix it so that's not necessary," I told her, but I didn't have an idea in the world how to get out of there.

It was about half an hour after Thomas left that Vernon came down from the office carrying bowls of food. "Real beef, folks!" he said cheerfully. What other jail treats its guests that well?" He opened a little slot in the cage down close to the ground and pushed them through, then closed it and went back upstairs. He was right about them having real beef in them. You couldn't mistake the smell. But there was another smell there, too, although very faint—the smell of some sort of medicine. And then I remembered Betty Harrison saying there had been a medicine smell in the room at the Hotel Gascar that Adele Hopkins had shared with Atkinson, and someone had vomited there, too.

"He's got this food doped. It's a way to keep me under control and get you to where the others are. You think you could fake getting sick?"

She said she'd try. So we waited about 10 minutes and then threw some of the food out on the floor, bent down and made ourselves retch. In a couple of minutes, Vernon came back down.

"Ah, now, that's too bad. Food didn't agree with you?" He unlocked the door to the cell, taking his gun out first, but obviously not thinking he'd need it. The girl was all curled up in a corner making herself retch and I was lying on my face. He came toward me holding the gun in his right hand, and when I figured he was right above me; I went straight upward, coming up under the gun and ramming my fist into his groin.

The gun flew up to the ceiling and clattered on the ground. Vernon bent over making a gasping sound like air rushing out of a tire. I yanked his hands away from where I'd hit him and hit him there again, and he fell up against the side of the cages with his face all twisted and looking as though he couldn't move.

"ALL RIGHT," I yelled. "Give me details." I bent over to yank his belt off and tighten it around his neck. "Where's that Christian charity of yours?" Then I took the long end in my hand, put him belly-down on the floor, put my foot on his back and yanked up hard. He yelled in pain. He didn't like that one bit. But I had more in mind for him. I was just getting started.

I told Vernon to relax and then just when he gave me an incredulous stare I grabbed under both armpits and hauled him off to the bathroom, kicking the door open with my boot. He was beginning to panic but I knew I'd get him to talk.

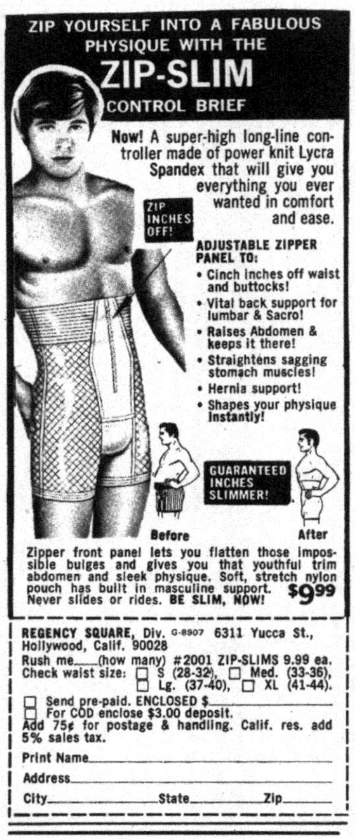


The next thing he knew he was in the tub and the water was on full force and he was gagging and sputtering. But I wouldn't let him talk. Not yet. Not till I was ready to let him tell me what he now wanted to tell me very badly.

"Vernon," I said calmly, "I'm going to drown you." I pushed him down, the water swirling around and Vernon struggling and making gurgling noises. I let him up after a minute, pulling him by the hair. "Now," I said. "It's your last chance."

Vernon talked.

He said there were a group of them that had put up a lodge in the woods. They called it Sierra Vista and talked girls into coming out to it by promising them jobs as hostesses at what they described as a "fabulous resort." When the girls got there, though, they were given certain tranquilizers to make them manageable and then they were used as brothel partners by well-to-do businessmen who paid $500 for three days with them. Most of the girls were persuaded to come by the job promise, but others turned it down and a number of these were tranquilized first (as with Adele Hopkins), and then brought to the Lodge by Sierra Vista recruiters.

"And what about tonight?" I asked, yanking up on the belt again when he was slow in answering.

"A group of our customers is coming into San Francisco," he wheezed. "Jesse is going to meet them there and bring them to the lodge by car."

"That means we'd better move along if we're going to get there first," I said. "You're going to do the driving and I don't want any clowning around, so maybe I better give you a little workout first so you'll know what you're in for."

I took the belt off him and spent the next couple of minutes working him over around the head and belly with my best kicking toe. The hippy girl whispered all the time. "Oh, that's so ugly. Must you do that?"

"Don't worry about him. He's a big believer in the meek inheriting the earth and when I'm finished here, he's going to be about the meekest thing that ever came down the pike."

It was like kicking a rubber mat by then, I got a final one in against his throat and the girl screamed as the blood spurted out of his mouth like a college pennant.

Photo shows building similar to one where white slavers held girls captive.

THEY had a big police van for hauling prisoners behind the station and that's what we took. Vernon drove, and all I had to do was move a hand or shift in my seat and he'd flinch. The girl sat on the other side of me. When we'd been driving about an hour and were well into the woods, she said, "Would you let me off here?"

"What do you want to get off here for? You're in the middle of noplace."

"No, I recognize it! My friends are close by."

I asked her what she was going to do when she caught up with them.

"All I want to do is drink some good wine and try to forget everything I saw here tonight," she said.

I had Vernon stop the car and opened the door for her to get out. She slid off into the darkness.

We left Route 51 awhile earlier to get onto something that wasn't much more than a path twisting through the woods. We kept following it in a generally downward direction as though we were circling toward the bottom of a slope. Finally Vernon said, "All right, this is it," and braked us to a stop.

"What are chances of Thomas and your customers being there already?"

"No chance," he said, "He could never make it this fast."

"What about getting down there? Is he going to come the same way we did?"

"That's the only way there is."

"All right, we'll back the van up under these trees overlooking the path, and I'll tie you up so I won't have to worry about you while I'm down there looking over the lodge."

He just sighed and shrugged. So we backed the van uphill a little ways till it was about 10 yards above the path and facing down toward it. Then I had him get out and wrap his arms around a pretty good-sized tree. I tied them in front around the wrists and tied a gag in his mouth. Then I started out toward the lodge, tire iron and Vernon's police revolver in hand.

I'D ONLY been going about 10 minutes when I saw lights through the trees. That was the lodge, all right! A great looking place—big, well-built and well-situated, too. Vernon had said there would be some hunting and skiing for any of their customers that wanted it. You could see the spot where they'd located the lodge was perfect for it. About 50 yards from the lodge, a dog rushed me, but I laid it out with the tire iron and went the rest of the way without any trouble.

Coming up next to a first floor window, I looked inside, seeing an enormous room with a bar and a great many soft chairs and couches and a couple of fireplaces. The three recruiters were playing cards at a card table, the two gunners wearing overcoats and Appleton wearing a checkered shirt and no tie. Appleton looked a little tense, darting his head around as though he were getting nervous waiting for his customers.

There were lights at all the windows upstairs and by standing back, I could see girls in some of the rooms. Or rather, I saw vague shadows moving around behind some of the curtains there, and I figured it had to be the girls. I also saw Thomas's jeep off to one side of the building, which I took to mean he had taken the big station wagon to Denver to pick up their customers.

After I'd had my look, I hurried back to where I'd left Vernon and the van. I still wasn't sure what I was going to do, but just as I reached the van, I heard men's voices singing "Side by Side" a distance off, harmonizing, and that cut down on my choices. There was really only one way to play my cards from that point out.

I got up beside the van and opened the door so I could get a hand on the stick shift. It was in reverse to keep it from rolling downhill. I got a foot inside the car where I could bring it down on the clutch in a hurry. Then I stayed like that, waiting.

The voices of the men singing grew louder. I could hear the sound of the station wagon's motor, grinding a little because it was moving over rough terrain. Then I saw the first gleam of headlights.

IT WAS with the station wagon a yard short of being directly in front of me that I put my foot down on the clutch, put the stick into neutral and got the van rolling. My timing couldn't have been better. The van lumbered smack into the side of the wagon. The wagon swerved around sideways and I ran around to the driver's seat—the side the van hadn't hit. As I reached it, Thomas was getting out, his face as wooden as ever under his sombrero.

"I guess I should have killed you back there, Franklin," he was saying.

"Yeah, that was a mistake!" I lunged straight into him and swung at his head with the tire iron. He hunched a shoulder up to take the impact, but the iron bounced up over it and continued on into his jaw, and he fell up against me clawing for his gun. I had him by the shirt and began hitting him with the iron and each shot sent a jolt up my arm, so I knew I was making good contact. Seven or eight blasts straight down on his skull, and then I let go of his shirt and stepped back, letting him fall there unconscious.

Most of the customers had gotten out of the wagon by then, and they were standing around looking dazed. I shouted, "Look, you men, I don't know what the sheriff here told you about the girls you'd be partying with, but I doubt if he told you it's a white-slave operation."

A murmur of anger and fear went through them. I shouted: "That's right! That's something to be worried about. Most of you have wives and families and responsible jobs, don't you. Getting yourself a little tail from time to time is one thing, but white slavery is something else. The girls are kidnapped. The girls are drugged. Thomas didn't tell you any of that, did he?"

"The son of a bitch!" one man said. "I can't take that kind of a chance." Others nodded and said the same thing.

"Well, there he is," I said, pointing to Thomas on the ground. "And here's another member of his group tied to this tree, here. Hang on to the two of them for me until I get back. Then we can see about getting you back to San Francisco and on planes back to where you came from. Maybe we can still keep the whole thing as quiet as though it never happened."

Toni, Adele and I went back to New York by plane. They were both hospitalized in Frisco first to recover. I waited there until they were released. We went to the airport from the hospital by cab. Adele sat in the front with the driver, while Toni and I finished up what we'd started in the Cherry Arms Hotel in Valencia Hills, draping a couple of coats over us in the back seat for privacy. ///

# *Art* and men

**MAM publishers usually had more than one MAM in their line, and had few compunctions about later reprinting stories and illustrations in their other titles—sometimes altered, sometimes as is.** It could lead strange and amusing disconnects between art and story, such as this one.

By the 1970s, *Man's Life* was recycling a lot of older artwork. So the uncredited illustration accompanying "God Help Me—They're Biting Me to Pieces!" likely first accompanied a different tale, though we haven't yet been able to ID it. The story itself isn't bad—a grim, noirsh killer creature story in the vein of "Chewed to Bits by Giant Turtles" (pg. 174). But the art director was either asleep at the switch when pairing story and illustration, or they really, *really* hoped readers weren't paying attention.

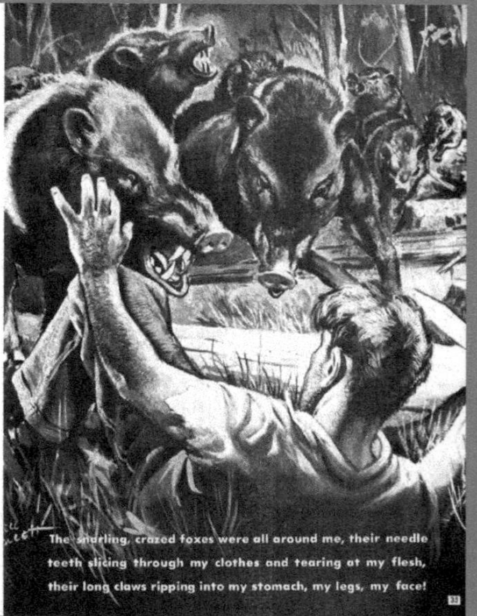

## "GOD HELP ME— THEY'RE BITING ME TO PIECES!"

by WILLIAM O'BANNON

EVELYN was a long way below me. And at first I thought I was hearing things. But then I *heard* and hot needles coursed through my legs. Without stopping to reload, without thinking of anything other than her safety, I plunged through the last of the hardwoods into open, rock-strewn tundra.

"O'Bannon!" she sobbed, a wail that hung over the autumn woodlands. "Please! Help me, O'Bannon—"

I'd spooked a big whitetail buck at the base of the timberline a moment before; I'd snapped off three clean-miss .34?'s at a fleeting silhouette and had stood there, sweating, angry with myself as I always was when I blew an easy one.

I'd yelled, "Evelyn! Buck coming through!"

She'd replied, *"Foxes—they're eating me!"*

"Leave the foxes alone—shoot the d-damned buck!" I yelled back angrily, but nothing happened except that the strawberry blonde yelled louder. So then I cut out through the last fringe of timberline and came out on the flat.

"Foxes! Foxes!" Evelyn wailed.

Three foxes. Big as small police dogs, three rabid foxes were tearing the strawberry blonde apart. From where I stood, Evey's lovely long body writhed in agony with one fox fast to her left leg, another leaping at her throat, the third hanging tenaciously to her right wrist.

I plunged through the deadwood onto the tundra, running and shouting, *"I'm coming, Evey! I'm coming—"*

As I raced toward her the saliva welled in my throat hot and sour. I could see Evey's blood spurting in the bright fall sunlight of a Saskatchewan morning. The wrist fox hit an artery and her rich red blood like a fountain spewed the air. Even as I ran I could hear the ripping of bluejeans and the distinct cracking of bones. Evey's sobs racked over the tundra fusing with the shrill, excited, demented ululation of her attackers. Foxes. Rabid foxes. I watched her go down under a flurry of fur, but still didn't risk a pot shot. I shoved one boot into a posthole instead and fell flat on my face.

"Please, help!" Evey sobbed, "O'Bann—"

Crimson smeared her yellow blouse as snapping fangs shredded the strawberry blonde. She was still writhing on the ground, whimpering pathetically as I got up again and ran. All I saw were the foxes and they covered her.

EVERYTHING went wrong that year. It was November, 1964, and up in the Canadian wilds where I had my camp there was supposed to be a deer season. It was more like Indian summer, hot, sticky, unseasonable weather for spooking bucks. But it was the only time I had to hunt, and the strawberry blonde who was scheduled to become my bride in December, insisted on taking the vacation together.

"I won't change anything—no curtains, no clean dishes!" Evey insisted while I was still half yes, half no about bringing her up. "Please, O'Bannon. Pretty please?"

"I'm out of my mind to be taking you up—or even *talking* about taking you up!" I snapped.

"That's nice," Evey Blanchard cooed, settling in my arms. Her lovely face plastered against mine until the room spun. "I knew," she whispered after a mite, "you'd see it my way—"

BESIDES Evey Blanchard, hunting was my passion. Every year I'd haul up to the little $5,000 shack I'd slapped together out of baling wire and old boards, and maybe every other year I'd bring down a nice eight, ten-pointer to Toronto. I was thirty-seven, a veteran of the Canadian Army and, for a guy of my age, reasonably rugged yet. I had no intention of ever missing a deer season if I could help it, so I accepted my future bride's offer.

It didn't occur to me to ask about rabid foxes. Hunting season always featured something unhappy in the woods country. One year we had bears galore—so many bears they were paying $50 bounty for each head a man lugged in. One year the blowflies were so thick a dead, ungutted deer was spoiled meat if it didn't get stuffed or hung in an hour.

We arrived at camp two days after the season inaugural, loaded for bear. My camp was a two roomer built for rugged living with(Continued on page 54)

34

33



*Man's Life*, June 1971
Artist uncredited

Sorry, let's read that again:



OK, got it. Moving on…

At auction in 2008, the nudity in this Gil Cohen paint-ing *(opposite)* raised eyebrows among collec-tors—though not for the obvious reasons. When it first appeared on the December 1967 cover of *Men (left)*, not only were the women clothed (albeit skimp-ily), they were body-painted! But a few years later, the Nazi

*Men,* December 1967
Illustration by Gil Cohen

officer with a flair for decorating had swapped his brush and palette for a cigar, while the ladies' body paint vanished completely—along with their tops. Subsequent investigation revealed the painting had been altered and reversed for repurposing in 1971, when it illustrated a story by none other than Walter Kaylin, writing as Roland Empey.

*Man's World,* August 1971
Illustration by Gil Cohen

**Beware the ides of March!** Whether he's trying to survive the sacred rites of a Bolivian "spider tribe" in *Action For Men*'s March 1969 issue or the remarkably similar ritual of Peruvian "scorpion cultists" a few years later in the March 1971 *For Men Only*, the adaptable protagonist of Earl Norem's illustration is not going going to have an easy time of it.

—*Wyatt Doyle & Robert Deis*

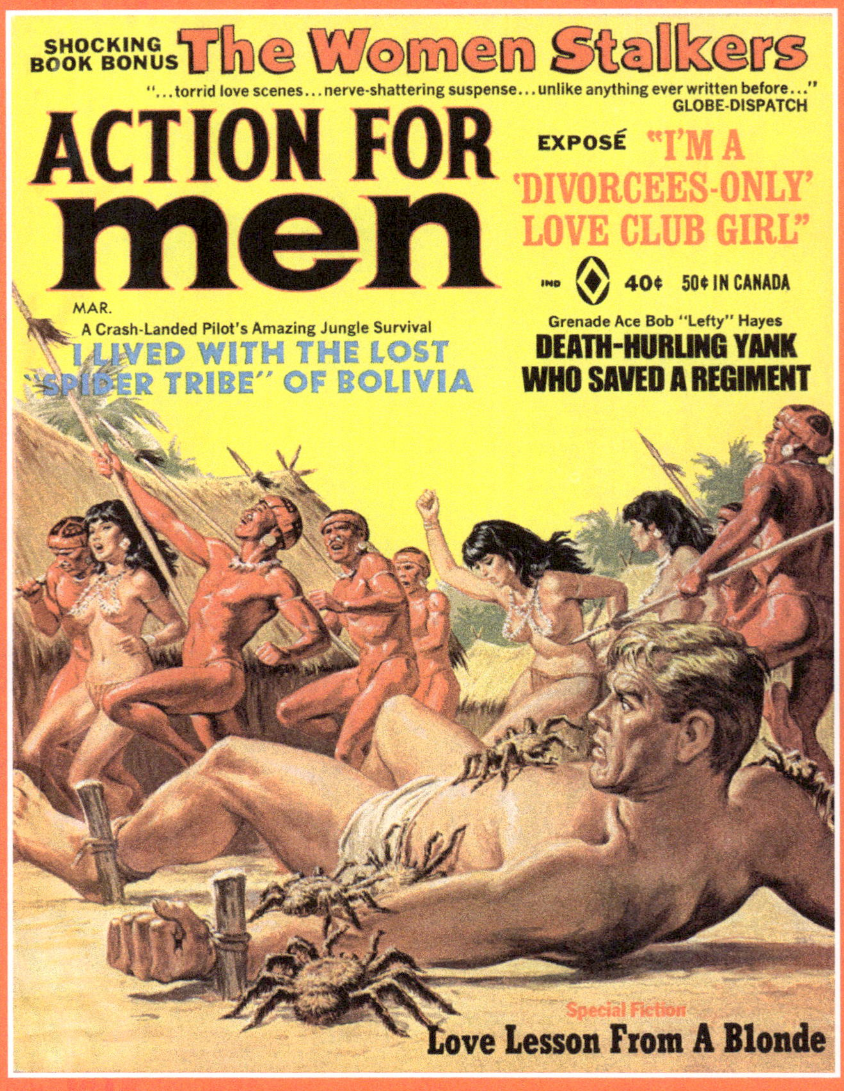


*Action For Men,* **March 1969**
**Cover by Earl Norem**

*For Men Only,* March 1971
Cover by Earl Norem

# ABOUT JANE DOLINGER & KEN KRIPPENE

JANE DOLINGER *is one of the most interesting women associated with men's adventure and bachelor magazines of the 1950s and 1960s. She's the only woman who was both a pin-up model and a writer of exotic travel and adventure stories for vintage men's mags. Her nickname back then was "Jungle Jane" and she was called "the most glamorous travel writer in the world." More recently, she has been called "a real-life Lara Croft" and a "female Indiana Jones." During her remarkable career she wrote more than 300 magazine stories and eight books.*

*The story of how Jane became an adventure travel writer is amazing in itself. She left her parents' Pennsylvania home at age 19, looking for a career that would fit her impressive intelligence and adventurous spirit. She ended up in Miami, where she saw a "Help Wanted" ad in the local newspaper that intrigued her. It read:*

> AUTHOR needs adventure-loving Girl Friday.
> Must be free to travel. Excellent pay.
> Reply Box M-569, giving full particulars.

*The ad was placed by the veteran adventure travel author and Hollywood scriptwriter Ken Krippene, whose travel and adventure stories appeared in major magazines like* National Geographic, True *and* Argosy, *as well as in less widely known men's magazines. (Krippene's story for* Sir!, *"I Married a Jungle Savage" can be found on pg. 289)*

*Krippene was preparing to head out on an assignment to South America with professional cameraman Bob Farrier. Dolinger responded to his ad and the two hit it off.*

*During the next year, Ken and Jane traveled together to Peru, went deep into the Amazon interior and lived for months with primitive tribes. She developed her own skills as an author. They both wrote magazine articles based on that trip and others that followed, many of which were published in men's adventure and bachelor magazines.*

*In 1955, Jane published her first book,* The Jungle Is a Woman: The Adventures of an American Girl in the Green Hell of the Amazon. *She followed that up with* The Head with the Long Yellow Hair, *a book about*

*Jivaro headhunters published in 1958.*

*Not long after their initial travels in South America, Krippene and Dolinger were married. She was in her early twenties, he was in his fifties. In 1954, they were married in Peru. They remained happily married and*

Adventurous Jane has also tried hand at bull fighting.

**The Witch Doctor Took Five Days to Shrink the Girl's Head. Then the Orgy Started**

# I Watched A Head-Shrinking Orgy

Jane and guide Taisha examine freshly severed head of Jivaro girl which was shrunken to size of orange in 5-day ritual.

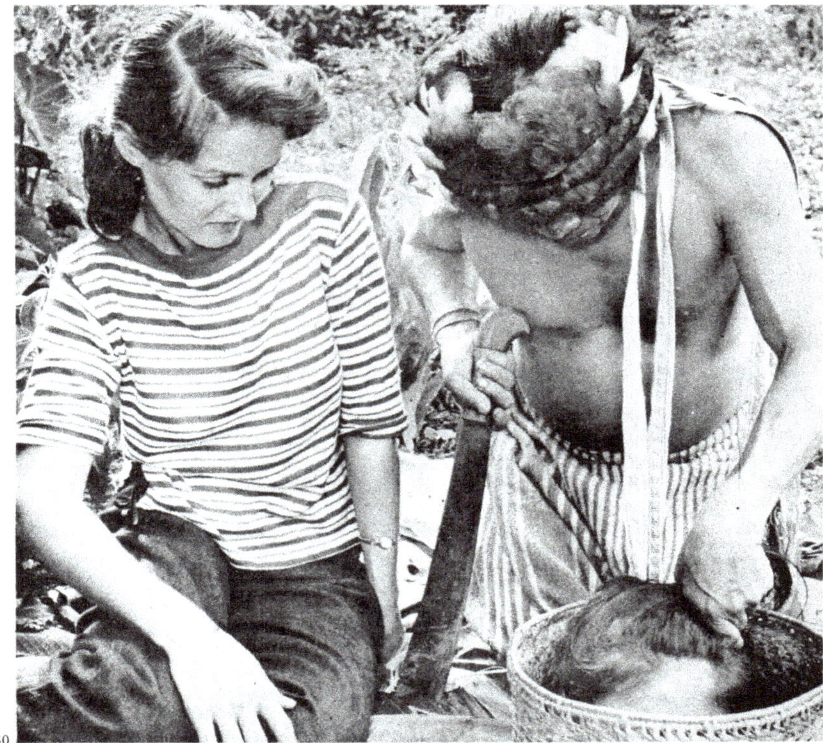

**South Sea Stories, July 1960**

*continued their globe-trotting writing careers until Krippene's death in 1980.*

*Jane died of cancer fifteen years later. When she passed, the world lost one helluva woman.*

*For more on "Jungle Jane," I recommend the biography* Jane Dolinger: The Adventurous Life of an American Travel Writer, *by Lawrence Abbott.*

—*Robert Deis*

This Jivaro warrior wears necklace of unused flash bulbs, which Jane gave him in return for shrunken head he holds.

While Jivaro mother watches, Jane prepares for bed. Huts sleep 20 or more; there's fire at foot of each bed.

Jane is believed to be first white woman to ever witness a Jivaro head-shrinking orgy.

**"I Watched a Head-Shrinking Orgy" by Jane Dolinger**
***South Sea Stories,* July 1960**

## "MY EXOTIC ADVENTURE AS A GIRL 'CRUSOE'"

— JANE DOLINGER —

*Escape to Adventure*, March 1959

COVER ARTIST: VICTOR OLSON

by JANE DOLINGER

## The fantastic true story of two women who lived in primitive freedom on a tropical isle

**Left:** The author (right) on lobster hunt with Debbie, her "Girl Friday." Picture at top of page shows shore of Fernandina, where Miss Dolinger lived just as original "Crusoe" had done.

# MY EXOTIC ADVENTURE AS A GIRL "CRUSOE"

**S**OME of you brawny he-men may think only your sex can find real adventure in the modern world. But you've got another think coming if you do. You're about to be told how I, a dainty (but not scrawny) girl spent two weeks in one of the wildest places left on the globe, accompanied only by a native maiden.

The place I chose to get back to nature is not only full of primitive danger today, but has a history of weird, exotic peril matched by few spots in the world.

Six hundred miles west by northwest off the coast of Ecuador and surrounded by the sparkling blue waters of the Pacific lie the Galapagos Islands, one of the most fantastic and unusual archipelagos in the seven seas. Spewed up from the bowels of the earth in the backwash of civilization, these islands, numbering approximately twenty-seven, have been visited in past gen-

the held until ahead of him
he stretch was only the speed-
Isaiah. At the wire, he caught
favorite for a dead heat. Shock-
had not expected either horse
be claimed. He won some more
ney and shared the purse, but

racetrack with $1,000 in his pocket,
which he shortly ran up to $25,-
000. He was next seen at Saratoga,
where on opening day he won the
astounding sum of $108,000; on
another day $50,000 and on the
closing day $15,000. Since then his

Rooney was
friend at Sara
brought to hi
which he had
disqualified. I
went right on
another occasi

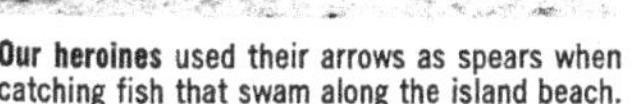

**Carefree** (and almost clothes-free) Debbie does impromptu "dance of the fish net" to Jane's primitive flute accompaniment.

**Our heroines** used their arrows as spears when catching fish that swam along the island beach.

**Close-up view** of fish and its fetching feminine captors. Since girls were alone on island, Jane took pictures by setting the camera for delayed shot before posing.



the three men. She had a
lar schedule, sometimes chang-
companions three times a night,
at others only once a day.
ut as the Baroness began to
of even this lush diet of male

to a shuddering, screaming pulp.
After that the Baroness had the
Germans take turns making love
to her in Valdivieso's full view,
so that he could "see what a real
lover is like."

**SOME** of you brawny he-men may think only your sex can find real adventure in the modern world. But you've got another thing coming if you do. You're about to be told how I, a dainty (but not scrawny) girl spent two weeks in one of the wildest places left on the globe, accompanied only by a native maiden.

The place I chose to get back to nature is not only full of primitive danger today, but has a history of weird, exotic peril matched by few spots in the world.

Six hundred miles west by northwest off the coast of Ecuador and surrounded by the sparkling blue waters of the Pacific lie the Galapagos Islands, one of the most fantastic and unusual archipelagos in the seven seas. Spewed up from the bowels of the earth in the backwash of civilization, these islands, numbering approximately twenty-seven, have been visited in past generations by many of the world s most illustrious and colorful adventurers.

Herman Melville, as a twenty-one year old seaman, first came to the Galapagos in the autumn of 1841. At that time there were many active volcanoes which spread a gray pall over not only the islands but a great portion of the Pacific surrounding them. His fertile imagination in this land of smoke, fire, brimstone and desolation, ran the gamut of emotions and later he incorporated many of his personal experiences on the islands in his immortal classic, *Moby Dick*.

In 1831 Charles Darwin set out on an oceanic survey around South America and eventually ended up on the Galapagos. It was here that he formulated his theory of evolution. Of primary interest was his study of the giant *galapagos*, or turtles, after which the archipelago was named. Every island he visited had its own quota of giant tortoises, each of a separate and distinct species. Although distances between islands were sometimes only a few miles, Professor Darwin was astounded at the fact that there never appeared to be any inter-breeding or mixing among the various types. The separate kinds, developed to various degrees of complexity, clearly illustrated how evolution works.

Early explorers of the Galapagos stated that the giant turtles were so numerous that it was possible to walk the breadth of an entire island without once stepping off their shells. Many of them weighed in excess of 750 pounds. Since the Galapagos were first discovered by Inca Emperor Tupac-Yupanqui in the middle of the 15th century, thousands of ships have stopped at the islands for the sole purpose of capturing the huge turtles, which were used for food on the high seas. From a study of the log books of 19th century whaling ships it has been estimated that over 200,000 giant tortoises were taken from the islands within a period of thirty years. Today the turtles are becoming scarce and in a short time may possibly become extinct.

Other illustrious people known to have been to these islands include the poet Lord Byron, and Sir Francis Drake and Sir Henry Morgan, famous British sea rovers who went there not only to replenish their water supply but to bury their precious treasures of gold and priceless jewels.

In spite of the fact that Professor Darwin's book, *On the Origin of Species*, was written from material collected only after long years of research in the islands, two other people actually did much more to publicize the Galapagos in a never-to-be-forgotten manner.

The first of these was a beautiful young honey-haired, blue-eyed German Baroness by the name of Eloisa de Wagner Wehrborn who, in 1932, arrived at the island of Floreana with two handsome German men—Rudolf Lorenz and Robert Phillipson—and one Ecuadorian named Valdivieso. Within a short time they had built a small house on a rising knoll and with utter disregard for their neighbors lived together as one happy family. The baroness, whose background was, and still is, obscure, emerged a gay, carefree vixen who had come to Floreana for the sole purpose of leading a wild adulterous life. Evidently a woman of wealth, she brought with her cases of champagne and exotic foods and delicacies. She quickly became the envy of four other German immigrants on the island who were forced by penury to live off the land and sea.

Snug as the proverbial bugs in a rug, the beautiful baroness and her three paramours proceeded to lead a riotous life and thought nothing of parading around the island in the nude, while their nights were spent drinking bubbly champagne and singing German songs to the accompaniment of phonograph records which the baroness had brought with her.

After a few months her Ecuadorian sweetheart, Valdivieso, weakened and ill, decided he had had enough and returned to Ecuador. With her lovers now reduced to two, passions mounted in the baroness' tropical paradise. The once docile girl became a sadistic monster and began horsewhipping her two lovers much in the manner that she mistreated her cattle. Even today bleached skulls of her animals can be found on the island.

While all the details of the Baroness' strange reign as queen of lust are not definitely known, enough information seeped out to give a pretty clear picture of her regime.

Eloisa had apparently concealed her sadistic inclinations from all three members of her male harem when they went with her to the island. At first she merely took turns in having "normal" relations with the three men. She had a regular schedule, sometimes changing companions three times a night, and at others only once a day.

But as the Baroness began to tire of even this lush diet of male companionship, her perverted instincts came more and more to the fore. Like some of her fellow frauleins who would be running concentration camps in a few years, she began to require cruelty as a prelude to sex activity.

Casting about for an excuse to inflict punishment on one of her trio of lovers, she chose Valdivieso as her initial victim. First she demanded that he, being a Latin, undertake the heaviest schedule of lovemaking, romancing her every other day, while the two Germans took turns on the alternate days. For a while Valdivieso was very pleased with this arrangement, but it was inevitable that he would soon find himself unable to satisfy the insatiable Baroness.

With that, she denounced him as a "scurvy pig" and insisted on her right, as leader (and financier) of the little colony, to inflict appropriate punishment on him. Drawing a gun, she commanded the two Germans to strip poor Valdivieso and tie him to a tree. Then she inflicted a hundred lashes on his bare body, reducing him to a shuddering, screaming pulp.

After that the Baroness had the Germans take turns making love to her in Valdivieso's full view, so that he could "see what a real lover is like."

It was small wonder that the Ecuadorian soon returned to his native land. But his departure by no means brought peace to the Baroness' realm. Her passion for cruelty grew stronger, and soon she demanded that Phillipson and Lorenz each submit to 20 lashes of her always-ready whip as the price of making love to her.

Both men were constantly scarred from their encounters with the depraved Baroness, yet neither rebelled at first, apparently because each hoped to become her favorite, perhaps even her only lover, by catering to her whims.

After a few weeks, however, Eloisa began showing a preference for Phillipson, the blond Viking, whereupon Lorenz suddenly made a dramatic declaration of independence. One day while Phillipson was out fishing for food, Lorenz disarmed the Baroness and announced that he was leaving her domain—but not until he had his full measure of revenge for the cruelty he had suffered at her hands.

At gunpoint Lorenz forced the shocked Eloisa to strip raw and lie prone on her cot in the shack. He then seized her whip and applied it thoroughly to her buttocks, thighs and back until she was screeching for mercy. Instead of that, he gave her one more violent, painful taste of his manhood, then left her sobbing on the bed while he departed from her life for good. Taking a gun along for protection, Lorenz moved down the beach a bit and built his own shack..

The weird adventure reached its mystifying climax a few weeks later, when the Baroness and Phillipson disappeared without explanation from Floreana. There were rumors that they had gone back to Ecuador, and some newspaper reports that she had headed for Paris. But it has since been definitely established that there was no ship at or near the Galapagos at the time of the disappearance, and it would have been impossible for the couple to leave by sea. In any case, neither of them has ever been heard from or seen since, and their sudden vanishing from the face of the earth still constitutes one of the great unsolved mysteries of this century.

And to add to the confusion, several weeks later two bodies were found on the island of Marchena and identified as those of Lorenz and a Norwegian fisherman. Cause of their death was unknown.

The second of the unusual characters who made history on the Galapagos was a Scotch sailor who in 1703 was marooned on the island of Fernandina and was forced to live the life of a castaway for the next four years and four months. On January 31, 1709, a ship, the Duchess, under the command of William Dampier, anchored off the island of Fernandina and sent a small boat ashore to collect turtles and firewood and to refill its water casks.

As the sailors disembarked, an Englishman dressed in goatskins approached them. His face was covered with a straggly beard and perched on top of his long matted hair was a peaked fur hat. In halting English he told them he was Alexander Selkirk, and, falling to his knees, begged them to take him back to civilization. The story of his lonely four-year vigil so intrigued the world when it became known that later the celebrated author, Daniel Defoe, drew upon the life and experiences of Selkirk for his now classic book, *Robinson Crusoe.*

QUITE frankly, I have read this book on many occasions and often wondered how it would feel to actually be marooned on such an island and how one could live, even with the companionship of a mythical Man Friday whom Defoe wove into the fabric of his story. Well, there was only one way to find out. Why not go to the Galapagos Islands and spend some time on Fernandina, the same island once inhabited by the world's most celebrated castaway?

Since the early days of the buccaneers the Galapagos have changed but little. Out of twenty-seven islands only four—San Cristobal, Isabela, Floreana and Santa Cruz—are inhabited, and the total population is less than two thousand. Fernandina still remains practically uninhabited, just as it was in the days of Selkirk.

Arriving in Guayaquil, the main port of Ecuador, I quickly made arrangements for a trip to the islands. Although the voyage was to take four days, the fare on a small, disreputable looking freighter called the *SS Galapagos* was only $12.00. I was the sole passenger, and because there were no staterooms or other accommodations, I slept in a hammock which the captain had strung for me on the upper deck. Our fifty-year old tub was certainly no *Queen Mary,* and two days out of Guayaquil the water pipes burst and drinking water was rationed to two glasses a day. What I didn't drink, the captain told me, could be

**We thought** you'd like to see what Jane looks like when she's wearing her red panties (and the rest of her regular clothes). As you can see, she looks the part of a regular girl, as well as explorer.

**While still** in Guayaquil, Ecuador, Jane saw cacao beans drying in streets. They are a leading export.

**Giant sea** iguana suns itself in Galapagos. Some of these monsters measure well over six feet long.

**Jane on** the 50-year-old freighter which took her to Galapagos in a four-day trip for twelve dollars.

used for bathing.

On the morning of the fifth day, our ship anchored in the bay at San Cristobal, the capital island, and after presenting my credentials to the governor I was free to proceed to Fernandina. Fortunately, I was able to hire .a small sailboat, and three days later arrived at San Salvador, a practically uninhabited island of volcanic cinders and clinkers. It was here that I met Debbie, a pretty young girl of twenty, whose father, a Danish refugee, made a precarious living as a fisherman on the island of Marchena. I suggested that she accompany me to Fernandina, and she was more than happy to come along. After all, Robinson Crusoe had his "Man Friday" and the least I could do was to have a feminine counterpart!

Debbie was an uninhibited "Girl Friday" who generally ran around the islands in her birthday suit, and she actually looked aghast when I suggested that for photographic reasons she would have to wear some clothing—not much, but enough to fall within the confines of good taste. Her wardrobe consisted of four or five skimpy pieces of animal skin.

Sailing in and around the Galapagos was a never-to-be-forgotten experience. In the deep blue waters around our small boat we saw giant sharks, many of them thirty feet in length, innumerable whales spouting gigantic streams of water toward the sky and iridescent porpoises

**Since they** didn't have a flag, the girls raised Jane's lacey red panties on pole as banner of their island realm. Author didn't need them anyway, since she wore only animal skins.

casting silver sheens in our wake. We were completely surrounded by terrifying denizens of the deep.

Fernandina, our home for the next two weeks, was similar to all the other islands. Tree-high cacti soared skyward. Huge chunks of volcanic cinders, interspersed with pink and blue coral rocks, reached inland as far as the eye could see. Gnarled old trees and clumps of strange-looking bushes covered the ground. It was as forlorn and desolate a place as I had ever seen, and yet beautiful in a hellish sort of way.

We had no flag, so my red lace panties hoisted high on a slender pole became our insignia of freedom. The island was filled with springs of cool clear water.

Debbie and I quickly made a small overnight shelter from the branches of trees and within just a few hours I became as uninhibited as my Girl Friday. Dressed only in the minimum of clothes, we lived the wild carefree life that Selkirk endured for over four years.

It has been said that Robinson Crusoe often danced with his cats and goats on his primitive island. Not to be outdone, I had brought along my bamboo Inca flute from Ecuador and Debbie, out of sheer ecstasy and the exuberance of living, danced along the stony beach with impish glee.

As in the days of Professor Darwin, who visited the islands just one hundred years ago, strange creatures, giant sea iguanas (many of them over six feet in length) closely resembling dinosaurs, came out of the mysterious depths of the ocean to sun themselves on the rock strewn beaches, but at our approach they would dive headfirst into the sea and silently disappear. While these water iguanas are not considered edible, another species that lives on land is captured by the natives for its delicious and succulent white meat.

Although it was comparatively safe living along the beach, natives from other islands warned us that to climb the lava cliffs in the interior could be extremely dangerous, as it was in the higher altitudes that the once-domesticated animals, now turned savage, foraged for food. In the hills roamed ferocious bulls, more dangerous than those faced by matadors in the bullrings of Spain. In addition to the cattle, wild boars, one of the most feared of all animals, attacked human beings without provocation, and even the once-gentle little tabby cats had turned savage, stalking their prey much in the same manner as the jungle jaguar.

We had come to Fernandina armed only with a machete and some primitive bows and arrows, certainly not the type of weapons one could use when faced with a charging thousand pound bull or when attacked by a herd of vicious wild boars. With our area of freedom limited by these hazards, I naturally became worried about how we would be able to survive and what we could find to eat. My fears were dispelled by Debbie. The sea was filled with a great many edible fish, and in addition, giant lobsters were easily found under the rocks near the shore. Early in the morning dozens of tortoises crawled onto the beach and because they were slow-moving, we had little trouble tipping them over on their backs, rendering them helpless.

Debbie showed me how to dig in the sand for turtle eggs, and with simple snares we captured several large birds, all of which were edible and extremely delicious. The island abounded in a variety of fruits such as oranges, papayas, avocadoes, bananas and date palms, so our diet was well-balanced and ample. Fortunately, we dug up an old iron pot (it might have belonged to Selkirk) and we used this for cooking our food.

On our enchanted island hideaway, time was a forgotten factor. Oftentimes we would be up at four o'clock in the morning. Just as the first brilliant rays of sun came zooming across the blue of the deep Pacific, we left our crude shelter and after a quick dip in the ocean foraged for our breakfast. Each morning we took our small sailboat and explored not only our island, but others nearby.

Only alone on an endless sea can one realize the immensity of space, and as far as I was concerned I became a Columbus, a Magellan, and a Pizarro, all rolled into one.

Debbie, who had lived all of her life in the islands, knew many exciting places. She showed me great limestone caves where the early pirates once buried their stolen treasures, and under-sea grottoes whose beauty was unmatched by man-made edifices. Now I knew why, since man first discovered the Galapagos, they were called *Las Islas Encantadas*, the Enchanted Islands. Here was a place where life was serene, simple and beautiful. Money was unimportant and a beneficent Nature took care of all our physical needs.

But all things must come to an end. After all, I was not Selkirk, and even though I hated the thought, I knew that I had to return to civilization. There were new horizons still to be conquered.

But, in retrospect, I came to the conclusion that the German Baroness had the right idea. A Girl Friday is good for a storyline, but next time I revisit the Enchanted Islands I must remember to take along a handsome "Man Saturday" instead.

Paradise, anyone? ▮▮▮

## "I MARRIED A JUNGLE SAVAGE"

— KEN KRIPPENE —

*Sir!*, November 1959

COVER ARTIST: UNCREDITED

hose I've run into down around the Amazon Basin. If you pay close attention to what they say, you can get some good tips on where to go for extracurricular excitement—and that includes sex!

A few months ago in Pucallpa, Peru, a small jungle community on the banks of the Rio Ucayali, I met a young preacher who had just returned from a trip into the jungle interior. Although still in his 20's, his hair was graying around the temples, and the incredulous look in his eyes reminded me of the first time I'd gone to a bawdy house, back in my schooldays in Chicago.

# I MARRIED A JUNGLE SAVAGE

**The Cashibos Go in for Husband-Trading. The Gal You Kiss Good Morning Usually Isn't the One You Kiss Good Night**

Author with Cashibo girl who stole his mosquito net; act constitutes marriage. She later sold him for 2 fish hooks.

Ark, a small, decrepit single-decked job with a flat roof. As I walked up the gangway I noticed that the craft listed to port, probably due to the heavy cargo of twelve cows which were already aboard. Juan, the toothless old river pilot, told me that the passengers rode on the roof and at night sleeping hammocks would be set up to ward off the hordes of mosquitoes and vampire bats which always appeared after sundown.

which followed us for miles. azure-blue sky was identified Several long-necked white b lows on either bank were eg are highly prized by the Indi

Later in the afternoon, as t to the shore, huge crocodiles and into the river. They were creatures with tiny red

**GENERALLY,** missionaries are nice Joes, especially those I've run into down around the Amazon Basin. If you pay close attention to what they say, you can get some good tips on where to go for extracurricular excitement—and that includes sex!

A few months ago in Pucallpa, Peru, a small jungle community on the banks of the Rio Ucayali, I met a young preacher who had just returned from a trip into the jungle interior. Although still in his 20s, his hair was graying around the temples, and the incredulous look in his eyes reminded me of the first time I'd gone to a bawdy house, back in my schooldays in Chicago.

"I saw some horrible things," the preacher said, shaking his head. "Why, those Cashibos have no sense of modesty. Imagine those young Indian girls practicing polyandry, and there was nothing I could do to stop them!"

I did a double-take on the word "polyandry," and dug back into my memory to classify it. Then I had it. Polyandry is a sexual gimmick, where women take on more than one husband at the same time. I knew they practiced it in Tibet, probably because the ratio of men to women is about five to one, but here in the Amazon it's just the opposite.

I took the poor preacher to the Turista Hotel and bought him a square meal, the first he had had in several months. Of course, I didn't do it entirely out of the goodness of my heart. I wanted to know more about those sexy little sirens of the jungle. Naturally, I didn't come right out and tell him I was interested in visiting the Cashibos. After all, I was a middle-aged amateur anthropologist; I had to attack the situation from the scientific angle. I had a cold bottle of beer while the preacher drank his potato soup, then lit into a plate of fried fish.

"About these Cashibos," I began. "Are they friendly?"

He rolled his eyes like a sick cow. "Friendly! Why, do you know, sir, those conspiring females tried to get me into their clutches.' They wanted me, a man of the cloth, for a husband And," he went on, "some of them were mere children, 13 or 14 at the oldest. I tell you, they had no sense of modesty!"

I agreed with him, but very carefully questioned him about the

location of the tribe and the number of days it would take to reach
them. Hell, I wasn't any missionary; just a scientific guy on the prowl.

I walked the preacher to the airport, where he caught a plane to
Lima. After waving him a fond farewell, I ran back to the waterfront and
found that a river steamer was scheduled to leave the next morning for
a trip to Atalaya and the home of the Cashibos. I bought passage and
went back to the hotel.

An hour before dawn I got out of my room, gulped down a cup
of coffee, picked up my overnight bag, and threaded my way down
the narrow litter-filled path to the river. The boat looked like Noah's
Ark, a small, decrepit single-decked job with a flat roof. As I walked
up the gangway I noticed that the craft listed to port, probably due to
the heavy cargo of twelve cows which were already aboard. Juan, the
toothless old river pilot, told me that the passengers rode on the roof
and at night sleeping hammocks would be set up to ward off the hordes
of mosquitoes and vampire bats which always appeared after sundown.

I climbed the rickety stairs and worked my way forward through a
maze of crates and boxes. I found a broken-down chair and sat in the
front of the boat so I could get a complete view of both sides of the
river. I was the only passenger.

We nosed into the deep channel and in just a few minutes entered a
bend in the river and Pucallpa disappeared. It was like entering a new
and beautiful world. Towering masses of green foliage extended along
both banks as far as I could see. The calm was broken only by the put-
put-put of our motor. Occasionally we passed palm-thatched huts of
Indian farmers who wrested a precarious living out of the jungle. Each
clearing had its quota of banana trees and yucca bushes, the two basic
foods upon which life depended. Even at this early hour Indian women
were at the river's edge washing clothes, while their broods of naked
youngsters frolicked in the muddy water.

The Ucayali is not only one of the swiftest rivers in the world, but
decidedly one of the most dangerous. We passed tremendous floating
islands, some of them a mile long and a half-mile wide, all moving
steadily toward the Amazon. Many times Juan had to change his course
in order to avoid colliding with huge trees, logs and other debris.

I took off my shirt and pants, marks of civilization which were
no longer necessary. The wind swept across the river, cooling my
body and tousling my hair. I felt free and, for some strange reason,
exceedingly happy.

Around noon Juan turned over the boat to his young Indian co-
pilot and joined me on the flat top. After lunch Juan pointed out several

Cashibo men perform duel with heavy wooden clubs. The winner brings high price if wife decides to sell him.

interesting things. The Ucayali was filled with schools of fresh-water porpoises which followed us for miles. A green mist against the azure-blue sky was identified as a flock of macaws. Several long-necked white birds feeding in the shallows on either bank were egrets, birds whose feathers are highly prized by the Indians for headpieces.

Later in the afternoon, as the channel took us closer to the shore, huge crocodiles slithered off the mudbanks and into the river. They were squat, loathsome-looking creatures with tiny red eyes and gaping mouths. They watched us suspiciously until we passed.

Just before sundown Pedro, Juan's assistant, came upstairs and set up our hammocks and mosquito nets. I asked him if we kept on traveling all night; he said it was impossible to go on after dark. Shortly afterward I heard Juan cut the motor, and we drifted slowly to shore. While it was still light we ate a hasty supper, and just as the sun was setting I got my first real taste of jungle mosquitoes. They came in clouds, thousands upon thousands, until they were a gray mist all around us.

It was impossible to beat them off. By 6:30 we were all under our mosquito nets in our hammocks. It was the first time in my life that I had gone to bed at that hour and, of course, I found sleep impossible.

The motion of the water made my hammock sway lightly. I wanted to turn over on my side but found it impossible. Mosquitoes hummed around the net, trying desperately to get inside. Juan and Pedro were snoring peacefully, but I wasn't that fortunate. I wondered how people made love in a hammock.

Finally I fell asleep. When I awoke the next morning, we were already underway. The sky was dark and gray. A delightful breeze swept over the river, cooling my naked body. Turning, I reached over the side of my hammock, groping for my cigarettes. Then, for the first time, I saw that during the night we had taken on some additional passengers. Squatting on their haunches and eying me soberly were a half-dozen Indian women. Two of them were about 15 years old, and one was a decrepit, white-haired, toothless creature whose withered breasts looked like two pancakes. They were all nude from the waist up and wore short wrap-around skirts which barely covered their thighs. Their faces were painted in intricate designs of blue and yellow, and their long black hair fell down around their shoulders. The two youngest looked mature and evidently knew what life was all about. When they saw me watching them, they started giggling and talking in *quechua*, their native tongue. I quickly donned my shorts, swung over the side of the hammock, and crawled out from under my net. Their eyes followed me as I went downstairs to the lower deck.

I found Juan at the wheel and asked about the Indian women. He told me they had boarded the boat just before dawn and belonged to the Cashibo tribe. They were the very women I had come so far to see. Not bad, I thought. Not bad at all! Their village was located farther down the river and our boat would dock there for the night.

Old Juan knew all about them. The Cashibos were one of the few matriarchies in the Amazon Basin. The tribe was ruled by the women. If a Cashibo woman found a man to her liking, she simply went to his family hut and brought his mosquito net into her own house. This act constituted marriage. From that moment on the husband assumed his wife's name and had to fish and hunt for her family until such time as she tired of the union. When this occurred she simply threw his net out of her palm-thatched house and she was legally divorced. According to Juan, some marriages lasted only one night, and nets moved from one hut to another with lightning speed.

"But," I said, "suppose some guy doesn't like his new wife. What then?"

"It's just too bad for him," Juan answered. "If he doesn't behave like a good boy he might be sent into exile by the tribe."

This was an entirely new twist. I hadn't known there was a pure matriarchy still in existence, but I was curious to see the Cashibos and spend a few weeks in their village.

Our second day on the river was a great deal like the first. Palm-thatched shacks were becoming scarce, and there was an abundance of birds and tropical flowers. During the afternoon Juan and I watched a giant anaconda, or water boa, slowly emerge from the river and disappear into the jungle. It must have been at least 30 feet long and its skin was a beautiful golden-yellow, crisscrossed with irregular black markings.

Toward sundown the Indian women became excited. They pointed ahead and talked rapidly. A few minutes later we tied up at their village. It consisted of eight large palm-thatched huts, each holding between twenty and thirty people. I immediately noticed the absence of men. Juan explained they went on fishing trips which often lasted days or weeks. While they were gone the women occupied their time by

weaving clothes from wild jungle cotton and gathering yucca, bananas and other fruits.

Juan asked me if I would like to go with him as far as Atalaya, where the Cashibos had their main village, but I declined with thanks. This suited me fine, and I knew there was enough river traffic at this point to work my way back to Pucallpa in case I wanted to escape.

Pedro carried our hammocks and nets into one of the larger huts. It finally dawned on me that the *jefe*, or chief of the tribe, was the white-haired woman who had been on our boat. The way her glittering black eyes followed me, I began to wonder if she had designs on my net. That would have been the end, I thought.

After eating a dinner of monkey stew and fried bananas we went down to the river for a quick bath. Some of the women followed us, squatting on the riverbank and watching us as we swam naked in the warm water. By the time we finished, the women were gone. We hurried back to the village to avoid the swarms of mosquitoes which always descended at sunset.

Entering the hut, I discovered that my net and hammock were gone. The women clustered around Juan and me and giggled. Juan talked to them in *quechua* and they pointed to another hut a short distance away. We walked over to the house and there was all my stuff.

Juan pointed to the net and told me to lift it up. I did. Lying in my hammock was a beautiful little Indian girl of about 19. I crawled under the net and stood beside her, not knowing exactly what to do. She smiled invitingly and moved over to the edge of the hammock, making room for me. I looked at Juan.

"It is the law," he said simply.

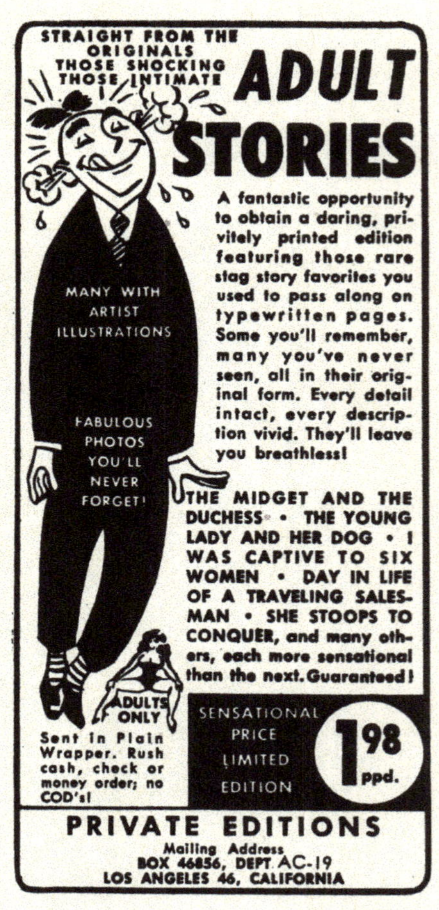

"The law of the jungle. You are now married."

Well, who was I to argue with the law of the jungle? After all, this wasn't the old white-haired witch, but a beautiful young savage whose eyes held an open invitation.

When I awoke early the next morning my jungle bride had already left the hammock, but on the dirt floor was a beautiful new *cushma*, an ankle-length garment hand-woven from the finest jungle cotton and dyed in bright colors. My clothes were gone, so there was nothing left to do but put on my new Indian dress, which looked more like an old-fashioned nightgown than anything else. I crawled out from under my net and looked around the hut. It was empty. Later I learned that all the women had rushed to the river bank because the men were returning from their fishing trip.

I found Juan and Pedro in another hut and walked with them to their boat. Juan told me he would stop by on his return trip in about a week; if I liked, I could go back to Pucallpa with him.

"On the other hand," Juan laughed, "you may be gone long before I get back." He winked knowingly.

I didn't know exactly what he meant, but it didn't take long to find out.

During the next few days I found out a great deal more about the Cashibo way of life. Each morning the women would meet in one of the huts and the old Jefe would assign the day's work for the men. Some were sent out to hunt, others to gather fruits and pick cotton. The rest had to go out and fish.

As an American I had been used to a certain amount of female domination, but this was going too far! Whether she knew it or not, this old dame ruled the village like a Roman despot.

The first day I was put on the fishing detail. These jungle men didn't fish with rods and reels. Fish was considered one of the basic foods and we had to bring back several boatloads or suffer a tongue-lashing from the *jefe*.

At daybreak we took our machetes and dug up dozens of barbasco roots. These we crushed between stones until they reached a pulpy consistency. The barbasco was then dumped into several canoes and we took off downriver to a quiet little stream which teemed with over 1400 varieties of edible fish. Our canoes were made of hollowed-out logs and tipped easily. I soon learned to sit very still, for both creeks and rivers were filled with hungry crocodiles which could take off a man's leg with one powerful crunch of a massive jaw.

Reaching the designated spot, the Indians covered the mashed barbasco roots with river water and swished it around in the bottom of the boat with their squat paddles. When the water had turned to a milk-like substance it was dipped out into the stream. Immediately we paddled downriver for about a mile and awaited results. An hour or so later hundreds of fish of all shapes and sizes came to the surface. All we had to do was reach out, pick them up and dump them into the boat.

When our quota was filled we returned to the village and the women went to work. They laid the fish on specially prepared racks where they could get the full benefit of the sun. In four or five hours the fish were sun-cured and as hard as bricks. Later the women stacked them up like so much cordwood, to be used as needed.

Strangely enough, the poisonous barbasco root didn't affect us at all. My only objection was that the Indian women never cleaned the fish before frying them. They considered the entrails a delicacy.

After a hard day's work you'd think a man would be entitled to go home and get some sleep, but that was not always the case. First of all, you were never sure who your wife would be that night.

Old husbands were traded away for just a couple of fish hooks, with maybe a piece of ribbon thrown in to close the deal. Handsome young men brought a much higher price. Some were worth at least two machetes or a piece of cloth.

You could kiss your wife goodbye in the morning when you were sent out to work, and be forced to greet a new one on your return. Whoever came up with the expression that variety is the spice of life must have learned it the hard way, living with the Cashibos.

In the beginning I thought that because of the color of my skin I was destined to become the big chief in the wigwam, but things didn't work out that way. When the old *jefe* saw that I couldn't use a blowgun, she sent me out with a cotton-picking detail, a back-breaking job at best.

This squad of unhappy men was comprised mostly of old coots and young boys who hadn't yet reached the age of puberty.

Late that night, when I finally got back to the village with my quota of cotton balls, I was so tired I tumbled into my hammock and in two minutes was sound asleep. This, I learned later, was a fatal mistake. The next morning I was sent out with a couple of toothless old men to cut bananas. This sounded easy. I thought all we had to do was bring back a few dozen bananas for the evening meal. How wrong I was! Each of us had to carry back a stalk weighing almost 40 pounds. These stalks, I found, as one of the huge hairy insects began crawling up my back, were loaded with tarantulas. I staggered down the jungle trail with my heavy load, cursing the day I'd ever heard of the Cashibo.

Nearing the hut, I saw the women sitting around in a circle on the dirt floor, laughing and giggling. I lowered my banana very quietly and crawled up behind them. If there was anything to laugh at, I wanted to be in on it. After five years in the jungle I understood enough *quechua* to figure out what they were talking about, and I soon discovered it was me. I was being sold down the river, bartered away to the highest bidder. At least, I thought to myself, I'll bring a high price. Then I saw a middle-aged woman named Taisha cautiously place a fish hook on the ground in front of her. Well, that was only the first bid. I expected to see machetes, cloth, everything, piled up in the center of the group as payment for my services.

The women continued to giggle and talk. *Come on, girls*, I said to myself, *let's get out the loot*. But no loot was forthcoming. Finally the old *jefe* placed two fish hooks on the ground, one of them rusty. There were no other bidders. So that was my price—two fish hooks! Well, I wasn't going to play house any longer. If that was all I was worth, it was high time to shove off.

I couldn't go back into the hut because I was afraid the old lady might claim me as her new spouse. Quickly I looked around. None of the men were in sight, so I beat a path to the river. I jumped into one of the canoes and began paddling furiously downstream. Later I knew I would be missed, but not too much. After all, a guy worth only two fish hooks wasn't entitled to any VIP treatment, even from a bunch of Cashibo dolls.

A couple of hours later I came to a good-sized village, not run by women, thank goodness, and got permission to sleep in one of the huts until Juan picked me up the next day. Needless to say, I willingly returned to civilization: a little exhausted, to be sure, but definitely wiser in the ways of jungle love sirens! **///**

# Men's Mart

A quick way to protect, as well as beautify, your flower beds and lawn, is with this new folding 10-gauge zinc-plated (non-rusting) steel wire fence that opens to 10 feet, stands 18 inches. It conforms to any contour— round, oval, oblong, heart-shaped or square. Each section is detachable so that fence can be lengthened or shortened. $3.98 ppd. Order from Lord George, 1270 Broadway, N.Y.

This new blue-steel German automatic fires blanks and doesn't require a permit to own. A 6-shot repeater, gun is fully automatic, has positive safety catch, self-ejecting clip. Machined with the care and precision of West German armament experts. Ideal for sporting events, it measures 4" long. It comes for $7.95 ppd. Order from Big Three Enterprises, 1109 6th Ave., New York, N.Y.

1898. That's when these helmets were made, and incredibly enough, this firm has found some that, though 58 years old, are *brand new* surplus. U. S. Army issue for Spanish-American War and Philippine Insurrection, all cork white linen helmets are duplicates of British African one. 2 sizes, small and large, both adjustable. $3.95 ppd. and a buy! Kline's, 329 East 65th St., New York.

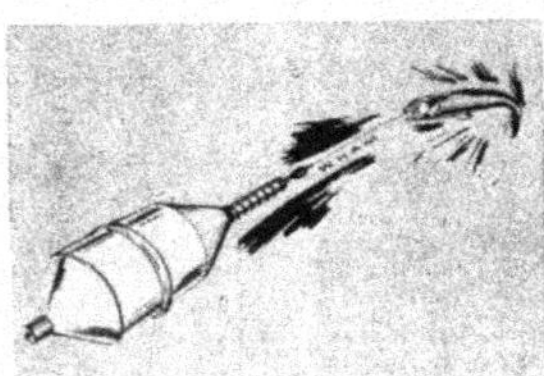

This new invention automatically catches fish because of an automatic trigger that sets the hook firmly in the mouth of the fish in just 1/50 of a second. It's called the "Bob-O-Matic" casting float. It takes just a second to reset trigger. Light and compact, it fits easily into any fishing kit. Might help increase your catch, boys. $1.98 ppd. Wegman Co., Lynbrook, N. Y.

The good man that makes this little beauty says it's the ideal gift for a guy who has everything. We've heard that before, but this time the man may have something. Yep, it's the proverbial fur-lined potty (with real fur, no less) that ought to get a chuckle out of anybody. Could even be used as a TV seat. Dealer inquiries are invited. $3.95 ppd. Lincoln Products, 411 Lincoln Bldg., N.Y. 17.

Keep this perpetual calendar handy and you'll always know the date. Just adjust the knob each month and the days fall in their correct sequence. All steel, it has a brass finish, sturdy stand. It measures about 4" long and 3" high. Useful for home or the office, calendar comes for $1 ppd. Order from Barclay Distributors, Dept. 664, 86-24 Parsons Boulevard, Jamaica, New York.

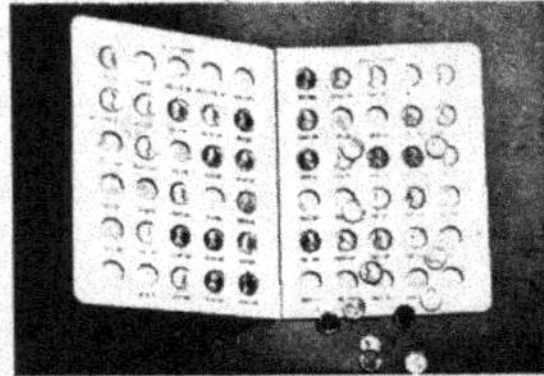

Object you're looking at is an unusual album for Lincoln head pennies—there's a place for 59 pennies, some easy to come by, others hard to find. Idea is to fill the album, naturally, but when full it'll be worth $16. Album's $1 ppd. from BYBY-MAIL, Box 67, Dept. E-2, Oakland Gardens Sta., Flushing, N. Y. If you fill album they give you $16 and $1 purchase refund.

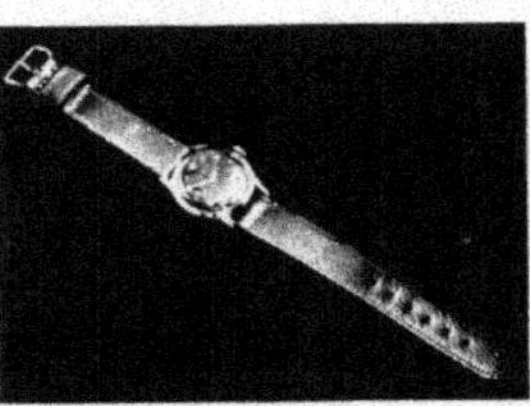

This 17-jewel watch has a high grade Swiss movement, and is waterproof, shockproof and anti-magnetic. It has an unbreakable mainspring and crystal, and is easy to read. Ideal for outdoorsman, it has luminous dial and hands, sweep-second hand. Electronically timed and adjusted, it has a 2-year guarantee. $14.95 ppd. Karron Enterprises, Dept. E, 2 S. Main St., S. Norwalk, Conn.

It's getting so that if you like cheese you either settle for the thin gummy concoctions stores stock, or send away for it. This Cheddar isn't processed, colored or pasteurized—just aged for two years. And until you try it you don't know what long aging can do to a rich whole-milk cheese. Sharp, crumbly 5½ lb. wheel, $6 ppd. Milder 3 lb. one is $4 ppd. Sugarbush Farm, Woodstock, Vt.

# ABOUT "I WENT INSANE FOR SCIENCE"

STORIES *about drugs are common in vintage MAMs. Many are "exposés" in the* Reefer Madness *vein. Others, though sensationalized to an extent (like virtually every story in a men's pulp mag), were a bit more thoughtful. Some were actually ahead of their time.*

*When* Man's Magazine *published the story "I Went Insane for Science" in August 1956, relatively few people were aware of the psychoactive drug involved—lysergic acid diethylamide. At that point, LSD was known primarily to certain pharmacology experts and psychiatrists, the Central Intelligence Agency and some of the human guinea pigs used in early experiments with the drug.*

*The CIA started testing LSD in 1953 in secret "mind control" experiments, code-named MK-ULTRA. (One of the test subjects was future novelist and Merry Prankster Ken Kesey, who helped make LSD a cultural phenomenon in the following decade.)*

*By the mid-1950s, psychiatrists at a number of "mental hospitals" were also experimenting with LSD. They were intrigued by the fact that it caused hallucinations and other effects similar to schizophrenia. By giving LSD to "normal" people, they hoped to understand that disease better. They also tested drugs that counteracted the effects of LSD and thus held potential for the treatment of schizophrenia.*

*The CIA's MK-ULTRA project wasn't exposed publicly until the 1970s. But in the mid- to late '50s, there were occasional articles in the popular press about the more well-intended psychiatric experiments.*

*"I Went Insane for Science" is an interesting example about a doctor who voluntarily took LSD for an experiment at a medical facility. He's called "Dr. Robert H----" in the article, to protect his real identity. It's written as a first-hand account, in the "as told to" style that was common in MAMs.*

*It's often hard to figure out if a story in an old men's pulp mag is true, partly true or total fiction. However, based on the level of detail in the story and on writer William Michelfelder's involvement, I think this one is at least based on fact. Michelfelder had a long career as a journalist and editor at many newspapers, including the* New York World-Telegram and Sun.

*Interestingly, the doctor shown in the photos used for the story is Dr. Carl Pfeiffer of Emory University. Pfeiffer was a pioneer in "orthomolecular psychiatry." In the 1970s, it was revealed that he was*

**Man's Story** (August 1968) weighs in on the LSD question with typical reserve.

also one of the scientists who conducted secret LSD research for the CIA's MK-ULTRA project.

According to a caption for the photos, LSD gave Pfeiffer "a schizophrenic reaction to Rorschach ink-blot test." One photo shows him laughing, so he seems to have enjoyed it. Dr. H----, who told the story of his own experimental acid trip to Michelfelder, didn't find his LSD experience so amusing. Instead of laughing during his LSD trip, like Dr. Pfeiffer, Dr. H---- ends up screaming.

On the positive side, the article notes that LSD research like Dr. H---- volunteered for did give psychiatrists a better understanding of schizophrenia. It also led to the development of new drugs that were effective in treating some schizophrenics—and, later, freaked-out Hippies on bum acid trips.

The example mentioned in "I Went Insane for Science" is the drug Frenquel, which worked fairly well. It was eventually superseded by a similar drug that became much better known, under the name Thorazine.

—Robert Deis

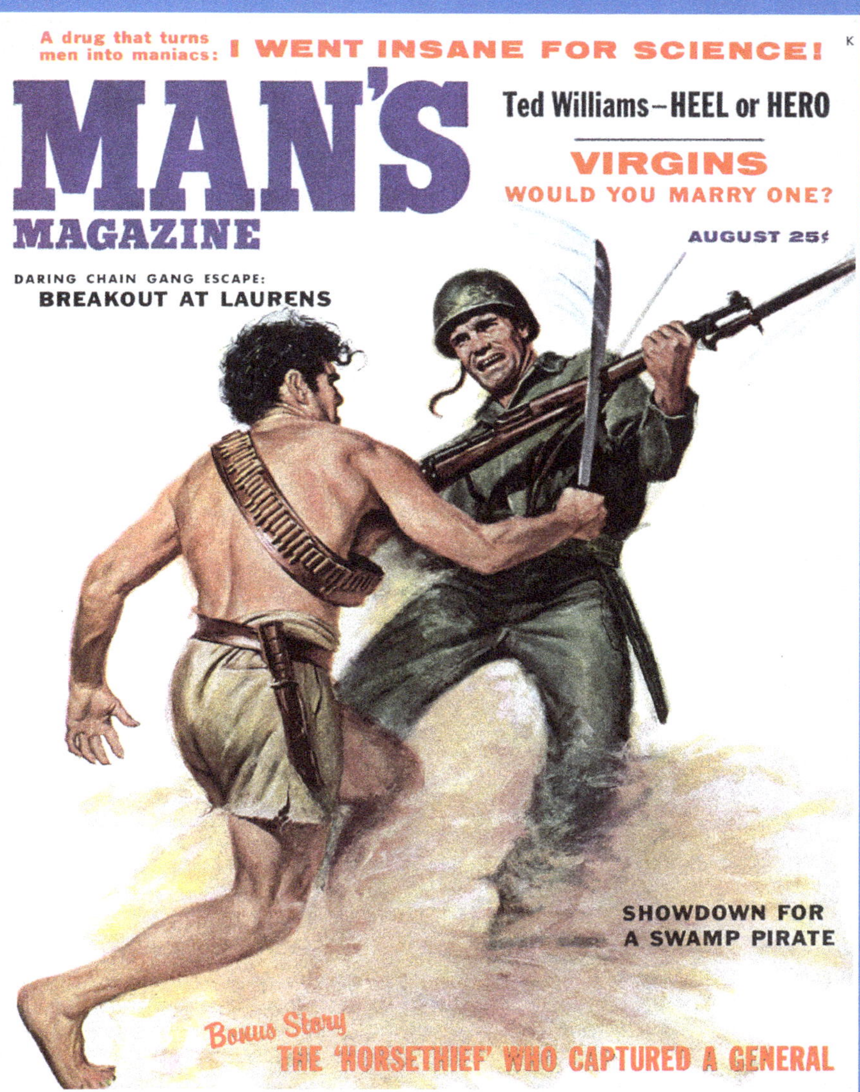


## "I WENT INSANE FOR SCIENCE"

### DR. ROBERT H. (WILLIAM MICHELFELDER)

*Man's Magazine*, August 1956

COVER ARTIST: TOM RYAN

not enou[gh] Of all the mental diseases, it is the most
baffling. We know its symptoms, *but we do not know*
*much of what goes on inside these patients.*

In a few minutes, when the dose of LSD-25 I swallowed
begins to take effect, I am going to live in that dark, un-
fathomab[le]
what re
doctors
I must
expose a
what I
subconsc
As I
why I s
water. S
How ca
torted w
phrenic
By sw
slab in
I believe
Lying
pound of
the theor
doctors,
phrenia –
in the h
I think
a person
has lost
A person
those wh
his viole
death-lik
And I
snake-pit
"Schiz
fable,"
before I
ing on a
gether t
they sep
together
"So .
they fou
tolerably
berserk.
or woma
One o
napkin.
tightenin
somewhe
light ab
sane . .

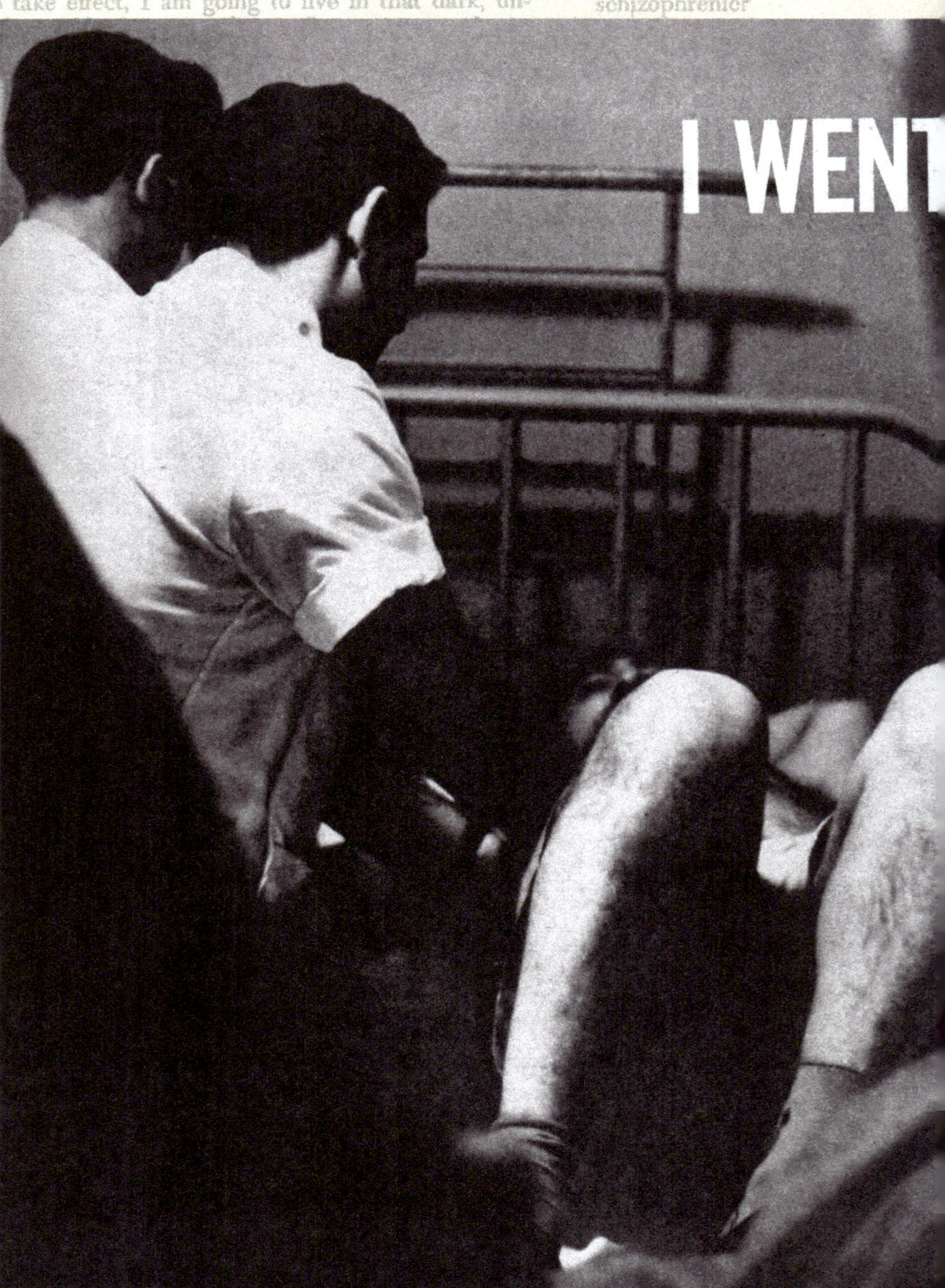


What about the pioneers like
Edward Evarts at the National
took LSD-25 and returned to o
Max Rinkel, of the Boston gr
fabulous data from his own s
did so much to improve the
schizophrenic?

I TELL
one. There is solace and security in knowing that
other sane people have tried this experiment. Right now
at Boston Psychopathic Hospital, at Brooklyn State Hospital, at the National Institute of Mental Health, at several
midwestern hospitals, doctors and staff workers are taking
LSD-25 and trying to bring back the story of the mad-

zinc. . . .
(Patient makes four guttur[al]
straint.)
*"I want to tap my head but n*
*there is the train pulling out*
*burning port and starboard lig*[ht]

ED
L!



305

# INSANE FOR SCIENCE

**I think about the schizophrenic's nightmare life — his violent moments, the hours he spends in a death-like trance. And I am frightened — for I am about to leap into his snake-pit world by taking a drug that turns men into mental patients.**

By DR. ROBERT H——— as told to WILLIAM MICHELFELDER

I AM SITTING on a tiny white stool in the seclusion room of a state mental hospital. Ninth floor, Section "G" is the polite clinical name. To the doctors here, privately, it is known as The Jungle. This is the place where they hide the worst of them.

Two colleagues stand over me, for I, too, am a doctor . . . Dr. Robert H————, a healthy young interne who some day hopes to be a first-rate psychiatrist.

I am about to voluntarily lose my mind.

The doctor standing on my right, one of the great new pioneers in the field of psychiatry-and-drugs, holds a glass in his hand. It is filled to the brim with six ounces of a clear, tasteless liquid.

"A few minutes after you drink this," he says quietly, "you will start to withdraw from the outside world. It is a venture into madness, you understand. For six hours, perhaps longer, you will undergo a full-fledged psychotic experience. You are likely to say anything and do anything — and yet you must come back to face what you have said and done.

"You do not wish to withdraw from the experiment?"

I glance briefly at the second doctor. Behind his back he conceals, rather shamefacedly, a new straitjacket. And beyond him in the shadows wait three of our strongest attendants, ready to leap. I am a muscular fellow and could be quite troublesome.

Do I wish to withdraw? I ponder the doctor's question. No answer can be found in this dim-lit cubicle; the answer comes from The Jungle, where I hear the monotonous cries of the deranged, and the creaking of bed springs as a number of those lost souls thrash in leather restraints. They are my reasons.

"Let me swallow that, please," I hear myself say, and reach for the glass. . . .

But even as I swallow LSD-25, the lysergic acid that has already played horrible tricks on other volunteers — men like myself — I can't help wondering if I'm not tempting fate too far.

After all, it's practically begging for trouble to risk my own sanity with a dosage of a strange drug. Especially when I know for a fact that medical science has been unable to bring some of those volunteers back to normality. I could be another such case. . . .

Some 5,000,000 Americans today are living on the brink of an insanity known as schizophrenia. Often they are obscure people in small jobs, nursing some secret maladjustment, hovering on the fringe of reality. These people need help before it is too late. Before they, too, wind up in 9-G or some other jungle.

There are more than 300,000 schizophrenics in our mental hospitals right now. Some 150,000 new cases develop annually, a steady and frightening increase year after year. We doctors have made some progress fighting this terrifying mental disorder, but

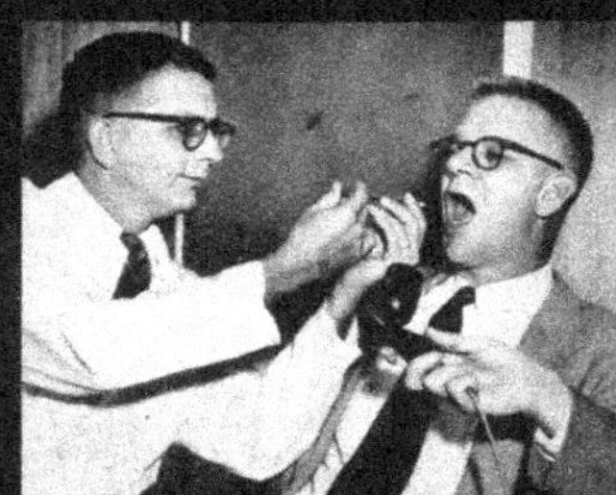

Dr. Harry Williams injects LSD-25 into Dr. Carl Pfeiffer, of Emory University, during Atlanta experiments. Pfeiffer, below, is under effects of drug and gives a schizophrenic reaction to Rorschach ink-blot test.

continued on next page

**I AM** sitting on a tiny white stool in the seclusion room of a state mental hospital. Ninth floor, Section "G" is the polite clinical name. To the doctors here, privately, it is known as The Jungle. This is the place where they hide the worst of them.

Two colleagues stand over me, for I, too, am a doctor… Dr. Robert H____, a healthy young interne who some day hopes to be a first-rate psychiatrist.

I am about to voluntarily lose my mind.

The doctor standing on my right, one of the great new pioneers in the field of psychiatry-and-drugs, holds a glass in his hand. It is filled to the brim with six ounces of a clear, tasteless liquid.

"A few minutes after you drink this," he says quietly, "you will start to withdraw from the outside world. It is a venture into madness, you understand. For six hours, perhaps longer, you will undergo a full-fledged psychotic experience. You are likely to say anything and do anything—and yet you must come back to face what you have said and done.

"You do not wish to withdraw from the experiment?"

I glance briefly at the second doctor. Behind his back he conceals, rather shamefacedly, a new straitjacket. And beyond him in the shadows wait three of our strongest attendants, ready to leap. I am a muscular fellow and could be quite troublesome.

Do I wish to withdraw? I ponder the doctor's question. No answer can be found in this dim-lit cubicle; the answer comes from The Jungle, where I hear the monotonous cries of the deranged, and the creaking of bed springs as a number of those lost souls thrash in leather restraints. They are my reasons.

"Let me swallow that, please," I hear myself say, and reach for the glass….

But even as I swallow LSD-25, the lysergic acid that has already played horrible tricks on other volunteers—men like myself—I can't help wondering if I'm not tempting fate too far.

After all, it's practically begging for trouble to risk my own sanity with a dosage of a strange drug. Especially when I know for a fact that medical science has been unable to bring some of those volunteers back to normality. I could be another such case....

Some 5,000,000 Americans today are living on the brink of an insanity known as schizophrenia. Often they are obscure people in small jobs, nursing some secret maladjustment, hovering on the fringe of reality. These people need help before it is too late. Before they, too, wind up in 9-G or some other jungle.

There are more than 300,000 schizophrenics in our mental hospitals right now. Some 150,000 new cases develop annually, a steady and frightening increase year after year. We doctors have made some progress fighting this terrifying mental disorder, but not enough. Of all the mental diseases, it is the most baffling. We know its symptoms, *but we do not know much of what goes on inside these patients.*

In a few minutes, when the dose of LSD-25 I swallowed begins to take effect, I am going to live in that dark, unfathomable world of true madness. I am going to know what really happens to a man in the grip of what we doctors call a "self-induced psychosis."

I must remain anonymous because a tape recorder will expose all the deep-down, intimate things that make me what I am—all the frustrated desires, evil wishes and subconscious tortures I normally keep under control.

As I wait for the drug to take effect, it is clear to me why I swallowed that dose, 100 micrograms in distilled water. Somebody has to if psychiatry is going to advance. How can we learn about schizophrenics and their distorted world if we can't get a true picture of the schizophrenic as he sees himself?

By swallowing that dosage, by lying down on that slab in 9-G, by entering that first convulsive nightmare, I believe I am helping my profession.

Lying on the slab, I think about LSD-25, an acid compound of a class of chemicals called indoles. I think about the theory, now being advanced by a number of reputable doctors, that many kinds of insanity—including schizophrenia—are actually caused by a chemical imbalance in the human body, and not always by emotional stress.

I think about the nightmare world of the schizophrenic, a person who lives in a waking dream state, a person who has lost contact with the world the rest of us live in. A person who cannot disentangle external events from those which take place in his dream world. I think about his violent moments—about the hours he spends in a death-like trance.

And I am frightened—for I am about to leap into his snake-pit world.

"Schizophrenics are like porcupines in the old German fable," one of the psychiatrists said to me, a few hours before I agreed to swallow this dose of LSD-25. "Freezing on a winter's day, they at first crowded so close together that their quills produced intolerable pain. When they separated, they nearly froze and were driven back together again.

"So...they moved backwards and forwards until they found a mean distance at which they could most tolerably exist. If they cannot find the mean, they go berserk. That, doctor, is the horrible torment of the man or woman today who lives on the fringe of schizophrenia."

One of the doctors carefully wiped my lips with a paper napkin. Nothing much happens, at first. I feel a strange tightening in my jaw bones. There is a peculiar quiver somewhere in the middle of my spine. The single white light above me whirls like a silver moth. But I am still sane...still able to think about my guinea-pig role.

I TELL myself I'm a martyr for science—a minor one. There is solace and security in knowing that other sane people have tried this experiment. Right now at Boston Psychopathic Hospital, at Brooklyn State Hospital, at the National Institute of Mental Health, at several Midwestern hospitals, doctors and staff workers are taking LSD-25 and trying to bring back the story of the madman's ghastly inner world.

As I lie back, feeling the tightening grip of the attendants and the coming scream I know I can do nothing about, I think:

What about the pioneers like Drs. Charles Savage and Edward Evarts at the National Institute of Health? They took LSD-25 and returned to our world. What about Dr. Max Rinkel, of the Boston group, who "returned" with fabulous data from his own self-induced psychosis and did so much to improve the "reaching inward" to the schizophrenic?

Nearly all their experiences, and those of their trained assistants, are today locked up in confidential vaults. Few laymen have ever read them. Nearly all of their experiences and monologues, carefully preserved on tape, are brutal invasions of the privacy of a human spirit. They should be kept from prying human eyes. They have value for doctors only. This I have always believed. But I also believe, in laying bare to a newspaperman for the first time the highly personal record of my own journey into madness, that some public good will come of it.

THAT is why I am releasing the tape recording of my experience.

Now… Now… NOW the LSD-25 is taking effect. I look up into the thoughtful, compassionate eyes of my colleagues as THEIR world begins to swim away from me. Already I have a feeling of a gulf between me and their environment. I cannot communicate.

And I know I am screaming. I have a strange sense of timelessness. I am plagued, pounded and weighed down by something. I have a suspicion and fear you will find out something about me. I have no common point of reference with the real world. I must do as much as possible to make no mistakes. I must stop the screaming. I must come back this very minute… I must not let my mind ramble….

*"So I was always thinking of Trixie. I walked along, turned the corner where the long silky hair streamed from the cornices and it was bleeding, bleeding. Those things kept following me, pushing against me with their stiff-legged gait and their noiseless speckled wings.*

*"Go away! Go away! The avenue is a forest of upthrust bare woman's arms. I see the vanishing blue light. And I say to you, doctor, it was not Trixie who rejected me, but I, Trixie, and I knew all the time this would happen. It is that rejection making the first part of my wished for….*

**(Patient screams and lapses into senseless gabbling. Violence ceases and he begins to talk in a low, child-like voice. No restraint is necessary.)**

*"…My head is now glued to the executioner's block. The crosstown bus has an axe raised on high and I wait for the final descending bloody chop. I am some evil inherited in a sad century cutting myself off from you*

*forever, Trixie.*

*"I walk into a dark closet on the avenue and lie down there and dream away my sins, hoping to wake in the backyard of my Uncle Jimmy's house. I've got here in my hairy shirt a zinc penny which is burning a hole straight through my breast. Water, do you hear? I must have gallons and gallons of water. I must fight the burning zinc....*

**(Patient makes four guttural screams and fights restraint.)**

*"I want to tap my head but nothing comes out. Besides, there is the train pulling out...red and green lights burning port and starboard lights. I've got damp strange sheets and the thing in the speckled wings is on me and I hear the clopping of the old horse on the cobblestone streets. Look out, here comes the damned horse and Trixie has a bloody knife.*

*"Dirt beneath the fingernails and lying down in the back of the car with Susan, and Trixie will never know... Don't cry, honey. I've got you in the September woods and I see the ducks flying and the tickering, ordered wheels of the fire engines.*

*"See the sharks coming with the funny laughs. Remember the movie with Spencer Tracy and the bing bong bing of the peanut shells we threw in the ball park that day at the Yankees? Is that a purple cat crawling along the fence beyond the phlox and roses, or is it Trixie, absolutely naked except she's a cat?*

*"I've got a pain now. Help me, doctor!*

**(Patient's eyes open for the first time. There is a sign of half-consciousness.)**

"The cramp is rising inside, doctor. I'm being clawed in the kidneys and stomach and wherever else. The furious birds are wheeling, all purple, and I see a shingled skyscraper in the moon and there is a sound of thunder of cannons..."

Hours later, the rantings stop. I begin to come out of the LSD-25 jag, and the conversation goes like this:

"Good afternoon, Dr. H____, do you remember where you are?"

"Hello."

"Who am I, Dr. H____?"

"I don't know for sure. You're a doctor, aren't you?"

"Yes, do you know who you are?"

"Maybe. I think I've seen you before."

"Where? Or do you still hear those voices and feel cramps? Is Trixie still a cat?"

Right then I sit up with a jolt. "Look here, doctor, you are referring to my fiancée!" I shouted, with my brain suddenly clear as a bell. "What are you talking about? Trixie a cat!"

Then I remember the LSD-25, and I realize my questioner is a kindly psychiatrist in the little cubicle of 9-G. It has been a frightening experience, but I am back—back in the world of sane people.

Friends, who know about the experiments, ask me how the mouthings of a normal man caught up in the seizure of an LSD-25 self-induced psychosis, can help the insane. Well, in the files at 9-G, they have similar tape recordings taken from patients under leather restraints.

MANY of them slip in and out of that schizo world from day to day. The psychiatrists in 9-G took my "stream of insanity" and compared it with the monologues of true schizophrenics. Here are a few of their conclusions:

Mental illness, particularly schizophrenia, may be caused by disturbed chemical actions in the human body. It is possible that the

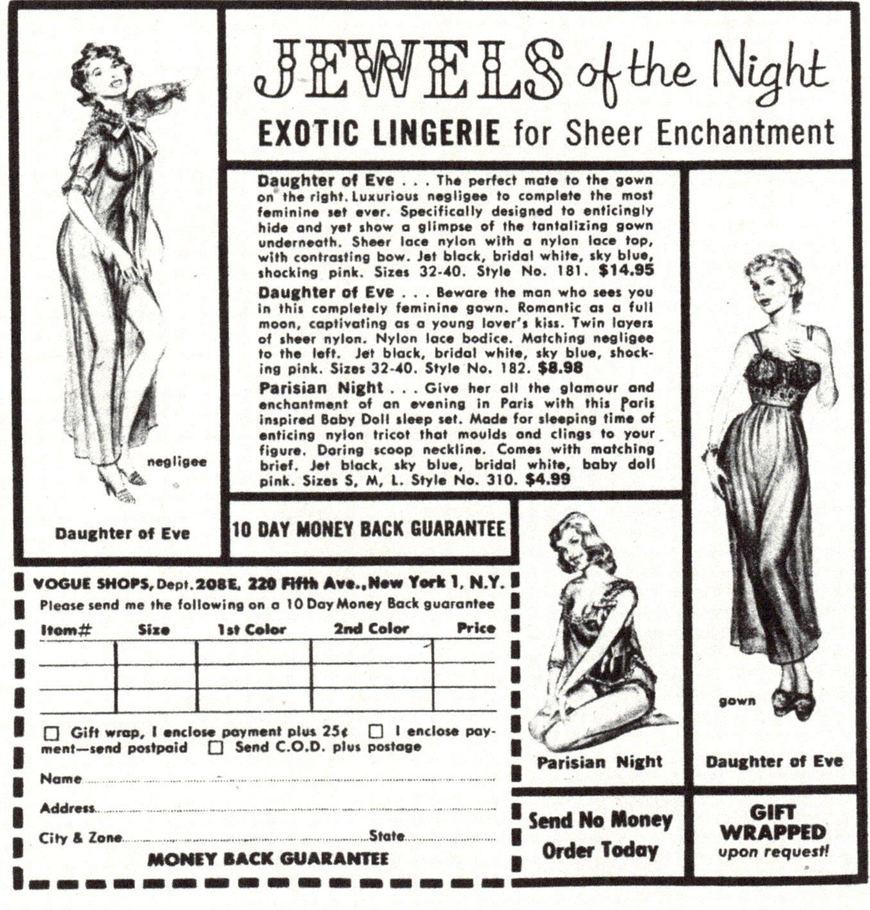

cause of schizophrenia is a mysterious chemical which originates in the human body itself.

The self-induced psychosis in the normal person may be the key to "reaching" the true schizophrenic.

If we can reproduce the "artificial madness" in a sane person, you might ask, how does it follow you can cure the poor soul who is in the steel grip of the REAL psychosis?

Well, there is an ironic twist to the answer. Earlier, sane volunteers took doses of LSD-25 and it played a horrible trick on them. Psychiatrists found, to their horror they could not bring some of these people back to sanity. Of course, they eventually brought them back; sometimes it took 15 months, or longer, with standard psychiatric therapy.

One of the most remarkable stories in psychiatry today is the story of how the LSD-25 captive is "returned."

The average human guinea pig (like myself) comes out of the LSD-25 self-induced psychosis in six hours, or less. There are no serious toxic after effects. But the sane persons who DID NOT shake off the dream world set off frenzied research in a dozen hospitals for another drug. They hoped it would "break" the LSD-25 psychosis.

Such a drug has been found. It may help LSD-25 be the key to schizophrenia. And here's why.

The pharmaceutical tag of this new drug is "Frenquel." It has been used, with considerable success, in the psychiatric wards of Christ Hospital, Cincinnati; at Galesburg State Hospital,

Galesburg, Illinois, and on "normal" human guinea pigs at the Bowman Gray School of Medicine, in Winston-Salem, North Carolina.

Frenquel differs from other known drugs for mental illness in that it blocks hallucinations in LSD-25 self-induced psychoses *and in true schizophrenics without using any other sedatives.*

This has staggering implications. For example:

TRUDY J. was a normal and healthy nurse in this same hospital. She was administered the regular 100 micrograms of LSD-25 in distilled water and fell into a deep "self-induced" psychosis. Here is a fragment of her monologue:

*"I saw Van Johnson 20 feet high and he was nude and I was all feathered balloons caught upon strings. There is one continuous honking of auto horns and the walls are beyond peeling of Communist plaster and I see city lights looking at me with mourning eyes.*

*"God give me back Michael Castle who is an eye weeping strange blue droplets all over the cloud of butterflies put into my safe-keeping.*

*"Finish, I say, finish. I want to die. There is a smell of a land in the earth to which I must return and dim bulbs hang on every landing in the house of my sister where I feel the touch of silken sleeves and the odor of armpits.*

*"I am shoved down in a thousand sharp cuttings from the tomato cans. I see the bum below the basement grating looking for the coins. The florist comes with a rope to throttle my neck and there is a swarm of wasps over America with whom I shall fly and I shall never be a good nurse for I am dishonest with the cocaine in the pharmacy closet and divided peach pies have been thrown into my teeth and I am choking, choking...."*

At the end of 13 frightful hours nurse Trudy J_____ came to a final, hoarse stop. But she was not out of the psychosis. She would not eat. She would not stand up. She would not dress. She sat for days in one of our seclusion rooms. She sat there all day with her legs drawn up under her chin, gazing off into space. Lift her arm and it would fall back lifeless and limp; talk to her and you would get no answer—no response of any kind. It was then that the chief of the psychiatric division gave her 10 mg. of Frenquel, orally. In less than eight hours she began to come around. At the end of 10 hours she sat up, dressed herself, ate a good meal, asked for pencil and paper, and wrote this impression of her "coming out" with the aid of Frenquel:

"THERE was some defect of attention. I don't feel too sharp mentally. But I have experienced this same sort of a feeling when a hard day's work in the children's ward has tired me out.

"I feel I have the situation under control. I have no hallucinations. I still have a dry mouth and a tight jaw. It was a tough fight. But I won."

But what did my colleagues find in the bizarre gibberish that flowed from our mouths while we were in the LSD-25 self-induced psychosis? Plenty. My case proves that. A good deal of what I said is of an extremely intimate nature, and I reserve the right to sit on my own private life. But I will tell you this much:

The doctors were right in diagnosing my constant allusions to Trixie (my fiancée) as a mild anxiety neurosis, with sexual overtones. The "dark closets" and "cobblestone streets" and the "sad century cutting myself off from you forever, Trixie," were a going back to my childhood and to "dream away my sins" in the backyard of Uncle Jimmy's house had a lot to do with a girl, a childhood playmate, with whom I had an early sexual experience.

The difference between this one "theme" in my psychosis and a similar one found in the tape recording of a hopeless schizophrenic (16 years a patient) was that I could relate some meaning between the inside and outside worlds.

The true schizophrenic—to be identified here as Bed 21—was not given LSD-25 and was permitted to talk into a recorder while in one of his periodic outbursts. Later Bed 21 was administered a dose of LSD-25 while in a trance-like state and he repeated, in substance, his monologue given previously without the inducement of LSD-25.

A fragment of Bed 21's talk went like this:

*"Meadows and young again, dogs dog dogs Lennie in the foyer flightless feathers Wang Wang Blues submarine light plasma and juices taxi taxi horse and horse cold in the throat clean the hall mirror Mama please seaweed marbles marbles over to the bridge please…"*

The doctors found here as in other true schizophrenics, a lack of pattern to relate some earlier experience with an actual contact with the external world. On one occasion, the chief of the psychiatric division told me, Bed 21 repeated Wang Wang 207 times before falling again into a waking trance.

But like the other human guinea pigs, I was of invaluable assistance to my clinical observers because as I emerged from the psychosis I was able to write down what the feeling was like. How I was able to catch hold of the chain of reason and pull myself back.

This is what I wrote for the doctors:

"I found my mind untangled and yet not untangled. I could hear my voice saying thoughts it should not and I struggled to stop it because I did not want you to find out things about me which were not true.

"I began to see those visual hallucinations like a strange picture on a distant movie screen. I had a feeling of helpless numbness and ye I was breathing heavily. The mind was racing, but not away from me, and I reached out to steady that racing.

"Then I heard the doctor and saw him and heard him say distinctly, 'Good afternoon, Dr. H_____. do you remember where you are?' and then I knew I was okay and on the way back."

It has been proven, incidentally, that LSD-25 creates a mental disorder in a normal person and makes the true schizophrenic even sicker. It points strongly to the implication that schizophrenia may start in any human being when there is a sudden change in chemical metabolism.

THE use of LSD-25 has opened a new field of "counter-drugs" for schizophrenic seizures. Experiments at this hospital, and at the University of Cincinnati neurological division, have clearly demonstrated that as many as 6 of 10 mild schizophrenics have had their hallucinations "blocked" by a small dose of Frenquel. As many as 3 of 10 have been kept permanently out of schizophrenic states by steady use of Frenquel.

This points, somewhat conclusively, to the fact that some unknown chemical in the human anatomy "kicks off" the schizophrenic seizure, just like LSD-25 is able to do it. This is a vital discovery. Perhaps a better "counter-drug" than Frenquel will eventually turn up.

Dr. Paul H. Hoch, chief of research at the Psychiatric Institute of New York says:

"Frankly, we are. using these drugs for diagnostic, prognostic and therapeutic purposes… Their great value is in experimental work."

But volunteer work with LSD-25 is one of the great boons to medical science. The doctors in 9-G have taken my blabbering and subconscious yearnings to another part of the hospital. There, they sit and listen to the recordings of the truly insane and compare them with mine. These are some of the questions they ponder—and they could have never done it without LSD-25 and the volunteer who goes insane for science.

That's why I was glad to take my "shot" of LSD-25 and I would do it again. I am proud to have taken the risk of "losing" my mind for science. It was a small favor to extend to thousands of Americans who live in a troubled darkness not of their own making. ///

Suit
$44.95

Things happen when you wear
ELEGANZA!

The boldest collection of dashing apparel and
dramatic imported footwear anywhere.

FREE! Send for full-color catalog of the latest
ELEGANZA fashions for men . . . from the world's
largest mail order house of its kind.
SEE eye-catching SLACKS: two-tones . . .
double-knits . . . dashing designs, fabrics,
colors . . . flared, pleated or straight
bottoms! SEE attention getting SUITS:
walking suits, slack suits, shirt suits!
SEE sensational SHIRTS, designed to
make every head turn your way!
SEE our exciting collection of imported
shoes and boots from all over the world.
See these and more — sold by mail only
and unconditionally GUARANTEED!

MAIL COUPON
TODAY FOR
EXCITING NEW
FREE
CATALOG

Eleganza

Suit
$44.95

Slacks
$17.95

Shoe
$27.95

Rush me your FREE full color
catalog showing plenty more great styles like these!

Name

Address

City

State                         Zip

Eleganza

703 Manley Street, Brockton, Massachusetts 02403

# ABOUT "'GHOST' BEAR"

*UNLIKE most animal attack stories in men's pulp mags, Bob Dorr's "'Ghost' Bear That Terrorized a Town" shows unusual respect for the animal involved—which is one of the reasons I particularly like it.*

*Bob had forgotten about it until I sent him a copy, and I was intrigued by Bob's response to seeing it again after all these years:*

When I reread "'Ghost' Bear," I scratched my head and tried to remember what I was thinking when I wrote it. After the passage of several decades, I couldn't. I did remember, however, that times had changed in America and that the men's adventure magazines flourished in a different era with different values. In those days, hunters were good and wild animals were bad. The cavalry was good and the Indians were bad. We live in a different world today, so when I set forth to refresh my memory of "'Ghost' Bear," I asked myself the obvious question: "Gee, I wonder if the bear is going to be alive at the end of this story?"

In most men's adventure magazine stories, the wild animals are portrayed as bloodthirsty beasts that love to attack humans, usually without provocation, even if they wouldn't in real life.

In 1975, when "'Ghost' Bear" appeared on drugstore newsstands, the nation was just becoming aware of environmental issues and was a long way away from having anything resembling an animal rights movement. I was busy in my government job, moving from one country to another, and raising a young family. I hadn't had any kind of pet since childhood—although I've since become a dog person, inseparably attached to my Labrador retriever.

In writing "'Ghost' Bear," I wasn't thinking beyond trying to emulate stories of similar ilk that

318

I'd seen in men's magazines. If it reads differently
today than other wild-animal stories of the era, it
must be for some subconscious reason that I can't
explain. I like the straightforward, functional style
of the story. It shows how the men's magazines
could be an excellent training ground for a writer.

*The two stories in this volume only provide a small taste of Bob's amazing
output and range during his men's adventure years.*

*Among other things, I'm looking forward to reprinting some of the wild
sexposé yarns he wrote, especially "The Erotic Stewardess Tapes" from the
May 1973 issue of* Male. *I'm very curious to hear how he did the research for
that particular "aviation history" story.*

—*Robert Deis*
[2011]

A polar bear attack story from *Stag*, Dec. 1972; cover by Mort Künstler.
Coincidentally, this issue also includes "Yank Who Flew the $2 Million
Secret Airlift," by "'Ghost' Bear" author Robert F. Dorr.

# "'GHOST' BEAR THAT TERRORIZED A TOWN"

## — ROBERT F. DORR —

*Male*, February 1975

# 'GHOST' BEAR THAT TERRORIZED A TOWN

## By TOM SWEENEY as told to ROBERT F. DORR

I WAS standing in a frigid sub-zero Alaskan gale that howled across the ice into my face. Yet I could feel sweat forming in the tight, cramped places inside my parka. Less than 20 yards away, staring at me with deadly intent, was the biggest polar bear I had ever seen.

A looming, dirty-white giant, it must have been twelve feet long and weighed a thousand pounds. The nomadic species of polar bear, this one had opened its mouth to expose gleaming, dagger-like fangs. Its black eyes bored into mine as it sized me up for the kill.

"Sweeney," I had thought aloud, "you're a fool!"

The fear knotted my stomach. I glanced to my left where I'd parked my snowmobile on the open ice 14 miles from Haevix, Alaska. I could see the butt-end of my high-powered rifle sticking up from the driver's seat, mocking me. The distance to the carbine was a hundred yards. By stupidly becoming separated from my weapon, I'd vastly increased my chances of becoming a dead man.

The polar bear stood there for a moment longer, breath-ing urgently, flanks quiver-ing. Its great white head was lowered like a battering ram. I knew polar bears didn't normally attack men and I had just enough time to think that maybe the huge creature wouldn't come for me after all. Then the bear let out a deep, (Continued on page 68)

BEARS deprived of normal sources of food by settlements may "raid" garbage dumps, attack unwary humans. Bear lost this encounter ...

14

Deke, Doc Kelley and I helped others to unload the lean, mangled, blood-spattered body of Morris Truefoot, 60, an Eskimo and one of the last remaining people in town who made his living by trapping. We laid Morris out on a table and Doc Kelley began working on him, but it was too late. Less than a half hour after his arrival, he died.

A lean, angular man, Richards was trembling and babbling almost incoherently as he merged with the crowd. Deke Hammerman reached him first, grabbed him by the shoulders, and coolly slapped him across the face.

"Come on, Jed, straighten up! What is it?"

"*Listen, everybody!*" Jed cried out,



**No one would believe his story about the huge beast that was roaming the trackless area just beyond the oil rigs. Then they began finding the mangled bodies . . .**

Hammerman had won. They'd agreed to hunt down the crazed animal.

"I owe you an apology, Tom. We're going to get some men together with rifles and go after that bear. We'll have to hunt it down and kill it before . . ."

Suddenly, everybody around us was

Through a window, we saw the faces of the men—trapped.

Normal crude oil isn't even inflammable, let alone explosive. It's just a thick dark jet. But the 50-gallon drums scattered around the toolshed didn't contain normal crude.

**I WAS** standing in a frigid sub-zero Alaskan gale that howled across
the ice into my face. Yet I could feel sweat forming in the tight, cramped
places inside my parka. Less than 20 yards away, staring at me with
deadly intent, was the biggest polar bear I had ever seen.

A looming, dirty-white giant, it must have been twelve feet long and
weighed a thousand pounds. The nomadic species of polar bear, this one
had opened its mouth to expose gleaming, dagger-like fangs. Its black
eyes bored into mine as it sized me up for the kill.

"Sweeney," I had thought aloud, "you're a fool!"

The fear knotted my stomach. I glanced to my left where I'd parked
my snowmobile on the open ice 14 miles from Haevix, Alaska. I could
see the butt-end of my high-powered rifle sticking up from the driver's
seat, mocking me. The distance to the carbine was a hundred yards. By
stupidly becoming separated from my weapon, I'd vastly increased my
chances of becoming a dead man.

The polar bear stood there for a moment longer, breathing urgently,
flanks quivering. Its great white head was lowered like a battering ram.
I knew polar bears didn't normally attack men and I had just enough
time to think that maybe the huge creature wouldn't come for me after
all. Then the bear let out a deep, growling sound, and came at me.

It wasn't exactly graceful. And it wasn't exactly fast. I had a split-
second to suck in my breath, calculate the spot where the huge beast
would pass and heave myself out of the way.

Hurtling in opposite directions, the polar bear and I brushed against
each other. Even that nudging blow had a powerful impact, and I knew
that I'd have been crushed if I'd landed beneath it.

I rolled on the ice, gasping, my lungs spilling a heavy opaque vapor
into the cold air around me. "Damn!" I cursed. "Damn… Damn…"

The polar bear, recovering balance, turned to come at me again.

It must have been a damned fool idea I had then, but it was the only
thing that came to mind. I tucked my head into my arms and curled up
into a ball, fetus-like, on the ice—playing dead. I didn't dare look up.
The bear was sniffing at my body. In a corner of my vision, I glimpsed
one of the creature's jagged-edged claws poking at me tentatively.

Maybe if I'd let the huge beast sniff and paw around me for a few seconds, it would lose interest and saunter away. But fear got the best of me.

So I leaped to my feet and started running.

Only started.

Behind me, the polar bear's right front paw lashed out.

It caught me low on the back, at the kidney, and it was like being hit by a pile driver. The pain burned across my back. I stumbled, feeling the sudden cold against my skin where a large fragment of my parka had been ripped away.

But I didn't fall. The huge creature had thrown itself off balance for just an instant and in that interval hobbled across the ice, collapsed against the snowmobile and got my gloved hands around the stock of my rifle. I yanked the weapon free and spun around to see the bear charging me,

I fired.

The weapon kicked in my hands and in the cold, open air the gunshots were surprisingly not very loud, I was sure I saw a red spot open up high on the polar bear's shoulder. Then the powerful, lunging animal collided with me and nothing made sense for a long time after that.

The interior of the medical clinic at Haevix, Alaska, was a maze of septic odors, tinkling sounds, and ceiling lights that spun around me like planets thrown out of orbit.

Haevix isn't much of a town, Population 380. A hamlet of trappers and fishermen until the early 1970s when they discovered oil on the Alaskan North Slope, Because it nudges against the Arctic Ocean, Haevix is one of the northernmost towns in the United States.

Its medical facility isn't much. The clinic was actually a Quonset hut, flown up inside one of the C-130's which had also carried the oil derricks up. The town's doctor was also its mayor, 50-year-old John Kelley, and he didn't have much help. So I figured I was lucky to be staring up at my friend Deke Hammerman's craggy, stubble-bearded, twisted-up features.

"Hi, how are you feeling?" he said.

"I hurt like hell," I said,

"The oil company helicopter spotted you pretty much by accident, Tom. Wasn't for that, you'd have frozen to death out on that ice floe."

"I was attacked by a polar bear."

Deke's gaze dropped. He couldn't look me in the eye. "We'll talk about it later," he said.

"Deke! I'm not crazy! *I was attacked by a polar bear and that's the truth!"*

"Sure," Deke said. Angry at his reaction, I propped myself up in bed, trying to clear the cobwebs from my brain, and Doc John Kelley walked in. Thin and bespectacled, his friendly face was grinning. He slapped me on the back, right where the massive bear's paw had struck, and to my astonishment I felt nothing except a vague, tingling numbness.

"I used a new anesthetic on you," the Doc explained. "Stearic Inoculation Fluid, or SIF. It erases all pain in the area of the wound. I gave you thirty cc's. A hundred would have knocked you into a coma. That's why you're having trouble getting your thoughts together."

So they didn't believe me! I'd been assaulted by a polar bear and nobody believed me! But damn it, I *was* getting things together. Right then. I even knew the date: March 15, 1974; I remembered who I was: Tom Sweeney, age 34, unmarried, originally from Ardmore, Oklahoma, by way of Vietnam and other places. I was a roustabout who followed the oil wells, even to this Alaskan hamlet within shouting distance of the Arctic Circle.

Things didn't improve in the pre-dawn hours of the following morning, when I woke again and still was in pain, even in the area numbed by anesthetic. Deke was there. Standing beside him was the only really eligible girl in town, Dianne Kelley, 20, the doc's daughter, who also happens to be my girl.

"Easy, Tom," she whispered. She was a tall, slender brunette with high breasts and a shape on her that wouldn't quit, and every other oil-derrick jock envied me."

"Damn it all, Deke—you too, Dianne—I *was* attacked by a polar bear out there! I know polar bears normally shy away from contact with humans, but this one had something…well, something *special* about it. A strange way of acting. Desperate, kind of. Or maybe just hungry. I don't know. But I'm not lying! The bear rushed me, and I hit it with a .30-caliber shot that may have gotten a lung, and if you don't believe me, you'll find its carcass out on the ice."

Dianne sort of nursed me during those early-morning hours, helping me to walk around for the first time since the accident. I began to have doubts. Could I have been mistaken about the bear?

"You're well enough to walk outside and watch the sunrise," she told me.

So we stepped out onto the porch, looked out at the slushy main street of Haevix and heard a helicopter approaching from the distance.

It was about 6 AM that morning when the oil company's helicopter crew brought back the horribly mutilated body of a man who was slowly dying in agony. They landed the chopper behind the clinic and Deke, Doc Kelley and I helped others to unload the lean, mangled, blood-spattered body of Morris Truefoot, 60, an Eskimo and one of the last remaining people in town who made his living by trapping. We laid Morris out on a table and Doc Kelley began working on him, but it was too late. Less than a half hour after his arrival, he died.

While they were talking about it, the townspeople and a guy named Tom Sweeney learned something.

*They* learned that the bear was real.

And *I* learned that I hadn't killed it after all.

The townspeople held a council of war. Some, like the doc, wanted to call the state troopers and have them go after the bear in snowmobiles. Others, like Deke and myself. felt we should get a group together and hunt down the man-killer. It turned into a long, confused meeting and at one point Dianne and I decided to go out and walk around. "It takes them awhile to agree on anything," she remarked.

"They're fools," I shot back. "The time to go after that animal is *now*,"

"We've got to go after that polar bear *now*!" I repeated to Dianne, pulling her along with me as we sauntered aimlessly down drab Main Street. "The guys in town are going to waste time arguing."

Whether anybody wanted to admit it or not, our town *was* under siege by that prowling, killer polar bear.

Take what had happened to Morris.

He'd been pushing his dogsled on snow-covered tundra only a half-mile east of town, heading out to check his traps, when his huskies abruptly halted and refused to move. The polar bear attacked him from behind.

Earlier, when it had left me unconscious on the ice, that huge white bear had ambled away in the direction of town with my rifle caliber slug imbedded in its shoulder. The huge animal's movements weren't impaired, but the wound was bleeding and the pain must have been intense. The creature managed to get off the ice island and reach the mainland near town before succumbing to the pain and holing up for the night in a cluster of trees.

We learned this later, of course-much later. when newspapers were claiming that our town had suffered a "siege of terror" and one reporter wrote that Haevix was "a town paralyzed with fear by a berserk, kill-hungry predator…"

Now, on the morning of March 16, Dianne and I stood in front of the saloon as the townspeople's meeting finally broke up. Judging from the grin on his face as he walked toward me, I knew that Deke Hammerman had won. They'd agreed to hunt down the crazed animal.

"I owe you an apology, Tom. We're going to get some men together with rifles and go after that bear. We'll have to hunt it down and kill it before…"

Suddenly, everybody around us was yelling. They weren't looking at me, Deke, or Dianne. Faces had turned to the west, to the end of main street at the edge of town.

One of the oil jocks, 30-year-old Jed Richards, was running toward us in the wild, nailing gait of a man gone near-insane. As he drew closer, I saw that Jed's eyes were wide with shock.

*"Hold it!"* he was shouting. *"Hold it, everybody!"*

A lean, angular man, Richards was trembling and babbling almost incoherently as he merged with the crowd. Deke Hammerman reached him first. grabbed him by the shoulders, and coolly slapped him across the face.

"Come on, Jed, straighten up! What is it?"

*"Listen, everybody!"* Jed cried out, struggling to shape his words. *"There's a polar bear loose in the oil field! He's heading straight toward the test samples of crude gas vapor; the stuff will blow up like an atomic bomb*

*and wipe this whole town out! He's heading toward it, running wild, and knocking down everything in sight!"*

THE HUGE white bear had appeared by surprise among the men who worked the thick jungle of high oil derricks on the tundra east of the town. The marauding polar bear had crashed and muscled its way through the oil field, trampling over everything in sight, and men scrambled to get out of its way.

A couple of them, ignoring the risky coats of ice that caked a derrick's ladder steps, had climbed frantically up the side or a rig as the heavy creature bulldozed past. swiping at them with powerful forepaws. A dozen or more men had locked themselves in a toolshed as the bear went by and one poor joker just lit out—high-tailing it away from the rigs in a wild, panicked run.

It took precious minutes for Doc, Deke, Jed and me to grab rifles, pile into Deke's Jeep and screech off toward the stick-like oil rigs that stood against the Arctic sun. Dianne had insisted on coming along and I knew, even better than the others, that it was pointless to argue when confronted with her stubbornness.

We reached the turn-out marking the end of the road and piled out, standing 1000 feet from where the huge bulk of the polar bear slammed against the tool shed with the men trapped inside. We heard the wood crackling and breaking as the great white creature smashed against the building like a battering ram.

"Too far to shoot!" Jed cried out. He was still terror-stricken and must have forgotten that the problem was far more serious than that. The Arctic wind washed into his face and his voice was muffled.

"We can't shoot anyway!" Deke cried, staring across the tundra. "We'll blow the town sky-high!" It was weird, seeing the bear slam its heavy paw into the side of the toolshed and hearing the impact seconds later. The wind was playing tricks. Through a window, we saw the faces of the men—trapped.

Normal crude oil isn't even inflammable, let alone explosive. It's just a thick dark gel. But the 50-gallon drums scattered around the toolshed didn't contain normal crude.

As part of an experiment aimed at developing a low cost home-heating fuel—the company's answer to the energy crisis—our guys had brought in some of the low-density oil derivative found at shallow depths above the major subterranean deposits. This stuff condensed on contact with air. The test-sample drums had unpredictable quantities of explosive vapor inside, and a rifle bullet, or even a spark from the bear's claws, would touch it off.

For a moment, I was hopeful that the bear would voluntarily break off its siege of the men in the tool shed. There was a deafening crash when the great, proud animal turned and bulled its way through stacked gear and tarp-covered machinery. But the creature turned again, returning to the men in the shed. It seemed to leave the ground on all fours and hurl its heavy bulk against the side of the structure. The impact was sickeningly loud.

"The bear'll break through the wall in just a second. *Those guys are dead…*"

Despite the risk, Doc Kelley dropped to his knees and braced his rifle. He knew the danger but he must have felt desperate to do something, anything, for those men trapped inside. But I threw my arm out and knocked his rifle barrel aside.

"Not that way, Doc."

"Tom, that shed will fall apart any second. The bear will mangle those men."

"We can't risk a blast. I got another idea, Doc. Your medical kit…"

"It's in the Jeep."

"Get it!" I turned to Deke Hammerman, needing his attention, seeing that the bear was about to crash through. Deke was raising his rifle, too, willing to risk a shot, willing to chance anything to save our buddies.

"We're not going to do it that way!" I shouted, reaching into the first-aid kit in Doc's hands, unraveling a roll of heavy adhesive bandage. "We can't risk blowing up the whole town! Besides, that animal doesn't know what it's doing."

Deke didn't understand. Nobody else did either. They watched, uncomprehending, as I pulled out the biggest syringe needle in Doc's kit, a foot-long, 2000-cc. job, and taped it to the front of my carbine like a bayonet.

"Tom," Dianne pleaded. "Those men…that bear…"

"I'm going to rescue them."

"I don't get it. Nobody understands you, Tom!"

"The anesthetic. The stuff the Doc gave me when I was hurt. Stearic inoculation fluid. SIF. A hundred cc's will knock a man out. (I'm going to try to get two thousand cc's into that bear."

We heard a heavy creaking, then a crash, as the bear's forepaw smashed through the toolshed door, splintering it, and one of the men inside screamed. Doc Kelley loaded my "bayonet" syringe with SLF while yelling at me through the howling wind, explaining all the reasons why it wouldn't work—I would have to hit a vein, I would have to depress the plunger. He wasn't even relieved when I threw away my ammo and jerry-rigged a wire arrangement that would enable me to plunge the syringe by pulling the trigger.

"Don't do this!" Dianne interrupted. "It won't work. You'll…"

Her voice was already fading into the wind behind me. Slipping and sliding on the mushy tundra, I left them there and treaded heavily toward the shed where the bear was pushing its way through the door jambs, shoving back the men inside.

The bear must have sensed me approaching from behind. Abruptly, it turned away from the trapped men and shifted its weight in the shattered doorway of the shed so that, like the men, it was facing outside toward me. I sidestepped around a row of the volatile oil barrels and started toward it more slowly, holding the carbine and "bayonet" out in front. The bear growled, squealed, and flailed out with its massive paws but didn't venture out of the shed.

The bear watched me, sinking back on its haunches, ready to spring. A low, snarling sound emanated from deep in its throat, a sound that was perhaps the most menacing of all. This was the way it had been when we'd met before except that I was now the one in motion, approaching from about 20 yards. *Just don't move!* I was thinking, cold with fear, the breath halted in my lungs. *Don't move!*

The bear leaped at me.

I remember, strangely, thinking of the savage beauty of the creature as a thousand pounds of blurred white fur came catapulting across open space at me, lethal claws and glinting teeth extended. There wasn't time to get out of the way. I dropped to one knee and held the rifle outstretched with both hands as the growling, spitting, thrashing beast came down on top of me.

The syringe jabbed into its throat and stayed there. My finger was squeezing the trigger when the weapon was wrenched out of my hands. Then the full weight of the massive polar bear crushed my legs into the tundra and a claw glanced off my shoulder and face, drawing blood.

A minute later, I blinked, uncomprehending, as the men from the shack, quickly joined by Deke and Doc, got together to shove the unconscious creature off me. Only the mushiness of the tundra saved me from being flattened to pulp. As it was, both my legs were broken.

"You did it, Tom!" That was Dianne's voice, behind my right ear. *"You injected almost the whole dose into him! He's out cold!"*

It's no comfort to the victims, of course, but the creature had preyed on us for a very simple reason: It was hungry. The animal had strayed from its usual habitat, to the northwest, where fish and other prey were readily available even in the dead of winter. Otherwise, it would never have attacked men, never "terrorized" us.

Doc, Deke and the other oil company guys rigged a sling beneath the helicopter, and the crew flew the unconscious creature back to more hospitable terrain. The polar bear was left at what seemed a suitable spot, about 75 miles from Haevix. When the chopper crew returned for a look-see the next day, it was no longer there.

I feel certain the big animal recovered, found some of its natural prey, and is still alive up there. I hope so. **///**

## "JUST WINDOW SHOPPING"

— LAWRENCE BLOCK (AS SHELDON LORD) —

*Man's Magazine*, December 1962

COVER ARTIST: MEL CRAIR

Illustration by **Ben Wohlberg**

**I CLIMBED** over the back fence and hurried down the driveway. They probably hadn't seen me at the window, but I couldn't afford to take chances. The police had caught me once. I certainly did not want to be picked up again.

It was horrible when the police caught me. I admitted everything but that wasn't enough for them. They put me in a chair with the light shining in my eyes so that I could barely see. Then they started hitting me. They used rubber hoses so there wouldn't be any marks. They hit me so much I nearly fainted.

The beating wasn't the worst of it, though. They called me names. They called me a sex fiend and a pervert. That hurt more than the beatings.

Because I'm not a pervert, you see. All I want to do is watch people. There's no harm in that, is there? I don't hurt anyone, and I never really bother anybody. Sometimes someone sees me watching them, and they get frightened or angry, but that's only once in a great while. I've been very careful lately, ever since they caught me.

And if they think I am a pervert, you should see some of the things I've seen. You wouldn't believe the things some of these *normal* people do. It's enough to make you sick to your stomach. Yet they are normal, and they call me a pervert, a Peeping Tom. I can't quite understand it. All I do is watch.

Ever since they caught me I have been very careful. That is why I left the window when the man looked at me. I'm almost sure he didn't see me, but he glanced toward the window and I hopped the fence and got away from there. Besides, it wasn't much fun watching at his window. The woman with him was old and fat, and I was getting bored with the whole thing. There was no sense in taking a chance for that.

When I got out to the street I didn't know where to go. I used to have a perfect spot. A pretty, young prostitute over on Tremont Avenue who saw at least 10 men a night. I could spend night after night watching her. The backyard was dark and I had a perfect view. But one night she saw me watching.

She was nice about it and sensible, too. She didn't call me a pervert.

But she said the men might notice me, that they wouldn't like it. She told me to stay away. It was a shame that I had to give up the spot, but at least she didn't call the police or anything. .

But I couldn't watch there anymore, and I had to find a new spot. I walked down the street looking for a lighted window. I stopped at several places, but there was nothing much to see. There were just people sitting and talking or listening to the radio or reading or watching television.

Finally I found a house with a light on that looked promising. The back yard was dark, too, which was important. It's harder to see out from a lighted room when there is no light in the back yard.

I stood close to the window and watched. A man and woman were sitting on the bed, taking their clothes off. I watched them. The man wasn't bad looking but my attention was confined to the woman. I'm not queer, you understand.

She certainly wasn't beautiful. Better than average, though. Her face was nothing to write home about, her breasts were rather small, but she had beautiful legs and a generally nice shape all in all. I watched her undress and began to get excited. This was going to be a good night after all.

They undressed quickly, which is not the way I like it. It's better when they take a good long time about it. But they just pulled off their clothes and turned down the bedcovers. I guess they had been married for some time.

I was really excited by this time, and my eyes were practically glued to the window. Then the man stood up and walked over to the wall He touched a switch, and the room was suddenly plunged into complete darkness. I was so mad I could have killed him. Why did be have to do a thing like that?

I stared through the window, but it was no use. The room was black as pitch. I couldn't understand it. How could he enjoy it with the lights out? He wouldn't be able to see a thing.

I was mad, and just about ready to go home and call it a night. But the little I had seen left me so excited that I could not stop there. I walked around, looking for another window.

By this time it was late and I had no idea where to go. Most of the people in the neighborhood were asleep by now. But I continued walking around, hoping against hope that something would turn up. I was just about ready to quit when I saw a lighted window on Bushnell Road. Never having been to that house before I decided to give it a try.

I approached the window and looked in. It was a bedroom window, with a woman sitting there. She had her back to me, reading a magazine. She was all alone.

ORDINARILY I would not have waited. Sometimes a woman will sit like that all night, just reading. But it was late and, having nowhere else to go, I waited. Besides, I had the feeling I would get a real show for my money.

As it turned out, I was right. She put down the magazine in less than five minutes, stood up and turned toward me. I was stunned when I got a good look at her. She was beautiful.

She was wearing a flower-print dress that made her look like a schoolgirl, but one good look at her would tell you she was nothing of the sort. Her body was far too mature for a schoolgirl's with proud, full breasts that nearly ripped the dress apart. Her face was pretty as a model's, and her hair was that soft reddish-brown that drives me crazy. I was ready to watch her forever.

She started to undress. I stared at her greedily. There was no one else around, and my eyes studied every detail of her body. She undressed slowly, tantalizingly, slithering out of her dress and hanging it up in the closet. Finally she stood there nude, and it was worth all the waiting, worth all the walking that I had done that night. She was like a vision, the most perfect woman I had ever seen.

I thought I would have to go home then. I expected she would turn off the light and go to bed, and if she had I would have been satisfied. It was enough for one night. Instead, she walked to her mirror and began to examine herself.

It was the perfect view for me. I could see both her back and the mirror image of her front. She looked at herself, and I watched her. Then she began to dance.

It was not exactly a dance. She moved like a burlesque dancer, but there was nothing crude about it. She knew how beautiful she was, and she moved in rhythm, making a symphony of her body and watching herself as she did. It was something to watch.

Finally she stopped dancing. She slipped on a housecoat and stepped through a door. I guessed that she was going to the bathroom, which meant it was the end of the show. I could have left then, but didn't. I wanted to get another glimpse of her. She had to come back.

I stood silently at the window, waiting for her.

Suddenly a door opened. I whirled around to find her standing there, in the doorway, pointing a gun at me. "Don't move," she said. "Don't move or I'll shoot."

I froze in terror, staring down the mouth of the gun, which looked like a cannon to me. "I wasn't doing anything," I stammered. "Just watching you. I didn't hurt you."

She didn't say a word.

"Look," I pleaded, "just let me go. I won't bother you any more. I promise I'll stay away from here." She ignored me. "I saw you in the mirror," she said. "Saw you watching me. I danced for *you*. Did you like the way I danced?"

I nodded dumbly, unable to speak.

"It was for you," she said. "I liked your eyes on me. I liked the way you looked at me." She smiled. "Come inside."

I hesitated. Was this a trap? Had she called the police?

"Come here," she said. "Come inside. Don't be afraid."

I followed her into the house, into the bedroom. "I want you," she said. "I want you." She slipped out of the housecoat and tossed it over a chair.

"Come on," she said. "I know you want me. I could tell from the way you looked at me. Come here." She set the gun on the dresser and motioned for me to step closer. "I want you to make love to me," she said.

I walked over to her, and she threw her arms around me. "Take me," she moaned.

I pushed her away. "No," I said. "I don't want *that*. I just wanted to watch you. I wouldn't do *that*."

She pressed against me again. "I want you," she insisted. She opened her arms and I felt her hot breath on my face.

There was only one way to stop her. I picked up the gun from the dresser. "Don't come any closer," I warned. "Leave me alone."

"Don't be silly," she smiled. "You want me and I want you." She kept coming closer as I retreated.

That's when it happened—when the gun went off. The noise resounded in the small bedroom, and she crumpled and fell.

"Why?" she moaned. Then she died.

The police beat me. They beat me harder than last time, and they called me a pervert. They think I tried to rape her, but that's not true. I wouldn't do a thing like that. **///**

# THE MAN AT THE WINDOW

SHORTLY *after Lawrence Block consented to our inclusion of his pseudonymous "Just Window Shopping" in this collection, a visit to a small bookshop opened the lid on a new mystery related to the story, rife with aliases, alter egos, hidden narratives and mistaken identity.*

*Sideshow Books in West Los Angeles has only been open for business since 2010, but it belongs to another era, when second-hand bookshops kept a wide variety of vintage paper and book-related curiosities among their stock.*

*Wall space not occupied with groaning bookshelves is crowded with prints, photographs, vintage advertisements and ephemera. Among their collection of original artwork from magazines and paperback book covers is an original gouache by Ben Wohlberg, circa 1962.[1] It depicts a man on a fire escape, hiding from view as he looks in an apartment window.*

*"This was an illustration for an early Lawrence Block story for* Man's Magazine *back in '62," I crowed to Tony Jacobs, Sideshow's proprietor. He regarded my "scoop" with polite skepticism.*

*"That was the cover to an Ed Lacy book,* Room to Swing*," he countered, then hunted down a copy on his shelves to back it up.*

*We were both right; the same painting was used for both works.*

*Though its use with "Just Window Shopping" suggests the story's unnamed narrator peeping through an apartment window at a scantily clad woman, Sideshow's original painting reveals a prominent element that's completely obscured in the* Man's *illustration: a second* male*, back turned to the unsuspecting woman…and he's brandishing a knife. (The magazine resolves this by dropping a large, blotchy shadow over that side of the window, crudely blotting out the sinister figure from a narrative that has no place for him.)*

*When Tony purchased the painting from a collector at a paperback show, he recognized it from the 1962 reprinting of the 1958 Edgar Award winner by Ed Lacy (pen name of Len S. Zinberg). Though* Man's *cast the man at the window as the story's unnamed, likely unreliable narrator, in its original context, the man at the window is Lacy's long-running character Toussaint "Touie" Moore, cited by crime writer Ed Lynskey as "the first credible African-American PI" in crime fiction*

---

1      In his later years, Ben Wohlberg worked in abstracts, as a fine artist. He passed away in 2024.

*Though he was unaware of the piece's second life as a MAM illustration, Tony wasn't surprised to learn it had been repurposed. The book was a Pyramid paperback, and* Man's *was a Pyramid periodical. MAMs frequently reused artwork, sometimes tweaking the piece—to various extremes and with varying levels of artistic skill—to adapt it to its new setting.*

*(It's worth mentioning that the story's triptych interior illustration has also been assembled from three clearly re-purposed pieces. Their origins were a mystery upon this collection's initial publication, but they've since been identified. For the full story, see the Men's Adventure Library's collection of Lawrence Block's MAM work,* The Naked and the Deadly.*)*

*Typically the original artists were not consulted, nor were they paid any royalty for the reuse. (A notable exception was Martin Goodman's Magazine Management Company, which artists Gil Cohen and Mort Künstler recall as being more ethical about paying for reprints than some of the smaller publishers.)*

*Tony suggests that while the protagonist's position in the shadows of the*

**Room to Swing (1962)**
**Pyramid F-709 1962**

**The man at the window in residence at Sideshow Books in West LA.**

*painting might well have been a stylistic choice, it was just as likely an effect of racial prejudices of the era, when covers of the comparatively few paperbacks featuring black protagonists tended to literally* hide those characters in the shadows *of the scene depicted—that is, when they were depicted at all. In the same way LP picture sleeves by Black musicians often eschewed artist portraits for images of (white) dancing teens or portraits of (white) models, faces of color were considered a liability, sales-wise. It wasn't until the 1971 reprinting that the cover art of* Room to Swing *featured unmistakably, unapologetically black figures—by then, a selling point. Times—and, more to the point, the marketplace—had changed.*

*The fact is, the man at the window is ambiguous enough for the artwork to support a variety of interpretations—or new uses. The race of the narrator in the Sheldon Lord story is never specified, but revisiting the story through the lens of the painting's original intent opens the door to an intriguing "hidden narrative" that's fascinating to consider: What if the narrator of "Just Window Shopping" is Black?*

*Considering the state of race relations in the US circa 1962, it's an alternate perspective that adds a discomfiting chill to an already strange and unsettling piece of writing.*

*—Wyatt Doyle*

# ABOUT "SLAVE OF THE SAVAGE BLONDE"

*BACK in the 1950s, most hunters read mainstream magazines like* Outdoor Life *and* Sports Afield. *And, for those men who liked grittier, spicier fare, there were several MAMs that focused on hunting stories.*

*One of the best was* Hunting Adventures, *published from 1954 to 1957 by Newsstand Publications (one of Martin Goodman's Magazine Management Atlas/Diamond companies).* Hunting Adventures *was like* Outdoor Life *or* Sports Afield *on drugs.*

*Expanding on that metaphor, the drugs would be a combination of testosterone, LSD, and Viagra. Maybe with a chaser of Cialis, mescaline, and Spanish Fly.*

*In addition to gory stories about great white hunters killing and maiming various animals (and/or natives) in remote places,* Hunting Adventures *offered exotic pulp adventures with sexy and often sex-hungry women.*

*"I Was a Slave of the Savage Blonde" is the longest piece in this collection, and with good reason—there's enough breathless action in this story for five lesser tales. In this "book bonus" from 1956, our narrator endures the MAM equivalent of a multi-car pileup: First an anaconda attack, then swarming piranha, hostile natives, and a nymphomaniac "white queen" with a rather unique approach to ending her romances… Eventually it all leads to a good old fashioned escape yarn, all delivered at a pace nothing short of feverish. Oh, and did we mention the zombies?*

*Hero "Jerry Gibson" is a field botanist who seeks out jungle plants that could provide new wonder drugs—much like Wade Davis, author of that great book about Haitian voodoo and zombies,* The Serpent and the Rainbow. *Like Davis, the hero of the* Hunting Adventures *story also runs into zombies of a sort. And, like those in* The Serpent and the Rainbow, *their condition is the result of a drug.*

*The credits for "I Was a Slave of the Savage Blonde" portray it as a true account, told by botanist Jerry Gibson to writer Emile Carlos "EC" Schurmacher. Unlike Wade Davis, Jerry Gibson was not a real person. However, Schurmacher was a real and very prolific writer. He started out as a newspaper journalist. In the 1950s and 1960s he wrote hundreds of fiction and non-fiction stories for men's magazines. He also wrote 17 adventure-oriented books before his death in 1976.*

*Emile undoubtedly never envisioned that someone, someday would view "I*

Was a Slave of the Savage Blonde" as a "classic." But in the realm of men's pulp adventure tales, it absolutely is.

—Robert Deis & Wyatt Doyle

A less ambitious MAM writer might have stopped at the anaconda attack. Fortunately, for Schurmacher that was only the beginning. (*His World*, August 1953; artist uncredited.)

## "I WAS A SLAVE OF THE SAVAGE BLONDE"

### — EC Schurmacher —

*Hunting Adventures,* Summer 1956
COVER ARTIST: Rafael De Soto

chopping firewood. We didn't need any firewood. He had stacked a plentiful supply earlier in the afternoon.

It is curious what a powerful fascination the report of a white person living somewhere alone in the wilds or the jungle has for the imagination. T... old Col... ple. He... jungles... still pr... hunting...

THAT... hamm... tering... seeking... and a... by, I s... blonde...

May... dyed or... myself... primiti... Campas... that Da... Argenti... one or... missing...

On th... very em... sive—a... and us... very m...

No, s... and trie...

But t... camp a... Pilcoma... she was... haps a... lone w... soon be... Guaran...

I trie... further... I drew... they be... told me... Rubia... who ha... that sh... maligna...

Okay... thought to myself, we'll let it go at that.

Just the same, I resolved to keep an eye out for anything which might contribute to the solution of what seemed to me to be an intriguing mystery.

Towards noon that day, as we approached a stream emptying into the Pilcomayo from an opening in the low-



ping paddle suspended in air. He shook his head.

"No, patrón," he objected. "This is an evil rio. It was here when the Pilcomayo rose and overflowed its banks in the rainy season that *La Estrellita* ...

# I WAS A SLAVE OF THE
# SAVAGE BLONDE

**"Kneel," she ordered, and my mind was too drugged to resist. Then her foot shoved my head into the dirt.**

**by JERRY GIBSON as told to E. C. SCHURMACHER**

▶ The huge anaconda struck our cayuco before we were actually aware of what was happening. A hideously bloated mass of shiny, greenish-black coils, it plunged down on us from a gaunt paratodo tree that jutted upward from the sluggish stream, bringing a rotted tree limb and a twisted network of lianas down with it.

The upper end of the branch caught me across the hips. I was sitting in the middle of the cayuco, leaning against my duffel bag. The blow smacked me backward and a heavy liana vine quivered and danced over my chest as though it were alive. (Continued on page 76)

bad reddi... body, a na... dish grour...
"I migh... you," I sa...
"Sí, pa...

same as I had observed along the Pilcomayo, but poisonous snakes and large anacondas, or water boas, as well as the more slender and shorter boa constrictors, were more numerous. There were sections of bushy banks which were infested with cascabels, a species of thick-bodied rattler. Some of them were more than seven feet

when I be... from the... faintly. h...

AT FI... ears... of a bird... brightly-... heard it...

en the Indios were on me from
side. They worked swiftly, bog-
me hand and foot.

e leader unbuckled my gun belt
fastened it around his own lean
. The holster looked ridiculous
his breech-cloth, swinging from

The Acaras were traveling over the
undulating hills, northward and away
from the stream. They carried me casually, without further word or glance.
The pain in my wrists and ankles became more and more excruciating with
each step of the way.

skirt below that c
curved torso mi
thigh. It struck
geniously designe
garment from th
conventional dres
"I am Luisa M
theatre voice tha

Jerry Gi
and—"
are you
Her
ery imp
what
ily as I
stared a
ocking
I had
playing
are you
e was p
a botan
d the s

ned. High and thin as a woman
ns. "Aaa-yuuu-daa!"
was the same voice I had
paddling the cayuco. The sound
made the Indios laugh again.
sense of humor left me cold.
there was something else. It had
me as soon as Felipe opened his
to voice his mocking scream. I

me up like a drunken man.
I stood there facing her then and I
for she was a beauty, no ordinary
pretty-faced blue-eyed blonde. There
was an alert, cat-like quality about her.
Her eyes were a bright blue. There was
a firmness and determination to her
face, a nose that was straight, a mouth

were bo
I put
any goo
of the way across
the time they fo
shack. A
a position in fron
lently threatening
his spear when I
out again.

As for Luisa M
appeared to be in

**Illustrations by Al Rossi**

**THE HUGE** anaconda struck our *cayuco* before we were actually aware of what was happening. A hideously bloated mass of shiny, greenish-black coils, it plunged down on us from a gaunt paratodo tree that jutted upward from the sluggish stream, bringing a rotted tree limb and a twisted network of lianas down with it.

The upper end of the branch caught me across the hips. I was sitting in the middle of the *cayuco*, leaning against my duffel bag. The blow smacked me backward and a heavy liana vine quivered and danced over my chest as though it were alive.

Just to the right of my head I saw a thick, slimy coil wound around the liana and I realized that the anaconda was also caught and trying to free itself.

I moved my head as far to the left as I could, horrified at the thought of that deadly coil finding my neck. I gave up all idea of groping for my holstered .38, somewhere on the bottom of the *cayuco*. All I could think about was freeing myself from the tangle and jumping over the side.

Behind me Jujuy, my stern paddler, was making his way toward me, stepping lightly though the mess of lianas with a machete in his hand. He paused and heaved the paratodo limb over the side.

"The pistol," I muttered, "I'll find the—"

I didn't finish. Tala's shriek from the bow cut me off.

"*El monstruo!*" he screamed. "It crushes me to death!"

Jujuy stepped around me and started for the bow, his machete up-raised.

Then Tala screamed again.

"*El monst—*"

The breath went out of him like air out of a punctured balloon. I caught a quick glimpse of him standing there in the bow with two great coils wound around his chest and belly. His eyes were bulging as if they were about to pop right out. His face was frozen in a hideous grimace of pain.

HE DISAPPEARED from view as Jujuy straightened up, swinging his machete. He chopped downward at the anaconda's tail, where it had found a purchase on the thick vine.

The tail came apart, spewing a dirty red over the bottom of the *cayuco*. I found my .38 then, jerked it out of the holster and started forward.

What happened next, I didn't see, for I was looking down at my feet, making my way carefully over the lianas. When I glanced. up, the snake had coiled around Jujuy's machete arm and he was clawing at it desperately with his other hand. Like a great whip, another thick coil suddenly wound around his neck.

Jujuy didn't even have time to scream after that. I heard him gasp, faint as a whisper, before the anaconda swiftly strangled him.

His body fell sideways across the bow, the snake still coiled around him. The monster's blotched, ugly head reared up and back. I saw its tiny, bead-like eyes.

I brought up the .38. My hand was shaking and the first two shots snapped the muzzle of the .38 up, scoring two complete misses. I gripped the gun with both hands, steadying the pistol. The bullet drilled through the monster's head, just below the left eye.

Somewhere I have read that the great constricting snakes relax their grip on their prey in their death throes. This was not true of the anaconda. It maintained its terrible hold around Jujuy's neck.

I couldn't get in any closer, for the monster's bloody tail lashed madly about, striking the sides and bottom of the *cayuco* with smashing blows. Seconds later, with Jujuy still in its coils, the dead anaconda dropped over the side.

They disappeared below the surface of the muddy water almost immediately. Part of the monster's body broke surface again and I saw shiny, greenish-black coils floating slowly away from the *cayuco*.

Suddenly, while I was watching, the sluggish water was churned into a frenzy. The body of the anaconda began to agitate violently. For a moment I saw Jujuy rise to the surface, face down. It was as if the great snake had come to life all over again.

My God, I thought, how much killing does this devil take? And then I realized what was happening.

Jujuy's body was jerking back and forth. Before my eyes his back was being rapidly stripped of flesh and I could see the whiteness of his spine and ribs through the frothing muddy water. I could also see the piranhas. The stream was swarming with the small cannibal fish. It was fantastic how quickly they had been attracted by the body of Jujuy and by the dead snake. They were making short work of both.

I looked away, sick to my stomach. Then I remembered Tala. He lay sprawled face downward in the bow of the *cayuco*, his body grotesquely twisted.

Bending over, I turned him on his back and felt for heart beats, hoping against hope that he might still be alive. But even as I placed my hand on his chest I realized it was futile. The anaconda must have broken every bone in his body.

I stared down at Tala's distorted face, numbed by the swiftness of the double tragedy. It was difficult for my mind to grasp the fact that it had all actually happened. My legs began to tremble as the reaction set in. I was drenched with cold sweat. Swarms of black flies were already settling on the *cayuco*—on the foul-smelling blood of the anaconda, and on Tala. I realized I had to do something about it pretty soon, before every damned insect in the Estero Patiño descended on me.

I roused myself and took another look over the side. The surface of the stream was now ominously quiet, but I wasn't fooled about the piranhas. I tried to steel myself to drop Tala's body over the side.

What the hell. I tried to reason coldly, when you're dead you're dead; and it doesn't make a damned bit of difference to a corpse who gets him—the jungle or the piranhas.

I started to lift Tala. His body buckled limply and the flies rose up in angry protest. I let Tala slip out of my grasp and fought them off.

I KNEW, then, that I couldn't dump Tala over the side. I'll find a piece of solid ground on the bank of the stream; I decided, give Tala a decent burial, clean out the *cayuco* and then head back downstream towards the Pilcomayo.

A good-sized *cayuco*, hollowed out of a single lagarto log, isn't easy for one white man to handle. It takes a couple of sturdy Guarani Indios, like the pair I had just lost.

I went back to the stern and picked up Jujuy's paddle. I started using it and found it awkward and heavy, but I got the *cayuco* moving.

I paddled slowly along the right bank towards a slight rise in ground. Above me, the big blackish sopilotes were already gathering, wheeling silently in the brassiness of the late afternoon sky. They knew that there was a corpse below and they were waiting.

I edged the *cayuco* up to the muddy bank. Several yards from the stream, I began digging near a clump of aromita bushes, using the paddle for a spade. It took me a couple of hours with the heavy paddle to dig a shallow grave, but it was deep enough and the sopilotes would not be able to get at Tala.

I carried him up from the *cayuco* and buried him. Afterwards I said a short prayer that I remembered. Then I went back to the *cayuco* and did what I could to wash it out with my canvas camp bucket.

It was almost twilight when I finished and the bats were darting above the aromitas against the purpling sky. I had no desire to eat an evening meal. Instead, I broke out the bottle of caña I had in my duffle and took a swig. It's a native Paraguayan rum, made of fermented sugar cane juice, and it feels like the business end of a plumber's torch as it burns down your throat, but it has its merits. Afterwards I lit a pipeful of cube cut and prepared to spend the night in the *cayuco*.

At daylight I'd head downstream to the Pilcomayo. Once I reached the river I shouldn't have any trouble finding a couple of Indios to paddle the *cayuco* back to Asunción.

But, that wasn't the way things worked out.

I have no one but myself to blame for what happened to me from then on in the treacherous, unexplored maze of swamp and jungle that Paraguayans call the Estero Patiño.

Losing my two Guarani Indios had been a tragic accident. It could have happened right on the Pilcomayo or, for that matter, on the Parana or the Paraguay.

But had I heeded the well meant warnings of Arturo Dalmana, Jefe de Asuntos, Ministerio de Interior in Asunción; had I listened later to Tala and Jujuy, I would not have been trapped like a wild animal by the Acaras, the most primitive Indians of the entire Chaco Boreal.

Sure, I can come up with several plausible answers as to why I made my Guaranis leave the Pilcomayo and head up one of the deviously twisting and unnamed streams leading into the heart of the Estero Patiño.

One of them is that I am a field botanist. It is an important part of my job to poke around in regions off the beaten track on a hunt for rare, perhaps yet undiscovered, plants and herbs which the pharmaceutical laboratory that employs me back home in Chicago might find useful in the treatment of arthritis or migraines or high blood pressure. In this respect, Paraguay—especially the Chaco area—is a botanist's paradise. One of the country's chief exports is tannin, extracted from the quebracho or "axe-breaker" tree. Another is *yerba maté*, whose leaves make a tea-like drink popular throughout South America. And there are numerous botanicals which still remain to be discovered.

ANOTHER answer for what I did is, I suppose, that human nature is human nature. I've got as much curiosity as the next guy. In the course of seven years of field work in tropical Central and South America, I've received a lot of warnings about staying out of unexplored territory. Mostly, I discovered, these could be taken with a double grain of salt. But about Arturo Dalmana and the Estero Patiño, I was dead wrong.

I had called upon Dalmana, in his office of the Ministerio de Interior at Asunción, to explain the purpose of my intended trip up the Pilcomayo. I had to have my Aplicación por Tráfico Interior okayed by him and, while I was at it, I wanted to have my passport visas double-checked.

The Pilcomayo is the boundary between Paraguay and Argentina for a considerable distance. With both countries scowling at each other across the river, I didn't want to get fouled up in red tape.

Dalmana was a dapper little chap with big horn-rimmed glasses, oiled black hair, and an aroma of eau de quinine. He received me cordially. He shook his head ominously, however, when the subject got around to traveling up the Pilcomayo.

"It is like no other river in the world, Señor Gibson," he said. "In truth it is navigable for some distance from either end. But it vanishes into the Estero Patiño, a swampy region of such vast magnitude that it staggers the imagination.

"*Pues*, it is reported to be like a prehistoric world, this Estero Patiño. Inhabited only by the savage Acara Indios, by many reptiles, some of the species not yet classified by our scientists. Even, so it is said, by unknown reptilian monsters."

I nodded politely. I've met plenty of officials like Dalmana. Ask them about something comparatively simple, like if the drinking water is okay, and you get a lecture on their government's water works projects. You've got to be patient with them.

"My intention is to hunt plants," I said when I was sure that he was finished. "I shall keep out of trouble."


He stared at me like a brooding owl. He shrugged his shoulders.

"Others have sat in the chair in which you now sit and assured me that they would stay out of trouble," he said. "There was a Bolivian geologist who requested a permit to seek oil in the Estero Patiño; an English explorer, and a woman anthropologist from Argentina."

"And they got into difficulties?" I asked.

"*Quien sabe?*" he said gravely. "When they were overdue on their return to Asunción, we sent planes and helicopters over the Estero Patiño to search the area. No trace was ever found of them.

"And, a few years ago during the rainy season, a small river boat, *La Estrellita*, vanished upriver near the Estero Patiño. No member of the crew, no passenger, nor yet a stick of wreckage has been found to this day!"


I received my permit and my warning. I might travel freely along the Paraguayan side of the Pilcomayo. But should I venture into the Estero Patiño, *ya lo creo*—the responsibility was entirely upon my own head.

I left Dalmana's office and strolled down Calle Independencía Nacional to the picturesque bay. I selected Jujuy and Tala from among the several Guarani river Indios who had *cayucos* for hire. They were muscular chaps, friendly and intelligent. They spoke Spanish as well as their own soft Guarani language.

Most of the Indios in Paraguay are like that. The proportion of Spanish blood is smaller than in any other South American country, and a good many Paraguayans have intermarried with the Indios somewhere along the line. The Guaranis even have their own theatre and native language books and periodicals.

It was not at all difficult for Jujuy and Tala to understand the object of my little expedition, although they were both somewhat disappointed that it did not include jaguar hunting.

"There are many big tigres to be hunted along the river, *patrón*," Tala grinned and showed his fine white teeth. "Also much good fishing, for the dorado and the pacu. *Sí*, and for many others."

"We shall see," I said, "but first there is work to be done."

We set out from Asunción early one morning a few days later. For almost two weeks we paddled along the northern bank of the Pilcomayo, past small Guarani villages and into the Chaco, while I made notes and collected specimens.

Day by day, as we headed into the Chaco, the country became more primitive. The river, with its numerous 'gators and schools of piranhas, also teemed with bird life: snowy egrets and grotesquely-billed toucans, jabiru storks, herons, duck, teal and many other species of water birds.

There were also a vast number of beautiful land birds in the Chaco, as well as the ungainly sopilote scavengers always hovering near our camp. One particularly ugly night bird, which I had never seen before, was called the eagle-owl or, in Guarani, *u'yara*. It made loud, snorelike noises from the nearby bush.

I visited several small Guarani villages and found the Indios to be hospitable and obliging. They kept us well supplied with fresh fruit and with dorado—a fine tasting game fish which somewhat resembles a salmon—with pacu, mandi and other fish.

When I showed interest in their work and asked questions the village medicine men, or aniros, showed me the drugs they used and volunteered to help me collect specimens I wanted.

One afternoon, when we were thirteen days out of Asunción, I left camp with Nameri, an accommodating old aniro from a nearby village. I had remarked that I would like to obtain a few pieces of bark from a small tohia tree which he used in the preparation of sleeping potions.

We were well on our way back after collecting the tohia specimens when Nameri paused to kick a tiny plant out of his way. I noticed that it was light green in color, saw-toothed, with scarcely any roots.

"What is it?" I asked curiously.

"Yaba," he muttered. "It is the plant that robs men of their minds.

There is much of it that grows in the Estero Patiño, but little to be found near our villages on the Pilcomayo. Which is good."

Must have some narcotic properties, I thought.

"How do you use this?" I asked as I bent over to pick it up. "Do you dry the stalks or—"

Nameri's unexpected reaction stopped the question and startled me. He quickly kicked the yaba again, this time out of my reach. And then he viciously ground it to pulp under his bare heel.

"No, señor!" he said sternly. He shook his head. "Yaba is not touched by aniros like myself. Nor yet by others like you who also seek to help men and make them well. It is used only as a thing of evil by bad brujos, by those who seek to enslave men, like La Bruja Rubia of the Estero Patiño."

It was the first time I had heard the name mentioned.

"The Blonde Witch?" I repeated. "Who is she?"

He did not answer. It was as though he regretted having spoken.

"Tell me then about the yaba," I said persuasively.

"It is a destroyer of the mind," he said grimly. "As surely as the piranhas in the river destroy the flesh."

He refused to say more. When I tried to question him further he lapsed into a sullen and obstinate silence, which he maintained all of the way back to our camp.

THAT night, after our evening meal, I tried to question Tala and Jujuy about La Bruja Rubia. They exchanged glances.

"It is said that she is a very bad *bruja, patrón*," Tala answered.

"But she is a *rubia*, a blonde," I persisted. "Is she then a white woman and not an Indio?"

"*Sí.*" It was plain from his uneasy manner that Tala hoped I would change the subject.

"Where is she to be found, this Bruja Rubia?"

"It is said she lives in the Estero Patiño among the Acaras *feroz*."

Tala didn't wait around for me to ask any more questions. He grabbed the camp bucket and started toward the river.

I turned to Jujuy. He averted his eyes, glancing at the fire. Then he picked up his machete and headed into the bush. Soon afterwards I heard him chopping firewood. We didn't need any firewood. He had stacked a plentiful supply earlier in the afternoon.

It is curious what a powerful fascination the report of a white person living somewhere alone in the wilds or the jungle has for the imagination. Take old Colonel PH Fawcett, for example. He disappeared in the Brazilian jungles way back in 1925, but they're still printing stories about him and hunting for him.

THAT night, as I lay awake in my hammock with the vampire bats fluttering vainly against the taut netting, seeking an opening to get at my toes, and a u'yara snoring somewhere nearby, I speculated at length about the blonde witch and her identity.

Maybe she's an Acara Indio who has dyed or bleached her hair, I thought to myself. I've known Indios of some primitive tribes like the Pijis and Campas to do so. I also remembered that Dalmana had mentioned both an Argentinean woman anthropologist and one or two female passengers on the missing river boat, *La Estrellita*.

On the other hand, Nameri had been very emphatic—though afterwards evasive—about the woman being a witch and using yaba. That didn't sound very much like a white woman to me.

No, she must be an Acara, I decided, and tried to forget about her.

But the next morning, after we broke camp and resumed our journey up the Pilcomayo, I wasn't so sure. What if she was a white woman after all? Perhaps a prisoner of the Acaras? Any lone white living among Indios might soon be regarded by the superstitious Guaranis as a witch.

I tried to question Tala and Jujuy further on the subject, but once again I drew a blank. When they were pressed they became sullen. No, patrón, they told me, they had never seen La Bruja Rubia. No, they had never met anyone who had seen her. They had only heard that she was white and *muy mala y maligna*.

Okay, my clammed-up amigos, I thought to myself, we'll let it go at that.

Just the same, I resolved to keep an eye out for anything which might contribute to the solution of what seemed to me to be an intriguing mystery.

Towards noon that day, as we approached a stream emptying into the Pilcomayo from an opening in the low-lying northern bank, opportunity appeared to beckon. When I asked my Guaranis where it led, they told me that it wandered somewhere up into the Estero Patiño.

"Bueno!" I exclaimed heartily. "After our midday meal we shall paddle up this stream."

Up in the bow Tala turned, his dripping paddle suspended in air. He shook his head.

"No, patrón," he objected. "This is an evil rio. It was here when the Pilcomayo rose and overflowed its banks in the rainy season that *La*

*Estrellita* vanished with all on board."

"This is not the rainy season," I pointed out.

He shrugged his shoulders. He had no answer for that one.

After we had eaten, I again announced my intention of taking the *cayuco* up the stream. Both of the Guaranis looked exceedingly grim and remained silent.

"What are you afraid of?" I asked sternly. "The Acaras? La Bruja Rubia? Vamos!"

I got to my feet and stalked down to the *cayuco* without a backward glance. I took my usual place amid-ships with my back propped comfortably against the duffle. I filled my pipe and lit it.

Out of the corner of my eye I could see Tala and Jujuy with their heads together. They were having quite a discussion. I didn't try to hurry them. I sat there, drawing on my pipe.

After awhile they came down the bank to the *cayuco* and picked up their paddles.

"The patrón wishes to journey up the little rio," Jujuy said slowly. "This is not our wish, but we go."

"Bueno!" I said approvingly. They were both good lads.

We headed up the sluggish stream that twisted and turned between low undulating hills, flanked by banks of reddish mud. We paddled past clearings of tall nacru grass and skirted impenetrable thickets of pink-flowering lapachos. Occasionally, there were paratodo trees which rose out of the water, festooned with lianas and many varieties of parasitic Bowers and air plants. Over the jungle-like walls of the stream and against the blue-molten brass horizon were silhouetted duapo palms and stands of the beautiful hardwood quebrachos.

The bird and river life was much the same as I had observed. along the Pilcomayo, but poisonous snakes and large anacondas, or water boas, as well as the more slender and shorter boa constrictors, were more numerous. There were sections of bushy banks which were infested with cascabels, a species of thick-bodied rattler. Some of them were more than seven feet long, but except when coiled they're slow movers.

On the second morning I had a bad scare as I stepped ashore. I almost put my foot down on a deadly little coralito, a snake related to the cobra family.

Luckily for me, Jujuy was at my side with his machete in his hand. He swiftly slashed the snake's head off. It had reddish rings on its dark brown body, a natural camouflage on the reddish ground.

"I might have died quickly but for you," I said gratefully to Jujuy.

"*Sí, patrón.*" He nodded his head gravely. "The little coralito bites and chews and holds on until a man is dead. But, *por Dios*, there are snakes even more terrible along this rio.

"Once, on the shore near the Pilcomayo, I saw a man from Hushui hunting deer. He was stalked by a jaca'upe more than 12 feet long. The snake was hiding in a hole in the ground, *patrón*. It was orange and white in color, and it followed swiftly after the hunter and struck him on the back like a tigre. Then it drew back and struck again and again until the man died. And then it struck once again in the throat to make very sure."

I made some notes about the jaca'upe. I had never heard of this snake before. I had no desire to encounter one.

We saw no signs of the Acaras. No sign of human life at all. From all indications, we might have been the first to have gone this far up the stream towards the heart of the Estero Patiño. We'll go on for one more day, I decided, and then turn back.

On the following day we paddled all morning. That afternoon the anaconda came crashing down into the *cayuco* and tragedy struck….

On the morning after I had buried Tala I started back downstream towards the Pilcomayo. Paddling the heavy *cayuco* single-handed, I made slow progress. After sweating with the paddle for several hours, I decided to let the sluggish current do most of the work and reduce my own efforts to steering.

The *cayuco* drifted along at not more than a mile an hour. As near as I could figure it would take me about a week to reach the junction with the river. Nevertheless, after what had happened I was satisfied to proceed slowly and with great caution.

It was well toward mid-afternoon when I beard the first scream. It came from the direction of the right shore, faintly, high-pitched, like a woman's.

AT FIRST I could not believe my ears. I thought I had heard the call of a bird, probably one of the many brightly-crested screamers. Then I heard it again, more distinctly. A long, drawn-out cry of *ayuda*—help.

I stared towards the bank. There was no *cayuco* drawn up on it. I saw no one on the reddish shore, nor on the small hill tufted with orange, yellow and scarlet chivato blossoms above.

"I must be hearing things," I muttered to myself.

"Aaa-yuuu-daa!"

The scream came again, as if in answer. Now there was not the slightest doubt in my mind that it was a human voice.

I paddled warily towards shore and grounded the bow of the *cayuco.* I pulled my .38 out of its holster and remained sitting in the stern, waiting for some sign of life.

For perhaps five anxious minutes nothing happened. Then once again I heard it.

The scream sounded more urgent, more despairing. It came from the hill, from the direction of a screen of the poinciana-like chivatos.

WITH a watchful eye for snakes and the .38 cocked, I stepped ashore and started for the hill through an opening in the scrub. The chivatos were not more than 150 yards distant. I'd walked about half way when suddenly the leafy ground beneath my feet gave way and I plunged straight downward. I was so startled by the unexpectedness of it that my .38 went off. I heard the bullet whistle past my ear as I damned near shot myself, and my feet hit bottom.

I found myself in a deep pit and my first, shaking reaction was indignation as having fallen in and relief that is wasn't a tambuchi, such as I have seen the Jivaros use in Ecuador with long, sharp-pointed bamboo stakes set in the bottom.

I'm damned lucky not to have been impaled, I thought angrily. The earth walls around me were perfectly smooth, and I decided that the trap had been dug to capture a large animal, undoubtedly a jaguar, alive. Getting out did not appear to be much of a problem. I could dig hand and foot holds in one of the earth walls around me and climb out.

Then I looked up and changed my mind. About a foot above my

**He flipped the rope over my head, around my shoulders, and jerked it tight.**

head the trap was ringed with needle-pointed bamboo stakes angled sharply downward. For the first time I realized that my chino pants and shirt were ripped and torn and that my arms and legs were scratched and bloody.

What the hell is this all about, I wondered with growing uneasiness, and felt my heart thumping. By now I had more than a suspicion that there was some connection between the screams I had heard and this trap.

"Those screams were decoys, Gibson," I told myself, "and you were one prize sap to fall for them!"

But who and why? The sooner someone came up with the answers and we had a showdown, the better. I'm not a very patient lad. Especially where a riddle or a mystery is involved.

I began to do some shouting then myself, for someone to come and get me out of the hole. I was damned sure that there was someone nearby. Several someones, in fact, for the screamer who had decoyed me here could not have dug this pit alone.

I kept right on shouting and yelling until my voice gave out. But it was at least two hours before anyone came.

A little trickle of earth rained down on my head and the back of my neck. Looking up, I saw that several Indios had silently appeared around the top of the trap and were staring down at me. They were stripped down to breech-cloths and they carried spears. I could not identify them with any tribe I had seen thus far in Paraguay. Like the Guarani, they wore their hair long, but across the upper part of their faces, like fiesta masks, they all had painted themselves red with achiote which gave them a weirdly bandit-like appearance.

Acaras, I thought.

I called out to them in Spanish to get me out of there. Not one of them moved. I tried again in the few words of Guarani I had picked up. This didn't budge them either.

ONE OF them, apparently the leader, muttered an order and two of the Indios disappeared from my view. Without haste the leader bent over with a machete in his hand. Splinters and pieces of bamboo showered down on me as he chopped away at the stakes above my head.

Soon after he finished, one of the two Indios reappeared with a rope woven of nacru grass. He made a loop in one end and lowered it down to me.

"Put it over your shoulders and under your arms," the leader called down to me in good Spanish.

For a moment, I was startled. I certainly hadn't expected a savage Acara to speak so well.

I did as he asked, thinking that the Acaras were not as primitive as they were reported to be. They hauled me up swiftly.

"Many thanks," I said, addressing the leader, "for getting me out of there."

He was taller and slimmer than the seven other Acaras with him. He stood there impassively with his machete in one hand, the end of the rope in the other. He said something in an Indian dialect that I could not understand. I gathered he was translating what I had said into his own tongue.

The effect on the Indios surprised me. They laughed uproariously, all but the leader.

Hell, it can't be that funny, I thought.

I began to loosen the rope around my chest. Abruptly the atmosphere changed.

The leader deftly flipped the rope from the end he was holding. A coil went over my head. As it came down over my upper arms he gave it a vicious jerk which toppled me off my feet.

"Hey!" I exclaimed. "What the——?

Then the Indios were on me from every side. They worked swiftly, hogtying me hand and foot.

The leader unbuckled my gun belt and fastened it around his own lean waist. The holster looked ridiculous over his breech-cloth, swinging from his naked thigh. There wasn't anything ridiculous about the wearer, though. He looked ugly and sinister as he gave an order.

One of the Indios came forward with a long, thick bamboo pole. He shoved it between my bound wrists, on down between my tied ankles. I suspected what was going to happen and I turned sick inside.

"Look here," I pleaded with the leader, "I don't know what this is all about. But I am an amigo…"

"My name is Felipe," he snapped. "You are not an amigo but a wild animal."

**I was slung between them, hanging from the pole like a bagged jaguar.**

"I am a man like yourself," I pleaded. "At least untie my feet and permit me to walk."

HE GRINNED at me, a tight-lipped, evil grin.

Ignoring me further, he called out an order to the Indios.

*"Ha'metse viri!"*

Two pairs of Acaras picked up the heavy pole and hoisted it to their muscular shoulders. I was slung between them, hanging like a bagged jaguar. I swung there, the weight of my body against the tightly tied ropes on my wrists and ankles soon becoming torture. They had already begun to throb painfully.

"Felipe!" I called out in desperation when I heard him give the order to march.

He answered by coming up beside me, staring down, his jeering eyes surrounded by the mask-like paint of red achiote.

"You are a wild animal!" he repeated. There was not the slightest indication in his voice that I might expect any mercy. "You were lured like an animal into the waiting trap. Thus!"

He opened his mouth and he screamed. High and thin as a woman screams. "Aaa-yuuu-daa!"

It was the same voice I had heard while paddling the *cayuco*. The sound of it made the Indios laugh again. Their sense of humor left me cold.

But there was something else. It had struck me as soon as Felipe opened his mouth to voice his mocking scream. I had glimpsed the shine of a gold crown on one of his upper teeth!

It looked, from the quick flash I had of it, like thoroughly civilized dental work. Whoever Felipe was, as much as he resembled the Acaras in his painted mask and breech-cloth, I was now certain that he was no primitive Indio!

The Acaras were traveling over the undulating hills, northward and away from the stream. They carried me casually, without further word or glance. The pain in my wrists and ankles became more and more excruciating with each step of the way.

At first I tried to hold my head up a little, but now the strain on my neck was unbearable and I was forced to give up the struggle.

My head fell back; a thick red mist rose before my eyes. It seemed to me that I was sinking into that red mist for a long time before I passed out completely.

When I did come to, God knows how much later, it was to see La Bruja Rubia, the Blonde Witch of the Estero Patiño....

I opened my eyes, still swimming through a reddish mist. I was lying on my side on the ground. There was a leaden numbness in my arms and legs. I scarcely realized that I was still tied hand and foot. Above me, I heard voices. I tried to turn my head and look upward, but a stab of pain darted through my neck.

My head cleared slowly; my eyes came into focus. Beside me were a pair of legs. Two tanned, slender columns tapering to slim, well-arched and sandaled feet.

I started to turn my head upward again, this time very slowly. I heard a voice above me, low and throaty, a woman's voice speaking Spanish.

"What have you here, Felipe?"

A sandaled foot prodded the side of my head impatiently. I gasped as the pain lanced through my neck again as her foot pushed my head upward. She was looking down at my face and I saw only her hair, an unruly mass of tawny gold backgrounded by the blueness of the sky. Her own face was veiled in shadow.

She gave an order in Acara. An Indio knelt beside me with a knife, quickly freeing my bound wrists and ankles.

"Get up!" Felipe snapped at me.

I tried to obey, but there was no life to my legs. An Acara grabbed me under either arm as I buckled, holding me up like a drunken man.

I stood there facing her then and I thought my eyes were playing tricks, for she was a beauty, no ordinary pretty-faced blue-eyed blonde. There was an alert, cat-like quality about her. Her eyes were a bright blue. There was a firmness and determination to her face, a nose that was straight, a mouth that was wide and sensual.

She wore only a single garment, snow white and of some sort of linen, held up over the left shoulder by a gold pin of unusual design, low-cut and slightly transparent. It was caught around her slim waist with a narrow belt of jaguar fur, forming a short skirt below that covered her gracefully curved torso midway to her tanned thighs. It struck me that she had ingeniously designed or improvised her garment from the material of a more conventional dress she had once worn.

"I am Luisa Monte," she said in a throaty voice that purred. "Who are you?"

"I am Jerry Gibson, an Americano," I said. "And—"

"What are you doing here?" she interrupted. Her voice had suddenly become very imperious.

"That's what I'd like to know," I said angrily as I glanced at Felipe.

Felipe stared at me with his jeering eyes, a mocking smile on his evil

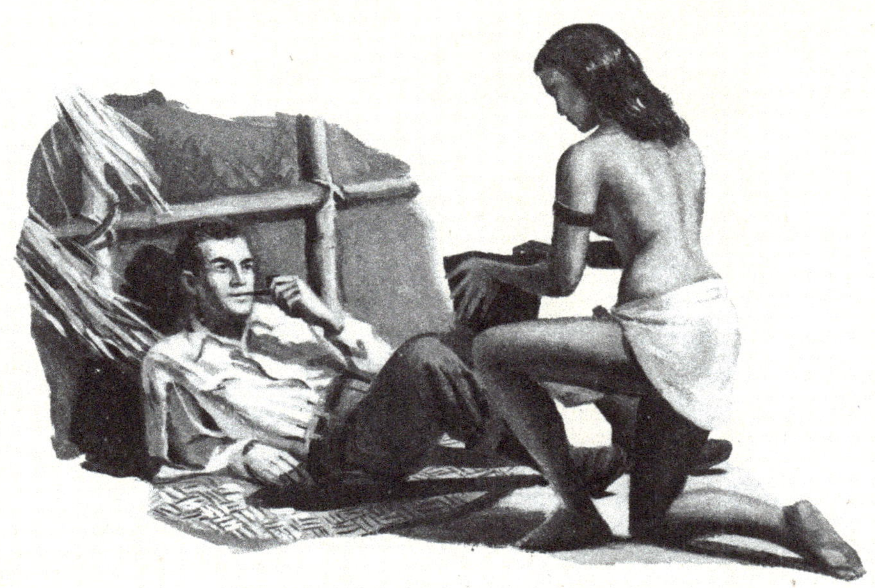

I heard the guard outside grunt and an Indio woman entered, carrying a large gourd.

lips. Somehow I had the feeling that these two were playing with me.

"What are you doing in Estero Patiño?" She was purring again.

"I am a botanist," I said, still trying to read the score. "What are you doing here?"

She didn't answer. She exchanged glances with Felipe. Again I had the feeling that they were playing with me.

My legs had become pins and needles. The circulation was coming back and there was feeling in my arms and legs again. I pushed the Acaras away. I was determined to have a showdown. The whole damned situation was exasperating and I had taken a lot of punishment.

"Now look here," I said, trying to hold my temper. "I'm tired of all of this fooling around. What's this all about?"

Luisa Monte gave me a quizzical glance. Then she turned to Felipe.

"You did well," she said approvingly. "This one has spirit."

He nodded and said something in Acara. The two Indios who were standing behind me suddenly grabbed me by the arms and started to drag me away.

"Let go, damn you," I said wrathfully, and tried to break loose.

THEY were both big fellows and, though I put up quite a battle, it didn't do any good. I fought them all of the way across the clearing up until the time they forced me into a small bamboo shack. Another Acara took up a position in front of the doorway, silently threatening me with the point of his spear when I tried to follow them out again.

As for Luisa Monte and Felipe, they appeared to be in animated discussion. They hadn't even turned around to take another look at me after the Indios started to drag me off.

Anger yielded to bewilderment and chagrin. I tried to look at my predicament realistically and decide what could be done about it.

This much I knew: I was a prisoner of Felipe's and of Luisa Monte, a beautiful blonde who I was convinced was the same Bruja Rubia that the Guaranis had mentioned so ominously. But *why* was I their prisoner? Who were they really and what were they doing here?

Your brain is blatting like a soap opera Gibson, I thought, grimly, better go easy, watch your step and your chances.

That made sense. It was the only thing I could do under the circumstances.

I looked out of the doorway and around the clearing. From what I could see of the village it was made up entirely of primitive shacks built of cane with thatched roofs woven of palm—with one exception. Off to the right and set apart from the shacks was a more pretentious structure. A house such as a white man might have ordered built in the jungle from material at hand.

It was also of cane, set upon log piles of quebracho about five feet above the ground. It had a porch with steps leading up to it. On the porch I could see some simple reed and bamboo furniture.

I moved back and sat down on a length of woven reed matting and explored my pockets. I still had my pipe and tobacco pouch and lighter. I also found my much-used jack-knife. This was the entire extent of my gear.

I stuffed the pipe thoughtfully and lit it, thankful that I had refilled the lighter with fluid only a few days before.

My pipeful was not quite smoked out when I heard the Acara guard grunt and an Indio woman entered carrying a large gourd. She was light-skinned and nude to the waist, wearing only a short skirt of a tapa-like cloth that the Guaranis call *pironuri*. She bore herself proudly. There was nothing of the subservient Indio woman attitude to men about her.

"Casira!" she said as she put the gourd down on the matting beside me.

The way she said the word it sounded like an order.

I glanced into the gourd. It contained only water.

Hell, I thought bitterly, are they going to put me on a diet of water?

I shook my head and put my fingers to my mouth, making motions of eating.

SHE WATCHED me in dark-eyed scorn. With a shake of her head she bent over and dipped her fingers in the gourd. Then she ran them lightly up and down my bare chest.

"Wash," I said to her, getting the idea.

"Was'," she repeated gravely after me and left.

I didn't expect her to return so soon. She caught me stark naked, taking a gourd-bath of sorts. She looked me over casually as she placed my food upon the floor. There was a lot of it, bananas and mahua palm-fruit, mangoes, and a large piece of cooked fish.

My eyes lighted up when I saw the fish. As soon as she left I tasted it anxiously. It was dorado and it was unspoiled and fresh. I knew then that wherever it was I had been taken in the Estero Patiño it could not be very far from a stream of fresh water. One into which the dorado had swum from the Pilcomayo. And with this discovery came my first faint hope of escape.

No one came into the hut that night. For the time being they appeared to have forgotten me. I stretched out on the matting, and after awhile my aching muscles relaxed, although sleep was a long time in coming.

On the following day the Indio woman came early in the morning and again towards noon, bringing food. She showed no sign of becoming any friendlier. Sometime during the morning the guard was changed.

About mid-afternoon I had a visitor, Felipe. He entered the hut with a cynical smile on his thin lips. He stood there arms folded, surveying me silently. I noticed that he was not wearing my gun belt and my .38.

"*En verdad,*" he said at length. "She has concluded that you are a fine specimen of an animal. And suitable."

"For what?" I snapped.

He eyed me insolently. I don't think I actively hated any guy before, not until I met up with this Felipe.

"You have a saying, you Americanos: 'Off with the old, on with the new'," he answered deliberately. "I heard it in my youth."

"In your youth you were not an Acara," I said angrily. I had a hard time keeping myself from tangling with the guy.

"Since you talk in riddles, let me tell you some answers," I went on. "As an Indio you are a phony. That gold crown you have on an upper tooth is good dental work, done in a large town or city. Furthermore—"

"*Pues,* you are observant," he interrupted. "What more do you know?"

My mind went back to my visit with Arturo Dalmana in Asunción. I remembered he had told me that an English explorer had disappeared in the Estero Patiño. Also a Bolivian geologist and the crew and passengers of a river boat. The way Felipe spoke Spanish I was positive he was no Englishman. I played a hunch.

"Suppose we say you are Bolivian," I said, "A geologist."

A startled light flicked on in his eyes and was gone. I knew I had struck home. I followed it up quickly.

"This girl friend of yours, Luisa Monte. Why is she called La Bruja Rubia?"

"No one names her so to her face!" He spat at me.

I started swinging then. I brought my right up hard and it caught him neatly on the chin. He went back against the reed wall and I measured him for a left. The Acara guard came rushing in, and I folded up as he clobbered me from behind with the haft of his spear.

Felipe snatched the weapon from him and stood over me, the point of the spear jabbing into my skin of my belly. I saw the look in his eyes and the tiny bubbles of foam at the corners of his straight mouth, and I thought it was curtains for sure. Then he controlled himself.

"No," he muttered. "When she's through with you, I'll get you, not the jaca'upe. I'll see to that. Come, she is waiting."

H E  PRODDED me to my feet and out of the door. I started across the clearing towards the house with the porch. The point of the spear pricked my back.

"To the left," he ordered, "and keep walking."

I did as he told me. As we headed towards the edge of the village and the screening thicket of aromitas beyond, I was chewing on what he had said, trying to remember where I had heard the word "jaca'upe" before. Abruptly it came to me. The snake Jujuy had told me about after killing the coralito I had almost stepped on.

We passed through an opening in the aromitas. I saw that all of the Acaras had gathered in a smaller clearing beyond. They sat on the ground in a great circle, and at the far end of the clearing was Luisa Monte. She was seated comfortably in a reed armchair. To the right, forming one half of the circle, were the women, bare breasted and short-skirted. Like Luisa Monte, they appeared to be very much at ease and were chattering animatedly to each other.

I knew that some sort of a rite or ceremony was about to take place.

The casual attitude of the women was somewhat reassuring.

I quickly revised my opinion, however, when I surveyed the male Indios sitting to the left of Luisa Monte. Their achiote-painted faces were grim and there was no talk among them. I noticed no spears or other weapons, only three or four small log drums with rawhide covers and two fife-like musical instruments of reed almost identical to the Guarani ilsas.

"Walk past the men," Felipe ordered from behind. "Stop when you have passed the last man in the group."

"What's this damned hocus-pocus all about?" I asked wearily.

He did not answer. Luisa Monte was watching me approach, an enigmatic smile on her lips. Her smoldering eyes scanned my face.

"You are angry, Jer-ree' she purred reprovingly. "Your face is like a thundercloud."

"Under the circumstances, what the devil did you expect?" I demanded. Her change in attitude took me aback. It was friendly, and I don't mean by this that she was acting coy. She was as direct as a man, not at all the coy type. She gestured with a hand.

"Sit here, at my feet," she said throatily.

"Why?" I snapped.

"You shall soon see. Because of you I have arranged this ceremony. You are the honored guest."

She waved her hand. As though in answer to the signal, a man entered the circle of Indios through the aromitas from the direction of the village. He walked slowly. As he advanced, the Acara women ceased their chatter. The circle was ominously still.

I inspected the new arrival curiously. He was tall and broad-shouldered. He wore a breech-cloth, but unlike the other Acaras he was not daubed with achiote paint across the upper part of his face.

I took a good look at his face and gasped with surprise. Dark as an Indio though he was, the features were indisputably those of a white man!

"So," I muttered, "there are more of us in the village! Who is he?"

She didn't answer. Glancing up, I saw that she, too, was intent on watching the man. He kept on coming towards us slowly, staring at her with expressionless eyes in which there was not the slightest hint of recognition.

She held up her hand when he reached the center of the circle. He stopped suddenly, as if he had bumped into a stone wall. He remained standing there.

It was an eerie thing to see. A small, cold chill started playing up and down the back of my neck. I felt that this man was either drugged or hypnotized.

Luisa Monte waved her hand again in the direction of the Indios to the left, and the drums began thumping. No, throbbing is much the better word. They were low and muffled, like the pulsing of one's own blood that one sometimes hears in high and sleepless fever.

ABOVE the throbbing of the drums the ilsas started wailing in an agony of torment. A sigh ran through the circle like a faint breeze through the tall nacru grass.

I gasped then. About six feet to the right of the man a snake was emerging from a hole in the ground. Long and slender, dull white with hideous splotches of orange, it poured itself out of the ground lithely and without haste. It was, I realized, remembering Jujuy's description, a deadly jaca'upe, a good 12 feet in length.

If the man was aware of it, if he was indeed aware of anything at all besides Luisa Monte, he gave absolutely no indication of it. He continued to stand there as though in a trance, staring dumbly at her.

I glanced upward, speechless with horror. Her beautiful face was serene, a study in impassiveness. She appeared to be viewing the scene with utter detachment.

"Stop!" I growled and started to get up.

A heavy hand clamped down on my shoulder, the nails biting into my flesh.

"There is nothing you can do," Felipe's voice spoke jeeringly behind me. "Nothing!"

He was right. Even before Felipe relaxed his grip the jaca'upe coiled and swiftly struck. It was like a flash of white and orange light as it buried its fangs deeply in the man's groin. Higher than I have known any other reptile to strike.

The doomed man took a few uncertain steps away and again the jaca'upe struck, this time in his thigh.

The victim's head snapped to the side. Tiny jets of blood spurted from his eyes. He tottered, fell, and was immediately dead. There wasn't the slightest further movement from him. I felt sick.

The jaca'upe crawled closer and coiled. For an eternity of horror it remained motionless and deliberate. Then it struck again—straight into the dead man's throat.

The wailing of the islas ended on a final note of anguish. The throbbing of the drums ceased. I shuddered and watched, transfixed while the long deadly snake slowly crawled back to the opening in the ground. Its head and upper part of the body looped downward. It flowed sinuously into the hole and disappeared.

THE HAND reaching downward beside me was cool and firm as it grasped my own. Luisa Monte rose from her chair calmly.

"Come, Jer-ree," she said.

I got to my feet, still dazed by the horror of the barbarous and incredible scene I had just witnessed.

Behind me I heard Felipe's voice, low and mocking. "I told you," he said. "'Off with the old, on with the new.' But fear not. In the end the jaca'upe shall not have you. I shall."

I started to turn, but Luisa Monte tugged at my hand.

"Come, Jer-ree!" she said again, and this time it sounded very definitely like an order.

I followed as she led the way towards the opening in the aromitas, not because I wanted to obey her. I think I would have followed the devil himself at that moment to get away from that awful clearing.

As we passed the Acaras they continued to sit silently in the circle. Luisa Monte held her head high. Her hair of tawny gold was picking up the reddish glints of the sunset.

She walked by the body without a single downward glance.

I FOLLOWED her to the village clearing. She stopped when she came to the house with the porch. Then she turned to me.

"This is my dwelling, Jer-ree,' she said. "Now you will share it with me."

"What do you mean?" I snapped.

"You know," she answered, gazing at me level-eyed. "You are not a child."

"You're damned right," I said. "Who was the man you just killed?"

The imperturbable expression on her face did not change.

"Jorge was my lover," she said calmly. "I did not kill him. You, yourself saw him walk to his death without uttering a word. You will take his place."

For a moment her words and calm assurance stunned me. This wasn't actually happening. It couldn't be.

I had a sudden impulse to run, as a man tries desperately to rouse himself and shake off a nightmare. I turned and three Acaras armed with spears were standing vigilantly behind me.

"Come!" Luisa Monte ordered.

She led the way into the house.

The interior was spacious and simply furnished, the comfortable reed chairs and bamboo table showing considerable craft in making. There were rugs of jaguar skins upon the quebracho hardwood floor, a few kerosene lamps upon the tables. With the exception of a wide, backless divan, also covered with jaguar skins, there was nothing especially feminine about the house.

Stacked on a table beside a lamp were several books, in Spanish: Haddon's *The Races of Man*, Malinowski's *Sex and Repression*, Hobhouse's *Morals in Evolution*....

She was standing beside me now, a quizzical smile on her lips.

"You will find my reading dull," she said. "But then there are other things...."

"Your books interest me," I cut in. "They are all about anthropology. Three years ago a woman anthropologist from Argentina left Asunción for the Estero Patiño. She disappeared and so did a geologist from Bolivia—until now."

"And an Americano?" she said, still with that quizzical smile, her eyes narrowing slightly.

"The Americano is now asking questions," I informed her grimly. "And also expecting answers."

"*Por seguro*, you shall receive your answers" she told me, "after we have eaten. *Suna!*"

She clapped her hands. From somewhere behind the partition which separated the large room from the rest of the house an Acara girl appeared silently, bearing food. Apparently I had been expected; there was plenty for both of us. I ate sparingly, having little appetite.

Instead of the inevitable *maté*, Suna brought coffee, black and fragrant. It was damned good coffee, and the first I had had in weeks.

Luisa Monte was now acting the part of a charming hostess. During the meal she treated me as a guest, not a prisoner, although when I glanced out of a window I observed an Acara watchfully on guard.

She didn't wait for me to ask her questions. She anticipated what was in my mind, speaking without reluctance and, I am convinced, with utter frankness. There was no reason for her to do otherwise.

She had come to the Estero Patiño three years before to find the Acaras and study them, hoping to live among them for a short time.

"Not only are the Acaras extremely primitive," she said with animation, "but, like many primitive tribes throughout the world, their social order is one of matriarchy. They strongly believe that the female, not the male, is the dominant sex, and they live accordingly."

She was smiling tantalizingly, and I knew she'd won again.

HER GUARANI paddlers had been ambushed and killed by the Acaras, she explained, but her own life had been spared and she had been brought to their village and treated with respect. She soon discovered the reason for this. Because of her sex she was *miyati*—literally, "safe from man-harm." She moved freely about the village, studying the tribe as she had originally intended to do.

Several days after her arrival a search plane flew over the village and once again on the day after. On both occasions she had hidden herself.

"I was not in need of rescue," she said matter-of-factly. "I was *miyati*. My studies of the Acaras were most interesting. I had an opportunity never given to any other anthropologist before. I wanted to stay longer. The village was ruled by several women. In time, I became their ruler. It was not difficult to bring this about."

She told me that while the Acara Indios were hunters and warriors, in their relations with their own women they were virtually slaves. If any of them stepped out of line the women had their own method of reducing them to submission. She did not go into details.

What she did tell me, however, was that she became fascinated with this little known aspect of her studies and learned quite a bit about it.

Then, almost a year later, the Acaras brought a white prisoner, Felipe Orsana, into the village.

"They expected that I, as their ruler would order him to be slain, according to the custom," she said. "Instead, I looked at this Bolivian standing so arrogantly and defiantly before me and thought to myself that Fate had sent me a guinea pig. I would put into practice that which I had learned.

"Within a week, this Felipe who had been so arrogant, who was newly arrived from the outside world where man, not woman, is dominant, knelt before me. In the village clearing before all of the Acaras he touched his forehead to the ground. I felt a strange new thrill of power and of triumph when I placed my foot upon his neck and told him that henceforth he was to be my slave and that he was to obey me in all things. And so he has."

I looked at her, reclining now on the divan, her hair, golden against the jaguar skin, her magnificent body's seductive curves.

"This Felipe," I said grimly. "He doesn't like me. It is because he was your lover?"

"For a little while," she admitted candidly. "But I soon tired of him. I found it more amusing to place him in charge of the hunters. To trap others and bring them to me."

"Like this man you have just killed," I snapped, "and like me?"

"Like Jorge," she answered evenly. "Like others. Yes, like you."

I sat there for a moment without moving.

There was a tantalizing smile on her beautiful face and my mind went back to the terrible scene I had witnessed in the clearing.

It was the smile that did it. That triggered me off and made me blow my top. I was out of my chair and by the divan, my hands around her neck.

I did not choke her. I shook her as a terrier shakes a soft white rabbit. She made no attempt to fight me off or to cry out. I think I would have killed her if she had.

I stood over her. My hands were still around her neck as I stared down at her.

Her glance crept upward. She looked into my eyes and I saw no fear in her own. Her arms moved slowly upward, encircling my neck. She pulled my head down to her.

I felt the hotness of her eager lips as they found mine and clung there in a kiss that was fierce and unrelenting. Her rounded breasts rose and fell beneath me, against my chest.

I fought to break free; my hands slipping from her neck and seeking her firm shoulders. Finding them, I pushed her downward among the jaguar skins and drew back from her imprisoning arms.

She lay there, not moving. I stood there shakily, trying to curb the flood of fever rising in my throbbing veins and pounding in my head. Knowing that disaster threatened if I yielded.

She sat up. Then impatience swept her to her feet and she leaped lightly from the divan. Again her arms were around my neck and she clung there, her body close to mine.

"You are not like the others, Jer-ree," she whispered. "You are so strong. So confident…"

In my heart I didn't believe her, but I kissed her savagely. Something in me snapped, for I had been tempted beyond all control…

When I awakened it was daylight. She was still sleeping, cradled in my arm. I gazed at her and saw a glorious animal in repose, a seductive human tigress who had devoured me with the ruthless fury of her passion.

Okay, I thought, last night she trapped you, but that was last night and where do you go from here?

I tried to figure out the answer, but I didn't get the chance. She had it all figured out for me when she opened her eyes lazily and smiled an invitation.

It was a strange relationship that I had with Luisa Monte. I soon discovered that she had a brilliant and daring mind as well as a beautiful body. She came to my arms demandingly, whenever she was in the mood. But this was not her entire interest. I did not have the slightest doubt that she was genuinely engrossed with her anthropological studies, although her approach, to say the least, was unconventional.

For the most part, the social order of the village appeared to me to be well established. It was, as Luisa Monte had pointed out, a primitive matriarchy in which the women were the dominant sex. She herself seemed to have the status of an uncrowned queen or chieftainess. Her orders were accepted and obeyed, by men and women alike, without question.

The Acara women did the cooking and raised the children. All other work was done by the men and they performed their many duties without protest.

Only the status of Felipe puzzled me. I could not make it out. As far as the Indios were concerned, he was undoubtedly a leader. But his relationship to Luisa Monte was that of a devoted slave. She seldom spoke to him except to give orders, and I often speculated as to why he had not taken off for Asunción. As far as I could see there was nothing to hold him back.

Unless he's in love with her, hanging around and hoping, I thought.

Still, that didn't make sense for a man like Felipe. He did not strike me as the kind of man who would be satisfied to hang around and hope. He was more the direct action type.

EVEN more puzzling was something that Luisa Monte had told me about him on the evening I had come to her house. Something about tiring of him as a lover and making him a slave. Maybe I would find the answer to that one in time, but not from Felipe. He and I had little to say to each other. The hatred was mutual. Although he kept his distance, I had the feeling that whenever I left the house his watchful eyes were always upon me. That I was never really out of his sight.

With almost nothing to occupy my time, the days passed interminably and I chafed my way through them. I read the books in Luisa Monte's scanty library for amusement. I took walks in the jungle, collecting species of flora and learning words of Acara from one or another of my Indio guards.

I am sure that Luisa Monte deliberately arranged it so that I would not have anything else on my mind but her.

One morning, while I was walking with C'bio, one of my guards, near a magnificent stand of quebracho trees some distance from the village, we came upon an Acara woman. I recognized her as Lulli, a childless woman of about 30 who lived with an Indio named Sart. The Acaras did not have any marriage rites although they were monogamous by custom.

LUILI appeared to be hunting for something in the nacru grass. I was curious, and asked C'bio what she was searching for.

"A little plant," C'bio told me, "for her man. Last night Sart visited the hut of another woman. Luili found out. Sart will not do so again."

"You mean, she's going to poison him?" I asked startled.

"No," C'bio answered. "She seeks the 'plant that steals the mind'."

Luili found what she was looking for while we were watching. It was a tiny plant, light green in color, saw-toothed, with scarcely any roots. I identified it immediately. It was yaba, the plant which old Nameri, the Guarani medicine man, had warned me about weeks before near his village on the Pilcomayo.

That afternoon Luisa Monte officiated at the judgment of the philandering Sart, in the village clearing, while the Acaras stood around and watched. She was seated in a chair in front of her house facing them, men to the left, women to the right.

The couple approached her, Lulli carrying a small gourd in her hand.

"Drink!" Luisa Monte ordered. Her beautiful face was impassive.

Sart took the gourd from his woman. For a moment he hesitated, then he gulped the contents. For several seconds there was absolute silence.

"Kneel!" Luisa Monte ordered, "touch your head to the ground." Sart obeyed and Lulli took a step forward, placing her right foot firmly upon his neck.

"Your man has become your slave to obey you in all things," Luisa Monte said without change of expression. "Is it your desire to have him further either as a man or as a slave?"

"No," Lulli answered. "I have wearied of him. I shall seek another man who is not a slave."

"Command him to rise!"

Luili did as ordered. Sarto got to his feet and stood quietly beside her. Then Luisa Monte spoke again, and as she did a sigh stirred through the watching Acaras and I felt my stomach tying up into knots.

"Beyond the far thicket of aromitas and the dwelling place of the jaca'upe there is a hill of devouring quipan ants. There your slave, Sart, is to die. Tell him thus."

Luili turned to him and repeated what had been said. Without a word he started walking to the left. The Indios dropped back to permit him to pass, eyeing him in morbid silence. I caught a glimpse of the expression on his face, like that of a man in a trance, like Jorge's.

No guard followed him as he walked to the far end of the village clearing and disappeared through an opening in the aromitas.

Thoroughly sickened inside, I turned to speak angrily to Luisa Monte. The reed chair was empty. She was gone, and the Acaras went about their various tasks.. As far as they were concerned, the thing was over and forgotten.

I remained there, brooding for quite awhile, trying to reconcile what I had just witnessed with scientific fact. I was familiar with several drugs which were hypnotic in effect. I knew of none like yaba, which apparently could put a man in a selective trance enslaved only by the person administering the drug.

Perhaps Sart hasn't actually gone to an ant hill, I argued to myself, perhaps he will wander around in the jungle until he is killed by a jaguar or a poisonous snake. From the expression I had observed on the faces of the Indios around me when Sart headed out of the clearing, I did not think this likely. Still, I was determined to see for myself.

Oddly enough no guard came up quickly behind me as I started walking towards the far end of the clearing. As I made my way through the opening in the aromitas I knew why. Felipe was there waiting for me. I came to an abrupt stop when I saw the 20-inch, razor-sharp machete in his hand. He gave me a thin-lipped, evil grin.

"You are alarmed?" he said. "*Pues*, your fear is needless. She has not yet given the word. You go sightseeing perhaps?"

"I am not alarmed," I growled. "I'll take you when I'm damned good and ready."

Dangerous words maybe, considering the machete he was holding, but he was one guy who kept on riling me. Had he goaded me any further I'm sure that I would have tried jumping him, machete or not.

He started off behind me when I skirted the second clearing. I came to a stop so fast that he bumped into me. I turned around.

"Okay, Felipe," I snapped, "You know where I'm going. Lead the way!"

"*Sí*, I know, but why do you want me to lead?"

"Because," I told him, "the very first jungle rule I learned is never allow a guy you don't trust to walk behind you with a machete in the bush!"

"You do not trust me," he murmured in mock reproach. "*Por Dios qué lástima*—what a pity!"

Nevertheless, he did as I asked. He led the way past the second aromita thicket, through some nacru grass, making for a chuapo palm. He halted about ten yards on the near side of the chuapo, grunted and pointed with his machete to a quipan ant hill.

Sart was stretched out on the hill and he was very dead. The loathsome, voracious quipans, the size and color of raspberries, were busily at work. They had started at his head, which they had already reduced to little more than a ghastly skull topped with long black hair, and were swarming industriously downward.

I turned away from the horrible sight, fighting off a wave of nausea.

I tried, not very successfully, to mask my feelings from Felipe. It was incredible that any human being, even in a hypnotic drug induced state, should deliberately seek out such a death.

Felipe was watching me intently. Tough as he was, I knew that he, too, had been affected by the horror on the ant hill.

"*Sí*," he nodded as if reading my thoughts, "yaba steals the mind and enslaves the body quickly. *Por Dios*, this I know."

"You should," I said. It was a shot in the dark. "Luisa Monte made you drink it after she tired of you."

He remained silent. I knew that I had scored. I kept at him.

"I am a field botanist, Felipe," I said. "You can't fool me. I know that no drug on earth can steal a man's mind permanently. No, not even yaba. Tell me, how long did the effect last?"

"Perhaps four or five days," he muttered. "Perhaps longer. *No importa*."

Maybe not important to you, I thought, but damned important to me. I had a hunch that yaba was habit-forming.

"After it wore off, you kept on taking it voluntarily?"

He shrugged his shoulders. "It makes a man forget that which he

I sprang for his throat, my thumbs digging into his windpipe.

does not wish to remember," he said.

I didn't ask him what he wanted to forget.

That evening I had a stormy session with Luisa Monte. She was waiting for me, impatiently. As I entered the house, she pounced on me and kissed me avidly.

She was strong and not easy to pry loose. I pushed her away finally and for a moment she appeared startled—for a moment only.

"Jer-ree," she murmured in her low, throaty voice, "I have been waiting for you."

"So it appears," I snapped. "I want to talk to you."

"Later," she said, and the word was an invitation.

"Now!" I told her. "Why did you kill Sart? I just saw him. He was not a pretty sight."

"Then look at me," she ordered coolly, "and you will forget!"

SHE WAS very sure of herself as she stood there, her magnificent figure lithe and imperiously demanding. The demand was difficult to resist.

"I cannot forget," I said. "Why did you kill him?"

"I have seen you read my anthropology books many times," she said. She waved a hand impatiently toward the table. "In many tribes, not all of them primitive, a man who commits adultery is condemned to death. Your Sart was an adulterer. By the laws of the Acaras he would have died in any case."

"Except that you picked a particularly horrible way for him to die," I said harshly.

The look she gave me was undisturbed. A slight smile hovered about her lips. When she spoke again she made me shudder. She might just as well have been politely discussing the weather.

"What matters how the man died?" she said idly. "Since it was necessary for him to die, he did so usefully, as a guinea pig. I only directed the method. His death, you will admit, is interesting proof that under the spell of yaba a human being will subject himself without question to any torture demanded of him. There is no reason for you to be angry, Jer-ree."

I stared at her. La Bruja Rubia, they called her, but she was more than a witch—she was a fiend.

As usual she won out. Slowly, smilingly, with that damned self-assurance of hers which was so difficult to resist.

The next morning, I awoke very early, determined to get out of the house while she was still asleep.

One of the guards, C'bio, was outside leaning idly on his spear.

He seemed a bit surprised that I was up and about so early. When I started off he followed me without question. I walked straight out of the village.

I had to think, to make what plans I could to escape before it was too late.

I knew now that it was not more than one day's hard march to the stream which emptied into the Pilcomayo. The fresh fish brought to the village by the Acaras had told me this weeks ago and since then, on one of my walks to the south of the village, I had come upon a faint trail and had seen Indio fishermen on it, I was certain that it led to the stream.

For some minutes I played with the idea of jumping C'bio and making an immediate break. I decided this was no good. With luck, I might get an hour's start. But Felipe and his Acaras would surely head me off long before I reached the safety of the Pilcomayo. Felipe had made no secret of the fact that he'd welcome just such a chance.

He's the key to this, I thought, Luisa Monte's faithful slave. I'll have to kill him before I try anything.

I headed back to the village determined to kill Felipe at the first opportunity. Without him, the Indio pursuit would be leaderless. I was confident that then I could escape.

He was waiting for me in the village clearing, a gloating look on his face.

"So," he said, "the day has come! She has tired of you as she has tired of all the others."

"Go on," I said, trying to keep my voice steady.

"*Pues*, that is all," he said with a shrug. "You should not be surprised. Even now she prepares the yaba for you. It did not take long to drain you of your manhood."

I JUMPED him much faster than he expected, before he could even bring his machete up to swing. I didn't throw a single punch but sprang straight for his throat. My thumbs dug in and he gasped like a drowning man as I kneaded them fiercely towards each other, trying to tear out his windpipe.

Somebody, I think it was C'bio, brought a spear butt hard up against the back of my head. I saw Felipe's bulging eyes through a blaze of glittering lights, but I didn't let go.

It was the second wallop from behind that knocked me out.

When I came to I was in a hut, Felipe and C'bio were jerking me to my feet.

"Come!" Felipe grunted.

He wasted neither words nor time. I was hustled out of the hut.

Luisa Monte was sitting in a chair before her house with the Acaras gathered on either side. She held a gourd in one of her hands. Her blue eyes surveyed me impersonally. As though I were a complete stranger to her.

I stood before her with Felipe and C'bio holding me by the arms. The back of my head was throbbing fiercely.

"Step away," she ordered, "he is yet a man!"

Felipe and C'bio obeyed her and she rose to her feet, holding the gourd out to me.

I reached out and took it automatically staring at her face. I saw not the slightest hint of either recognition or compassion. She was coolly going through a familiar ceremony, discarding another of her lovers.

"Drink!" she commanded.

For a moment I had the impulse to throw the stuff into her face and make a break for it. I took a look around me I saw Felipe grip his machete eagerly hoping, no doubt, for the order to use it.

I didn't have a chance. I raised the gourd to my lips; the yaba was bitter. I drew a deep breath and then I drank.

The effect was gradual, the way liquor creeps up on a man until he finally realizes that he is drunk. I was thoroughly conscious, but thinking had now become too great an effort. I was content to have someone else do all the thinking for me.

"Kneel," commanded Luisa Monte. imperiously. "Touch your head to the ground."

I obeyed her and I felt her slender, sandaled foot treading ruthlessly upon my neck.

"You are a slave," she said. "You will obey me in all things."

Kneeling there with her foot still on my neck a curious feeling swept over me. In a bizarre way it was almost one of relief. I wouldn't have to think. She would do it for me and tell me what to do. She removed her foot from my neck.

"Get up," she commanded. "You may return to your hut."

I got up slowly, walked across the clearing bland into the hut from which I had been taken. I lay down on the reed matting on the floor. I was tired now and wanted only to sleep.

I have no idea of how long I slept. It might have been round the clock for all I know. It was broad daylight when I awoke.

Someone had placed food inside the hut and I ate. Afterwards I went to the door. There was no guard outside. Sometime that day, or perhaps it was the day after, Luisa Monte summoned me to her.

"You shall live in that hut until I tell you otherwise," she told me. "Luili shall bring you food."

I nodded obediently.

For the next few days she summoned me to her house every morning and ordered me to do various little tasks. I cleaned her sandals, refilled the kerosene lamps, cut and brought firewood.

For much of the day I was free to wander about and I took walks away from the village. No guard followed me. It was needless. I had no desire to escape.

On these walks alone I gathered plants through sheer force of habit. I brought them back to my hut without any real interest in them. Occasionally, I saw Felipe in the village. We gave each other a wide berth.

IT MUST have been four or five days later that I gradually became aware of a change in me. My mind appeared to be becoming less clouded. At the same time I began to develop an inexplicable craving.

One morning, when I came to Luisa Monte's house, she apparently noticed it too. She gave me many orders and an unusual number of duties to perform. When I had finished she summoned me to her.

"You are in need of yaba," she told me. "Tomorrow I shall bring you a gourd. You will drink it and it will make you feel better."

"I will drink it," I repeated obediently. "It will make me feel better."

On the way back to my hut I said to myself, I am her slave, why should she be concerned with how I feel?

And suddenly it came to me. I was thinking! Reasoning again like a human being. The effects of the drug were wearing off.

Instead of going back to the hut, I headed out of the village.

The only way she can keep me enslaved is with yaba, I said to myself; tomorrow she expects me to drink it again.

And then came an alarming thought. I wanted to drink it! This was the unknown craving that had been gnawing within me. Like Felipe I would become addicted to it unless I could fight the craving off.

I realized that I would have to take drastic measures and I knew just what to do.

About half a mile from the village was a spinli bush and I made for it, gathering several twigs. Spinli, like ipecac, is a powerful emetic. I put the twigs in a gourd of hot water and let them steep all night.

On the following morning Luisa Monte came to my hut.

Imperiously she summoned me to the door and held out the gourd she held in her hand.

"Drink!" she commanded coldly.

Obediently I took the gourd.

She remained to make sure that I had drained the yaba then turned and left me without a word.

How long did I have before the powerful, mind-enslaving drug would take effect, I thought anxiously, three minutes, perhaps four?

I needed only ten seconds or less as I dashed into the hut and swallowed the gourdful of spinli.

I ran out and went behind the hut. I just about made it. For several terrible minutes I vomited and retched as if I would bring my guts up. Then I crawled back into the hut. I was as weak as a kitten but my mind was clear.

On the following morning Luisa Monte summoned me to her house. I responded quickly and obediently to her orders, playing the part of her faithful slave. She had no fault to find. My performance evidently was convincing. That night I waited until I was sure the village was asleep before I crept into Felipe's hut. He was snoring like a pig as I knelt silently down beside him.

My fingers were around his throat when he woke up.

"*Por Dios*, you!" he said.

Those were his last words. He gasped as the breath went out of him.

"This time I'll finish what I started," I muttered to him as his eyes began to bulge.

After he was dead, I looked around for my .38. I found it in a corner of the hut, still holstered. I strapped the gun belt around my waist and calmly checked the pistol. It was okay and loaded. Felipe hadn't fooled with it.

I picked up his machete and went to the door. Nothing was astir in the moonlit clearing. I darted across the clearing and to the porch of the house, then tiptoed through the doorway.

SHE WAS sleeping soundly on her jaguar skin divan.

I leveled the .38 at her. I had come to kill her as I had Felipe; she was a murderess—far worse than he had been. But, looking down at her, I knew that I couldn't go through with it.

I shook her roughly by the shoulder and she opened her eyes. She was wide awake instantly and recognized me.

"Jer-ree!" she exclaimed. She was startled to see me; and at the sight of the gun in my hand.

She recovered quickly. I had to hand it to her for her courage.

"Jer-ree," she repeated low and throatily.

"Stand up!" I snapped.

She got to her feet and I took a last good look at her in the moonlight. I steeled myself. I could not kill her, but I couldn't leave her to give the alarm just as soon as I started out of the door. I'd have to put her to sleep and gain some time.

She started toward me, all self-assurance. Her outstretched arms

were an invitation. I didn't move.

Just before she reached me I brought my arm up and swiftly downward. The barrel of the .38 crashed hard against her tawny gold head and she crumpled to the floor.

"I'll give them your regards in Asunción," I muttered grimly as I stepped over her and through the doorway.

Keeping to the shadows, I hurried to the edge of the clearing and took a last backward glance before striking out along the fishermen's trail. The village was still asleep. No one stirred. I hiked along rapidly, the .38 in my right hand, the machete that had belonged to Felipe in my left.



I thought a little about Luisa Monte and what she'd do when she recovered consciousness. First off, she'd probably summon Felipe and summon him in vain. When she discovered that he was dead, she'd send the Acaras after me with C'bio leading 'em.

I felt not the slightest twinge of conscience about having killed Felipe, only a sense of relief that he was not alive to direct the pursuit.

The trail twisted and wound through the jungle-like forest and across clearings of tall nacru grass. Those grassy spots were the worst and I traveled through them as fast as I could, always expecting to encounter a night-prowling jaguar.

About an hour after daybreak, I reached the stream and paused for a brief, uneasy rest. Although I detected no sign of pursuit I was not lulled into any false sense of security. I had to keep going, downstream towards the Pilcomayo.

Sometime that afternoon I had my first meal, wild mangoes and mahua palm-fruit. I ate it while walking along the bank of the stream and I kept on walking until almost twilight. Then I climbed a quebracho tree and spent the night in the fork of two big branches. I tied myself to the trunk with a liana. It was hellishly uncomfortable and I dozed fitfully. But I was safer there than on the ground.

At daybreak I was ready to start off again. I untied the liana and then, on a hunch which turned out to be inspired, I climbed higher to the upper branches of the quebracho and took a look around. Some distance to the South, over the green-fringed tops of the chuapo palms, I glimpsed a broad, muddy river. The Pilcomayo!

I reached the shore of the river early in the afternoon and a tiny Guarani village before nightfall. It sounds simple when you say it in a sentence, but I pushed myself like the devil to do it and I was damned near exhausted when I walked in on an Indio family. They treated me with typical Guarani hospitality and I remained with them for two days. After that I arranged with two of the village fishermen to paddle me downriver to Asunción.

I suppose that according to the rules of storytelling, the account of my own experiences in the Estero Patiño should end right here. But there is an epilogue.

A letter from Arturo Dalmana reached me in Chicago more than eight months after I had left Paraguay. His Ministerio de Interior may be slow in its paperwork, but I must admit it is thorough.

He began his letter by informing me that my Aplicáción por Trafico Interior had not been cancelled. He had kept it in his "open" file for many weeks and would I be so good as to mail him my original copy, or did I intend to use it again, in which case he would make the proper notation.

"By the way," he added, "we are now making some progress in surveying the Estero Patiño. I am glad that you heeded my advice and did not venture into it. As I warned you at the time, it is a most dangerous place. Recently one of our government survey parties discovered an Indio village which had been burned by savage Acaras.

"In the ruins of one hut was found the charred skeleton of a white man. In the ruins of a larger hut, the charred skeleton of a white woman. It is believed that both had been captured and held prisoners by the Acaras and killed at the approach of our party."

So, I thought grimly to myself, the Acaras finally killed Luisa Monte, La Bruja Rubia!

I can only guess at the reason, but I don't think I'm wrong. She was furious at the failure of C'bio and his men to recapture me and let them know it. Without Felipe around to keep them in line they finally turned on her.

Strictly my theory of course, but of one thing I'm damned sure: The savage Acaras will stand for just so much—even from a *bruja rubia!* ▰▰▰

# LESBIANS

AMERICAN *males who read MAMs had a special fascination with lesbians—a fascination editors were happy to accommodate.*

*The many purportedly nonfiction articles (and some fiction yarns) about lesbians in MAMs have sensationalized titles, headlines, and subheads, and are illustrated with titillating photos or artwork. The way lesbians were viewed and portrayed evolved over time. Most nonfiction articles in issues from the uptight '50s and early '60s depicted female homosexuals (and gay men, for that matter) as perverse and depraved. Lesbians in MAM fiction from those years were typically either sadistic villains or poor, misguided babes who just needed to be converted by some manly man.*

*During the swinging mid- to late '60s, homosexuality was still usually portrayed as an aberration. But the viewpoints of some stories were a bit less hysterical and condemning than in previous years. Some were even sympathetic, or almost accepting. There were articles like "Is Lesbianism a Cure for Frigidity?" (Real Men, April 1964) and "The Big Lesbian Boom—And What's Behind It" (Man to Man, March 1965).*

*By the 1970s, as increasingly explicit, hardcore porn mags dominated the men's magazine market, the last of the remaining MAMs tried to stay in business by following trends set by* Hustler, Penthouse, *and their clones. There are some old-fashioned sexposé style stories about lesbians in MAMs published in the '70s. But as many or more are oriented toward titillation or instruction rather than judgment or shock. Consider the informative classic, "How Lesbians Make Love—What 'Normal' Men and Women Can Learn From Them" (Men, December 1971).*

*Still, for most of the men who read MAMs in their time, about the only thing that could be more maddening and ego-shredding than the thought of their wife having an affair with another man was the idea that she could be having a* lesbian *affair. And as many of the magazines' "experts" were all too eager to remind readers, it could happen at almost any moment!*

*Was there reason for the manly readers of, say,* Man's Exploits *to worry about their own wives? Yes, indeed! At least according to a March 1964 article in that very magazine by one JH Berkely, who dared pose the question, "Is Your Wife a Secret Lesbian?"*

*Over the years, MAMs published a number of other helpful articles for readers who wanted more information about lesbian wives. Another interesting one from a cultural history perspective is in the December 1973 issue of* Man's Story, *titled "The Shocking Scandal of Suburbia's Lesbian Wives." And, yes, it actually links the spread of middle class, suburban neighborhoods in America to lesbianism. It also stokes the fear most men had about the burgeoning women's liberation movement. Author Frank Gorman lays out his case in the first few paragraphs:*

> The sexual revolution in this country has spawned a dark urge…lesbianism.
>
> Its growth in the past fifteen years has been phenomenal, or is it a coincidence that those same fifteen years have seen the mass migration to suburbia? There is a definite link between the two.
>
> Today, with a lesbian population in the US of about five million (that's a conservative estimate) there's reason to believe that with the influence of women's lib more and more suburban wives are turning to invert relationships.

*According to studies and experts cited in the story, "lesbianism is often the consequence of a disordered and confused society." (Mind you, the "experts" in such reports tended to be fictional constructs, while the "studies" were often complete bunk.)*

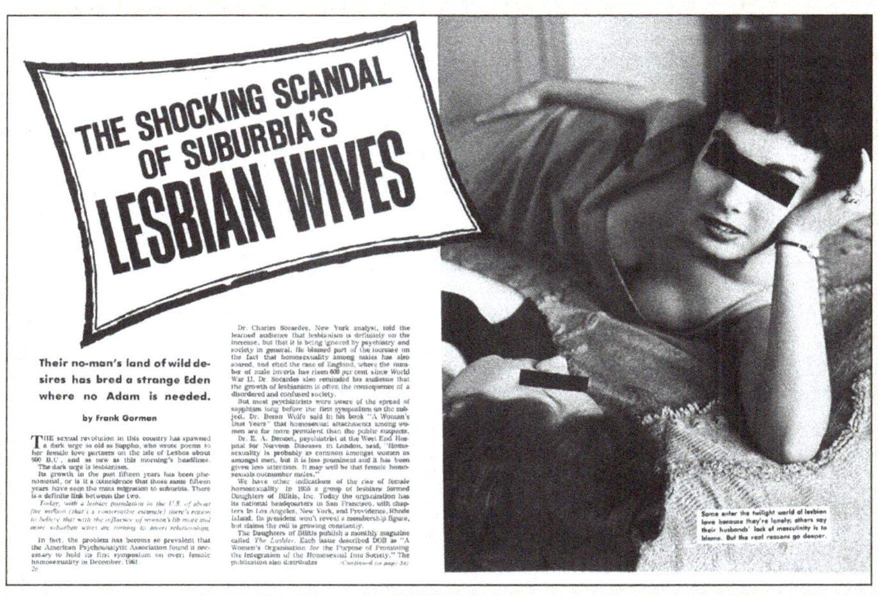


THE sexual revolution in this country has spawned a dark urge as old as Sappho, who wrote poems to her female love partners on the isle of Lesbos about 600 B.C., and as new as this morning's headlines. The dark urge is lesbianism.

Its growth in the past fifteen years has been phenomenal, or is it a coincidence that those same fifteen years have seen the mass migration to suburbia. There is a definite link between the two.

Today, with a lesbian population in the U.S. of about five million (that's a conservative estimate) there's reason to believe that with the influence of women's lib more and more suburban wives are turning to invert relationships.

In fact, the problem has become so prevalent that the American Psychoanalytic Association found it necessary to hold its first symposium on overt female homosexuality in December, 1961.

Dr. Charles Socardes, New York analyst, told the learned audience that lesbianism is definitely on the increase, but that it is being ignored by psychiatry and society in general. He blamed part of the increase on the fact that homosexuality among males has also soared, and cited the case of England, where the number of male inverts has risen 600 per cent since World War II. Dr. Socardes also reminded his audience that the growth of lesbianism is often the consequence of a disordered and confused society.

But most psychiatrists were aware of the spread of sapphism long before the first symposium on the subject. Dr. Benn Wolfe said in his book "A Woman's Best Years" that homosexual attachments among women are far more prevalent than the public suspects.

Dr. E. A. Bennet, psychiatrist at the West End Hospital for Nervous Diseases in London, said, "Homosexuality is probably as common amongst women as amongst men, but it is less prominent and it has been given less attention. It may well be that female homosexuals outnumber males."

We have other indications of the rise of female homosexuality. In 1955 a group of lesbians formed Daughters of Bilitis, Inc. Today the organization has its national headquarters in San Francisco, with chapters in Los Angeles, New York, and Providence, Rhode Island. Its president won't reveal a membership figure, but claims the roll is growing constantly.

The Daughters of Bilitis publish a monthly magazine called *The Ladder.* Each issue described DOB as "A Women's Organization for the Purpose of Promoting the Integration of the Homosexual Into Society." The publication also distributes (Continued on page 34)

**"The Shocking Scandal of Suburbia's Lesbian Wives" by Frank Gorman**
*Man's Story,* **November 1973**

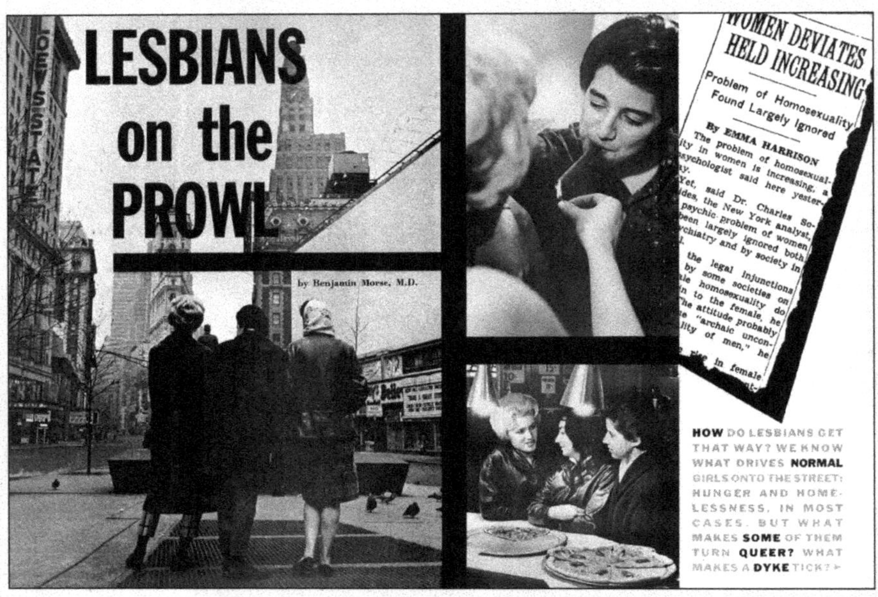


"Lesbians on the Prowl" by Benjamin Morse, MD (*aka* Lawrence Block)
*Man's Story,* November 1973

Our story, "I Went to a Lesbian Party," also dates from 1964, but it dispenses with paranoia in favor of an openly curious approach to the subject. Presented as a true, first-hand exposé, supposedly written by a heterosexual female reporter named Joanne Beardon (almost certainly a pseudonym of a male writer), the setting is not suburbia, prison, or a mental hospital, but a plush city apartment in a swanky building appointed with tapestries, crystal chandeliers and a doorman.

The lesbian party gets off to a rocky start when our "girl reporter" is cornered by an aggressive "big bull dyke" ("Tiny") who tries to stake an early claim on our correspondent. Beardon's night improves once she's able to mingle. She's even treated to a seductive "love-dance" by one of the other guests (described here in vivid, mating-ritual terms familiar to an audience well-versed in jungle-goddess pulp fiction). Joanne even finds herself (gasp!) unexpectedly attracted to the winsome temptress. But what will Tiny have to say about it…?

Despite leaning heavily on stereotypes, the writer's attitude is otherwise open-minded and more or less free of judgment. The story even concludes on a pronounced note of not merely tolerance, but affirmation.

—*Robert Deis & Wyatt Doyle*

## "I WENT TO A LESBIAN PARTY"

— JOANNE BEARDON —

*All Man*, May 1964

COVER ARTIST: UNCREDITED

**When the girls get together, anything can happen. A behind the scenes look at one of America's most shocking and degrading scandals!**

THERE WERE BUTTERFLIES as big as bats in my stomach as I rode up to the sixth floor of the plush apartment house. I didn't expect to like this assignment one bit, but my editor had said it would be an exclusive for the paper and it was all mine if I wanted it. I'm a newspaperwoman first and last, so naturally I wanted it.

All we had to go on was a report from our man on the police beat that folks in a certain neighborhood had been complaining regularly about loud, late parties. And that the complaints always mentioned large groups of girls and young women, never a word about brawls between drunken men or over-boisterous male voices disturbing the early morning peace. The editor, had smelled a rat that could sell a lot of papers and had called me on it.

As a night-life columnist, I had contacts in all sorts of places. I called an actress who knew her way around the more shadowy corners of our fair city. I'd once given her a plug in my column so she owed me a favor.

The actress had given me the name of the girl I would be meeting in a few minutes, and I had been assured that she would cooperate in every way. The only hitch was that I would have to cooperate too. Under no circumstances was I to let on that I was a reporter.

The elevator zoomed to a stop. As the heavy door slid spookily back by itself, I ran over my cover story in my head. I was an old school pal of the actress in town for two weeks and anxious to connect with some "congenial" friends. I found Apartment Six-B, rapped quietly and waited for my first look at a congenial friend.

After almost a full *(Continued on page 68)*

by **JOANNE BEARDON**

## A Girl Reporter's Exclusive

# I WENT TO A LESBIAN PARTY

20

than one of the apartment doors flew open revealing a blowsy leviathan of a woman with short, straight hair that lengthened in back and met in a duck-tail. Her massive hips were swathed in heavy brown corduroy that hung in huge folds over out-size legs. She had a voice to match her physique.

then following with my eyes that delicious line up to where it swelled into the fuller roundness of thigh and hip. Then it narrowed into a se-ductive slimness at her waist and finally disappeared under the bulky sweater.

She began to smile slowly at me [...] about [...] of the [...] a drink [...] self on [...] y hand [...] shoul-[...] black [...] e way [...] r. She [...] e was [...] about [...] e furi-

[...] oney," [...] u just [...] you'll [...] andle." [...] on my [...] crawl. [...] placed [...] ted to [...] nbered [...] s sup-[...] thing. [...] vas go-

[...] ing us, [...] all to [...] meet [...] iny a [...] k my [...] a quiet

[...] y, the [...] ts." [...] t hav-[...] ed and [...] e girl, [...] casual. [...] You're [...] know. [...] nks so [...] about

[...] ble at [...] ing. I [...] g so I [...] from [...] ted to [...] ow, it [...] re be-[...] e that



eyes I'd ever encountered. I can't remember ever being so thoroughly cruised by any man in my life. The thin summer sheath I was wearing seemed to melt away as her eyes traveled down my body, lingering in the places they found especially delightful. I really felt as though I

blonde, Fay, made a move before I was ready or had figured out how to handle it. If I just went along with whatever came up I wouldn't get much of a story although I might discover a new kind of experience. For the moment, however, I got my-self off the hook.

**THERE** were butterflies as big as bats in my stomach as I rode up to the sixth floor of the plush apartment house. I didn't expect to like this assignment one bit, but my editor had said it would be an exclusive for the paper and it was all mine if I wanted it. I'm a newspaperwoman first and last, so naturally I wanted it.

All we had to go on was a report from our man on the police beat that folks in a certain neighborhood had been complaining regularly about loud, late parties. And that the complaints always mentioned large groups of girls and young women, never a word about brawls between drunken men or over-boisterous male voices disturbing the early morning peace. The editor had smelled a rat that could sell a lot of papers and had called me on it.

As a night-life columnist, I had contacts in all sorts of places. I called an actress who knew her way around the more shadowy corners of our fair city. I'd once given her a plug in my column so she owed me a favor.

The actress had given me the name of the girl I would be meeting in a few minutes, and I had been assured that she would cooperate in every way. The only hitch was that I would have to cooperate too. Under no circumstances was I to let on that I was a reporter.

The elevator zoomed to a stop. As the heavy door slid spookily back by itself, I ran over my cover story in my head. I was an old school pal of the actress in town for two weeks and anxious to connect with some "congenial" friends. I found Apartment Six-B, rapped quietly and waited for my first look at a congenial friend.

After almost a full minute, the door swung briskly open. She was tall, with broad shoulders clad in a checkered sport shirt. A wasp-waist just barely widened into the slimmest hips I'd ever seen on a woman. The slimness was emphasized by the tight, rust-colored riding breeches. Her straw blonde hair was done in tight to the head, completing the picture of hard, disciplined beauty. Full, bright-red lips parted in a toothy smile.

"Sara's friend?" I nodded and was about to introduce myself further, but I never got the chance. She grabbed a leather jacket off the back of the sofa.

"Let's go." she said, and took hold of my elbow with an authority that left me feeling a little helpless.

Once on the street, she made no secret of who was escorting whom and who was running things. She stepped off the curb and gestured at the nearest cab. She opened the door for me, gave me a decisive shove and we were on our way.

While June—she'd finally gotten around to telling me her name— was describing the sort of girls I was going to meet and smoothly giving me the once-over, I took note of the neighborhoods the cab was taking us through. I've mentioned that June's apartment building was plush. It was a tar-paper shack compared to the monied castles that now rose on either side of the street.

We pulled up in front of an old but still elegant building that crowned the top of the hill. This was not one of those stiff, new, chromium and glass, paper-walled jobs that goes up in a week. This luxurious and ornate structure had that no-corners-cut, no-expense-spared look. A doorman swung open the paneled oak door and we stepped into the lobby.

While we waited for the elevator I kept up a chit-chat with June, carefully picking my way around her subtle overtures. At the same time my eye noted the deep-pile carpet and the rich, heavy fabric of the tapestries that adorned the high-rising walls. The massive chandelier that loomed above the lobby was of the purest crystal. It must have cost a fortune even in the last century when it was new. It had since been wired for electricity, of course, but it still had that old-fashioned, Old World opulence. It was obvious that the ladies I was about to meet were not just a gaggle of girls looking for kicks, or a tawdry collection of ordinary tramps. These would be respectable people you'd be honored to have in your home as guests. I fully expected there would be some whose names had turned up in the paper as financially or socially prominent. I began to worry that maybe I would be recognized as a columnist.

But I had no time to worry. The elevator was here and I was on my way to a party that would be like no other I'd ever attended—and I had not led a sheltered life!

The little gingerbreaded elevator carried us up to the 18th floor and stopped. The operator leered at me as we stepped out into the hall. No sooner had the elevator door closed than one of the apartment doors flew open revealing a blowsy leviathan of a woman with short, straight hair that lengthened in back and met in a duck-tail. Her massive hips were swathed in heavy brown corduroy that hung in huge folds over outsize legs. She had a voice to match her physique.

"June, Baby," she blared. "We've been waiting for you! Say, who's your cute friend?"

I saw my hand get swallowed up in her sweaty paw as I was being dragged into the apartment. As soon as we were inside, June disappeared, apparently she had her own fish to fry, and I was left in the clutches of this big bull dyke. It turned out that her name was Tiny (naturally!) and she was hosting tonight's bash.

"Just have a seat here, Sweetstuff," she said, "and I'll go fetch us a couple of drinks." I lowered myself onto the low-slung sectional sofa that encircled the room and watched old butter-buttocks waddle toward the bar set up at one end.

As long as I was alone, I took the opportunity to look around and get an impression of the place. I couldn't openly take notes, so I wanted everything firm in my mind and no mistakes. Unlike the rest of the building, this apartment was ultramodern—including the occupants.

There was the expected clutch of gaunt-faced, stringy-haired beatniks sitting in a closed little circle looking very intense and emancipated.

There were several older women whose style of dress and exquisite poise just shrieked "Success!" Whatever else may have been here, there was plenty of money. I felt there was a story here that would set the whole town on its ear—all I had to do was get it.

I stopped looking around when I spotted the slim blonde seated on the floor. She wore a tight black leotard topped with a bulky orange sweater. Her slimly tapered legs were stretched out to one side and she balanced a drink delicately on one knee. When she saw me looking her over she stopped her conversation.

This girl had the boldest pair of eyes I'd ever encountered. I can't remember ever being so thoroughly cruised by any man in my life. The thin summer sheath I was wearing seemed to melt away as her eyes traveled down my body, lingering in the places they found especially delightful. I really felt as though I were sitting there stark naked.

It seemed strange at first, but after a while I realized that I felt very flattered that such an exquisite creature should find me attractive. Maybe it was just a case of pampered feminine vanity at first. All I know is that I found myself admiring the smooth curve of her calf, then following with my eyes that delicious line up to where it swelled into the fuller roundness of thigh and hip. Then it narrowed to a seductive slimness at her waist and finally disappeared under the bulky sweater.

She began to smile slowly at me and just as I thought she was about to speak, Tiny burst out of the crowd and bore down on me, a drink in each hand. She settled herself on the sofa, shoved a glass in my hand and put one arm around my shoulders. I saw the girl in the black tights begin to laugh at the way Tiny was taking me over. She turned back to the group she was with and seemed to forget all about me. I found that this made me furious and I began to hate Tiny.

"So you're new in town, Honey," Tiny was gushing. "Well you just put yourself in my hands and you'll have all the fun you can handle." With that she put her hand on my body and my flesh began to crawl. Then she pulled me close and placed her lips right on mine! I wanted to break and run but I remembered my cover story and that I was supposed to like this kind of thing. Fortunately, June saw what was going on and rescued me.

"Tiny," she said, approaching us, "you can't keep little Jo-Jo all to yourself. She came here to meet people." Without giving Tiny a chance to protest, June took my hand and steered me over to a quiet corner.

"I saw you cruising Fay, the tall number in the black tights."

I was a little embarrassed at having been noticed. I stammered and said she was a very attractive girl, trying my damndest to sound casual.

June winked knowingly, "You're not telling me a thing I don't know. And everybody else here thinks so

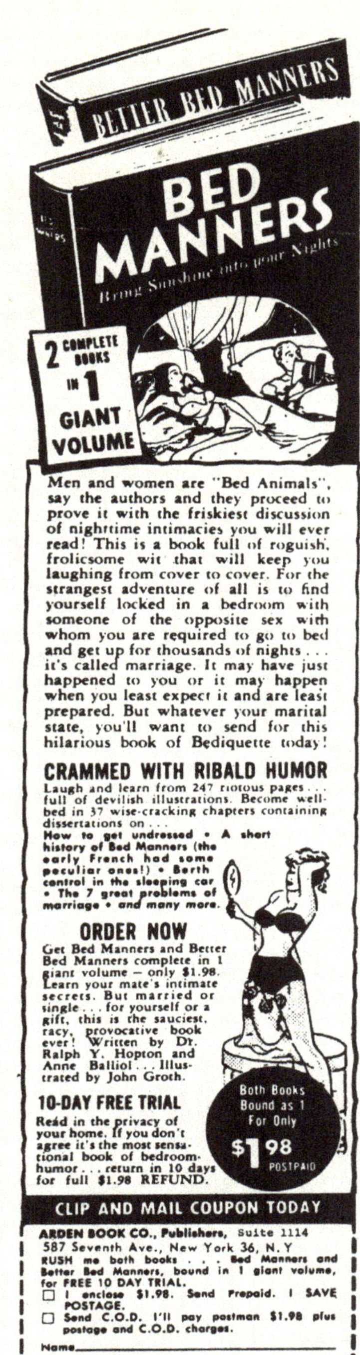

too. Anyway, she was asking about you. You're very lucky."

I felt a little uncomfortable at how fast things were moving. I wanted to get into this thing so I could put together a column from it, but at the same time I wanted to stay on top of the situation. Now, it seemed as though things were beginning to crowd me. Suppose that blonde, Fay, made a move before I was ready or had figured out how to handle it? If I just went along with whatever came up I wouldn't get much of a story although I might discover a new kind of experience. For the moment, however, I got myself off the hook.

"Well, really, June, there were a lot of others I liked too. I think I'd like to try and make my own contacts for a while."

"Sure, why not, you shouldn't have any trouble. I'll be around if you need anything." She gave my hand a squeeze and was gone.

The only illumination in the room came from the colored lights strung around the wall and the red revolving spot affixed to the ceiling. In the gloom it was hard to pick out definite faces. When the girls began to dance with each other, the whole scene just merged into a pulsating mass of sensuously slithering bodies with the erotic rhythm of the music overlaying it all. Through the murk, I spotted Fay's blonde head and bright orange sweater.

She was in the grip of an intense looking black-haired girl with a death-white face. The zombie, who was obviously leading, danced with strong definite steps and held Fay's supple, young, body pressed tightly against her. A surge of jealously began to grow in me and I found myself hating that black-haired witch.

I forgot about them, however, when I felt a soft hand drop onto my shoulder. I turned and looked into the demanding eyes of a full-blown redhead in a white sweater and black satin skirt. The sweater was tight enough and thin enough to show she hadn't bothered with anything so restraining as a bra. Although she hadn't said a word, I caught on that she wanted to dance with me. I nodded and smiled; she placed an authoritative arm around my waist, moved her body against mine and pushed me out onto the floor.

She never did bother about conversation. She just got right down to business and began flicking her tongue in an out of my ear while her breath played in little warm circles over my neck. She danced with her whole body, hardly moving her feet at all. Her breasts took on a life of their own, struggling against the flimsy material of the sweater as they moved over my own. I had never thought I would enjoy this type of attention from another woman, but this redhead was an expert.

Abruptly, the music stopped and there was a moment of silence before the whole gathering, as if by a signal, stopped dancing and found places to sit. Some chose the sofa, but most of them simply folded their legs like large insects and dropped to the floor. They had all paired off into closely clutching couples and seemed to be waiting for something.

I turned to ask my redhead what was up, but she had vanished. I located her on the far end of the room with a petite looking blonde in her arms. She was giving the blonde the same working over I had been getting only she was being much more thorough now. The blonde was moaning and squirming with delight. As I watched I found myself beginning to tremble.

Since everyone seemed to have paired off, it was strange that I should be left alone and that no one made a move to claim me. Even Tiny was keeping her distance. I thought that perhaps it was up to me, as a newcomer, to make a move, but I never got the chance. Suddenly, the whole room was plunged into darkness and the crowd became silent. A magenta spotlight flared on at the far end and there stood Fay. Her hair glistened gold while faint purple highlights followed the slim curve and taper of her body.

She stood still as a statue until the hush was complete. Then as soft, insistent music began to play, she started her dance. It was then I realized the significance of my having been left alone. This love-dance Fay was performing was aimed at me. She had made her selection for

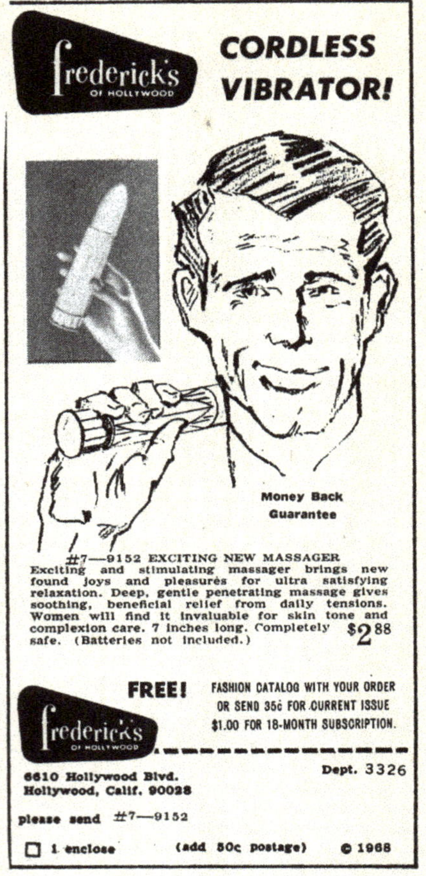


the evening and the dance was part of a ritual—as I discovered later that occurred whenever a new face showed up at one of these affairs.

Every eye in the place was on the softly undulating body of the violet-tinted love-goddess. Muscles in her thighs rippled invitingly and her eyes glowed like two purple fires. Rolling her hips in slow, tantalizing circles, she reached up and began to unbutton her sweater. A low murmur came from the watchers as the globes of Fay's breasts began to appear.

Then the music shifted from the softly sensuous to a blatantly sexy wail of a single trumpet. Fay's head flew back, a cry of animal ecstasy came from her lips and was echoed by the grappling couples on the floor. Fay began to step around the room, never ceasing the wild swiveling of her hips. The sweater was now completely unbuttoned and began to fall from around her ivory shoulders, exposing the full, velvet beauty of her ruby-tipped breasts. Now only the thin black tights remained.

She began to move closer to me. Her body, writhing as though in the grasp of a lover, answered the steady, penetrating thrust of the drum. When she was right in front of me, my pulse pounding like a triphammer, she stretched out her arms. The music stopped with a crash; the lights went out cloaking us in pitch blackness.

I felt a pair of smooth-tapering arms go around my waist and the roundness of Fay's body crushing passionately against me.

Fay's body gleamed whitely in the moonlight that streamed through the window. As I held her soft roundness to me I experienced wild thrills that no man had ever been able to arouse in me.

The passion and vitality of this blonde Venus were unbelievable.

She played on me until I was limp with ecstasy. When it came to sensuality, Fay was a virtuoso.

The other couples were just as active. From the far end of the room came a cry of agonized pleasure. The apartment was alive with sounds of rustling clothing, squeals, and moans of passion. The colored lights had come on again and a weird pattern of red, blue and violet undulated eerily over the straining and slithering bodies that covered the floor and furniture.

The room was a scene out of some mad mythology far removed from twentieth century real life—and the whole thing was even more unreal when I thought about the fact that there were no men at all in the place. I thought all this but the thoughts just didn't take hold. With Fay outdoing herself, and drugged by the new responsiveness I was finding in myself, I knew that, for the moment at least, I was right where I wanted to be no matter how far out of this world it was.

In the morning things were different. I was the first to wake up and when I had looked around and gotten over the first shock at the sight of so much nude female flesh, I began to pick up the threads of my everyday personality. Trying not to see the spent sprawled bodies around me, I gathered up my clothing and was dressed before anyone else was awake.

Only then did I stop and take a long look at Fay. The early morning sun played along the curves and planes of her body. In sleep her face was like an angel's, ringed all around with golden strands. She looked so helpless and appealing with her nude body stretched out on the white down rug, and the small half-smile on her lips. Although I could still appreciate that she was a beautiful girl I felt none of the passion or the compelling drive to possess that had gripped me last night.

I remembered the night with pleasure but had no real desire to repeat it. Maybe it was just the excitement or the strangeness of it all. Maybe I'd never react that way again after the first time. I don't know why it happened and I wouldn't care to predict how I'd behave if I were in that situation again.

What I do know is that there's still a lot of mystery surrounding human emotions, sex in particular, and passion can be a powerful thing. When I wrote my story for the paper I did the best I could to emphasize the strength of the emotions that are involved with Lesbianism. And the fact that Nature is Nature and natural impulses will always resist the controls imposed on them by "civilization." ///

# CARL EVANS' MAD MONKEYS

WHEN I interviewed Dr. David M. Earle, the author of All Man! (the excellent book about Ernest Hemingway and 1950s men's magazines), one of the questions I asked was whether there were any issues of men's pulp mags that were his particular favorites. He told me, "I of course love magazines like the August 1953 issue of Male, which features 'Monkey Madness.' Three guys in a life raft being attacked by hundreds of monkeys. It's just so ludicrous."

When I looked at that issue I didn't recognize the work of the artist who did the cover painting (also used inside in black-and-white). The credits said it was done by Edward Laning, an artist who is better known as a mural painter than an illustration artist.

I did recognize the story, and realized it was also one of my favorites. I first saw it in the January 1951 issue of Stag, under the title "Mad Monkeys Manned the Lifeboats." It's a cover story on both mags.

The Stag cover painting is uncredited. And, even my collaborator Rich Oberg, the world's foremost expert on MAMs, didn't know or recognize the artist. So I posted a scan of it in the Men's Adventure Magazines Facebook Group, where nearly 300 fans of vintage illustration art hang out, and asked if anyone else knew. Sure enough, it was soon ID'ed by Timothy Isaacson, one of the knowledgeable pulp art buffs in the group.

He recognized it as the work of John R. McDermott, a top vintage illustration artist featured on the indispensable American Art Archives site and in several posts on the excellent Today's Inspiration blog:

"That cover, 'Mad Monkeys Manned the Life Boat' from January 1951, was done by John R. McDermott (1917-1977)," Tim wrote in a post to the group. "McDermott started out has an animator for the Disney Studios in Hollywood after high school. With the outbreak of World War II, that job ended as he became a Marine in the Pacific Theatre, during which he became a combat artist and made drawings for the Corps' records of actions in the Solomons, Guadalcanal and Okinawa. When the war was over his drawings caught the attention of the folks at Blue Book magazine and his career as expert in military subjects and depictions of them was established. I think he did some work for Argosy as well."

In recent months, I ran across the "Mad Monkeys" story in three other MAMs. It was the cover story of Man's World in December 1957, under the title "Life Raft Madness." The painting for that cover is by artist John Leone, *who died in 2011 after a long and distinguished career.*

*The fourth appearance of the "Mad Monkeys" story I know of was in the August 1969 issue of* For Men Only. *In that issue, it's titled "The Most Horrifying Shipwreck Story Ever Told!"*

*And, although the cover painting used for the story is by Mort Künstler, the interior illustration is by Gil Cohen—another great artist who once did artwork for MAMs. Cohen is now renowned as one of the nation's top military aviation artists.*

**Stag, January 1951**
**Cover by John McDermott**

*The fifth reprint of the "Mad Monkeys" story I've seen is in the 1973 one-off,* The Best of Male *and* For Men Only.

*The title used in that one is "500 Starving Monkeys Are Eating the Survivors!" The illustration is a black-and-white version of Mort Kunstler's cover painting for August 1969 issue of* For Men Only.

*So what about the story?*

*This "killer creature" yarn is portrayed as a true story written by a merchant seaman named Carl Evans, but it was almost certainly penned by one*

**Man's World, December 1957**
**Cover by John Leone**

*For Men Only*, August 1969
Cover by Mort Künstler
*(left, as* Emmett Kaye*)*
and Paul Rader *(right)*

*For Men Only*, August 1969
Original interior art by Gil Cohen

*of the imaginative pulp writers who contributed to the men's adventure genre.*

*It's basically a horror story about the fate of a merchant ship that was carrying hundreds of African rhesus monkeys that were destined to be used as test animals in medical labs.*

*En route, the ship's boilers explode, killing most of the crew. As the vessel sinks, one of the surviving crew members takes pity on the monkeys and sets them free. His act of kindness turns out to be a big mistake.*

*Nine seamen who are left make it onto a life raft. Almost immediately, hundreds of desperate monkeys begin swarming onto the raft with them. This leads to a gruesome battle for survival. Not all of the men live through it. None of the monkeys do.*

—Robert Deis

**For Men Only,** August 1969
**Cover** *(detail)* **by Mort Künstler (as Emmett Kaye)**

## "MONKEY MADNESS"

— CARL EVANS —

*Male*, August 1953

COVER ARTIST: EDWARD LANING

# Monkey



There were 37 of us—nine officers and 28 seamen—aboard ship that trip, and you couldn't have found three who didn't think we were dead ducks. I sure as hell did. Not that the idea was in my noggin when we signed on in October—far from it. I was just jumping at the bonus-bait they waved under our noses, to get us to ship out in spite of the fact that we'd be lugging tanks and planes and other stuff for the Limeys, with the Jerry subs itching to do a little short-stopping. October, 1941—remember? All the war meant to me then was a chance to risk my neck and get a few extra bucks for doing it.

We were going round the Cape of Good Hope—FDR had closed the Mediterranean to U.S. shipping. Port Sudan and Suez were our destination—to get this Lend-Lease stuff to the Limeys before Rommel could get up steam. Don't ask me where we were exactly on December 7, because after Sparks slugged us with the news, nobody gave a damn about our position. All that counted was how long it would take us to get where we were going and then back to the States.

It would take a long time. And so, as I said, almost every last guy aboard figured we were as good as dead.

We dumped the cargo in Africa as per schedule and sailed in ballast for Calcutta. There we picked up manganese ore, talc, jute, mica, rubber—the usual. And something not so usual, too. We took a load of monkeys aboard, rhesus monkeys the docs back home wanted for experiments with infantile paralysis. Five hundred of those jabbering monks were brought on as deck cargo, 20 of 'em to a cage, piled up on the after deck. Nobody gave 'em a second thought. Not then.

Mostly, at the time, we were thinking about other things. I sure as hell was. Yeah—women. The ship was tied up at the Kidderport Docks No. 1, and just past the dock area was the native bazaar, crawling with people—including women. For as long as our ship was docked in Calcutta, I had me quite a time. Later I got to be awful glad about that because, for a while, particularly when it started with the monks, I sure figured I'd seen my last female.

But that's another story. I didn't start out to tell you that one—any sailor's done the same or *(Continued on page 80)*

from the S.S. *Halifax*, seven miles
...er us than the *Patence* had been. The
...e-crew was to stand by for orders.
...en Kelsey understood that the Old
... had to risk a boiler explosion, so
... we went into the engine room and
... the valves already dogged down,
...

Then the sixth shell ripped into us. If
it had come 40 seconds later, it would
have gotten me, for it entered below the
water line, directly above the boilers. The
engine room blast shook the entire ship.
I was blown against a bulkhead and
stunned for a moment. Live steam and
tongues of flame whipped up the ladder,
...

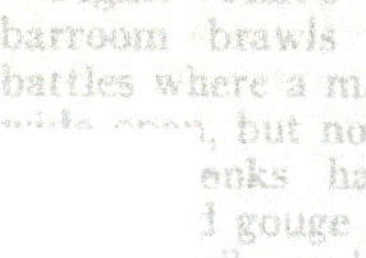

recovered our ba...
his footing and p...
it was... I could
and by that time
to fight it out on
Fight? That's
barroom brawls
battles where a m...
while open, but no...
onks ha...
d gouge
ell—and
d terror
hey scre...

# Madness

**Somebody opened the cages to give the monkeys a fighting chance—a chance to fight to the death for possession of the bobbing life rafts.**

as
told
to
CARL
EVANS

...atic, shook his fist at the Jap cruiser
...the fifth shell landed. The Old Man
...hed; the flag hung ...
...realized it was up to me to get the
... of the black gang on deck. As I
...ed the monkey cages, I saw that a
... had been blasted open by the last
... and Chips, who was on the after...

even as we stood there, every last one of
us paralyzed with horror, we saw blood
...
scream like a madman until the water
closed over his head.

Dozens of the creatures had reached
our raft and were pulling themselves
aboard. I don't know who leaped at them...

...EST isn't
...erted a p...
They s...
...ny of t...
ship, or the missio...
ing from posts in
...ma can t...
got it first-hand ...
the surviving five...
All the way back
about the Japs...
been picked up...

**Illustration by Edward Laning**

**EDITOR'S NOTE:**

This amazing story is absolutely true. It was told to Carl Evans by a seaman friend who lived through the nightmare. That man, however, is now in an insane asylum.

We tried checking with the steamship line that owned the vessel involved, and with the company whose cargo was aboard. Both gave us a polite but firm brush-off.

The story that follows, with a few names changed, is the information nobody wanted to release.

**THERE** were 37 of us—nine officers and 28 seamen—aboard ship that trip, and you couldn't have found three who didn't think we were dead ducks. I sure as hell did. Not that the idea was in my noggin when we signed on in October—far from it. I was just jumping at the bonus-bait they waved under our noses, to get us to ship out in spite of the fact that we'd be lugging tanks and planes and other stuff for the Limeys, with the Jerry subs itching to do a little short-stopping. October, 1941—remember? All the war meant to me then was a chance to risk my neck and get a few extra bucks for doing it.

We were going round the Cape of Good Hope—FDR had closed the Mediterranean to US shipping. Port Sudan and Suez were our destination—to get this Lend-Lease stuff to the Limeys before Rommel could get up steam. Don't ask me where we were exactly on December 7, because after Sparks slugged us with the news, nobody gave a damn about our position. All that counted was how long it would take us to get where we were going and then back to the States.

It would take a long time. And so, as I said, almost every last guy aboard figured we were as good as dead.

We dumped the cargo in Africa as per schedule and sailed in ballast for Calcutta. There we picked up manganese ore, talc, jute, mica, rubber—the usual. And something not so usual, too. We took a load of monkeys aboard, rhesus monkeys the docs back home wanted for experiments with infantile paralysis. Five hundred of those jabbering monks were brought on as deck cargo, 20 of 'em to a cage, piled up on the after deck. Nobody gave 'em a second thought. Not then.

Mostly, at the time, we were thinking about other things. I sure as hell was. Yeah—women. The ship was tied up at the Kidderport Docks

No. 1, and just past the dock area was the native bazaar, crawling with people-including women. For as long as our ship was docked in Calcutta, I had me quite a time. Later I got to be awful glad about that because for a while, particularly when it started with the monks I sure figured I'd seen my last female.

But that's another story. I didn't start out to tell you that one—any sailor's done the same or better! I'd like to see the guy, though, who can match what happened to our tub on April 6th.

We kissed Calcutta goodbye on April 4, bound for Colombo in Ceylon. It figured to be a five-day run, provided the ship stuck to ten knots all the way. That was what the First counted on doing, and as engineers go, he was a pretty hep guy. I'd been on his black gang for the whole trip, and he'd get my vote any day in the year.

Our ship was the usual freighter—you'll find 'em a dime a dozen in any US port—a 5,800 tonner built in 1921, black-hulled with red boot-topping and a buff funnel, masts forward and aft. You wouldn't enter her in a speedboat race, but all the same she was a solid job.

None of us was doing much horsing around when we lifted anchor. The news had been getting blacker and blacker. It was bad enough to have the Japs at war with us just when we were in their back yard, but then the *Prince of Wales* and the *Repulse* took nose-dives and the panic was on. Sparks, that sour old son-of-a-bucket, got a bang out of putting up bulletins to put the fear of God into us. Around the middle of February, he let us know, Singapore had fallen. Less than a month later Sparks used red crayon to tell us that Rangoon had fallen.

All you have to do is take a fast look at a map to see why we were jittery. Even before we'd left Calcutta, we'd learned that the Japs had swept the Limey fleet out of the Malayan Straits and it didn't take a military genius to guess that the Jap Navy might very well give the Bay of Bengal a going-over. Which, in case you've forgotten, is where we sat.

For 24 hours after we were on the move again, things were quiet. It was the day before Easter Sunday and those of us on the 8 to 12 watch were shooting the breeze about what we d be doing if we were back in the States. I was too busy chasing around oiling the engines, so I let the First and Kelsey, the fireman, do most of the jabbering.

At eight bells, when the second watch took over, the First and Kelsey and me went up to the mess hall to get our chow and to find out what was buzzing. Nothing was buzzing. Sparks had told the boys the wire was quiet. Well, I didn't like that worth a damn and I said so. It was too quiet—something had to be brewing. Belly-robber, our chief cook who couldn't cook to save his neck but who was a nice guy anyway, grinned and told me to go aft if it was noise I was after.

The ship's engines gave me all the noise I wanted, but just the same after chow I drifted aft to the poop deck. I had nothing else to do; and besides, it was just like being at a zoo to watch those monks.

Those brown-furred Indian devils were really something to see! With their bare faces and backsides, they looked enough like some humans I've bumped into to hand me a laugh. In each cage the oldest male grabbed all the females for himself and he'd beat the bejabbers out of any other male who made a move in the wrong direction. So the males messed around among themselves, unless one of 'em could steal a female when the bull boss wasn't looking.

You could hear the monks from some distance away. Just let a few get excited and pretty soon the whole pack would be cutting loose with that shrill chirp of theirs. And if they really got worked up, they'd grab hunks of leftover potatoes or carrots or stale bread and hurl it out of their cages. Once I got conked with a hunk of potato, but I swear the monk who did it was kidding around—soon as I turned my back again, he let fly with another hunk!

For as long as they were riding on our rust bucket, they were at the mercy of the bosun and the carpenter. These two washed the cages down with a hose every morning, fed the animals twice a day, put the sick in separate cages and dropped the dead overboard. Getting the sick and dead out of the cages could be risky business if the monks were worked up and if a guy wasn't careful. A two-foot bull has teeth that work like meat choppers, and when his hands and feet grab hold, you'd think he's got suction pads at the end! One of 'em wrapped himself around the bosun and it took two of us to tear him off.

Naturally the bosun and the carpenter got extra dough for the job—50 bucks, plus an extra 50 smackers if less than 10 per cent died on the way—so they were pretty damn careful. Chips, the carpenter, was a bull-headed ox with a queer mushy streak in him, and he worried about the monks like they were kids, and he swore bloody murder whenever one died. I nearly bust a gut to see him peering in every cage to find out if his little friends were okay, because I knew he was as tough as they come.

Chris, the bosun, was probably the only guy in the merchant marine who could have bunked with Chips. Chris was half-deaf, so maybe that's why. Besides he was a tough baby, too, and anyone who's ever sailed under him knows he's a miserable character—knows he was a miserable character, because he got his when the shooting broke out.

It's about time I got to that. But if you didn't know everything I've just told you, you'd never believe what happened.

Easter Sunday it started. Most of the day we'd plowed right along, calm as a Hudson River Day Line excursion. But along about 1600 hours, at the end of the second watch, Sparks picked up a few faint distress signals, too far away for him to get 'em clearly, but close enough for us to realize trouble was on the way. The only question was: how far off was it?

Orders came down from the Old Man to check guns and lifeboats. Guns—that was a hot one! We'd left the States unarmed except for a couple of .45s the skipper packed, which we might as well have traded in for slingshots. And at Suez we took aboard some heavy stuff—a Browning machine gun that sure as hell dated back to the first World War! Just the thing to scare the pants off a Jap cruiser!

As far as the lifeboats went, we were a little better off. Like most rust buckets her age, the Silver City had four lifeboats hanging from gravity davits on the boat deck. Besides that, before sailing from the States we'd rigged up two rafts on the forward deck.

THAT night the card games busted up early. I went on deck and found a couple of other guys there, saying nothing, just sitting around. It gave me the shivers—a blacked-out ship plowing ahead into a black night, no sounds except the throbbing beat of the propeller and the jibbering of the monks. I wound up with a real case of the willies, so I ducked below and hit the sack.

I'd be lying if I said I slept through the night. By 6:00 AM I was up and around, restless as the devil, and I wasn't the only one. But nothing was new and I just killed time until Belly-robber decided to give us chow.

I didn't have much of an appetite to begin with, and by 7:20 I had none at all. That was when Bliven, the ordinary seaman on the 4 to 8 watch, came down to make sure we were up. He was so pale his freckles stood out like splattered ink spots and he was clenching and unclenching his fists.

"Sparks just come up on the bridge," he said, "to tell the Old Man he'd picked up an SOS. The *Pawnee.* Shelled and sinking, 30 miles from here!"

"What's the skipper doing about it?"

"He's gonna head in for Vizagapatam," Bliven said. "That's our nearest port right now. And he's got the Chief on deck—I think they're aimin' to dog down the valves."

Kelsey and the First and me looked at one another. We were in for a nasty watch. The ship's boilers had been inspected and the safety valves set for 196 pounds where they'd been sealed. Now the inspector's seal would be broken and the lever shifted so that we could build up the pressure maybe to 250, only nobody knew whether the boilers would take it without blowing up.

Kelsey was all for trying to talk the skipper out of it. He was, that is, until shortly before we were due to relieve the third watch. One of the AB's came off the bridge to let the men know that Sparks had gotten a second SOS, this one from the *SS Halifax,* seven miles nearer us than the *Pawnee* had been. The entire crew was to stand by for orders.

Even Kelsey understood that the Old Man had to risk a boiler explosion, so when we went into the engine room and saw the valves already dogged down, none of us said a word. If the order was to get this tub to 12 knots, we were set to bust a gut trying.

As the pressure went up in the boilers, so did the heat in the engine room and so did the tension. My ears strained for the telltale sounds: the popping of rivets or the buckling of plates and tubes.

Then the lookout spotted a vessel on the horizon tearing along in our wake. At the same time, because of the heavy steaming our stack began to smoke. The Old Man blew his top and bellowed down to the First that he'd cut his heart out if the smoke wasn't cleaned up in ten seconds.

But already it was too late. That Jap cruiser was on our tail and we couldn't have given it the slip in a million years. Down in that hot hell-hole, where we couldn't see a thing, we knew anyway that the shells would soon be falling. The general alarm was rung, sending the rest of the crew to battle stations—which

for our ship meant fire-fighting posts and lifeboats—while we slaved in 120° heat to get half a knot more out of those engines.

Suddenly the ship shuddered and we knew we'd been hit. The First yelled to me to hop up on deck and see what the score was, because he couldn't get through to the skipper.

There was good reason why he couldn't. The cruiser had bracketed us with its two first shells, the third had torn through the shelter deck not far from the machine shop, killing one wiper and injuring a second as they were trying to secure the gear. A fourth shell had struck almost simultaneously, square on the bridge. The AB at the wheel was dead; the skipper's legs were shattered.

SPARKS, who'd been sending out an SOS ever since the cruiser hove into sight, made his way to the Old Man, carrying a bottle of Scotch with him. But the Old Man wouldn't stay on the bridge. He'd taken an American flag out of the locker and now, with Sparks dragging him, he made his way to the poop deck where he raised the flag on the after staff. Then, after Sparks started back to his station, the Old Man stood erect and, cursing like a lunatic, shook his fist at the Jap cruiser until the fifth shell landed. The Old Man vanished; the flag hung in shreds.

I realized it was up to me to get the rest of the black gang on deck. As I passed the monkey cages, I saw that a few had been blasted open by the last shell, and Chips, who was on the after deck with a fire squad, weeping with rage, seized a crowbar and began breaking the hasps on all the other cages. If only I'd had the brains then to stop him! But I didn't, and so out those creatures swarmed, climbing into the rigging in panic, their cries mingling with the screams of the wounded on deck, making my ears ring wildly and my flesh crawl.

Then the sixth shell ripped into us. If it had come 40 seconds later, it would have gotten me, for it entered below the water line, directly above the boilers. The engine room blast shook the entire ship. I was blown against a bulkhead and stunned for a moment. Live steam and tongues of flame whipped up the ladder, and though I tried to keep going down to see what I could do for the First and Kelsey and Borlund, the steam drove me back. But I knew that nobody could have lived through that.

Now the ship, its motors silenced, was eerily quiet. With all the lights out, I had to grope my way back in the dark. When finally I stumbled onto the forward deck, I found some of the men who were left alive gathering around the chief mate. Almost all of them were wounded, and the mate himself was soaked with his own blood. He ordered the rafts launched and told us to dive in after them.

WITH that he dashed back to the midship house and shouted to the men on the boat deck to lower their boats or else to jump overboard and make for the rafts. They tried to drop one boat but its lines were fouled and it capsized, so they let the others go and leaped into the sea. A few managed to climb down to the water level and start swimming from there.

So did most of the monkeys. Chirping shrilly, they swarmed over the sinking ship, riding it like a logger on a slow-spinning log, until they had to take the plunge into the water. We hardly noticed them.

Only 16 of us made the rafts. A few others were clinging to bits of wreckage. We yelled to them to stick close, if they could.

A monkey swam up to the raft I was on and Belly-robber reached down to pull it out of the sea. It too was a living fellow creature; no one wanted it to die. But suddenly I realized that hundreds of the monks were coming our way!

Someone screamed. Not 100 yards away we saw a seaman hanging on to a piece of timber—and, arms and legs wrapped around his neck, was a monkey, tearing at him with its teeth!

"Oh God!" groaned Belly-robber. "It's Sparks!"

Then I recognized the guy, only now his thin and sour face was convulsed with terror and his eyes seemed to be popping out of his head. As I watched, incredulous, I saw another monkey join the first, and still another, ripping away mercilessly to get that hunk of wood from him. And even as we stood there, every last one of us paralyzed with horror, we saw blood flowing from Spark's face. and he began to scream like a madman until the water closed over his head.

Dozens of the creatures had reached our raft and were pulling themselves aboard. I don't know who leaped at them first—maybe it was me. All I remember is that we became animals too, making wild sounds deep in our throats. Not all of us; some were too weak from loss of blood. But the others fought to keep the monks off.

It was horrible. We tried kicking their heads off, but they were so damn fast they could duck and swing up before we'd recovered our balance. Belly-robber lost his footing and plunged into the sea, and it was all I could do to drag him aboard; and by that time it was too late. We had to fight it out on the raft.

Fight? That's a laugh! I've been in barroom brawls and shore front gang battles where a man can get his skull split wide open, but nothing was ever like this. Those monks had four arms—because they could gouge our eyes with their feet just as well—and their teeth were razor-sharp. And terror had made them insane, so that they screamed wildly and their eyes rolled and twisted with rage.

Even as I got my hands on one, others were wrapped around my legs and I couldn't shake them loose. 1 managed to work my fingers onto the neck of the monkey I held and then I squeezed, ignoring the others until this one was dead. Then I seized his feet and used the corpse to beat at the others. Once I'd gotten them off me, I flailed away with the dead monkey at any that came near.

Even so, I was bleeding from several cuts, and I saw that a few of the men on the raft, exhausted by the ordeal of the sinking, could hardly raise their arms to struggle against the beasts. I gave the dead monkey to Belly-robber and waited for another to jump me.

This one was a bull, but I was set for him. He leaped straight at me. I let him grab hold of my left arm, and then I whipped my right hand around and got him on the back of the neck, tightening there. But before I knew what had happened, that bull rhesus had spun around behind me, his hands around my throat! Panic-stricken I reached back to seize his head. His teeth slashed my fingers, yet I kept on groping until I had him.

With that he sank his feet into the back of my neck and for an instant the shock and pain paralyzed me so that I almost let him go. But in a fury I took a tighter hold on his neck and, enraged. I twisted. I heard it snap. The body went limp.

I can't be sure of what happened after that. All I remember is that we used their dead to beat them back into the sea, and that when we had finally driven the last one off, two of the nine men on our raft lay there with blood gushing out of open wounds. One of them was Belly-robber. Within the hour they both were dead.

THE REST isn't important. Sparks' SOS had alerted a passenger ship bound for the US. They spotted us and took us aboard. Any of the businessmen on that ship, or the missionaries who were returning from' posts in Java, Sumatra. Malaya and Burma can testify to this tale. They got it first-hand from the seven of us and the surviving five from the other raft.

All the way back the passengers worried about the Japs. But for those of us who'd been picked up, there were other nightmares.

And me—I still have them. I wake up in the middle of the night, scared stiff and sweating like a pig, and not until I've got the light on do I believe that I'm not being strangled by insane monkeys. **///**

# "EVEN THE RHINOS WERE NYMPHOS"

## —— BRUCE JAY FRIEDMAN ——

**IN 1954,** after several rather pleasant, humdrum years of Korean War duty, I was employed as an assistant editor of *Focus* magazine, one of the many publications of a medium-vast company called Magazine Management. Editorial jobs were difficult to come by in the early fifties. (Have they ever been easy to come by?) A job at *F.Y.I.*, the house organ of *Time-Life*, had been dangled in my direction and then mysteriously withdrawn. I was quite nervous before the final interview series and trotted around the block several times, turning up in a heavy sweat which may have counted against me. My disappointment was great, since I had been assured that although I would not actually be working on any of the esteemed Luce publications, I would "get to visit every floor" of the building. I had tried *Collier's*, where I was instructed to start a file on myself and house it in the personnel department, tossing in items of interest that might come about in my everyday life. At the end of the year, "the three most interesting files" were to be called down and hired. I was given an upcoming issue of *Collier's* and instructed to study it in an attempt to worm out the secret of the magazine's prominence. The lead story was a photo essay on airports at night, transport planes slumbering peacefully in their hangars. The following piece offered readers a history of garlic. On my own initiative, I created a photo essay on Bronx playground bullies which failed to impress Dan Mich, the powerful editor of *Look* magazine. However, I was invited to a party at which male and female *Look* staffers went into a little room and then popped out, wearing each others' underwear.

I am not entirely clear on how I got to the Magazine Management Company, but somewhere in the picture is a chance encounter involving my mother and a furrier at the House of Chan restaurant. I believe the furrier's son-in-law worked for the company and helped me to get a foot in the door. My editor at *Focus* was a towering fellow named James A. "Big Jim" Bryans, whose view it was that in order to succeed at newsstand publishing, one had to hammer away at what he called the Big Emotions—that is, Hunger, Sex, Death, Jobs, etc. This advice has held up. I was introduced to Martin Goodman, the owner of the company, a congenial silver-haired gentleman of indeterminate age who looked a bit like Hopalong Cassidy. Although I was under the impression that I had already been hired, he looked me over, nonetheless, and said, "Alright, let's give him a try." I worked for the company for eleven years, and I am still not quite certain I ever pinned down the job. Through the time of our association, I found Martin Goodman to be a supportive friend, but at no time was I unaware of a chilling side to him, one that had sent scores of editors writhing into clinics with colitis symptoms. He was at his most quietly fearsome when some unfortunate new editor made the mistake of showing him a photo layout on logrolling. Part of the Martin Goodman legend is that his brothers called him Mr. Goodman. It was said that he was called Mr.

**MM mogul Martin Goodman (right, in dark glasses) with son Charles "Chip" Goodman (left), 1966.** *Photo courtesy Josh Alan Friedman; all rights reserved*

Goodman as a little boy. Once, flushed with confidence, having written a well-received novel, I attempted to call him Martin. I thought I had done well until I realized my voice had been an octave too high.

*Focus* was a peppier and saltier version of a magazine phenomenon called *Quick* which was

virtually bite sized and flourished in the early fifties. Most of the Magazine Management publications were peppier and saltier versions of other successful publishing ventures. That might have served as a motto for the company: A bit late, but peppier and saltier. We played Jayne Mansfield to the various Marilyn Monroes of publishing.

New magazines were created and done away with as casually as dimes are popped into Vegas slot machines. No sooner had I settled in as a *Focus* staffer than I was switched off to another bite-sizer called *Picture Life*. I believe that Martin Goodman began this venture because of his affection for the word "life." A genius at divining the buying habits of magazine shoppers, he had great faith in the pulling power of key words. I always felt he came a cropper in the case of *True Action*. Both "true" and "action" are clearly splendid words individually; when combined, however, they seemed to represent a ringing rebuke to a magazine called *False Action*, which, of course, did not exist.

*Picture Life*, alas, did not flourish. It predicted correctly that Floyd Patterson

**Bruce Jay Friedman, 1954**



would win the heavyweight title and received exactly one letter—from a dying man who was confident he would be able to eke out an extra month of life if only we were to run a six-page picture layout featuring Mitzi Gaynor sniffing gloves. No matter. A series of waggish freelance captions I did for a Magazine Management cheesecaker called *Tab* attracted the attention of Martin Goodman. I was pried away from my position beneath the thumb of "Big Jim" Bryans, given a secretary, an assistant, and the reins of a new entry called *Swank*. My three-man team was considered a large staff in MM terms; years later, when I visited the *Saturday Evening Post* and saw entire floors of people thrown over to the publication of one (skinny) magazine, I felt like Lemuel Gulliver on some weird and wasteful new island. (We were terribly arrogant at Magazine Management and always felt—much in the style of late-night drinkers who are convinced they can take over Haiti— that a handful of us could have "saved" *Life, Look, Collier's,* etc.) *Swank* had once belonged to Arnold Gingrich of *Esquire* and had published Hemingway stories in the twenties—but had never quite caught fire. I was instructed to "take off after *Esquire* and be classy, but not too classy." The advertising people refused to drop their truss ads, which were a trademark of Martin Goodman publications; I argued that you could not kick off each issue with a giant truss ad and then turn around and be urbane and classy (I now feel otherwise) but I was voted down. My first call to a literary agent—heady stuff—was to the distinguished

James Oliver Brown. My goal—acquisition of the rights to a Boileau-Narcejac suspense novel, for condensation in *Swank.*

"I don't like your price, Friedman," said Brown.

"I'm not too crazy about it either," I said.

Actually, the fee of one thousand dollars for a twenty-thousand word selection may have been an all-time Martin Goodman record breaker. In declining my offer, Brown said he had accepted one from Alfred Hitchcock for $150,000. (The novel was turned into the film *Vertigo.* To this day, I think of Brown's name as being James Oliver I-don't-like-your-price-Friedman Brown.

*Swank* published new stories by William Saroyan and Graham Greene, and God alone knows who read them. Truss ads and all, the magazine attempted to be classy and risqué. I assigned the late AC Spectorsky to do an article on girl pinching. He did one on girl bumping which I rejected. He did a second version on girl shoving; I sent it back. He countered with a third, on girl tickling. I returned it and paid him half his fee. Years later, he asked me to join him at *Playboy.*

"I am making you this offer," he said, "because of your quite proper refusal to accept anything but girl pinching."

*Swank* failed to set the world on fire. I could tell its sales were feeble because Martin Goodman would walk into my office each month, smack the current issue, and leave. *Playboy* and its legion of imitators in the lit-clit field were beginning to throw their weight around. Risqué was not enough. Though dismissed by some as an "armpit" publisher, Martin Goodman, tapping some strange vein of propriety, refused to "go all the way" and *Swank* faded out of the picture, eventually being sold to someone down the street. In an ironic rendezvous with destiny,

**Male,** January 1958
**Cover by Stan Borack**

the magazine was subsequently published by Martin Goodman's son, Charles, quite properly, as a class tits-and-asser.

In my early years at Magazine Management, I had shown some flashy moves in the backcourt, but my shots were simply not going in. I was Mr. Around the Rim and Out. Despite my disappointing stats, Martin Goodman decided I was the man to take over *Male*, which, along with *Stag*, was a cornerstone of the Goodman chain, a hot seller in the burgeoning men's adventure field. There was a clear-cut hierarchy in this chamber of publishing. High above all others, at a lonely, nosebleed-producing altitude, stood the mighty *True*, which had achieved its status through newsbreaking revelations about hanky-panky in the conduct of World War II. Several notches below, but sturdy nonetheless, was a slick looking Western cuspidor of a magazine called *Argosy*. There followed, at least in terms of "classiness"—if not circulation—*Saga*; and then, after a bit of a leap and a bound, one reached the nether world of the Goodman books (as our magazines were referred to at the time), *Male, Stag, For Men Only, Man's World, Action for Men, True Action*, and so on. By no means did Magazine Management represent the end of the line. There were legions of other titles that generally featured Gestapo women prancing around captive Yanks in leg shackles. When the men's field met local opposition, the broom used was generally a large one and we were miffed at being swept off the newsstands along with the leg schacklers. Standing off to the side, refusing categorization was a publication called *Man's* magazine, which both fascinated and disturbed Martin Goodman. It had a modest Circulation, was quite unflashy, and seemed to be morosely

**True Action, May 1959
Cover by Mort Künstler**

going its own way. It was, nonetheless, the only competitive magazine that Martin Goodman would smack. I think he was peeved that despite its sluggish appearance it had any circulation at all. And it wasn't his.

A regular activity at Magazine Management was the examination of current issues of *True* and *Argosy*—and perhaps some renegade magazine that had shown a flurry of sales—and the attempt to ferret out the secret of their various achievements.

"Do you think they have our books spread out in front of them?" someone would ask. (Do girls like it, too?)

"You're damned right," would be someone's brave answer—although it seemed unlikely that Fawcett's lordly Ralph Daigh would invest time in cutting his way through the underbrush of our truss ads to peek at a *Male* lead story. This was an era of great snobbishness. A *Male* editor would grow pale at a cocktail party when confronted by a

*Men,* December 1964
Cover by Bob Schulz

True staffer. A *True* person, on the other hand, would be unable to meet the eyes of a *Timer-Lifer*, who in turn was made uncomfortable by the presence of an Alfred Knopfer. There was no end to this, of course, and I'm sure that even Knopfers would feel one-upped by *Times Literary Supplement* people, and so on up to God—that is, until the era of camp and the put-on, when it became a strong social advantage to identify yourself as the managing editor of *Forced Enema.*

I became involved with *Male* at a time when both *Stag* and *Male* had built circulations in excess of a million copies on the strength of stories about people who had been nibbled half to death by ferocious little animals. The titles were terrifying cries of anguish. "A Grysbok Sucked My Bones"; "Give Me Back My Leg"; they seemed to have even more power when couched in the present continuous tense. "A Boar Is

Grabbing My Brain."

Salted in among these animal nibblers were backup yarns about third-rail executions. All this, in the supposedly halcyon Eisenhower years. I would have been only too happy to sail in and begin cranking out more of these—but there had been a sudden, unexplainable cessation of interest in these accounts of leg-nibbling ordeals. The men's adventure books had been holding the line with Sintown, or what I always thought of as "scratch the surface" yarns. (Outwardly,

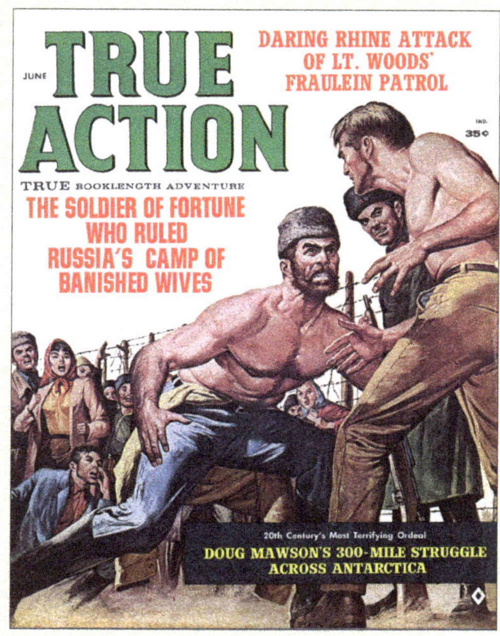


**True Action, June 1961
Cover by Charles Copeland**

Winkleton, Illinois, is a quiet, tree-lined little community… But *scratch the surface* of this supposedly God-fearing little town and you will find that not since Sodom and Gomorrah and blah blah blah.) Any town with a bar and a hooker would do—but somehow the unmasking of fleshpots did not quite do as a total diet for "our guys." We never did find out with any precision exactly who "our guys" were. They seemed to be multiple men's magazine readers who would buy Argosy and True and then return, with a certain petulance, and buy one or two of ours. Much in the style of someone who has eaten dinner, but requires a cup of chile to be put properly over the top. We were reasonably sure our readers drank beer and had some affiliation with Iwo. There may have been some migrant workers mixed in among them. My brother-in-law was the only reader I was able to pinpoint with any certainty.

We failed, finally, to come up with a concise formula, one that could be as crisply stated as that of, say, the confession magazines: "Sin, confess, repent." With a bit of tap dancing and some Nielsen-type research, we discovered what "our guys," whoever they were, liked and didn't. There were some surprises. Sports, for example, were of little interest. Fiction was weak. Forget about Westerns. There seemed, at the time, to be no appetite whatever for nostalgia. Perhaps there was a realization that the fifties were the past, even while they were going in. The Civil War could be slipped through as a theme so long as the writer concentrated on life in a vermin-infested cell. What we did find was a ferocious craving for what was actual and real (although, ironically, *Real*, as a title, did not work, a trusted employee of Martin Goodman's treacherously slipping off to try it and, with great embarrassment, failing instantly). Our staple product became the verifiably true story of some fellow who had survived a Japanese "rat cage," made a record-breaking Death Trek though Borneo, raided Schweinfurt, or helped to storm the Remagen Bridge. Dutifully, we served these up to "our guys," who were appreciative. There were, however, just so many Borneo death trekkers to be gotten hold of. Rather swiftly, *Man's World, Men*, and inevitably, *True Action* had been assigned to my group. This meant I had to purchase some fifty stories each month, an awesome number of death treks. (Most magazine publishers feel that if an editor comes up with one or two strong stories per issue, he is in good shape not so with Martin Goodman, who required no fewer than twelve. If the last story in *True Action* was a bit shaky, he would smack it.)

It was at this point that there arose the notion of simply making

"The Thrill-Kill Pack" by Mario Cleri (Mario Puzo)
*Male*, November 1965
Illustration by Bruce Minney

up "true" stories and providing them with full documentation. What a giddy and bracing sensation as we set about falsifying our first "true" jungle trek. No doubt Goebbels, W. R. Hearst, and various CIA operatives before us had experienced that same lift to the spirits. *Above left:* The wallet dropped by Howard "Copter" Gibbons as he was searched by Customs at Manila Airport in 1943; *top right,* Aita, the jungle girl who assisted Gibbons on the first 35 -mile leg of his 1,000-mile Borneo "Trek to Glory." There was, of course, no Howard "Copter" Gibbons. His photograph was that of a Hungarian gymnast, provided to us by Sovfoto, under the impression that we were doing UNESCO coverage. The agency finally got wind of what we were up to and threatened to sue if we did not stop using their gymnasts as Yank death trekkers. Secretaries around the office pitched in and helped us along with photographs of their boyfriends.

Once we had made our little "adjustment," we began with great verve to make up entirely new bombing raids, indeed, to create new World War II battles, ones that had turned the tide against the Axis and brought Hitler to his knees. The master of the latter technique was Mario Puzo, who would create giant mythical armies, lock them in combat in Central Europe, and have casualties coming in by the hundreds of thousands. Although our mail was heavy, I don't recall a single letter casting doubt on any of these epic conflicts. Many correspondents, however, scolded us for incorrectly identifying a tank tread or rifle designation in our documentation. It required minimal effort on our part to begin making up brilliant reviews for our Action Book Bonuses. These in turn were culled from mythical journals of criticism. "Absolutely stunning in its impact…"—*Record.* (Well, a few of us around the office loved it and we had sort of gone on record as feeling that way.) Since it was so simple and pure an idea, I would guess that the idea of inventing "true" stories first occurred to Martin Goodman. Nonetheless, a certain ritual had to be carried out—one in which he would appear in my office holding the layout of a fabricated GI landing "a bit north of Anzio, and hitherto unrevealed, but a thousand times more critical to the Allied fortunes."

"This one true?" he would ask.

"Well, sort of," I would say.

"Mmhmm."

He would then give the layout a light tap, not quite a smack, and disappear.

We were not so much altering tapes as creating new ones; monkeying around with existing tapes could be a tricky business. On one occasion, we ran a fully documented piece about a Canadian who died after a valiant death trek through Indochina. To spruce things up a bit, and to add a bit of salt to the illustration, we sent along a few jungle nymphos as companions for our man. When the magazine was on the stands, we learned that the heroic Canadian was alive, after all—the

**"The Strange Wild Women on Big Mike's Island" by Mario Cleri (Mario Puzo)**
***True Action,* November 1966**
**Illustration by Gil Cohen**

most popular minister in the Toronto area. A surefire lawsuit if ever there was one—once our Canadian edition crossed the border.

With the entire staff gathered round, I called a reporter on a Toronto newspaper and casually inquired about the fellow, learning that he had, indeed, been a popular minister, but had gone off to hunt bear and was believed to have perished in the wilderness. Covering the receiver, I hollered out: "He went bear hunting and he's dead."

A great cheer rang out and everyone returned happily to work.

In preparing our fabricated true adventures, it was important to maintain a degree of geographical balance. One day I glanced at the dummy of an issue that had gone to press and noted, with horror, that no fewer than three of our Yank "rat cage" survivals took place in Japan-dominated territories. George Fox, who was to share the screen credit on *Earthquake* with Mario Puzo, was dispatched by limo (the only limo dispatch in MM history) to the printer with instructions to reset the type, putting one rat cage in Germany and another in contemporary Rio.

Along with death trek and survival stories, yarns about tough cops

**"Blood Bandit Mountain" by Mario Cleri (Mario Puzo)**
***Male,* August 1968**
**Illustration by Samson Pollen**

who had embarked on county cleanups were surefire; also guaranteed to please were pieces that had anything to do with islands—storming them, hiding out on them, buying them at bargain rates, becoming GI king of them. (My favorite, written by the great Walter Kaylin, had to do with a seaman who took charge of one and went about ruling it while sitting on the shoulders of a weird little chum with whom he had washed ashore.) "Breakouts" were another highly successful feature. Any story called "We Go at Dawn" or "No Prison Bars Can Hold Me" would be read with satisfaction. It was preferable that the escape be from some death camp or other, but San Quentin did nicely and our readers enjoyed it immensely when people had to burrow their way out of mile-long tunnels. Another source of delight was the account of some GI who had attacked the enemy with an ingeniously devised contraption. For years, Glenn Innfield heroes went after the enemy with everything from lethal flying scooters to grenade-bearing chickens. Also popular was the revenge or "trackdown" yarn, one in which the hero caught up with someone who had behaved unattractively to him in a hellcamp (Remember me, Kraus?) and gunned him down in a postwar Ankara cafe. Additionally, our readers had a fine time with any story in which the author was in a lather about something, be it Furnace Repair Vultures Who Are Cheating You Blind or those So-Called Soviet Tuna Boats off Fire Island Which Are Stealing All Our Secrets. Our best man in this department was Joseph Millard, who could get himself into a snit on any subject and, indeed, did so some ten times a month. If America wasted too many of our hard-earned dollars on missiles, it got him hot under the collar. If not enough was spent, it got his dander up all the same. There was no pleasing the fellow.

As to the physical makeup of the "books," our readers seemed to prefer illustrations in which each hair follicle shone through with brilliance. Attempts at nonrepresentational, Chagall-like drawings brought out the worst in Martin Goodman. Illustrations were generally gotten up before the true adventures were created. No writer has ever been left quite so shaken as Mario Puzo, his first week on the job, when the author-to-be of *The Godfather* was shown a finished illustration for a thirty-thousand-word nympho jungle trek yarn he had not yet begun to write. Martin Goodman considered the "feel" of each magazine to be terribly important to its success and, like a newsstand alchemist, would brew up a different paper mixture each month—pulp, slick, semislick, four-color, duotone—giving each new issue a certain pimpmobile look to it.

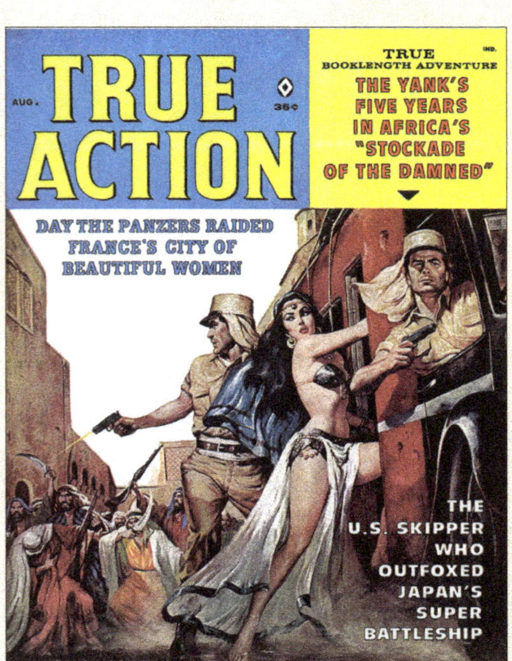


**True Action, August 1961**
**Cover by Charles Copeland**

Although Magazine Management had the reputation of being
something of a "sin pit," the Goodman magazines, at root, were
outrageously pristine, almost conventlike. Never before has there been
a case in which the name triumphed so resoundingly over the game.
Although "nymphos" abounded in the pages of *Male* and *Stag* (even
the rhinos were nymphos) and girls were mentioned frequently who
would do "anything and everything," one would have to look elsewhere
to discover exactly what that anything and everything was. Would-be
masturbators were made to settle for a few lubricious crumbs. "Throw
'em a few hot words," was Martin Goodman's edict when a nervous
editor suggested heating things up a bit for sales. These were along the
lines of "heaving breasts," "long shapely legs," "a flash of pink panties."
It may be that a "dark triangle" or two slipped by, but I rather doubt it.
In the pictorial division, each magazine ran a set of pictures of young
women in bathing suits throwing haughty looks over their shoulders.
The famed Magazine Management retoucher was Murray Schapiro,
whose coveted job it was to airbrush out nipple aureoles and pubic hair
strands on photos of cheesecake models who had been careless during
shooting sessions. There is no record that a single aureole or strand
ever slipped past his eagle's eye and made its way to the newsstand.
(From the look of the current heavily pubic issue of *Stag*, one gathers
that Schapiro has undergone a wild career change and now spends
his hours dabbing back in strands quite similar to the ones he spent
years erasing.)

Despite his essential innocence of heart, the Magazine
Management editor tended to walk about with a heavy sense of
insecurity and the feeling of being up to something a bit shady. The
cocktail party could be an unnerving experience, loaded with booby
traps. Inevitably, the question would be posed.

"What kind of work do you do?"

"I'm in publishing."

"That right. What type?"

"Magazines."

"Really. Which ones?"

"Men's adventure."

"You don't say." (And here the trap would start to close.) "That
*True* magazine stuff?"

"Sort of."

"What do you mean 'sort of'?" (Rare was the Inquisitor who failed
to pick up the scent at this point.) "What are the magazines *called?*"

"Well, they're sort of called *Male, Men,* you know…"

**Male and Farewell: The legendary Mel Shestack
presents BJF with a mock Male cover at Friedman's
MM sendoff, 1966**

"Oh, *those*. Haw, haw, haw. What'd you just call them? *Men's
adventure*. That's funny. Listen, tell me something truthfully, I've always
wanted to know… Do you get to screw those girls or not?"

Time has a way of adding a cosmetic touch to past love affairs,
old marriages, uneasy situations. I think of my years at Magazine
Management as being carefree ones spent in a happy environment. I
can also recall that MM editors had, perhaps, the highest divorce rate
in publishing. I believe we came in at 3.7 per editor at one point, nosing
out *Newsweek*. Quite regularly, one of our people, beset by domestic
woes, would run his head at full speed into the watercooler. I remember
giving it a hard tap or two with my own forehead. Still, there were
compensations—money seemed to fly around in small gusts if not great
blizzards. While salaries were kept low, Christmas bonuses were often
substantial and it was possible to supplement one's income by staying
awake all night and doing freelance assignments for the legions of
MM publications. Though I gave the impression of being skilled as a
death trek writer, I never actually *wrote* one of them and remained the
coach who had never actually played the game. I did, on the other hand,
create a column of short newsy items called *Stag Confidential*, which

told drivers how to rotate their tires effectively, encouraged job seekers to "hotfoot it" up to Vancouver, and advised rascally types on how to spot "joydolls" at a glance. This was a time of great and disciplined production for me. As editor of five magazines, and an annual or two, I was able to commute two and half hours each day, write three novels and dozens of short stories and magazine articles, work out at Vic Tanny's gym, play games with my sons, and, to a degree, continue on with my marriage. I don't recall actually working on the magazines. They seemed to come trotting out by themselves. This may have been attributable to my one useful insight as an administrator, which was to hire the gifted and the guilty. It got back to me that I was considered a decent fellow who hired people and bought material on a compassionate basis. Let me correct the record and state that not a single decision was made on the basis of anything but total self interest. The more brilliant the employee, the less I had to do. I recall spending most of my time ordering up cheese danishes and taking strolls through the MM corridors, looking in on Bessie Little of movie, confession, and TV; the great Stan Lee, whose empire of comic artists, which at first fanned out into the distance, was to shrink to a single desk (and no secretary), then blossom forth into an empire once again when college students made cult figures of the Fantastic Four. Afternoons, I might allow myself to be worked over by the legendary "gentle con artist," Melvin B. Shestack, whose ingenious cons never once redounded to his own enrichment. (On one occasion he had me convinced that J. D. Salinger had ended his retirement and was about to go entirely the other way, with appearances on the Johnny Carson show—and that his first planned visit was to meet the team of *Male*, a magazine he had admired while living in seclusion. Shestack managed his con by including that one perfect, seemingly unfakable detail. All his information had been passed along by Salinger's tree pruner.)

It took me a good year and a half to gather up the courage to say goodbye to MM, and about ten seconds to adjust to my new life as a gypsy. Magazine Management was great fun, but it was just one of those eleven-year things. I had occasion, recently, to look over the current men's adventure field only to find that there was no field left to speak of. The once mighty *True* had been purchased by a California company, whose policy, as enunciated in its first issue, seemed to be one of dealing with the New Sophistication by facing East and breaking wind. "What this country needs is…a magazine fearlessly dedicated to men, and men's pursuits. Without apologies to anyone… We're not anti-women, we're pro-men. And if that's male chauvinism, then snort!

oink! snort." With cover stories on Bob Hope, Johnny Cash, and Woody Hayes, *Argosy*, that once sleek, dangerous gunfighter of a monthly, would seem to be pegged toward retired police chiefs. *Stag* and *Male* appear to be beating an orderly retreat in the face of the *Gallery-Oui-Genesis-Game* onslaught, begrudgingly giving ground in the form of four-color "beaver" photos and articles calming masturbatory fears.

What happened to the men's adventure field? In terms of reader interest, the Korean War proved to be a bore. Long before Abbie Hoffman and Daniel Ellsberg, the prescient Martin Goodman was able to point out that you could not "give Vietnam away" on the newsstands. World War II receded, finally, too far into the distance and became parodistic by its nature. "Iwo" somehow became a laugh line, a Brooklyn joke. Mix in the power of Colombo, the appeal of instant replay, *The Towering Inferno*, the stampede of chic newsstand porn and you begin to get some answers. There is also the elevation-of-Falstaff (Dustin Hoffman)-to-hero argument for those who care to fiddle with such notions.

Recently, I walked into a handsomely appointed Madison Avenue cigar and magazine store in search of some of my old adventure books. The stalls were lined with row upon row of paperbacks such as *Anal Hatcheck Girl*—and racks of chic British import magazines, featuring color photographs of the labia minora of Victorian factory wenches. I asked for *Male* and *Men*. Looking me over carefully, the owner led me to a back shelf, glanced about furtively and slipped my two purchases into a brown paper bag. Taking my money quickly, he returned to the cash register and refused to meet my eyes.

We never did make it into the club, and I must say I was pleased to find that out. **///**

# ACKNOWLEDGMENTS

Our heartfelt gratitude to all the contributing writers for their generous support of this project. Special thanks to Susan Ellison (RIP), Lucy Kaylin, and Lisa Wager.

Thank you Rich Oberg, Mike Chomko, William Lampkin, and Jack Cullers at PulpFest, Tony Jacobs and Crystal Claire at Sideshow Books, Timothy Isaacson, Malcolm and Christine at Bookfellows, Mike Towry and Mark Stadler at San Diego Comic Fest, Thomas Clement of American Art Archives, Lynn Munroe of Lynn Munroe Books, Eric Blackburn, Duke Comby, Jason Cuadrado, Cormac Foster, Vic Nol, Paul Silva, Scott Somerndike, Innes Weir, Stanley J. Zappa, the Doyle family, and our friends in the Men's Adventure Magazines & Books group on Facebook.

# ABOUT THE EDITORS

Writer-guitarist JOSH ALAN FRIEDMAN sold his soul at the Crossroads of the World—42nd Street and Broadway—and moved to Texas in 1987. He is the author of *Tales of Times Square*, *Tell the Truth Until They Bleed*, *When Sex Was Dirty*, and *I, Goldstein* (with Al Goldstein). Featuring the art of his brother, Drew Friedman, he wrote the comix collected in two anthologies: *Any Similarity to Persons Living or Dead is Purely Coincidental*, and *Warts and All*. As "Josh Alan," he barnstormed the Republic of Texas for 30 years, winning three *Dallas Observer* Music Awards for Best Acoustic Act. He released five albums: *Famous & Poor*, *The Worst!*, *Blacks 'n' Jews*, *Josh Alan Band* and *Sixty, Goddammit*. *Black Cracker* was his first novel, and he is working on a second, *All Roads Lead to Great Neck*. Visit **BlackCracker.fm**

**ROBERT DEIS** owns one of the world's largest collections of vintage men's adventure magazines (MAMs) published in the 1950s, 1960s, and 1970s. In 2009, he created a popular blog about the genre, **MensPulpMags.com**. A few years later, Bob and Wyatt Doyle of New Texture launched The Men's Adventure Library, a series of books that feature classic MAM pulp fiction stories and artwork. That series now includes nearly 20 lushly illustrated story anthologies and art books. In recent years, Bob and Wyatt have been featured speakers at PulpFest, and Bob was listed in the book *Who's Who In New Pulp*. Starting in 2021, Bob began working with Bill Cunningham, head of Pulp 2.0 Press, to publish a magazine that features MAM stories and artwork, called the *Men's Adventure Quarterly*. He has contributed articles about MAMs to various magazines and fanzines and also writes two blogs about famous quotations, **ThisDayinQuotes.com** and **QuoteCounterquote.com**. Bob lives near Key West, Florida with his wife BJ (who graciously tolerates his fascination with vintage MAMs), their three dogs, and four cats.

**WYATT DOYLE** is ringmaster of New Texture, and he edits and designs most releases. His own books include *Stop Requested* (illustrated by Stanley J. Zappa), *Dollar Halloween*, *I Need Real Tuxedo and a Top Hat!*, *Buty-Wave Is Now Closed Forever*, and *Jorge Amaya Doesn't Live Here Anymore*. A retrospective of his photography was presented by Gallery 30 South in Pasadena, CA. With Robert Deis, he edits The Men's Adventure Library series, exploring vintage pulp fiction, illustration art, and history. With Jimmy Angelina, he created *The Last Coloring Book* and *The Last Coloring Book on the Left*, as well as *Be Italian*. Together with Hal Glatzer and Norman von Holtzendorff, he produced *Things That Were Made for Love*, collecting the Jazz Age songsheet art of Sydney Leff. He assisted in the publication of Georgina Spelvin's memoir, *The Devil Made Me Do It*, and published Josh Alan Friedman's *Black Cracker* and *Tell the Truth Until They Bleed* via his Wyatt Doyle Books imprint. He administers the creative estate of Rev. Raymond Branch, and curates **RevBranch.com**. His screenplay with Jason Cuadrado, *I'm Here For You*, was produced as *Devil May Call*. A member of The Stanley J. Zappa Quartet, a recording, *The Stanley J. Zappa Quartet Plays for the Society of Women Engineers*, has been released.

# MANY TITLES AVAILABLE IN SOFTCOVER, EBOOK, AND DELUXE EXPANDED HARDCOVER EDITIONS

## ROBERT DEIS AND WYATT DOYLE, SERIES EDITORS

### He-Men, Bag Men, & Nymphos
*Stories by* Walter Kaylin

Leaving an indelible mark on three decades of sweat-soaked pulp fiction, Walter Kaylin tackled testosterone-fueled subjects from Westerns to war, secret agents to sex sirens, Nazis to noir. His frequently over-the-top plots and characters scaled new heights of ingenuity and invention, while setting the standard for the kind of un-apologetic savagery and excess that made men's adventure magazines notorious, then and now. Includes reminiscences by Kaylin, his family, and his former editor, writer Bruce Jay Friedman.

### Atomic Werewolves and Man-Eating Plants: When MAMs Got Weird

*Featuring* Theodore Sturgeon, Manly Wade Wellman, Gardner Francis Fox, Gil Paust, Rick Rubin, HP Lovecraft, *and more*

Weird MAM tales of supernatural encounters, monstrous cryptids, vampirism, witchcraft, demonic death cults, killer robots, psychotic chicken butchers, and of course, atomic werewolves and man-eating plants!

"Hands down, one of my favorite books of 2023."
—Stephen Bissette (*Swamp Thing, Tyrant*)

## Recommended by The Washington Post

## Cryptozoology Anthology
*With guest editor* David Coleman
*Featuring* Arthur C. Clarke, John Keel *and others*

When American men had questions about the Yeti, the Loch Ness Monster, Bigfoot, and other weird beasts from the strange world of cryptozoology, they found answers in the hard-hitting pages of men's adventure magazines. Here are samples of sensational period reporting and wild, "true" accounts of savage, fist-to-claw duels between man and Sasquatch, man and fishman, man and monster! Plus expert analysis by crypto authority **David Coleman**, cryptid-by-cryptid commentary, and much, much more. Don't leave civilization without it!

**Recommended by The Washington Post**

## A Handful of Hell
*Stories by* Robert F. Dorr

Aviator, diplomat, and historian, Robert F. Dorr was uniquely qualified to write for men's adventure magazines, bringing sweat-and-blood, nuts-and-bolts authenticity to his stories of risk, combat, and sacrifice. Vivid, gripping tales of aerial conflict, battlefield heroism and action—some fact, some fiction, all adrenaline-fueled, white-knuckle adventure from one of the genre's greatest voices.

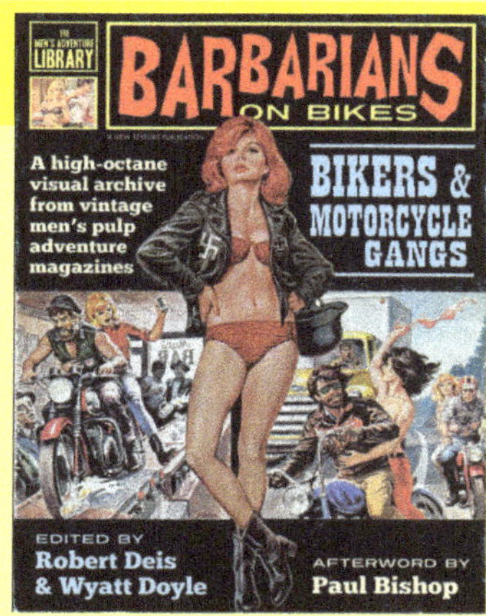

## Barbarians on Bikes
*Afterword by* Paul Bishop

An oversized color collection compiling three decades of motorcycle-themed magazine covers and interior spreads from the 1950s through the 1970s, most unseen since their original publication. Biker illustration art at its most savage. A biker movie between covers, **Barbarians on Bikes** is big, bad, and untamed… Think you can handle the ride?

A series of lush visual archives collecting some of artist Samson Pollen's most memorable pieces, selected from the hundreds of jaw-dropping illustrations he provided for men's adventure magazines (MAMs) from the 1950s through the 1970s. Pollen was equally celebrated for his abilities to effectively render action and movement, as well as his gift for painting beautiful and dangerous women. Illustrating work from authors like Mario Puzo, Martin Cruz Smith, Richard Stark (Donald Westlake), Norman Mailer, Ed McBain, Richard Wright, Don Pendleton, Erskine Caldwell, Walter Kaylin, and Robert F. Dorr, Pollen's immersive illustrations transported adventure-hungry readers from tropical jungles to brutal battle-fields to raging seas and mean city streets. Samson Pollen painted it all—spectacularly. Yet almost none of these stunning illustrations have seen print since their original publication. Until now.

Both **Pollen's Women** and **Pollen's Action** are drawn from the artist's own exhaustive archives of his original artwork for MAMs, while **Pollen in Print 1955–1959** is the inaugural volume of a projected series presenting his artwork chronologically as it appeared in the magazines, allowing us to fill gaps in Pollen's archive and definitively chart the trajectory of a remarkable career.

All three big 11" x 8.5" horizontal volumes include the late artist's reminiscences and autobiographical comments.

### Eva: Men's Adventure Supermodel
*by* Eva Lynd

Blonde Swedish countess Eva Lynd's multi-faceted career touches every aspect of 20th century popular culture. A model for leading illustration artists and top glamour and pin-up photographers of the era, she also appeared with some of the biggest names in entertainment on both the big and small screens. Eva shares her story in her own words and pictures. Includes artwork from pulp masters such as Norm Eastman, Al Rossi, Mike Ludlow, and James Bama.

### One Man Army *by* Gil Cohen

Exploring the incomparable talent of Gil Cohen via the unique perspective he brought to the Mack Bolan universe as one of **The Executioner** series' most celebrated cover artists. **One Man Army** showcases Cohen's spectacular and original paintings for the bestselling action paperbacks, chronicling his seminal role in establishing the Bolan mythos for millions of dedicated readers worldwide.

### Mort Künstler: The Godfather of Pulp Fiction Illustrators

Celebrated for his ability to present large-scale action while never losing sight of essential details, **Mort Künstler** is a master of capturing conflict in paint—both its spectacle, and human cost. At last, here is a stunning selection of his finest pieces from the MAM era in this long awaited collection. A close study of an unequaled career, every page explodes with action, color, and artistry.

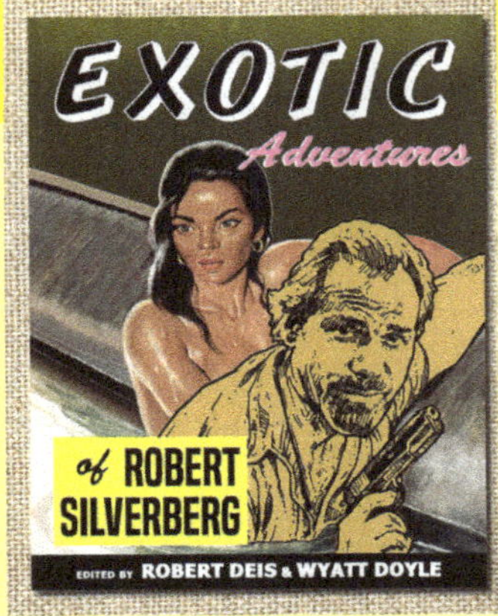

## Exotic Adventures of Robert Silverberg

From safari to bordello, from smugglers' cove to opium den, Robert Silverberg's lost pulp exotica returns to print for the first time since its original 1950s publication, presented in bold new facsimile re-creations that look fresh off the newsstand, circa 1958. Strap in for fully illustrated globe-trotting adventures from the vivid imagination of one of speculative fiction's most honored talents, working incognito.

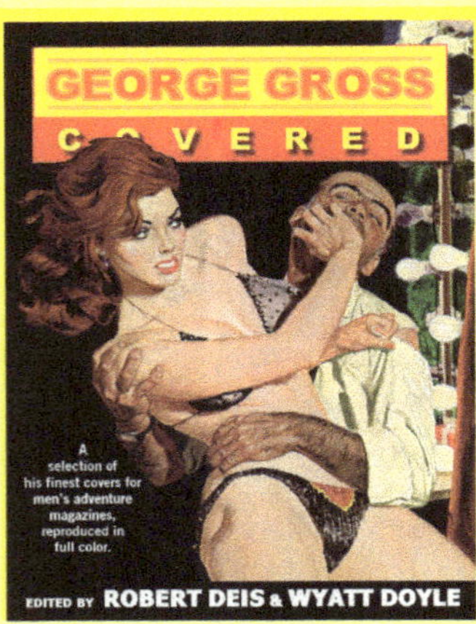

## George Gross: Covered

A top artist for pulps, men's adventure magazines, and paperback covers, George Gross's artwork spans decades, and helped establish a visual vocabulary for action/adventure and hard-boiled fiction. A unique talent who led the way for generations of artists, his imagery continues to inspire and influence. Spotlighting dozens of his memorable covers, this full-color collection includes contributions by historian David Saunders and artist Mort Künstler.

## The Naked and the Deadly
*Stories by* Lawrence Block

Spicy detective stories, international intrigue, and bedroom secrets… Before the bestsellers, Block cut his teeth on MAM fiction and nonfiction articles, collected here in their complete and uncut versions for the first time since their original publication. Includes a new introduction by the author.

THE
MEN'S ADVENTURE
LIBRARY
JOURNAL

THE
MEN'S ADVENTURE
LIBRARY
JOURNAL
I WATCHED THEM
Eat Me Alive
Killer Creatures in Men's Adventure Magazines
EDITED BY ROBERT DEIS & WYATT DOYLE


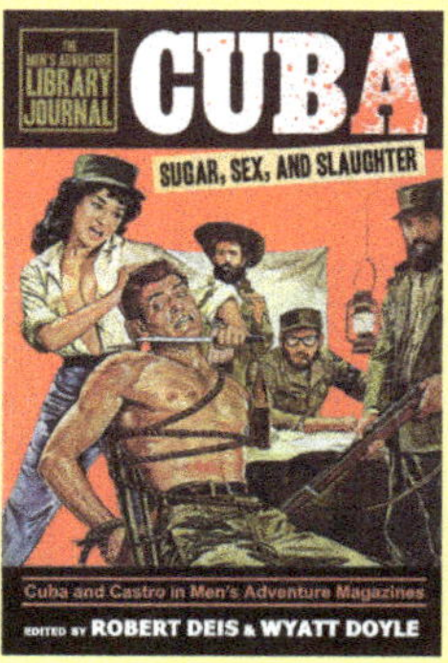

THE
MEN'S ADVENTURE
LIBRARY
JOURNAL
CUBA
SUGAR, SEX, AND SLAUGHTER
Cuba and Castro in Men's Adventure Magazines
EDITED BY ROBERT DEIS & WYATT DOYLE


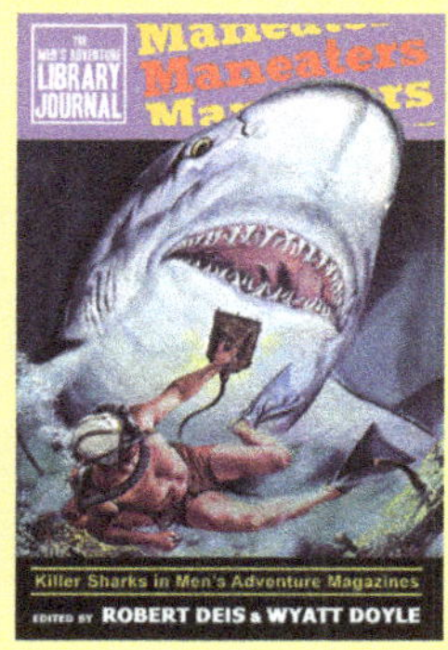

THE
MEN'S ADVENTURE
LIBRARY
JOURNAL
Maneaters
Killer Sharks in Men's Adventure Magazines
EDITED BY ROBERT DEIS & WYATT DOYLE

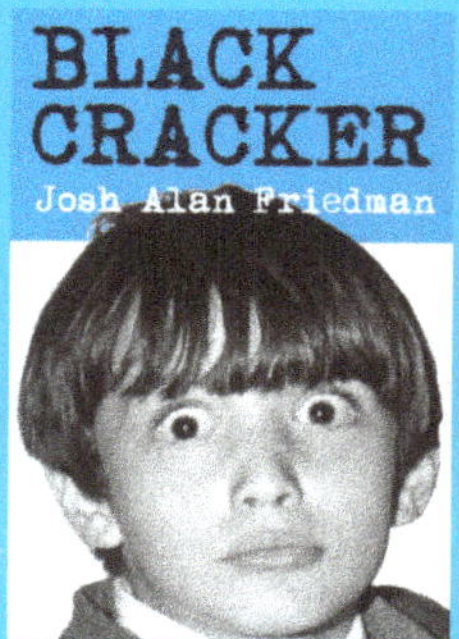

**Black Cracker**, *an autobiographical novel by* Josh Alan Friedman

1962, flashpoint of the civil rights struggle. And young Josh is the lone white boy in a segregated grade school. An unflinching funhouse tour of a Long Island boyhood, and its now-forgotten poor Black shantytowns. Hilarious and heartbreaking.

———————————

**Tell the Truth Until They Bleed**, *by* Josh Alan Friedman

Up close and personal with important and unsung figures in blues and rock 'n' roll: the self-made, the self-serving, and the self-destructive. Illuminating parts of the music industry most don't talk about, this is show business without the showbiz.

———————————

**Stop Requested**, *stories by* Wyatt Doyle; *illus.* Stanley J. Zappa

"A series of rueful, witty and occasionally heartwrenching stories about riding the bus in LA. Doyle finds consequence in the inconsequential. He's Bukowski without the nasty streak. And he's real good. Highly recommended." —Marc Campbell, *Dangerous Minds*

———————————

**nu luna**, *a novel by* Andrew Biscontini

After 400 years of colonization, the moon is home to nearly a billion people, living in a crowded industrial police state on the verge of collapse. *nu luna* is a deeply personal matinee space adventure, spun through an improbably plausible future history. The future is beautiful and dangerous.

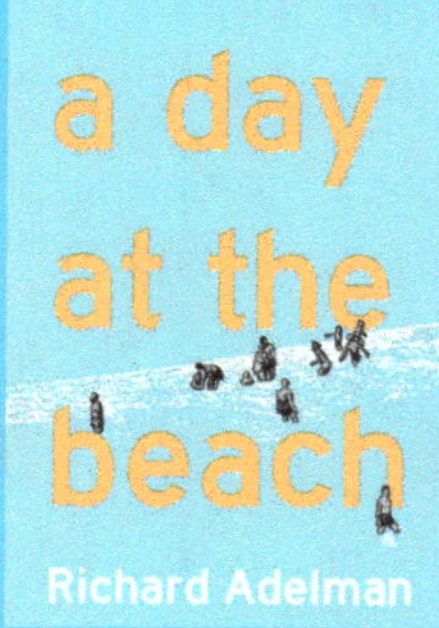

**Teacher Tales**, *a novel by* Richard Adelman

For 40 years, Mr. Kessler has kept his head down and not made waves. But new acquaintances and bad decisions in his final year before retirement bring his ordered world crashing down around him—tragically and hysterically. A smart and darkly comic novel.

---

**A Day at the Beach**, *a novel by* Richard Adelman

Atlantic City, summer of '63. A boy. A girl. And the other boy, who reluctantly pretends to date her to help his pal. A funny, nostalgic novel of young love, best friends, and poetry, capturing one 12-year-old's last great summer as a kid down the shore.

---

**Nimrodia**, *poems by* Eric Reymond

Visual art and ancient history are the starting point for most of the poems in this collection, as the modern world intersects with these domains again and again. Though language, culture, and time may divide us, these are also the forces that link us together.

---

**Sub-Sub Librarian, Extracts on a**, *poems by* Eric Reymond

The title poem imagines *Moby Dick*'s Sub-Sub Librarian experiencing transcendence and illumination through his wide readings. Additional poems find inspiration in texts as diverse as contemporary poetry, vocabulary quizzes, and course syllabi.

**Things That Were Made for Love: The Songsheet Art of Sydney Leff**
Wyatt Doyle, Hal Glatzer, Norman von Holtzendorff, *editors*

The first-ever songsheet art collection presenting the cream of the Jazz Age illustration artist's work on songsheet covers from 1924-1932. A gorgeous visual feast that playfully captures the moods, elegance, and style of an era.

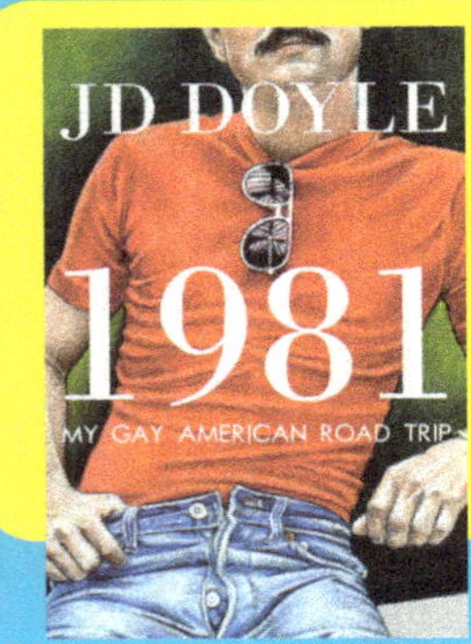


**1981—My Gay American Road Trip**
*by* JD Doyle

A playful, intimate, one-of-a-kind illustrated record of gay life, love, lust, and liberation post-Stonewall, in the heady days before the devastating crisis that would change everything.

## #new texture Music

### CD / DOWNLOAD

**I've Got Heaven on My Mind**
Reverend Raymond Branch

**Sixty Goddammit** Josh Alan

**Jimmy Angelina** s / t

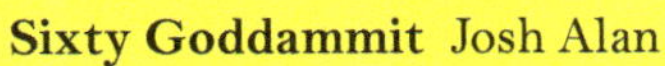


**Cursed** Carolina

**Continental / International**
Jon E. Edwards

**Map of the Moon**  s/t

**Sing-Song Songs**
Stanley J. Zappa

**Free / Refuse**
Hall, Skrowaczewski, Zappa

**Live a Little**
Manzappaczewski

The Stanley J. Zappa Quartet
**Plays for The Society
of Women Engineers**

**Crossing Guards**
Carter, Leffue, Sikora, Zappa

**Turkey Bacon Donuts Bitches**
MANZAP REBORN

**Balloons**

Daniel Carter,
Nick Skrowaczewski,
Stanley J. Zappa

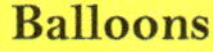

**# new texture**   Words and Pictures and Music

# new texture